# Releasing Trophies

BY
Shannon David
Hamons

To Capt. Wensing!
Very glad our paths crossed in
Hawaii. Best wishes for continued
calm waters. – SH

**Publisher:**
**Shannon David Hamons**
**Harrison, Ohio**

**Printed in the United States of America**

Publisher's Note: This is a work of fiction. Any references to historical events, real people, or real places are used fictitiously. Other names, characters, places, or events are products of the author's imagination. Locales and public names are sometimes used for atmospheric purposes. Any resemblance to actual people, living or dead, or to businesses, companies, events, institutions, or locales is completely coincidental.



**Releasing Trophies/ Shannon David Hamons**. -- 1st ed.
Paperback: ISBN 978-1-7326282-0-5
E-book: ISBN 978-1-7326282-1-2

To My Family & Friends and to Those Still Searching

*Chaucer said time heals all wounds...I have a lot of wounds, not enough time.*
*– Anonymous*

# ACKNOWLEDGMENTS

This book may have been years in the making but took a lifetime to develop within thoughts and living. Thanks to my wife Joy, who has shown me unconditional love and encouraged me to press on to tell a story about facing fear, pushing yourself, and deciding what is important. Telling that story to my daughter Chelsea and son Connor is only reflecting the ideals of kindness, courage, and perseverance they have consistently taught me over the years. I have to extend deep appreciation to my sisters Sharon, Claudia, and Michelle, who were always my biggest cheerleaders and made me believe I could do almost anything. I am thankful to my parents William and Lucille, both of whom overcame lives of hardship to give their children all they could; but mostly, they made us aware that "doing the right thing" and treating others with respect were most important. I am also indebted to my brother Larry, who died before I was born, but whose legacy has spoken to my heart many times about choosing a better path. I am grateful also to my grandsons Eli and Jonah, and perhaps those grandchildren yet unborn, for reminding me of the importance of what is yet to come in life. Thanks also to my stepchildren, Gabrielle, Zach, and Garrett, for showing me that the care of family often transcends the typical borders. Thanks to my many relatives, friends, and co-workers who have provided words of encouragement and displayed countless examples of honor and sincerity. Many thanks also to Mitch and Gerilyn Jobe of FourNine Design for their boundless creativity in designing the cover jacket. Finally, thanks to Diana Grabau at *Seize the Day Edits* for tirelessly working with me to create something of value.

# CONTENTS

# Chapter One

The coffee and bacon smell glorious.

Autumn sun cascades through the diner window and mixes with the smoke hanging above the farmers' green John Deere and blue Ford tractor hats. A scrawny county inspector charged with monitoring the restaurant smoking ban sits on a stool at the end of the counter nursing a Marlboro and a decaf. Between puffs he watches local newspaper publisher Frank Barnett in the corner table having a robust conversation with a sheriff's deputy. The inspector risks being late for his first appointment as he lingers over his eggs to see how the apparent dispute will end. He wonders what could cause Frank so much anguish while the deputy appears relaxed, almost serene.

The humble Sarah's Diner in little Le Fleur, Ohio, has been witness to a vast assortment of similar disagreements over the decades. Hearty debates have always been a favorite side dish here, where everyone comes to chew on the comfort food, mull the veracity of the town's fast-spreading news, and make outlandish bets. Last week, geezers Loomis and Red got into it over which of the two had the baldest tires on their pickups, with the matter settled only after the entire place emptied into the side parking lot for a vote. Red had to buy Loomis's breakfast—the traditional prize for winning an argument—judged by a show of hands. The winner usually ends up ordering an extra side of meat just to tweak the loser a bit more.

Sarah's has weathered gracefully and remains the unofficial bull-session bureau for a dwindling number of the town's crotchety males. The younger farmers prefer McMeals in paper wrappers behind steering wheels while texting each other. Still, the tradition of real plates, silverware, and flirting with the waitresses lives on at Sarah's, where the old men have freedom to share tales away from their wives' incredulous stares and guffaws.

Frank the newspaper man remains a regular at the diner, and has a deep, silent fondness for its radiant owner, Julie. The publisher and the restaurant boss share mutual admiration that is borne by their need to engage in any stimulating conversation that is not of farms, football and the local Fireman's Festival. The two have developed a genial way of sharing glimpses of bigger dreams over cups of coffee and slices of pie during slow afternoons. They enjoy a friendly closeness; however, they guard their greatest secrets, which they fear would reveal too much of their self-perceived flaws.

Even at this moment Frank is unaware that Julie is closely monitoring his conversation with the deputy. If need be, she would deftly step in to quash his angst in a way that only an authentic ally could do without causing embarrassment. Julie's unfailing warmth gives Frank solace when he is troubled. He has needed that comfort more regularly lately, and this may be one of those days which require second helpings.

The consistency of Julie and the diner provides another layer of normalcy to the routine for Frank and other residents in tiny Le Fleur. The old-timers have little fondness for change but deal with it grudgingly when it comes. So, it is no wonder that the late owner and matriarch Sarah O'Meara is given highest honors with a huge framed photo over the milkshake blender. She looks down from the heavens over her daughter Julie with her timeless smile to ensure the farmers don't get too zesty with the language, the bets, or the condemnations of the meddling government and the dastardly banks.

Frank has heard the story a hundred times how, on one splendid Indian summer morning about thirty-five years ago, just before the breakfast crowd arrived, the young Mrs. O'Meara of barely forty-two years fell dead while stirring a big pot of boiling spaghetti. Her sudden death and subsequent robbery of the cash register by Willis Booker as she lay on the kitchen floor are still deliberated in the diner now and then—except by Frank, who would never share in such gossip and risk arousing painful memories for Julie. Unfortunately, the passing decades mangle the truth with imaginative color and outright fabrications better than the antique blender whips up milkshakes. Depending on the storyteller, any version could be the gospel, or "Nothing but the manure from my hogs," according to eighty-nine-year-old Red.

One fact that has never been disputed is how Sarah's poor little Julie walked into the diner that chaotic morning to find Police Chief Benson Wells calling for an ambulance on his walkie-talkie. Julie pushed her way past him to the horror of her mother lying on the floor in a pool of warm noodles and water. Little Julie always stopped by the restaurant on the way to school to pick up a kiss and her lunch that Mom so lovingly prepared by using leftover specials from the day before. Kids at school would do their best to barter for some of Mom's delicacies, particularly the pieces of homemade pie. Julie would delight in the fact that her classmates usually had nothing that was worth a trade.

Everything changed for Julie on that crushing fall morning. Part of her youthful exuberance drained in uncontrollable tears onto the diner's kitchen floor and forever clung to Sarah's lifeless body as Chief Wells and two EMTs finally pulled her away from the scene. She grew up years that day within screams of devastation usually reserved for world-weary adults. Julie never talks to Frank about the loss of her mother, and Frank never treads into that lingering heartache.

Despite the awful experience of finding Mom dead at the diner, Julie expertly fills her mother's space behind the warping counter. She listens carefully to all that is said and all subtly implied by those around her, and chats kindly and keeps everyone's confidential fibs. She also preserves all the recipes and continues to make Mom's wonderful pies, even adding a couple new varieties taken from a diner she loves to visit on her way to Lake Erie. She has made Sarah's Diner her own, not only so Pop will stay occupied, but also to ensure the memory of her mother will live on in Le Fleur.

Julie now works feverishly six days a week, from 4:30 a.m. to 3:30 p.m. During the afternoon preparation for the next day, a straggling farmer or two will drop by for a late lunch and another conversation with her. On the verge of forty-five, she maintains the vigor, figure, and youthful look that encourage both Frank and the old men to get up at dawn and drive into town for bacon and eggs when they have plenty of both at home.

The congenial and ever-smiling hostess toils beside her round little father who is pushing eighty-six. Pop shows up every day too, although he has taken over the less strenuous jobs of wrapping silverware in paper napkins and drying glasses. High school and community college students comprise most of the wait help.

Two older Mexican brothers handle the cook duties with a precision and speed that would put any of the students to shame. Eduardo and Gerardo, now Ed and Gary, bustle around the kitchen with spatulas blazing, the neatly arranged griddle sizzling, and plates soaring to the counter. They had been migrant workers who came out of the fields in nearby Celeryville more than twenty-five years ago. They work as intensely here as they did in the black muck farmland and even taught Spanish to Julie and Pop as they were taught English.

One other long-time waitress, Marilyn, has taken on the weathered persona of the scruffy tabletops. Usually missing in action during slow periods as she sucks on her coffee and cigarettes out back to refine her gratingly raspy voice, she transforms into a dazzling dynamo during the peak breakfast and lunch periods. She and Julie employ a magical ballet as they instinctively pirouette around each other, never spilling a drink or dropping a fork, seemingly in a race to get everything to customers before they even know they want it. Marilyn was a classmate of Sarah's and is a revered link to the past who knows almost every detail of every farmer around the lunch counter. Everyone talks to her, but no one dares cross her. She acts as a substitute mother and protects Julie just as much as Frank.

Julie, Pop, Marilyn, and even Mom, looking down over the cash register, demand everything in *their* diner—from the food to the debates—remain comfortingly sincere. A large plastic pickle jar transformed into a "cuss bucket" sits on the end of the counter where offenders caught swearing by Julie or Marilyn will drop a dollar through the slotted lid. Pop can no longer hear them, or he chooses not to. Around Christmastime, all the money in the bucket goes to several needy families in Le Fleur.

Publisher Frank and the deputy sitting in the corner booth aren't keeping with the O'Meara rules of congeniality. Their conversation has stalled, and their hash and eggs cool from disinterest. The two now sit motionless at the table as the waitresses buzz by with full plates and steaming pots. The lanky, older Frank slumps with a reddened face in his lengthy hands. Phil, the younger heavyset deputy, stares and wonders what sudden reaction will spring forth because of the story he just told.

Curiously, there is no quick reaction. Frank just sits, trying to digest the lawman's story. Phil's pudgy face grows more perplexed with each passing moment, until he must break the silence.

"Frank, say something," he demands.

But Frank only keeps his face buried in his wiry fingers. His thinning hair and big ears are the only things visible. His knobby elbows on the table and his stiff back combine to form a perfectly balanced tripod for his frozen head.

Frank, a picture of vitality for most of his life, is now gaunt, tired, and haggard. More than six foot three, he had always been on the muscular side, with a chiseled face and brawny limbs. He could have been pegged as a stereotypical, strapping American farmer for advertising campaigns. The only thing that would give him away as a marketing imposter would be his supple hands. Instead of decades pushing tractor levers and fence posts, he has hammered only at a keyboard and managed a few paper cuts. Those ad-man looks have faded over the last few months, with decline further exaggerated by sagging clothes on a dwindling frame. Even a weather-beaten farmer would now choose a different marketing stand-in.

"Frank? Aren't you going to say something?"

Frank slides his hands to the bottom of his chin and looks pitifully at the deputy.

"I haven't talked to you in years," Frank chokes out, "and you call me last night to meet you here for breakfast to tell me this? You could've told me anywhere. You could've told me on the phone. But here? You really are a damned idiot!"

Caught off guard by Frank's abrupt comment, the deputy attempts to suggest, "Frank why don't you—"

But the dumpy deputy cannot complete the question before Frank jumps up with one hand still on his face, pushes the chair back with a screech, and darts through the door, ringing its bell violently.

Julie almost spills her coffeepot as she stops at the table. "Phil," she crackles, "What the hell did you say to upset Frank?" She holds up the pot menacingly, waiting for an answer, while Phil sheepishly mumbles at his plate.

"I only told Frank something that he suspected was true for many years."

Julie yanks up his uneaten plate of food and barks, "You jackass. It's pretty clear you should've left him wondering about it! You should go back to Mansfield now. We need the table for our regulars."

Phil throws some money down on the table, grabs his round-brimmed deputy's hat, and slinks to the door. He is uneasy and unbalanced, the way a big man would try to glide. He grabs the antique doorknob and pauses to look back at all the old farmers staring with contempt. Though raised in Le Fleur, Phil knows he is not in the fraternity of this breakfast club. Worse yet, he has offended Frank, who belongs as an honorary member and who is admired for his even disposition, behind-the scenes benevolence, hearty handshakes, and neighborly talks. Phil also knows he had better leave now before a dozen prickly farmers gladly place dollar after dollar in the pickle jar as they cuss him like a tattered pickup truck.

He also knows the farmers could not care less about his Richland County sheriff's badge. The sheriff's office has been a bane to the farmers for years since Le Fleur lost its own police department to ineptitude and strained town budgets. Fortunately, the farmers complain a little less now about slow deputy response times or aggressive ticketing since the new, improved version of the Richland County Sheriff won office.

To Phil's surprise, the farmers say nothing. There is no swearing—no barbs of any kind. The blank looks and growing quiet feed the unease. Ed, however, peeks out over the order counter and bellows, "Es major dejar ahora Phil antes de que venga y te golpeo con una espatula!" Even the farmers who cannot understand Spanish realize that a spatula could soon be involved in a beating.

Phil turns red at the mysterious insult and finally blurts, "Well, damn it. You all smell like hogs anyway. Go back to your Irish slop."

A coffee cup whizzes across the room and shatters into the doorjamb just inches from Phil's head. Marilyn takes a threatening step toward Phil so he cannot mistake the culprit. Her spiteful look is enough to prod him to give the bell his own ringing note of abrupt departure. Once outside, Phil looks down the street and sees Frank shuffling along the sidewalk. Even from fifty yards Phil can see Frank still holding his face, maybe rubbing his eyes. Phil starts to yell something but then decides to suck back his words. He grumbles under his breath, jumps into his patrol car, squeals a U-turn in the square, then speeds toward his post in Mansfield some twenty miles away. His windshield perspective is liberating.

# Chapter Two

Frank slouches down the street as if walking the deck of a ship while trying to avoid motion sickness. He drags himself toward a small elderly woman who waddles up to him. "Hi, Frankie," she quips in a motherly tone. "Thanks so much for sending that young boy over to fix my steps. That's just like you to look out for others."

Frank nods, mumbles something, and lumbers on while amber leaves fall unnoticed onto his head and shoulders. The streams of warm sunlight that pierced the diner window are now consumed by roiling clouds, and the promising morning now builds into a wind-whipped, blustery, late-September day.

Strangers observing Frank's stagger would surmise he is much older than his years, with no direction left in life; perhaps he is the village idiot who wanders aimlessly. Le Fleur residents know Frank is no idiot. They have great respect for his quiet intelligence, community leadership, and humble way of life. If the town rallies around a cause, Frank is usually behind it financially and almost always anonymously. Most can figure out he is the usual benefactor who every year makes sure the painted red thermometer bursts out of its top on the Community Chest billboard in the square. He also sponsors the town's entire Little League each season, but modestly, his company's name no longer appears on the uniforms, programs, or outfield signs. He gets to the field several times a week to take action photos, eat peanuts, and stand along the right-field fence to gab with the fathers and grandfathers he has known forever. He serves on the organizing committee for the Le

Fleur "Fireman's Festival" and even serves as a pie-tasting judge and referee for the mud volleyball games.

Frank inherited a once-profitable newspaper, 2,200 acres of farmland (leased and farmed by others), a number of once-busy downtown buildings, and the town's only gas station. Talk around the village is that he also stands to inherit a fortune from his ailing mother, thanks to his grandfather's prohibition-era Lake Erie bootlegging. His grandfather used his newfound riches to start the newspaper after prohibition. Frank has no need to continue publishing a small-town newspaper to make a living, which is fortunate because the paper is barely getting by, and no one else would do such a foolish thing in today's marketplace of internet news and mindless blogs. But, as reflected in the modest frame house in which he was raised and still lives, social strata hold no value to him, and wealth is just another predicament to put up with.

Frank describes himself as a spiritual person, but veers away from the formality of regularly attending church. He says the "noise of self-righteousness" drowns out the feeling of reverence. He leans on his mother's gentle paraphrasing of scripture about "shutting your door to pray in secret, and in secret God will reward you."

Despite not being a regular in the Sunday pews, Frank is good friends with Pastor Harold, who is president of the town's Clergy Committee. They meet occasionally for lunch and talk about community service projects, baseball, and comedic television. But the pastor will always stealthily lead discussion toward life's struggles and the hereafter. The brotherly pastor has tried for years with no luck to get Frank regularly under the steeple. Harold recently decided that a one-on-one ministry during lunch a couple times a month is a more effective way to get the names of God and Frank used in the same prayer. So far, so good.

Frank often tells Harold of his admiration for the *worthy* people who are able to fashion works of beauty through emotional expression. Those people who top his list of "creators" are capable of eloquently revealing their impressions of reality through fine art, music, literature, scientific advances, architecture, imaginative designs of stunning automobiles, and even the patient coaxing of barley mash into fine spirits. Frank never finished college but attempts to capture the essence of worthiness in articles he writes in the little weekly paper delivered to doorsteps every Wednesday afternoon. The paper has collected thirty-four awards from the Ohio Newspaper Association over the decades, but neither he nor his late father James, nor even his grandfather, ever published a single article announcing those big achievements. That would appear too much like veiled self-adoration.

Regardless of the awards, Frank now realizes he and his ancestors have fallen short of worthiness. Frank knows this thanks to Phil's story and now fears the town's residents may soon realize that the paper imparts mere childlike fabrications that reflect smudged interpretations or outright bias.

As Frank shuffles along Main Street, his thoughts drift to a long-ago conversation when his high school girlfriend tells him that he has struck a perfect balance between pessimism and optimism, never leaning too far to either. He gasps a deep regret as he remembers her coldly saying to him, "You're just a boring realist. You don't even know how to dream. You'll be stuck in this place forever." That made for a tense senior prom night.

She stopped returning Frank's calls right after graduation and started dating the class clown. She and the jester are now married and own one of the largest commercial real estate brokerage firms in Cleveland. Maybe realists like Frank cannot be mystical, inspired, spiritual, or even cynical enough to be really creative and worthy—at least to cheerleaders with big dreams.

Ironically, without a healthy dose of editorial mysticism or cynicism, the readers of the *Le Fleur Sentinel* get only fleeting glimpses of a larger world. Subscribers pay five dollars a month for watered-down, highly filtered doses of pabulum that show up on their doorsteps and computer screens every Wednesday afternoon. They are given a safe bubble of distortion that cloaks them in a soft, fuzzy blanket of small town-ness.

The leaves blow angrier past Frank as dark clouds tumble at the end of the street behind him. Wind whisks the dusty sidewalks, and shadows recede into a lifeless pall, but the growing tempest has no effect on Frank's tunnel vision as he hobbles along unaware. A thunderbolt ruptures the elusive peace and light rain falls unnoticed. When it begins to rain harder he reaches up mechanically to adjust his hat, only to realize he has left it, his jacket, and his umbrella at the restaurant. Even so, he continues to walk slowly past the stores, ignoring the available protection of awnings and the many residents who wave, say hello, and call his name. The growing deluge saturates his clothes and washes the tears from his face.

The sensation evokes memories of youthful games of chase in a rainstorm on this very street when friends wanted the athletic and usually unflappable Frank on their team. Frank had a certain calm about him that helped him excel in baseball. But somewhere, below the usual composed exterior lay a raw, impatient nerve, that when plucked by someone's apparent stupidity, could instantly cause him to swell into a fireball of wrath. Most people knew how to deal with the occasional, sudden fury that would quickly fade; a few others who didn't know how to cope with the verbal outbursts just chose to avoid him altogether.

One friend who knew how to endure Frank's quick, periodic episodes of anger was childhood friend Dave. Frank imagines Dave sprinting behind him and yelling for him to slow down. "No," Frank would instruct in a gruff tone, "you need to learn to run faster; you're too slow!" Frank was only a few months older than Dave but was always trying to be the big brother, since neither had one of their own. They did everything together and knew each other's dreams and fears. Later, as adults, they had many laughs golfing and fishing, and even shared a few manly tears when they were thrown unhittable curve balls of life. Sadly, the men grew apart with different perspectives of cause, and the rain droplets that used to provide refreshing coolness to the spirited young boys now melt those memories for Frank with a chilling melancholy.

Frank stops his shuffle and stands at the bottom of a doorless stairwell, wondering how he arrived here without remembering the journey. He looks up at the sign hanging over the doorway just to make sure he is really at the landing to his second-floor office. The sign, "Le Fleur Sentinel—Founded 1934," flaps in the strengthening gale, deflecting a stream of water onto Frank's upturned face. He closes his eyes but keeps them skyward to let the water flow over his brow and down the front of his shirt collar. He eventually studies the flight of stairs before him and the daunting climb upward.

His heavy, sodden clothes smother any final remnant of tenacity he may have had as the day began. Glancing to the left, Frank sees that the baker has been watching him through his store window. He forces himself to nod to the kindly storekeeper, then skates through the empty doorjamb to begin his slow climb up the stairwell. Only the deep smell of fresh bread from the bakery reminds him that he still has reasons to live.

Each step creaks under the weight of slow upward plodding, and shoes squish out water twenty-four times until the summit is scaled. Frank stands before the cloudy glass door with "Le Fle-- Sentinel" printed neatly in Century Schoolbook letters. He wonders how long the "u" and "r" have been missing on the end of "Le Fleur." He gives a slight grunt of amusement and pulls off the drooping "Fle" and throws it down on the landing.

Frank opens the door slowly but draws attention with long, strained squeaks. Closing it slowly is another major blunder. He braces himself for the onslaught of questions that will be flung at him by the three reporters at the back of the room and the even more curious front-desk staff. Gloria looks above her glasses over the reception counter but says nothing. Frank peeks up from his mushy shoes to see baffled looks around the newsroom. The mute reporters study him like the farmers gawked at Deputy Phil in the diner. He slogs down the hallway as if nothing is amiss, and everyone goes back to work as if that were true.

After maneuvering around the ancient wooden office desk, Frank plops down in his equally archaic leather chair and leans back to shut his eyes. He gets only a moment's peace before Gloria plunges into the room in antipathy.

"Frank, what on God's good earth are you doing walking around in the rain without your jacket and umbrella? You know you shouldn't be doing things like this in your condition."

She barely finishes the sentence when her hand flies to her mouth and her eyes grow wide in dread.

Frank glares around with a pirate's grimace as if a drunken shipmate just shouted out where "X" marks the spot of the buried treasure.

"I'm sorry Frank," she whispers as she reaches behind and gathers the door to a close. "But you know better than this. You need your strength."

They simultaneously exhale feeble resignations, knowing that even catching pneumonia right now probably would not matter much to Frank's long-term condition.

Gloria eases around to sit on the edge of the desk. She tenderly picks up Frank's cold white fingers in both of her warm brown hands, like a mother consoling her son who just came home from a schoolyard fight.

"Frank, I've worked for you and your dad a very long time. You're like my family. This paper has been my love…" She searches for the words lost between her head and heart.

"I've had troubles of my own. I saw troubles with your dad, but I don't think I can take what's happening to you. Tell me why you were out in the rain and look so depressed. Are you having a spell?"

A tear begins to roll down her beautiful mahogany cheek as she pulls Frank's pale hand against her face. Somewhat surprised, Frank notices Gloria's eyes swelling with hurt and stands to gently hug her without getting her too wet, while she covers her mouth to conceal growing sobs.

"Gloria, please—please—shhhh—don't cry. You know," Frank half laughs, "I'm not good at this emotional stuff."

He gives her a couple pats on the back then puts his mouth to her ear. "You've always been here for me like a sister. We've grown up together, in a way. You and Russ have been my family for so long now."

He moves away to look out the window and change the subject. "I'm not having a spell, as you call it."

Gloria gathers composure from under her sobs. "Then what is it? Why are you so upset? I can see worry all over your face."

"Gloria, I just had a conversation with Phil. You know Phil, the horse's ass deputy that comes over from Mansfield and stirs things up once in a while."

Gloria hisses, "Yes, I know that—that—"

"Well he just gave me some information that is a little unsettling, that's all. I might have to do a little investigative work to clear some things up. It might make for a messy article and hurt some people, though."

Gloria looks at him with puzzlement.

"You want to talk about it?"

Frank turns away and looks out the window again. "Not right now. I'm a little tired and cold. We'll talk about it later."

Gloria opens the closet in the corner of the office, reaches inside, and takes a hanger off the door that holds pants, sport coat, tie, and neatly pressed shirt. She then reaches up on a shelf and pulls down a towel, a change of underclothes, and dry shoes.

She emerges from the closet, wipes her cheek on her shoulder, builds her composure, and demands, "C'mon, Frank, if you don't want to talk and you aren't having a spell, get these on before you chill!"

"Boy, you sure love it when these fancy clothes come in handy every couple years, don't—"

She throws the towel in his face before he can finish. "Just do as you're told and don't talk back!"

Frank chuckles. "Well, I better find some congressman to interview so this outfit doesn't go to waste while I sit around here and do the obits."

The term "obits" spawns awkward glances.

"Oh, hush up. It'd do you good to wear a tie once in a while and look like a publisher for a change."

"Well," Frank says, "you're determined to get me in my funeral clothes early, aren't you?"

"Listen Frank, please don't talk like that. You know I can't stand to hear it."

"Yeah, I know. Sorry."

Gloria helps Frank out of his clothes. She turns away when he gets down to his underwear and puts her arm out behind, waiting for him to deposit the wet article in her hand. She takes the briefs from him in pinched fingers and leans down to pick up the pile of clothes. She deposits the laundry in a bag that hangs on the back of the closet door and turns around to Frank just as he pulls up the slacks. They stare at each other and grin, then shake their heads critically.

"Get to work, slacker," Gloria demands. "Russ is waiting for that story on the new art gallery, and you have a ten o'clock with the mayor."

Frank roars, "Oh yeah—that fool's coming in today!" as he slips on the white dress shirt without the T-shirt.

"Yes, you have to see Hank today. You've been putting him off for two weeks, and he wants his reelection campaign story to run next week."

Frank leans his head back in disgust as he buttons up. "The windbag might as well be running unopposed. O'Brien is a bigger fool than he is. Why the hell does he care about a story?"

Gloria walks away and Frank yells down the hall at her, "Well at least I don't have to wear a tie for that jerk."

"Frank, that isn't Christian-like," she shouts back. "By the way, you're the one going to look like the jerk, wearing a nice shirt without an undershirt on. I just can't teach a white country boy anything, can I? Now, get busy."

"I will," Frank howls, "but tell Russ to stop rewriting everyone's stories so damn much. By the time your son's done cutting, we've lost half the week's copy. He needs to leave some of the descriptive details in there. Not everyone wants *just* the facts. Hell, everybody's working twice as hard around here 'cause he keeps cutting so damned much."

Frank's complaint goes unanswered as Gloria returns to the front desk. He slumps down in the chair and puts on a sock, pauses, then opens the desk drawer to take out a bottle of Dewar's scotch. It is a few minutes after nine o'clock, but his head is throbbing, and that chill foretold by Gloria arrives in earnest. He takes a drink, rolls his head around, and breathes out an invisible flame.

He lowers the bottle back into the drawer next to a beautifully carved box. Keeping his eyes fixed on the wooden rectangle, Frank takes out the bottle again for another long drink. He sets the bottle off to the inside of the drawer, pulls the box out to place in front of him, and opens the lid to reveal a glistening nickel-plated short-nosed .38 revolver. He runs his finger from the sight on the barrel, over the revolver openings, across the hammer, and down the grain of the wooden handle.

Frank takes the pistol out of the box, leans forward, shuts his eyes, and puts his forehead on the desk. He turns the .38 over and over in his hands, out of view below the desktop. The weapon's superb balance and craftsmanship bring a weak smile to his face. His grin widens as his growing imagination is crowded with competing possibilities for using the steel sculpture.

# Chapter Three

A tapping noise in the corner of the office interrupts Frank's alternating thoughts of mayhem and heroism. Frank looks up to see a stately older man sitting across from him, gently rapping an umbrella tip on the edge of the small meeting table. Startled, Frank stands up and raises the gun up above the desktop for the man to see. He doesn't point the gun, but the message is clear.

"Who are you and what are you doing in my office?"

The old man, neatly dressed in a dark blue suit, white shirt, and red tie calmly looks at Frank without saying anything.

"Who the hell are you?" Frank persists.

Still, no answer.

Frank turns toward the door and shouts, "Gloria, who's this guy in my office? Some guy just walked down here into my office. Gloria? Gloria?"

There is no answer from the front desk or newsroom.

"Everything is all right, Frankie," the stranger enunciates calmly.

Frank is stunned that the stranger knows his name and even adds the "ie" on the end. He studies the old man's creviced but noble face to look for clues of identity that may have been missed. He still cannot discern having ever seen the man.

"Okay, Old Man, what's going on? Who are you?"

"Who do you think I am?"

"Jesus, mister, don't start playing games with me. Who the hell are you?"

The stranger chuckles softly. "I am not playing games with you, Frankie. I was in the diner this morning when Phil upset you."

"That's bull! I didn't see you there. You'd of stood out pretty damn easily. No one goes in there wearing a suit. And how do you even know Phil, anyway? What the hell is going on here?"

"Oh, I was there, all right," insists the stranger. "Perhaps you don't bother to look at the faces anymore or notice anything that's going on around you. That's not a good habit for a newspaperman to get into. You have to keep an eye out for the details."

Frank looks away from the old man and slides open the desk drawer.

The stranger holds up a box of .38 rounds. "Looking for these?"

Frank studies the shells in the man's hand, then looks back at the drawer and shuts it, his voice less confident.

"How'd you get those? How'd you get in here? What do you want?"

"It's not what I want. I will help you get what you want, though—and help you do what you need to do."

"Damn it," Frank sighs. "You aren't making any sense. What do I need to do?"

"We will figure that out," says the old man. "We can work things out together over the course of time."

Frank puts his hand on his forehead. He is beginning to sweat. He puts the gun on the desk, then rubs both temples. He tries to calm his breathing and gather himself, then shuts his eyes to think about the next question he should ask.

"What things are we—" Frank looks up to find the man gone. He looks around the room and down the hall but sees no old stranger. Frank rubs behind his ear, opens the drawer, and fumbles around for the bottle of scotch. He stops searching and startles in amazement that the box of .38 shells are returned to the top of an old Bible. He grabs the bottle and takes a deep swallow, then grabs the bullets and bangs them and the gun onto the desk with a thud. "What's going on?" he whispers.

# Chapter Four

Gloria bursts into Frank's office to find him slumped in his turned chair, staring out one of the side windows. Her words catch in her throat as her fierce demeanor melts into concern.

"Frank, what's the matter?"

Frank doesn't say anything. He stands and pretends to look at something of great interest on the street below.

Gloria probes more insistently. "Frank, are you going to tell me what's wrong?"

Still staring out the window, Frank softly responds, "Gloria..." then stops to search for the rest of his thought. Gloria patiently waits while Frank lifts his hand to his face, rubbing it over the stubble on his chin. He continues massaging and searching, but Gloria knows what he wants to say, so she says it for him.

"You had a really bad spell this time, didn't you? I was buzzing your phone to let you know Hank's here for his interview, but you never answered."

Frank drops his head to look at the floor and barely mumbles, "Yes...yes, I think I had another spell and this one was intense."

He turns to her and picks up strength, "But this time it was so real...it was *so real*! And it really scared me. I called for you, but you didn't answer and there was no noise from the newsroom. I didn't hear you buzz me, either. But there was this old man sitting right there. He said he was here to help me do something."

Gloria cuts off his story. "My God, what are you doing with a gun and bullets on your desk? For God's sake! You weren't..."

"No!" Frank snaps. "No, I wasn't going to shoot myself, if that's what you were thinking. Jesus, Gloria, you know I wouldn't do that!"

With calculated movements, Frank slides into his chair and picks up the revolver and shells, opens the drawer, and places them back into their safe places. He pulls out the whiskey again, slowly unscrews the top, and takes a sloppy swig. He extends the bottle in mocking fashion to Gloria, but she closes her eyes and grunts in disgust.

"So, what were you doing with that gun on your desk? Where did you get the damn thing, anyway?"

Gloria never swears, so even her uttering "damn" is jolting to Frank.

"That gun has been in my desk for years. My dad gave it to me a long time ago, not long before he died. Now let me finish my story.

"This old man was just sitting right there as calmly as can be, all prim and proper, and he said he was going to help me do something and that we would figure it out together. I showed him the gun, and he just had this nutty look on his face and then he showed me that he had the shells in his hand. It was not like the other spells, Gloria. The others were all just fleeting images with no real substance to them. I'm telling you, the guy was sitting right there. We had a conversation!"

Gloria used her best calming voice. "Didn't Doc Phillips tell you that you'd see and hear all kinds of things as the tumor continued to grow? I wouldn't put much stock in it."

"Gloria, you don't understand. He was here, as real as you are now and then he was gone. It was like time had stopped and you and the others weren't in the newsroom. He spoke so clearly. And it seemed I knew that voice from somewhere."

"Okay, Okay, Frankie. We can talk about this some more later, but right now Hank is here. He's been waiting."

"Oh, that bastard. Tell him to just go—"

"Frank! Hush! That's not like you. He'll hear you!"

Frank squeezes his lips together as though ready to spit out a watermelon seed, for he knows that this is a lost argument if he continues. "Tell that slimy SOB to come in," he mumbles.

Hank, with his wrinkled suit and stained tie, bumbles into the office and plummets with a dull rubbing noise into the leather guest chair in front of Frank's desk. There is no offer of a handshake or warm greeting from either man. Hank crosses his legs, and Frank pushes back to put his feet up on the desk.

Frank opens with an abrupt, disinterested volley. "So, Hank, rumor has it that you're running for reelection. Don't you think you've put this town through enough misery? What are you, seventy-eight? Seventy-nine? Don't you think you should hang it up and give someone else, like O'Brien, a chance?"

This spawns a wide smile in Hank. There is no better sport than sparring with the newspaper publisher. Hank loves all notoriety—anything to keep his name in the paper—but he has deftly managed to keep Frank from making him look bad on the front page.

Most people in the town love Frank and detest the mayor on a personal level. They consider the politician the butt of ongoing humor. Still, the mayor has gotten some things done for this little town over the years, and most residents look at the negative stories as a humorous, personal hatred between the two men. Besides, Hank has never really been *caught* cheating, stealing, or lying. His major crime has been political grandstanding—a small price that residents are apparently willing to pay for consistent trash pickup, few potholes, clean parks, and the return of a solvent town budget.

Frank isn't sure why he has always despised Hank. Perhaps it is the mayor's knack for taking undue credit for others' hard work around the city and placing unjustified blame on staff when things fall short of residents' expectations. Maybe Frank's detest for the mayor grew because the previous publisher, Frank's dad, had come to despise Hank. Perhaps the dislike festers because Hank always looks disheveled and a bit pompous in his cheap suits and crazy ties while everyone else walks around this humble farming town in jeans and Carhartts. Most likely, Frank's animosity festers because he has not been able to reveal the mayor as the true scoundrel he believes he is.

"Frank, you know this town needs me." Hank oozes the words through his smile. "Besides, you also know O'Brien is a drunken idiot and womanizer. People may dislike me, be indifferent about me, or think I am a bag of hot air, but they know O'Brien beats his wife, and that's why he got fired from teaching. That poor man needs help with his demons. Besides, you know a Democrat hasn't won an office in this county for decades. That poor, misguided soul is just wasting his time."

Frank slaps his hand on the desk. "Oh, I can tell you're really concerned about him. Maybe when you win your election you can give him a job on the street crew, so he can get insurance and the psychological help he needs."

"Well, you never know, Frank. That sounds like a good idea. Maybe you can put that idea in your editorial supporting my reelection!"

Frank slowly digs at his forehead. His words become measured and strained.

"Hank, you're a self-centered bastard. You know it, I know it, and just about everyone in town knows it. I guess...I guess..."

Frank pauses and rubs the palm of his right hand above and slightly behind his ear in a circular motion. After a few moments he clasps his hands behind his head, leans back a bit further, and takes a couple deep breaths, eyes shut.

"You okay?" Hank asks with forced concern.

After a few moments Frank opens his eyes, leans forward, and grabs the edge of his desk. "Don't worry. You'll get your damn story, one way or the other. I'm sure you don't care which way it comes out."

Hank's leer confirms Frank's assumption.

Frank lifts himself and walks on wobbly legs around his desk to an enormously deep countertop running the entire length of the wall between the windows. Under the counter are shelves divided into dozens of sections, looking like a gargantuan letter organizer. However, those shelves have widths and depths measured in feet instead of inches. He runs his hand down the stacked shelving unit until he comes to the one labeled "1982—2nd half." Bending down, he reaches into a shelf and slides out a huge leather-bound book that contains original archived newspapers. He struggles with it and flops it on the countertop above the shelves. Frank carefully opens the cover and puts his hand into the pages about a third of the way and gently flips a large section of the newspaper pages to the front. He then leafs through pages individually until he reaches the item of interest.

"Here it is, Hank. Wednesday, September twenty-second, nineteen eighty-two. Do you know what happened just a couple days before this issue was published?"

"Well, not right off. That was a hell of a long time ago."

"Yes, it was." Frank sighs. "Come over here and take a look."

Frank lifts up the edge of an original issue of the *Le Fleur Sentinel* which has been bound and stored in the cubby for decades. There is a blaring headline and accompanying photograph at the top of page one.

"Surely you remember this. You were a much younger man and had been mayor for only a couple years."

The mayor struggles to his feet and limps over to the shelf. The self-confident smirk melts into some other grimace that had been lying just below the corners of his mouth.

"Oh yeah, the Booker arrest," he mutters with feigned disinterest.

Frank challenges sternly, "The Booker arrest? You mean the Booker framing! You know what really happened—you were part of it!"

Frank bangs his fist on the old newspaper and leans forward to continue his interrogation. "You know Phil Wells, don't you? Phil, the Richland County deputy, son of former Le Fleur Police Chief Benson Wells. He gave me some interesting news this morning. You know what really happened back in '82 to Booker. You know, and you never said a word to a soul!"

Hank stares into Frank's eyes with a cold, malicious squint. The moment drags a bit until Hank murmurs nefariously, "You've finally gone mad, haven't you? Either you've lost it, or your illness has gotten the best of you."

Frank's face drains into a white paste and then saturates back into a ruby hue. He drops the corner of the archived newspaper and slams the leather cover shut.

"You son of a bitch! What the hell do you know about my illness?"

"What do I know? Lord, Frank, the whole town knows. You don't think people see you goin' in and out of Doc's office? The doctor-patient confidentiality is about as good as the privacy between a reporter and his sources! You're no longer that big strapping ball player. Look in the damn mirror, man. People can see and know without being told. Aren't you supposed to know what townspeople know? Or do you think they only know what you print in your little paper?"

Once again Hank has managed to deflect the tough question, to turn the tables and change the subject away from something he wants to avoid. This skill has been honed through more than thirty years of running for and keeping office. He has used it on Frank with varying degrees of success, but today was its best employment.

Frank turns away to face the big book lying on the counter and puts his hand on the black-grained cover, stroking down the edge of the binding. He lowers his head and closes his eyes and softly says, "Screw you, Hank. Get the hell out, you smug bastard."

"Well, that was some interview," Hank snorts. "I hope you have enough info for my endorsement editorial. Let me just tell you this—you can't take everything as gospel that people dredge up about an event that happened so many years ago. People think they know things, but they only remember the colorful fragments. If you keep going down the road you're on, just be prepared for what you find. It may lead to a story not worth telling, or to one worth keeping buried because it would only hurt you and those you love. I say none of this for my own sake, because my conscience is clear. I sleep like a baby."

Hank confidently glides out of the office to leave Frank meditating over his book of questionable history. He opens the book back up to the story of Booker's arrest and glances down at his father's byline—*James Barnett, Publisher*. He looks over to the picture above the fold at the credit. *Photo by Frank Barnett*. The young, enthusiastic photographer was eager to get in on the story and prove to the people of Le Fleur he was a real newspaperman and not just the son of the publisher.

He refreshes his memory of the story he has not read since the day it was printed almost thirty years ago. The article vividly recounts how Willis R. Booker, 49, was arrested at his home by Police Chief Benson Wells on the afternoon of

September 20 after a search warrant was executed on the suspicion of robbery of the diner.

The article states that Chief Wells said he had requested the search warrant after he observed Booker hurriedly walking down Main Street, away from O'Meara's Diner, with a brown package under his arm. At the time he noticed Booker, Wells said he was entering the diner just before the 6:30 opening and heard Sarah O'Meara weakly calling for help. He said he then found Sarah on the floor gasping for breath and the drawer to the cash register open. He was quoted as saying it appeared Sarah went into cardiac arrest and that he immediately called paramedics and began performing CPR. Unfortunately, she was pronounced dead upon arrival at Willard Hospital.

Chief Wells and several other Le Fleur officers arrived at Booker's Trux Street home approximately 3:45 p.m. and found Willis Booker and his wife at the kitchen table. Wells confirmed that a subsequent search of the property led to the discovery of a brown bag of cash totaling four hundred seventy-three dollars in a toolbox in the Booker garage.

Chief Wells said that the cash found by officers nearly matched the four hundred seventy-eight-dollar total of the diner's previous day's receipts, according to Charles "Pop" O'Meara. Booker was to be held in the Le Fleur jail until being transported within a couple days to the Richland County Jail for arraignment at the county courthouse.

The article stated that the Booker arrest spawned widespread anger among the residents of Le Fleur. Many residents stated being upset about Booker's heartlessness in finding Mrs. O'Meara lying on the floor of the diner in distress and then making off with the previous day's sales. Some said Booker deserved severe punishment if found guilty of robbing, and some speculated he may have even knocked Sarah to the floor. A few others stated that the crime couldn't have been committed by Booker, because the family was so selfless and giving to everyone.

Le Fleur High School Principal Fred Loomis was quoted as saying, "Even though the Bookers are one of just a few black families in town, Willis has often donated his time to Le Fleur causes, and his wife Clara headed up the annual Community Thanksgiving Dinner at Lincoln Elementary School." He also pointed out that their son, Freeman L. Booker, was the star running back at Le Fleur High School from 1976–80 and was named to the All-Richland County team his senior year.

Chief Wells was quoted near the end of the story that he would have officers stationed at the Booker home "until further notice to protect Mrs. Booker from any unruly behavior."

Reading the passage now, Frank interprets the comment as the chief slyly recommending that someone should make an enflamed action against the family. Two days later, on the Wednesday afternoon the *Sentinel* was being thrown on doorsteps, someone broke into the Le Fleur jail, bludgeoned the guard, and shot Booker dead in his cell before he could be transported to Mansfield. That night a cross was burned in the Booker front yard and officers gathered to make sure the rage of Booker's brothers was kept in check. Those new front-page stories had to wait another week to be published.

Of course, every detail of the Booker robbery had been spewed all over town since the moment of the arrest. The accounts blazed through Le Fleur on Monday morning, from grocery store to barber shop to hair salon to hardware store. The *Sentinel* only rehashed the events two days later and put a stamp of legitimacy onto the storytelling. The paper was a twenty-five-cent verification of the widely accepted *facts*.

Frank slams the big cover shut and stumbles back to his chair, easing into the leather to avoid damaging it or himself. He sits for a moment, gazing aimlessly at the wall behind his desk where more than thirty framed photographs hang in a semi-organized pattern. Some of the photos are decades old and some just a year or two young.

There are shots of the typical ribbon cuttings, smiling faces, kids in uniforms emblazoned "Sentinel," a couple of engulfed house fires, and a stark photo of a large black man being led off his porch by police. Five smaller images are gathered together in a cluster off to the right side—a collection of photos of the same black man in a jail cell in various poses of anxiety and contemplation. Next to these five images hangs a certificate that states, *First Place Photography—Ohio Newspaper Association, Frank Barnett, photographer.*

Frank scans back to photos hanging to the left and stops at a more pleasant image. The photo shows several men standing on either side of a tall sign that reads "Lewiston Landing." Above these large letters, formed in a curve at the top of the sign, are smaller letters that read "Village of Lewiston, NY." Between the two lines of text is a carved salmon that brings color, vibrancy, and a focal point to the sign. Three men stand on the left side of the sign and two on the right. Hanging from hooks at the bottom of the sign are eight large salmon. A man at each end of the group holds a salmon by the gills.

Frank stands up, takes the photo from the wall, and looks deeply into the men's faces. He knows them all but can barely remember them being this young. Tenderness and affection for his friends fills his head. He rubs his finger over the glass and lets it linger on the image of Dave and him standing together, smiling by the sign. The reflection in the glass of his now-scoured face startles him. He replaces the photo on the wall and takes down an older photo of his father standing at the same sign with Chief Wells and a couple other men. His fury builds until he carelessly tosses the framed photo to the side of the credenza and the glass breaks from one corner to the other. He plops down in the chair again, swivels toward the computer screen, and types in the name “Joe Cinelli” on his contact list. He clicks on the number and the speaker rings out loudly.

After two rings, a confident voice booms out. “Hello, this is Joe.”

Frank is startled that the call was answered. It takes a moment of throat clearing before he picks up the receiver to speak.

“Hello, Joe. This is Frank Barnett. I didn’t expect you to pick up. I thought I’d get your voice mail.”

“Yeah, you caught me at home for a few days. I’ve been traveling a lot for work and decided to take a week or so off. How the heck have you been? It’s been a couple years since I’ve heard from you. What’s new?”

Frank pauses a moment, trying to decide if anything new was worth commenting about.

“Well, you know, just busy trying to keep this newspaper afloat and staying out of trouble. How are Ingrid and the girls doing?”

“Oh, the family’s great,” Joe gushes. “The girls are doing really well. They’re getting grown up fast.”

“Yeah, I can appreciate that. I remember when they were first born. Seems like just a few years ago.” He pauses briefly. “Hey, listen, I was wondering if you or your brother Chris would have any open dates for fishing anytime soon. I haven’t been up there for a while and I just wanted to see if I could get back up for some salmon.”

“Well, I told Ingrid I wasn’t going to do any fishing over the next week and would just stay around the house. But she and I both know if a good customer really wanted to go out, I wouldn’t be able to resist. If I tell her it’s you, she’ll be all for it. You interested in going out Saturday or Sunday? It might be a bit early for the salmon run. The bass are really hitting off

Buffalo, but if you want to go for salmon, we may be able to land a few out on the lake."

"Damn, Joe. Sunday would be great! I really want to try for the salmon, though. Whaddaya think?"

"Okay, we'll go out of Lewiston and see if we can't get us a couple big ones out on the ledge. Or maybe we will see what's happening up in the river. If nothing else, we'll probably land a couple good lakers."

"Awesome. I can't believe I got you on the phone and you can take us out so soon. It's going to be me and one other guy. I think we'll drive up Saturday and stay over at the Youngstown Motel, then we can get an early start at the landing on Sunday. Can we still get our licenses at that place over the hill in Lewiston?"

"Yeah, if you get up here early enough Saturday, you'll probably find the owner there. She's usually open till six. By the way, who's coming with you?"

"He's a young man named Russ who works at the paper. His mom Gloria is our business manager. I think you may have talked to her a few times over the years. Russ doesn't know anything about it yet, but the trip is a work assignment, so he can't say no. See you Sunday morning, Joe."

"Looking forward to it. See you at the landing at six-thirty sharp on Sunday. Can't wait to catch up with you."

Frank eases the receiver into its cradle and takes a deep breath of satisfaction. He pauses, then presses a button on top of his phone. "Russ, come in here for a minute."

The meticulously dressed and groomed young reporter bustles into Frank's office.

"Yes, what is it?"

"Russ, you and I are going to leave Saturday morning to go fishing up at Lake Ontario. This is a reporting assignment for you, so you can't say no."

“Frank,” Russ mumbles in disbelief, “I’m not sure I can go. Ann’s parents are coming into town and the baby has been sick the last few days. It isn’t a good time to—”

Frank cuts him off, but only half sternly.

“You just have to tell Ann that your reprehensible boss is making you do this crummy assignment and that your job depends on it. She can hate me all she wants, which she already does anyway, but she can’t take it out on you. Now get out of here and get all your copy read today and tomorrow. I know you work at home on Saturdays to catch up, but you can’t do that this weekend. We’re going fishing, young man! And by the way, I’m taking tomorrow off, so you all have to pitch in and cover for me. I want you to write next week’s editorial. It’s time you learn to fill that space.”

Russ stands frozen, eyes wide. “What the heck am I going to write about?”

“Don’t worry. You can read all your copy and come up with some good material for a column before you leave work Friday. And I’m leaving it up to you to get everyone scheduled in advance to cover the city council and school board meetings on Monday night because we won’t be home until late that day, and you’ll be too damn tired to cover anything when you get back. Now, get out of here and start acting like the managing editor. You’re getting a promotion and a raise, young man. It’s long overdue.”

“Frank, I...”

“Shut up, Russ, and get the hell out. You don’t have any time to waste!”

Russ turns in disbelief and walks with purpose down the hall. He has squinty satisfaction on his face that has been missing a long while. A promotion to managing editor, a raise, and a fishing trip, all in a matter of seconds. The best part is that he has a weekend pass from a fussy toddler, badgering wife, and insufferable mother-in-law. He cannot even be made out to be the bad guy this time—this assignment is from his "son-of-a-bitch" employer, after all.

Frank watches Russ trot down the hall, then picks up the phone again and punches a number.

A pleasant woman blurts, "Good morning, Rocket Chevrolet. How may I help you?"

"Hi, this is Frank Barnett. Could I speak to Sid, please?"

Sid greets the call with great enthusiasm. "Hey Frank! How the heck are you?"

Frank wonders if there is a hidden question below the question but moves on to the important issue.

"Sid, you still have that yellow Stingray on the showroom floor?"

"The convertible? Sure do."

"Okay, I'm coming over in the morning to buy it. I want it polished extra shiny and gassed up. It's time I stop kicking its tires and pull the trigger!"

"Is this some kind of joke, Frank? You haven't bought a new car since my dad was here. Then all of a sudden you're going to buy the most expensive car in the place? What the hell?"

"Just have it ready," Frank demands. "I'll be there at eight tomorrow morning."

"To hell with that! I am not going to let you wiggle out of this one. I'll drive it over to your house personally tonight and have it there by seven!"

"That's a deal, Sid. I'll have the bank call you for the details and have them deliver a check. And by the way, I expect a good year-end deal on this, and no bull."

Gloria walks in from the hallway after listening to much of Frank's conversation.

"Are you serious, Frank? You're buyin' a Corvette? You think that's a good idea? And what's this about you naming Russ the managing editor and you two going fishing this weekend? What the heck are you doing with all of these things?"

"Don't worry. It's all going to be good. Call Rodgers over at the bank and have him work with Sid on the Vette and have Fenton put it in the ownership of the paper. Then you need to keep herding Russ and the others to get the work flow managed. I am counting on you, Gloria. Russ may be the new managing editor, but you're the business manager and a better publisher than me. We both know you keep this place going anyway—the rhythm and soul of the paper, as I've always said."

"Oh, very funny."

"Really. You and Russ are the best people I know. In fact, I should've promoted him long ago. You know, I won't be able to work much longer. You both will need to carry on without me soon. He'll be a good editor, but you're the one who'll make him succeed—just like you did me."

He turns back to the computer screen, voice cracking. "I'm gonna finish the obits, then I'm gonna get out of here and I'm taking off tomorrow, too. Russ and I will leave Saturday morning and be back late Monday. Now go tell Russ I'll pick him up at his house Saturday morning at nine sharp."

"Frank, what—?"

"No more questions. I can't take another one. Just help me out with this. And one more thing—make sure the masthead gets changed for the next edition to reflect Russ as the managing editor."

Gloria turns in befuddlement and continues down the hall, knowing life will be different from this moment forward. She pulls a hanky from her pants pocket and wipes her cheek as the sound of Frank's keystrokes fill her head. Frank's presence within the paper has been decreasing over the last few months, and the three "newsboys," as he calls them, have picked up the slack with composure and pride. Many of the big decisions have fallen to Gloria, and she has managed, with learned confidence. She makes it to her desk to sit, unsure and terrified, just like the young woman who came to work for Frank's dad so many years ago. She picks up a photograph from her desk to study a young black woman holding her baby. She is flanked to the right by the stately older Barnett with a pipe and on the right by young Frankie in a ball cap. They were the entire staff back then.

In his office, concealed from the world, Frank bangs away, chronicling the life of Carmen H. Bunch, 91, who passed after a long illness. Between keystrokes he hears, "That was a good thing you did, Frankie."

Frank slowly turns to the corner from where he heard the voice. No one is there. Frank looks around the room and down the hall, then turns back to the computer screen with indifference to the voice and completes Bunch's obit and several others. He takes more care than usual to cram consequence into just a few column-inches of little life stories.

Frank saves the obits in the computer folder titled "Sept. 20 edition," shuts down the machine, turns to his desk, and opens the drawer. He pulls out the whiskey bottle and screws off the lid with measured care before hoisting it to his lips for a very small taste. He caps it, then places it in the outer pocket of his beat-up leather satchel. He reaches down and pulls out the gun and shells and carefully puts them in the wider inner pocket of the bag. Throwing the strap over his shoulder, he shuffles to the door, then turns to examine his ripened office. He explores the space for small details, as a policeman would a crime scene. The photos behind his desk are all slightly askew and he puffs in amusement at the clutter. In the corner where the strange visitor's image and voice emanated, he sees only the empty chair, to which he speaks softly.

"So, it was a good thing, was it? What? Making Russ the managing editor? Making Russ go fishing? Buying the car? What?"

He flips off the light switch and makes his way down the hall and stands before Gloria's counter. She looks up from her seat through swollen reservoirs, bites her lip and then pinches her mouth between her thumb and finger. A seemingly invigorated, younger-looking Frankie, one she remembers, looks away from her to the back of the newsroom.

"Okay everyone, I am going to be gone for a few days, so you'll need to pull together to get the next issue out. Russ is your new managing editor, and he'll go over the assignments with you today and tomorrow, but he's going with me this weekend and will not be here Monday. I know you guys can do it, just like you do when there's a short holiday week or when folks are on vacation. Gloria will buy everyone lunch on Monday and pizza Monday night. You...you guys are good at what you do. Thanks for your dedication. Russ, be ready to go Saturday morning and be sure to pack some warm clothes and your rain gear."

Frank turns and bolts through the door before anyone responds, or before Gloria again catches his eye. He barely touches the steps as he skims his way down to the sidewalk. His pace is lively down the street as the sun breaks through onto his cheeks and a cool breeze gently pushes back against his collar. He takes in all the smells, sounds, and small-town minutiae that bind Le Fleur in commonality to other kindred hamlets.

He makes the brisk three-block walk to his house on the border of downtown. Stopping at the front gate, Frank looks up at the well-kept white two-story house and its neatly manicured lawn and large wrap-around front porch. The neighbor boy, Tommy, grooms the grass and edges with great precision. Every kid in town wants to take care of the Barnett lawn because the owner pays well for a job well done. The last youth caretaker actually kept the job into his community college days because Frank was so generous a boss.

After a few seconds admiring Tommy's yard work, Frank is up the porch steps and through the unlocked door to kick off his shoes next to the umbrella stand. He stops in the hallway to open a shadowbox and removes a crusty, antique baseball glove. Rolling it over in his hands close to his face, the musty smell of leather brings a torrent of memories of days in the sun with friends who were as close as brothers. It is a moment of deep satisfaction that he doubts could ever be felt again, but he wants to try.

He puts the glove back into the box and makes his way to the rear sunroom, flips on the ceiling fan, and settles into his favorite overstuffed chair while pulling out two pill bottles and the whiskey from his satchel. He fumbles with the human-proof bottle caps but finally manages to get two pills from each. He washes them down with a big swig of whiskey, then leans back to put his feet up and is instantly asleep.

There is a knock at the door. "Frank, Frank, are you home? You in there?"

# Chapter Five

Frank comes slowly back to groggy awareness to lift himself out of the chair as Sid approaches the sunroom.

Sid puts his hand out for a shake. "Taking a nap, heh, Frank?"

Frank weakly clasps Sid's palm, still rough from when he learned about cars as a mechanic at his father's dealership.

"I was banging at the front door for a couple minutes and didn't hear anything, so I thought I'd pop my head in. Told you I'd have the Vette here tonight. It's out front, all gassed up and waxed."

Sid glances down at the end table where the pills and whiskey bottle sit. "Everything okay?"

"Why the hell wouldn't it be?" Frank pulls his hand back. "It's just been a long week. Getting the paper out this week was kinda tough with the computer issues we had, that's all. Thought I'd catch a nap before my trip this weekend."

"Oh, yeah? Where ya goin'?"

"Well, I'm going to run some errands tomorrow and then Saturday I'm taking Russ—you know, Gloria's son—up to Niagara for some salmon fishing."

Sid's eyes widen in envy. "Damn, that sounds like fun. I remember our dads talking about those trips up there and the huge salmon they caught. He wanted me to go with all of you as I got older, but I never was much interested. Besides, when he went, I had to stay and run the lot."

"Yeah," Frank says, "Dad started taking me up there more than twenty-five years ago. After our dads died, I just kept going up with some other guys. Now those guys are gone too—or some of us just don't speak anymore. You know, Russ is like a son to me in many ways. I don't know much about my own boys, so maybe I can just pass this thing on to Russ."

Sid wasn't prepared for the personal direction Frank was going despite all his salesmanship and skill at pretending to care about the lives of his customers.

"C'mon, Frank. Let's go out and I'll show you the Vette's features and we can go for a ride. You're gonna take it on your trip, aren't you?"

"Damn right I am. But I don't need to be tutored or take a test drive. I already bought the damn thing, didn't I? You get things worked out with the bank and my attorney?"

"Sure, but I think I need to show you a few things about the car—how to change the suspension settings, put the top up, stuff like that."

"Jesus, Sid. I think I can figure that out. If I can't, I'm sure it's in the manual. Chevy did put a manual in the glove box, didn't they?"

"Well sure, but this thing's really powerful. It has over four hundred horsepower and can go almost two hundred miles an hour. You have to ease into understanding what this beast is all about."

"I know it isn't my old truck, but I'll manage. Why don't you sit down and have a glass of whiskey with me to celebrate the purchase?"

Sid looks over to the table. "Well, I would, but it looks like that bottle is pretty much killed. You got another one?"

"Oh damn, no I don't. I guess I'll just have to go get one. Maybe I'll take the Vette out for her maiden voyage to pick up a bottle."

"You want me to go along with you?"

The question has a tinge of concern and a bit of begging in it.

"No. I tell you what. Let me spend the evening exploring the car and I'll stop by the lot tomorrow with any questions. You have a cover for it? I could pick that up tomorrow too."

"Yeah, we have a cover to give you at no charge and, damn it, I was going to bring it. But I'd be happy to go for a ride with you tonight if you want and we can stop by the lot to get it."

"No, that's all right. I am going to jump in the shower, then go downtown to get something to eat."

"Okay, Frank. Come by in the morning to pick up the cover. I've already put the temporary tags on the car for you."

The two men walk together to the front door. Frank holds open the screen as Sid hands him two sets of key fobs, then hops down the porch steps. Frank stares at the gleaming Corvette, which looks a little out of place on the street of this modest neighborhood.

"Just be careful," Sid yells back. "You won't believe how this thing wants to roar, even in first gear. It's like a jet fighter taking off. Be gentle with the clutch. Small moves to start, small, easy moves. You'll be in third gear and sixty before you can believe it. It'll be like trying to keep a wild horse restrained."

Frank closes the door and watches Sid get into a Cadillac driven by one of his salesmen. He alternates between looking at the Vette and watching Sid ride away, with a moment of doubt about his impetuous purchase. He arcs his back, breathes deep, and rubs his hands over his chest and then, with a lengthy exhale, he sighs the release of insecurity.

"What the hell, I can handle this car."

He looks at the "racing yellow" composite-fiber monster at the curb and slowly pushes the screen open again. He is already mentally practicing the small moves encouraged by Sid as he stands and gawks from the porch. Frank gazes up and down the street to see if anyone is watching. He is a little embarrassed that this expensive piece of American automotive engineering is sitting in front of his house for the entire world to see.

Frank eases down the steps and warily approaches the shiny missile. He gently glides his finger along the rear fender on the passenger side, down the slope of the door, along the rise of front fender, and finally to the headlight housing. With a sensual touch he thinks he feels the car responding with a subtle charge. It desires to sprint. It wants to leap. It needs to be unleashed, now.

Frank moves to the front of the car and puts his finger in the small scoop opening at the lower front of the hood and runs his hand around the edge. It brings a smile to his face as he senses this outlandish thing begging for attention just sitting still. He moves to the driver's side and gently puts his fingers in the flush handle to open the door. The inside is a serious cockpit, like a fighter plane, and just about as small. Frank grabs the leather-wrapped steering wheel, eases himself into the supple driver's seat, and senses his butt dragging on the ground. He throws one of the key fobs over to the passenger seat to land on the invoice sticker that he hadn't noticed was there. He picks up the price sheet and glances over the long list of features of the *3LT with Z51 Performance Package* but doesn't bother to inspect the many optional features. He tells himself, "I guess it doesn't get much meaner than this."

He looks at the left portion of the invoice sticker and reads, *Estimated 15 miles per gallon city, 18 miles per gallon highway. Assembled in Bowling Green, Kentucky.* The bottom right reads, *Manufacturer's Suggested Retail, $76,510,* then down to the final total of *$86,415*. He asks the sticker, "I wonder how much I actually paid?"

He folds the sticker and tucks it in between the passenger seat and console. He presses the clutch, puts his foot lightly on the accelerator, and pushes the keyless start. The car bellows with a strong, deep rage. The growl grows heavier and subsides as he presses and then lets up on the accelerator several times. With seriously controlled timing, he places his hand on the shift knob to make sure it is in first gear, lets up on the clutch, and gives it a small amount of gas with his right foot. The car leaps ahead and stalls. The first test with the car is a failure.

He starts it again and this time gives a more precise dose of gas and clutch release. The Vette moves ahead slowly, and he makes a right turn into the driveway. He eases up the drive and maneuvers to the open left side of the garage next to the scruffy pickup truck. Frank routinely leaves his garage open twenty-four hours a day, never worrying about anyone walking off with anything. He thought the neighbor kids would have taken something by now, but they have never bothered anything, as far as he can tell.

The Corvette fits neatly into the garage. Frank gives the car a couple blasts of accelerator with the clutch firmly engaged, to listen to the lion roar approvingly for its new den. He feels the energy rumble in the gearshift knob, the steering wheel, and the seat of his pants. A perfect blending of man and machine. He lets his foot off the gas and clutch with clumsy timing and the car jumps forward to push a bicycle into the front garage wall.

"Damn it."

Frank gets out to examine the scar he has already given the creature. "Sorry. I'll get better." He is relieved to see no noticeable blemish caused by the bike.

He closes the door with both hands with a sound that is pleasingly precise. Standing tall over the low-slung car makes him feel powerful. He thinks that every car, especially a *super car*, needs to have a name.

"You look like a lion," he says. "That's your name from now on. The Lion."

He studies the graceful but glitzy lines and thinks about the next day and his command of the brawny brute's instant responses. He walks to the house and looks back to the Vette as he enters the back door. He presses the button on the kitchen wall to close the garage. He cannot remember the last time the garage door was lowered.

His thoughts fade from the car to a shower, knowing that the warm water will relax him after such a trying, puzzling, and emotional day. There is a throbbing in his head and he rubs his fingers over the area behind his ear. Frank lumbers to the sunroom and plops down in his beloved chair, opens the pill bottles, and takes two from each. He struggles a bit to swallow them with the few drops of remaining whiskey. He yearns to sit, just for a moment, before showering. He leans back into the softness, puts his feet up on the ottoman, and begins to snore.

## Chapter Six

The ambient light softens the sunroom as evening drifts onto Le Fleur. The home's otherwise silent calm is periodically broken with Frank's labored breathing. The dimming of the day creates a sense of desolation in the tidy but dated house. The furniture had originally been expensive but now shows its age and would be replaced if left behind for some new homeowner.

Except for Frank, there are no living things in the house. No plants, no pets, not even a goldfish with which to converse. A large fishbowl sits on the antique dining room hutch, but it is filled with pencils, scissors, several pica rulers, newspaper blue-line pens, an array of knobs, buttons, tacks, and other useless items that have waited years for a chance to provide service.

It has been this way since Brenda left thirteen years ago with the twins. The furniture, wallpaper, and area rugs that cover most of the hardwood floors were old even then. Now they are just residue from a time when things were tolerable for Frank. But most things seemed unbearable for Brenda. She grew increasingly depressed from being a widow to the newspaper and extremely disillusioned with Frank's frugal nature. She had the boys and house to keep her busy and friends to lunch with, but she felt alone and ignored in a one-sided relationship. She wanted desperately to be an adoring and caring wife, but Frank was rarely around to share her passion, or too tired to respond with any compassion when he was there. She felt deserted and remote from the man who in college had promised her never-ending exhilaration. When Frank was home, Brenda would often accuse him of unleashing that sporadic impatience and temper onto her and the boys without justification, which in her eyes outweighed his normal composed benevolence.

She spawned many arguments by threatening lavish home renovations, perhaps because it was the only method she could contrive to ignite any kind of vigorous spark in him. He would not consider something so foolish when nothing, as far as he could tell, was worn out. Instead, he diverted those funds to repair buildings he owned or to some new equipment needed for the newspaper. Brenda often objected resentfully that Frank's tenants and employees enjoyed better surroundings than she and the boys did.

Instead of worrying about fancy things, he wanted Brenda to share in his love of words and to help out at the paper. He thought it noble to carry on and be a pillar of the Le Fleur community, like his parents and grandparents, and was perplexed at her ability to dismiss his family's honorable and gallant mission. After all, he was writing about real life, of people they knew and institutions his family helped build. He envisioned that one day his sons would take up the historic tradition where he left off and that they, too, would become virtuous defenders of small-town mores. Though he tried to coax and prod her into an understanding of this selflessness, he finally judged her to be greedy, uncaring, and unmoved about greater circumstances beyond new living room curtains. Brenda judged Frank to be more interested in anything apart from their home and those who waited for him to be there.

Brenda took nothing material but the family minivan, clothes for her and the boys, and many of the family photos. The divorce "in absentia" was handled by their lawyers. Brenda and Frank had not spoken to or looked each other in the face since the Friday morning he left for work and she went to the bank to drain the shared savings account of $249,355. She left him with all the stocks, investments, buildings, and land, and a spiteful $20.34 in the savings to keep it open. She then sped away with the boys for an unknown future that would at least provide a sense of freedom and that elusive exhilaration once promised her.

The bank manager, Martin Rodgers, tried to delay Brenda from making the withdrawal while calling Frank's office and pager to let him know what she was up to, but Frank was out chasing some police issue. Rodgers could not prolong the withdrawal any longer since Brenda was equally on the account with Frank, which was separate from the newspaper bank accounts. Rodgers finally reached Frank after nine o'clock that night, but by then, Brenda had long since deposited the enormous check into the secret account she had opened at another bank in Shelby several years previously. Frank did nothing to fight the issue.

He received a few scathing letters from Brenda during the first several years apart. The only comfort Frank found in them came from scant updates about the boys, along with an occasional photo documenting their smiling faces and healthy growth. Frank knew that Brenda wanted to emphasize, wickedly, that the boys were doing very well without his influence, but he cherished the photos just the same. He wrote back asking to see the boys and for a telephone number to call, but she never agreed, and he never pressed the issue.

Brenda's letters became less frequent and stopped arriving altogether about four years ago. Frank had court-ordered visitation rights to the boys, but he never pursued them since Brenda had taken the boys to the east coast. Brenda took full advantage of the fact that Frank had forgotten to request in the divorce agreement that she must live in close proximity in order for him to be able to see the boys. His attorney, Jerry Fenton, was on a three-week drunk during the case and did not realize the omission until after the case was final. As usual, Frank was too busy at the paper to read the divorce decree in great detail.

After Brenda's brief accounts stopped arriving, the birthday cards with checks to the boys were returned to him unopened. Sometimes nine or ten of Frank's cards and letters to the boys would come back bundled in a large envelope.

The last news Frank received was from a private investigator he hired to find out all he could about the boys. The report stated that Brenda had married a pharmaceutical executive in Boston and the boys wanted for nothing. Apparently, they had thrived at one of the city's finest private high schools, enjoyed an impressive social circle, and were now excelling in college in the sport of lacrosse. Frank came close several times to hopping on a plane to fly to Boston to show up at the front door and ask to see his sons. But he understood that the returned letters meant his ex-wife and the twins were done with him, and he obliged. He imagined many times how his surprise arrival would play out but concluded that Brenda's false indoctrination of the boys about their father would prove too great a chasm to cross. The investigator still gives Frank three- to four-page updates with several clandestine photos of the boys twice a year. He keeps them all stored, preciously, in a trunk by his easy chair and looks at them from time to time.

Brenda took none of the photos that contained Frank, and she smashed and discarded any of her and Frank together. She did leave several framed pictures of Frank, Jeff, and Joey on the coffee table in the living room. Frank wondered at the time if she left them out of a small remaining kernel of kindness, or if she did it to make an emphatic statement about what she had taken from him.

One of the fading photographs depicts Frank and the boys standing together on a pier at Kelly's Island on Lake Erie, each holding up a fish they had caught. There is another of the three taken at the Little League baseball field with the boys in their *Le Fleur Sentinel* uniforms and their dad bending over between them. The photo was taken the year Frank was the infamous head coach who managed to show up to less than half the games because of some big story, school board meeting, car crash, or house fire he had to cover. "Had to" was a matter of fierce debate between the mom and coach.

The montage of memories slips in and out of Frank's jumbled mind to form a cold darkness. The pain seeps through and raw images stab at his thoughts. His breathing grows a bit more labored as he tosses himself to one side of the chair and props his head on the arm. Sweat beads on his forehead as his legs flail and twitch.

His visions emerge into a gray despair that devours the corners of the house as he stands near the front door watching Jeff and Joey sit at opposite ends of the kitchen table doing their homework. The lone light above the table is all that illuminates the study session. Brenda sits between them at the tableside reading a book and asks periodic questions of the boys. Frank quietly leaves for the paper, of course. It is a Tuesday night and the news from this afternoon's city planning commission meeting must be filed for the next morning's paper. Most study sessions happened this way—mom tutoring and dad leaving for the office.

The images dissolve into a scene years later of Jeff and Joey ripping open their Christmas presents in earnest as the phone interrupts the festivities. The boys stop the gleeful commotion as Frank listens to the phone and nods his head in understanding.

Brenda asks in mock concern, "What is it, Frank? Whose cat is up a tree and requires your immediate attention?"

Frank eases the phone onto the wall while scolding her with descriptive language.

"For your information, Principal Loomis slid his truck off the curve at North Street and ended up in the Blackfork River. The medics are there now, pulling him out of the water. That would be a great photo."

Brenda stands and points angrily to the boys.

"For God's sake, Frank, it's Christmas Day! Call one of your reporters and tell them to go!"

"I couldn't have them go out on Christmas morning. I have to go myself. I'll be right back."

Naturally, the photos, interviews of the police and medics, and trip to the hospital to check on Loomis mean Frank gets home well after Brenda and the boys finish opening their presents. Frank opens his gifts later that evening as Brenda and the boys half-watch with disinterest. Frank's sadness and growing humiliation of missing the boys' pleasure of opening gifts, all bought and wrapped by Brenda, is poorly masked by contrived appreciation for his presents that he knows were bought out of obligation and not gratitude. He tells himself that the importance of doing his job well benefits the family. He believes that someday they will understand.

The dream brightens as Frank sits at his desk on a brilliant Saturday afternoon, editing several stories written by one of his young reporters. One story describes how an area farmer hired a company to clear-cut a stand of majestic virgin forest to sell for lumber. The logging created a mild controversy in the town because it has long been believed that the woods served as a temporary encampment for Col. William Crawford on his way to the 1782 campaign against some "hostile Indians" during the Sandusky Campaign. Frank's infatuation with the area's historical tidbits is a personality trait that exasperates Brenda and some others at the paper.

While Frank absorbs the story about the demise of the trees and Colonel Crawford, Joey is being mobbed by teammates after a three-run homer in the bottom of the sixth inning to lead the Tigers over the Reds in youth baseball. Brenda calls Frank at the office to relay the majesty of the feat and slams the phone down before Frank can utter a word. He edits one more story about a three-car wreck on Route 98 before heading home to congratulate Joey.

While this memory rises through his subconscious, Frank feels the sorrow just as he did on that summer day that slipped away years ago. Once again, he feels his chest cave in on itself from remorse for choosing to edit these damn stories instead of cheering his son on to home plate.

He recalls walking home while practicing his speech of praise, but sadly remembers it had to wait because Joey had gone to spend the night at a friend's house—the home of the assistant coach—who had taken the boys to Curley's Drive-In for an ice cream celebration. The next morning before he, his brother, and mom went to church, Joey recounted his heroic feat for his dad. Joey brushed off his dad's well-meaning acclaim in the usual way, with absolving thanks and pretense of no hurt. Frank promised to be at the next game. He meant it. But of course, he could not have foreseen the house fire over on Maple Street.

The images in sleep seem as real as when they occurred years before. They are both comforting and agonizing. He is proud of his sons. He relishes their smiling faces. But watching their smiles weaken as he walks out the door during one of his hundreds of ill-timed departures melts the images into a puddle of misery.

Frank's shirt is now sweat-drenched, and his face is flushed with stinging distress. His scant, damp hair is riotously scattered in all directions, with a bit matted to his forehead. He struggles, half conscious, to wake himself from the cruel affliction of memories. He is well-practiced in keeping the past mostly suppressed within neatly sealed boxes, lowered deeply into a well of spousal blame and contempt. Rarely do the voices of Brenda or his sons escape the confinement. But, when the dreams do manage to leak out, they are vividly chastising, a penance for abusing time and losing the opportunity to share his love with wife and sons. They wondered, as he did, about how to reach in and pull out at least a thread of heartfelt devotion. At one time he had wondered how to do that with his own father.

The frail, sweaty, trembling man wakes fully and pushes himself up by kicking the ottoman and leveraging against the arms of the chair. He knows he has to fight his way out of these visions. He raises himself as a pain in the back of his head causes a muted grunt and a longer, audible exhale as he finally awakens. Reaching for the pills is a feeble maneuver that results in most of them being ejected all over the wooden floor.

"Son of a bitch!"

Frank grabs two from his lap and chews on them and swallows in disgust as the rancid metal taste fills his mouth. These pills are supposed to be taken whole with significant water, but he is too drained physically and mentally to drag himself to the kitchen for such an indulgence. He swipes at the remaining pills and they fly off toward a matching chair in the opposite corner of the room. He is glad for the severe banishment of them and the brutal force he mustered in their flinging.

Several of the tablets congregate curiously on the floor around the soles of shiny black shoes. Frank examines the feet, then moves his eyes slowly upward along neatly pressed pants to a tidy suit coat and tie, then finally upon that stoic, aged face.

Frank shouts, "You! You! Holy hell! Not you again!" He cowers back and demands, "What are you doing here? Why the hell can't you leave me alone?" He lowers his head onto his shoulder as he grabs himself in a hug. Looking away, he denies his senses and yells at the top of his lungs. "You aren't real, you aren't even there! You are my imagination! Go away, damn you. Just go away and leave me alone!"

Frank's rage trails off into an anguished muffle as his face contorts and rivulets of tears further dampen his sweat-moistened face. He curls up in a fetal position, grabbing his knees. His sobs grow, and he pities himself, with shrieks reverberating throughout the otherwise quiet house and then he passes out, exhausted. No dreams or pain this time.

# Chapter Seven

Frank slides into the cockpit, cleanly shaven, thoroughly medicated, caffeine laden, toast filled, and without any morning hallucinations. The snort of the brawny V8 soothes the remaining muscle soreness not smothered by the hot shower. He is mastering the timing of the gearshift, clutch, and gas, maintaining the triangulated control between hand and feet. His fingers curl around the eight-speed knob, and his left hand grips the responsive leather steering wheel. It gives him a sense of control he has not experienced in many months.

During the past summer and early fall, he has felt influence over very little—not his disjointed thoughts, not his cranky disposition, and most certainly not the sketchy plans for the remainder of his life. The only matters he has administered well are related to the execution of his estate. He has entrusted those details to Rodgers at the bank and an alcohol-recovering Fenton. The attorney has been on the wagon for several years and managed to rescue his bourbon-plagued career from the edge of a deep trough.

The morning dampness skids over Frank's head as the Lion cuts corners with precision and scatters startled songbirds with growling bursts of exhaust. Each strong push and pull of the gearshift brings stares from pedestrians and delight to Frank. Speeding is rare for Frank, but today he does nothing but exceed the limits. He imagines each onlooker wondering, "*Can that really be the boring editor? Is that really him, driving that brutish, glaring machine?*" He greatly relishes being unlike himself—now fearless, ruthless, and frenzied.

The Vette screeches to a halt within inches of a shiny red tailgate and massive bumper of a new F-250. Frank pushes the gearshift into slot number 1 while keeping his clutch foot plastered to the floor. He slowly presses and retreats from the gas pedal several times and leers criminally when the car rocks from potential to kinetic energy being expelled from the bawling quad tailpipes.

He jumps out of the car with newfound strength, with no acknowledgment of the mannequin people gawking at him in astonishment. Skipping up the walk to the law offices, he relishes his taut skin and powerful muscles that have longed to be stretched. This must be how the Corvette felt as it pulled out of the garage before this morning's drive. He felt the same purpose in his youth when he hit his game-winning homeruns and his teammates slapped his back, thankful that the strongest and best player was on their team. At those glorious moments he was in control, and it did not matter that his dad was at the office buried in work. His mother was at the field to witness, and he was a hero to her. The car has reminded him that those sensations of strength were there to be retrieved—he is thankful they could be summoned at all. He presses his own gas pedal further up the walk.

As he swings open the heavy wooden door of the historic office building, he nearly runs into Julie O'Meara, exiting from the diner. Both are startled as Frank grinds his braking shoes to a halt and Julie looks up as her apparent despair melds into confusion.

"Frank?" she asks with hesitation.

"Oh, Julie, I'm so sorry! I wasn't paying attention. I was going so fast. Let me hold the door for you."

"Frank, you look good. You doing okay today?"

"Oh, yes. I'm doing just fine! How are you and your dad doing?"

"Well, we're doing well. You know, okay, I guess. You—you sure look better than when I saw you yesterday. You were so upset, and you left in such a hurry. You left your jacket, hat, and umbrella too. Are you sure everything's alright?"

Frank pauses a moment to digest the fact that his departure from the diner the previous day may have startled patrons and employees and caused a burst of discussion, arguing, and bet-taking.

"Oh yeah, everything's fine," he says convincingly. "Just going to do a little bit of business with Fenton, and I'm getting ready to go fishing. Everything's great!"

She smiles widely. A sparkle returns to her pretty eyes, and kindheartedness erases her somberness.

"Well, that, um, that sounds good, Frank. Why don't you come by later for lunch and get the stuff you left? It's 'fish Friday,' you know. So, you can have some in case you don't catch any on your trip."

Frank is momentarily lost in the silkiness of Julie's tender voice. He has often thought that if Le Fleur ever had a building tall enough and someone needed talked off the ledge, the sheriff should get her to do the coaxing. He always savors sitting across the counter from her, if only to swim in her soothing tones of calm and compassion.

"That's a great idea. I think I'll do that!"

They stare at each other as both search for some way to end the conversation. They have always admired each other, but a mutual barrier of apprehension has existed between them. Frank has a deep infatuation with Julie—her work ethic, her quick smile, and her genuine zest for the important place that she and the diner have maintained in the community.

Julie attended Ohio State University, only two hours away in Columbus, but to her it seemed like a different planet. She earned a bachelor's degree in biology while Pop, Marilyn, and the students ran the diner. At one time she thought about getting a master's degree in marine biology and doing some kind of work around the islands of Lake Erie, one of her favorite escapes, when she manages to get away at all. She loves to sit on the pier at the OSU research lab near Put-In-Bay on South Bass Island. She pokes around the shoreline and talks with graduate students at the historic facility. But the only place Julie ever really feels whole and completely in control is in her little town at the diner, next to Pop. She loves the people, she loves the stories, she loves the smells, and she adores her soft-hearted and cuddly dad. It is in the diner that she feels closest to her mother.

Julie comes to work impeccably made up, her beautiful, wavy, reddish-blond hair restrained in a ponytail and bow. Her constant smile spreads a glow to her graceful face and her statuesque figure fills out a crisp white blouse. Her black slacks and white apron are donned in a way that a fashion magazine would artfully portray "Diners of the Midwest."

At one time Frank had considered asking Julie to date but decided not to for reasons he cannot comprehend. The best he could rationalize was that his ex-wife Brenda had once accused him of having an affair with Julie. Perhaps he imagined that asking Julie on a date after the divorce would give Brenda's allegation some belated credence. Frank would never want others to think that Julie was the cause of his divorce, even if he waited years after Brenda left to ask Julie for a date. The fact that Brenda spread false innuendos all over town about Frank and Julie having had clandestine meetings seemed to taint any future dating plans. Perhaps Brenda knew that there'd been no actual affair, but she'd seen the potential and intended to foil those possibilities before leaving Frank and the town behind. Brenda wasn't happy, so why should Frank stay in Le Fleur and find contentment? Maybe that was her devious plan, or perhaps that was Frank's vivid imagination creating excuses for his inaction.

Frank supposed that Julie admired him, but he had no idea how true that perception was. Julie rarely dated, and rumors circulated that she was more attracted to women than men. Julie has one very close friend in Lindsey Patton, with whom many evenings are spent, long weekend trips made, and local dances and festivals attended. Lindsey badly wants to date men, but her ungainly appearance and frumpy nature repels potential suitors.

Despite her ungraceful demeanor, Lindsey has a heart of gold like Julie's, and the two are the closest of confidants. In fact, Lindsey is the only person in the world that knows Julie desperately wants to marry Frank. He happens to be the only person in the county that Julie thinks kind enough and truly worthy of her love and dedication. Julie had made a pledge to herself long ago to make it happen, and that pledge has prevented her from getting close to other men.

Lindsey frequently tells Julie that she should date other men to make Frank jealous, so he will act before it is too late. Julie will not even hear of the scheme to use others to get to Frank, but neither will she take the offensive and ask him out. It is part of that "risk aversion" she learned when her mother died. She needs him to be the old-fashioned provocateur. Today, standing in front of the law offices and asking him to come for Friday fish at the diner is about the closest she has ever come to an inducement, and the closest he has come to thinking about the possibilities of acting on his desires.

"Okay, great!" Julie found an ending to the stare-down. "Make sure you get there before one-thirty, because you know the fish goes fast!"

"Oh, I will, Julie."

His skin now even tighter and his back a little straighter, Frank watches with reverence as Julie glides down the walk with a fluid, ladylike gait. He feels like a man who could again hope for a time and place where the past didn't matter and where a future could still be written with her.

Taking the risk of an obvious stare, Frank fixes intently on Julie as she slides into her fourteen-year-old Volkswagen parked in front of the F-250, rattles it to a start, and rumbles down the street. He sees, or imagines, hopefully, that she turns to look out the back window at him.

Frank navigates the heavy wooden door, which seems lighter now, and makes his way down the marble hall to an equally impressive door with "Jerry Fenton, Esq." painted on its glass. Fenton's use of the abbreviation for "Esquire" always makes Frank chuckle with thoughts of how this term, used to describe someone with nobility, has been commandeered by attorneys of Fenton's small-town pedigree.

Frank enters the office and greets the receptionist. "Hell-oh, Helen! How are you doin' today?"

The grandmotherly Helen swings her chair around with well-rehearsed smoothness.

"Well, well, if it isn't good ol' Frankie Shmankie!" Frank hates that moniker and she knows it, although he never confronts her about it. "You are a bit early, my young man. I'll let Jerry know, since he just got done with his last appointment."

In an instant she is on her phone. "Jerry, the newspaper tycoon is here. Go on in, Frankie."

Fenton turns from placing an armful of files on the credenza behind him. "Hey Frank, always punctual as usual. Have a seat, my friend."

Frank simultaneously sits and pulls up toward Jerry's desk in a nearly threadbare, blue wingback with a field of golden-stitched anchors.

"Hey Jerry, was Julie just in here with you? Is everything okay with her?"

Jerry replies emphatically, “You know I can’t talk about that with you. She may have been here, but her business is her business.”

Frank looks astonished as he considers pressing Jerry for more details but resigns himself that it really is not his place to know, at least not now.

“Okay then, let’s get these papers signed so everything is set to go. I don’t want to spend all day here. You’re gouging me in fees as it is.”

The men smile because they both know the fees, if anything, are way too low, even for Le Fleur. Fenton turns back to another mound of files on the credenza and opens one on top of a tall stack, then turns again and leans forward to hand Frank a document.

“Everything’s in order, Frank. You want to go through it all point by point to make sure it’s exactly as you want?”

“No, just let me give it a quick glance. I trust you’ve got everything in. I don’t expect any omissions this time.”

The “this time” stings them both a little, but it is a point well taken by Fenton, even though Frank laments the reference to the divorce error. Fenton sits quietly as Frank glances at each page to catch the major points while skipping all the *wherefores, therefores,* and *in consideration of* language. After a few minutes Frank finishes the ninth page and slowly closes the document.

“Well, it all looks fine. I guess that’ll just about do it. My last will and testament is finally put to bed. Just one thing, though, you misspelled the name of the foundation on page seven. Please change that after I sign the last page, would you?”

“Oh dammit, Frank, I’m so sorry.”

“No problem. One other thing, if you don’t mind. I’m going over to the dealership when I leave here, and they’ll send over the title to the Vette I just bought. You’ll need to add it to the ownership in paragraph four on page two.”

"Sure thing. I hear you look surprisingly good in that yellow race car."

Fenton does not wait for an answer and continues stating the obvious. "In fact, there will be a lot of surprises for the people in the will, won't there?"

Frank tosses the will on the desk and leans back with a grunt.

"Yeah, I guess there'll be some surprises in there. It's my last chance to call some shots the way I need 'em, and the way they should be, I guess."

Frank shoots up from the chair and extends his hand.

"Thank you, my friend," Frank says softly. "Please take care. Remember that you're a good man and that you have great strength and you've overcome a lot. You have all my trust and I know you won't disappoint. Most of all, just be good to yourself and that wonderful family of yours."

Jerry gets up and firmly grasps Frank's hand.

"I don't like how you said that. You make it sound like the end is here—right now—like this is the last time I'm going to see you."

"Oh, you'll see me again. I'm just going fishing, which you probably already know, since Gloria always calls you the moment anything happens. But I'll be back in town Monday night. I just needed to tell you that you're my friend and that I believe in you. I should have said it a long time ago."

Jerry tries to avoid teary-eyed contact as he picks up his phone to call Helen. Frank and Fenton sign the last page of the will, and Helen notarizes it to make things official. After she clamps the notary press on the lower left of the last page, Frank hugs Helen, to the surprise of all, especially himself.

"Okay boys and girls, get back to more important work." The last word is barely uttered as Frank leaves the office and makes his way outside and down the walk to scramble into the Vette. The car screeches away from the curb and makes a left turn at the intersection toward the Chevy dealership. As Frank contemplates the words he spoke to Jerry, he wonders if he rushed through them too fast, failing to emphasize his caring.

# Chapter Eight

The trip to the Chevy dealership seems like an instant. The car turns in with a muted squeal of tires and Frank climbs out, slowly closing the door with care as if he is gently touching the shoulder of a beautiful woman. Out of the corner of his eye he sees several salesmen stop what they are doing to watch him. Even they cannot believe Frank bought the most expensive car on the lot, not counting the big Chevy farm trucks out back—but those are not exactly driven for pleasure or speed.

"Frank! You actually made it here in one piece!"

Frank is startled by Sid's stealthy approach.

"Damn it, Sid! You shouldn't sneak up on a guy like that. Where the heck were you hiding?"

"I wasn't hiding. I was standing over by the pickups and even waved at you when you pulled in. You seemed so intent on whipping that baby into the lot without smashing into the showroom. Thanks for not driving it through the building, by the way. So, waddaya think? Pretty damned awesome, huh?"

Frank leans over, puts both hands on the door, and looks in at the interior.

"Yep, the Lion's pretty incredible. Never drove anything like it before, but I got it all figured out. She may be strong, but she lets you tame her if you pay attention to her."

"Sounds like you got it solved—and you even named her. You must be smitten. Fenton took care of all the papers, so let's go get that cover before that love wears off."

The two men walk side by side through a wide door left open for another car to be driven into the showroom to fill the spot where the Lion once sat. As they walk across the showroom, Frank looks at the replacement car with surprise.

"Hey, isn't that your dad's '66 Impala?"

Sid smiles widely. "Yep. That was Dad's. We had it over in the collector garage with a couple of his others and thought it was time to bring it out for air. Only has twenty-one thousand original miles on it. We've been offered a lot of bucks for it, but it's not for sale. I thought it would be a good conversation starter and attract a few lookers to the showroom, though."

"Not for sale, huh? How much you been offered?"

"Well, I figure it's worth maybe thirty-five thousand since every bit of it is original, but a guy over in Ashland offered me fifty for it. Not bad for a car that sold for less than four grand new, but I told him it was worth much more because it was Dad's, and he babied it so much. Ya know, dad loved this car more than any Vette that ever came down the line. Hell, I think he loved this car more than me or Mom."

Sid rambles, seemingly without breathing. "It is a pretty rare car. The 427 SS convertible with manual, wire wheels with the spinners, and the gauge clusters wasn't a common package. This is the original Danube Blue, too—never been painted."

Frank finally interrupts. "My dad never was much into cars, but he sure admired your dad's passion for taking care of this one. I remember he tried ta get your dad to drive it up to New York on a fishing trip a couple times, but Will wouldn't hear of it. He told Dad that he wasn't going to let guys get in it to fart, spill beer, and slosh fish juice all over the place. It was probably a good thing he wouldn't drive it up. Who knows what kind of condition it would've been in when they got back."

Sid nods. "Yeah, that's funny, 'cause I remember Dad telling me about how James tried for weeks to talk him into taking it fishing. Dad just wouldn't go for it. By that time, the car was already a collector's item but still looked as new as in '66. Ya know, Frank, I think James even tried to buy that car from Dad because he wanted to drive it to New York so badly."

Frank steps to the car and touches the chrome door handle. "Hmmm. I didn't know that. I never thought my dad was ever actually interested in cars."

"Yeah, it's interesting what you find out about dads after they're gone, huh? I remember finding out after my dad died a few years ago, that he had a girlfriend who worked for Chevy up in Detroit. Mom was the only person who knew about her, and for some reason, she put up with it for years. Just last week I asked her about it again and she said, 'Your dad had certain needs and so did I. We both got what we needed.' I was stunned to hear her say that, being such a churchgoing woman and all. I never dreamed she would let him do that stuff and never call him on it."

Frank is surprised to hear Sid jump with such ease from the Impala to his father's infidelity. Sid waits for Frank to respond with some in-kind, juicy tidbit about James. Frank lets the bait drift by.

"Well, I guess my dad had secrets, but mostly about other folks in town," Frank finally musters. "You know, my dad didn't talk much or tell too many stories, unless it was about the fish he caught—or almost caught. He did his storytelling in the paper every week, I guess."

Frank stands for a few moments looking at the '66 and bending this way and that to admire the timeless design, the time-frozen perfection, and the gaudy chrome.

Impatient, Sid says, "Well, come on up to my office. I asked a salesman to put the cover up there. I'm giving him the commission, but I wanted to be the one to give it to you since it's such a historic occasion. Heck, we might even need to take a once-in-a-lifetime photo of you driving off!"

Frank cocks his head to one side, wondering if he should be offended or flattered by Sid's comment. Flattery wins as he chuckles and follows Sid up the stairs and into the austere, dated office. Three glass walls afford great views of the showroom and the outside sales lot.

"The only real question, Frank, is whether you want the extended warranty on the car. I bet the salesman a pizza that you wouldn't want it, so—"

"Hold on a second. I think I might go for that. Someone other than me might be driving this car soon. How much is it to increase the three-year warranty to seven years?"

Sid scans Frank's face to see if this is a joke but realizes it's a real inquiry.

"Well, probably around four thousand, but I'll have to do some checking to make sure. I gave you about five grand off the sticker, so adding the extended warranty would take it back up close to the original price."

"Gee, thanks for the big discount," Frank snickers. "Let's go for the extended warranty then."

Sid snaps up the phone to the salesman and asks for papers to be brought up for the warranty. Before Sid finishes and hangs up, Frank moves over to the glass to look down over the showroom floor.

"Go ahead and get that ready, Sid. I want to go down and check out another car. I'll be back up in a minute."

Sid finishes the call and gets up to watch Frank, already down on the floor, scrutinizing a fire engine-red Camaro and a white Malibu sitting next to the '66. He walks around one, then the other, all the while biting his lip and scratching his cheek.

In a few minutes Frank ascends the staircase and Sid scurries back to his desk to pretend he had not been watching.

"Sid, make that salesman's week and start up the papers for the purchase of the Camaro and the Malibu. I'll have Rodgers and Fenton take care of the details for those too. Fenton will tell you where to deliver the cars come Monday."

"Holy Mary Mother of God, Frank! Are you shitting me? You don't buy a new car for ten or fifteen years and then you buy *three* in one day? What the hell is going on with you?"

Without emotion or expression, Frank just stands next to the window and looks down on the sales floor.

"Don't pretend you don't know what's going on. You know I'm not long for this world, and you can't take it with you, as they say."

Frank moves to the desk and signs the papers for the Vette's extended warranty and shakes Sid's hand.

"Thanks for your help on this. Maybe I'll bring you some salmon next week."

Before Sid can collect his whirling thoughts into words, Frank is down the steps, out the showroom door, and squealing tires off the lot and onto Route 61 back toward Le Fleur. No one had time to snap a photo.

In between shifting, Frank calls Fenton on his cell phone.

"Hey, Jerry, Sid's going to prepare sales documents for a couple more cars. The white one goes to the person on page three and the red one to the person on page four. Yeah, okay, I know. You need to execute those sales on behalf of the newspaper...Yep...Yep, I know, damn it. I'll see you Monday."

Frank picks up an incoming call and hears a nearly frantic Russ describing a police situation.

"Okay, I'll be right there," Frank says. "Two minutes tops."

# Chapter Nine

The trailer park is engulfed by a half-dozen Richland County patrol cars with lights flashing. Eight officers lean over the cars and point their guns toward the front of the double-wide. Three other policemen who had come over from Shelby on a call for backup are keeping area residents behind hastily arranged police tape. The periodic shouting of the officers to "Come out peacefully, Fritz," are met only with a repeated "Go to hell!"

The deputies frown at each other and shake their heads. They wait for the sheriff and a couple of hostage specialists to arrive. No one wants to be the first to do anything stupid and raise Fritz's tension.

The sound of a breaking window shatters the lull, and everyone crouches behind whatever car or tree is nearby. The window next to the trailer door is busted out from the inside, but there are no shots and no visible signs of a gun barrel sticking out. After a few moments of waning fear and growing curiosity, everyone stands a little taller to see what Fritz is doing inside the trailer.

A car pulling up at the end of the street catches everyone's attention. To the amusement of many and the angst of the deputies, it is not the sheriff. Frank claws his way out of the Vette and weaves over to Russ, who leans on the roof of a patrol car next to Deputy Phil.

Frank says, "Thanks for calling, Russ. What's going on?"

Phil exhales and lays his pistol on the roof as he turns to Frank.

"Same old shit, Frank. Dumbass Fritz drank all night and won't let his wife leave for work or the kids for school."

"How long's this been going on?" Frank asks.

"A couple hours. I guess he knocked her around pretty bad, too. She finally managed to get her cell phone to call the office. Guess that probably got 'er busted a bit more."

Frank looks at Phil oddly. "Why the hell doesn't someone go up to the door and talk to him and find out why he's so ticked off?"

Phil blurts, "You're such a law enforcement genius, Frank! You don't think we've been trying to talk to the fool? It's the same old drunken crap, except he's taken things to the next level this time. He says he has a gun and will start shooting if we come up to the trailer. Claims he just wants to talk to the sheriff. He just broke out the window and we think he might be getting ready to start shooting."

As Phil finishes lampooning Frank, the sound of more falling glass and a thud regains everyone's attention. The crowd crouches again and looks toward the trailer at what was thrown out the broken window.

"What the hell?" Phil says.

Russ says, "It looks like a baseball with a note taped to it."

Phil looks at Russ with disdain. "And what the hell makes you think it's a baseball and not some goddamn hand grenade?"

"Look over on the left. You can see the red stitches."

Phil leans left toward Russ and then pushes more with his hip, which causes Russ to push further left into Frank.

Phil strains his eyes a bit and nudges his glasses higher on his nose to get a better look.

"It could be a baseball, I guess," Phil concedes. "It's hard to tell. You just can't take those kinda things for granted. We better wait till the sheriff gets here before we decide to mess with it."

Everyone's attention snaps toward the trailer again as angry words tumble out of the window.

"Okay, damn it, I put a note on that there ball," Fritz grumbles. "The note says what I want. Somebody better come get it!"

Phil shouts back, "Or else what?"

"Jus' come and get the damn ball, you big fat sissy," Fritz demands.

Frank looks at Phil. "Well, you big fat sissy, you better go and get it."

Phil closes his eyes. "Shut the hell up, Frank. The minute anyone goes after the ball Fritz is going to start squeezing off rounds. He's baiting us to come closer for a good shot. That ball and fake note are bull. He just wants to play with us."

Frank cocks his head. "Jesus, Phil. Don't you even have the slightest bit of curiosity about what the note says?"

Phil sneers. "It doesn't say anything. It's just a trick."

Russ and Frank grunt and can feel the crowd bearing down on Phil with their stares and growing contempt. The deputy re-aims at the window and grips his revolver with both hands. Someone to the far left of the semicircle attempts to move toward the ball, but another deputy hauls him back by the shirt collar.

Damn it, Phil," Frank says, "You're just gonna let that man hold his wife and kids in there and let the ball lay on the ground? You really are a coward! Some kid's gonna break free to run up and get that ball if you don't do something. Then the sheriff's gonna kick your ass for not getting it. But I guess you don't care as long as the old man walks up there and does it for you."

Phil straightens. "Well, hell, why not let the sheriff get the ball? He makes three times as much as I do. Besides, his kids are grown and long gone."

"You useless bag of skin!" Frank shouts.

Most people in the crowd can now hear the exchange.

"You just like playing with other people's lives, don't you? Yesterday morning in the diner—what was that all about, anyway? You had to get that little story off your chest and now you pull a stunt like this? You're a piece of crap with a badge, just like your goddamn father!"

The crowd takes a collective gasp. Few have ever heard Frank swear—and now he targets Phil's father, too.

Phil slowly turns toward Frank and nudges Russ back to speak past him.

"Listen, you prick. You better just be careful. Once the shooting starts, crossfire can be a hell of a thing."

Russ's eyes grow large. Frank responds in a soothing, muted voice.

"Don't worry, Russ, the guy doesn't have the balls to shoot me at close range, although I'm sure he would love to do it. No, he doesn't have the balls his evil father had."

The hum in the crowd builds and several heads nod toward Phil. One older man points to the frumpy deputy and cracks the drone of voices with clarity.

"C'mon, Phil," the old man cajoles, "Why don'cha get out there and git the damn ball? It's your job, man!"

Some take off their ball caps and scratch their heads while others in small clusters creep toward the front edges of patrol cars. The uneasy minutes stretch beyond real time as baking sweat droplets form on Phil's jowls just below his large sideburns.

Fritz's booming voice shatters the pane of tension. "C'mon, somebody!" "Come and get the ball. I'm tired a' waitin'!"

Frank glances at Russ, grins slightly, and begins to move.

"No Frank, no!" But before Russ can get a good hold of his sleeve, Frank moves toward the end of the cruiser. The crowd gasps again.

A man under a big oak tree to his rear shouts encouragement. “God be with you, Frank!”

Frank’s concentration is broken, and he wonders who the man might be.

“Take it easy now, Fritz. It’s Frank Barnett, and I’m coming up to get the ball. Just take it easy, buddy!”

Most of the spectators hunker down a bit and officers steady their aims, except for Phil. He pulls his gun off the car roof and yells, “My God, Frank! What the hell are you doing? Get your ass back here!”

Frank doesn’t look back. “Don’t worry, Phil, this could be your big chance to take out Fritz and me at the same time.”

Frank walks with slow, steady purpose toward the ball. Everyone lowers more.

“Everything’s okay, Frtiz! I’m coming to get the ball and see what you want. Just take it easy. I can’t hurt you.”

“You don’t have to worry, Frank,” Frtiz shouts back with a bit of kindness and relief. “I guess you’re the only one out there who’s got any damned guts. Don’t worry, I ain’t gonna shoot ya!”

“I know you’re not, Fritz. Are the wife and kids doin’ all right in there?”

“Yep. The kids are watchin’ TV and Betty’s pourin’ them some cereal. They’re all doin’ just fine.”

Frank shuffles to the ball and looks down at it, then over to the broken trailer window, back over his shoulder to Phil, to Russ, and side to side along the entire length of gawkers, all fixed on him. He bends down to pick up the ball and gingerly removes the tape holding the note.

*You came this far, now come on in.*

Frank yells without looking up from the note. “Fritz, I thought you were going to tell us on the note what you want.”

“That’s what I want. The note wasn’t meant for you, but since you picked ’er up, I guess you’re elected. It’s better you come in anyhow than any of those dumbass deputies with guns. That could really scare the boys!"

Frank eases to the trailer and climbs the three steps up to the entry landing. The crowd, uneasy, murmurs behind him. Several deputies' revolver hammers click into place. He whispers, "Jesus, I hope Fritz didn't hear those."

He looks at the faces staring back at him. He scans their worried eyes, then looks past them to survey the neighborhood. He was in this trailer park a thousand times as a kid to play with his friend Dave and pitch a tent outside on weekends and summer nights. Comforting thoughts about their lifelong friendship give him a moment to breathe deeply. The regret for the waning of that friendship allows angst to filter back into his head about the risk he is going to take.

He glances down the street and notices that the ends of each trailer strung along Dogwood Drive are lined up at a repetitive angle. Cars and trucks in various states of rust and disrepair, bicycles and toys strewn about, and haphazard piles of wood and lawn furniture leaning up against many of the homes clutter the trailer park.

Frank examines the yard around Fritz's trailer. From where he stands, the lawn appears to be an oasis within the neighborhood. The yard contains no clutter, and it appears the trailer has recently been power-washed. It looks much newer than the rest of the abused, unkempt trailers.

The lawn is uncharacteristically green and is neatly trimmed along the driveway and around the mailbox. The big white wooden box has been recently painted and new metal numerals attached. Frank is startled by the address—1111—a reoccurring number that frequently pops into his consciousness. He remembers reading that some believe a mystical quality is attached to it and may mean a change is coming, perhaps a moment of clarity.

"Okay, Fritz, I'm at the door."

"Come on in. You ain't gonna get hurt."

The screen door opens smoothly, and Frank half-steps inside the inner door. Fritz sits in a red, fake-leather recliner in the left corner, up against the divider spindles that separate the living room from the small kitchen area. He looks casual enough to be watching a ballgame, in his boxers and T-shirt. His feet extend out on the raised footrest, but his relaxed appearance is shattered by the army issue .45 handgun resting on his thigh.

Fritz's relatively good physique is borne from his lifelong manual labor. Only his plumpish middle and faintly graying flattop and sideburns hint at his age. A USMC tattoo on his right forearm and his father's photo in marine dress uniform on the wall behind him proudly announce the family's military heritage.

Fritz is well known around town for being slightly off-kilter. Though never arrested, he picks an occasional verbal fight with some unsuspecting soul who happens to cross his path. He alternates between being jovial and kind to everyone he meets and being incensed after misinterpreting someone's benign comment.

For the most part, he kept that attitude in check in the marines until he became a sergeant and developed a paranoia of being secretly monitored. His superior officer finally convinced him it was time to retire before things ended badly on his service record. His last job for a tree-trimming company ended a month ago when he threatened his boss with a limb for telling him to put on his yellow safety vest.

Trying to keep his focus on Fritz, Frank sees the two boys, about eight and ten, in his periphery. They are lying on the floor to his right, watching cartoons on the old television at the end wall. They chomp on cereal in plastic sandwich bags, empty juice glasses off to their sides. Betty, at least ten years

Fritz's junior, sits on the sofa with her legs crossed, to their far right.

The furniture in the trailer is old, but the living room and kitchen are immaculate, and the faint smell of lemon cleaner lingers in the air. Everything is orderly; the newspapers and magazines are stacked with precision on the worn TV tray that functions as Fritz's side table. Hot Wheels cars and action figures line up with exactness on top of a well-used wooden toy box. An old coffee table in the middle of the living room shines with a mirror finish and serves as a pedestal for an enormous, historic-looking Bible, having been opened and placed on top of a doily in the center. The massive book with browning pages is flanked by two white cherub candle holders with red candlesticks. The only style theme of the furnishings is cleanliness.

Frank asks calmly, "You all right, Mrs. Weggling?"

"Yes, I'm all right. There's nothing bad here."

Fritz jumps in. "You're damned right she's okay! That's one sweet lady, Frank! Hell, we just gave each other big, long hugs!"

Frank glances over at Betty. He sees a red spot on her cheek, but she is not bruised or cut anywhere. She has a calm worry, as though she has been through this many times before, but with an understanding that the gun being waved around is a new variable to possible endings.

"Fritz, the deputy said that you were hitting Betty and you were keeping her and the kids in here against their will. Is that the case?"

"Sounds like you've been talkin' ta that dirty skunk Phil."

"Well, that's what he told me a little while ago. That's not what's going on?"

Frtiz looks Frank in the eyes, wanting to make sure he believes. "Me and the missus get a little riled up once in a while and raise our voices a bit, but I wouldn't ever hurt 'er—

or those kids. I'm the one who told her to call the cops. I listened when she was on the phone. She didn't say anything to the cops about me hittin' her. She just said I was upset and that she and the kids weren't gonna leave me alone until someone came to talk to me."

"Is that right, Mrs. Weggling?" Frank asks.

"That's pretty much the way it went—and please, call me Betty."

Formalities over, Fritz says, "Now Frank, you're a pretty good fella, I think. I'm damned lucky you're the one who picked up that ball and came in here. That's best for Betty and the kids too. You know me and even talk to me down at the diner sometimes. You even treated me real good in that story you wrote years back when I had that little scrape down at the hardware."

Fritz pauses to pick up the .45 off his thigh, gesturing and pointing the barrel around as his substitute finger.

"But take those deputies out there. Most of 'em ain't even from around here. They don't know anything about any of us except what they hear, or maybe what they dream up as they drive over here from Mansfield. They think I beat my Betty, but you know that ain't true. I may push her out of the way some, but I *never* hit her. You know that's right, huh, Frank?"

"Well," Frank pauses for a moment and considers his words carefully. "I suppose that's how it is. I know you don't ever want to hurt her...or the kids."

"You're damned right!" Fritz leans forward like an excited preacher driving home a point. "I'd never hurt Betty or those beautiful kids. It wouldn't make sense for me to hurt 'em. They're all I got in this world!"

"Yes, Betty's a fine woman and those are great kids. I saw their names in the honor rolls a few weeks ago, didn't I?"

"Hell, yes you did!" Fritz settles back in solace. "Got three copies of your paper. Those kids are so damned smart, I don't know how they're mine. But they are, 'cause they got my eyes, nose, and ears, poor kids. At least God gave 'em brains I never had."

"Okay, then. How about those kids get off to school so they can keep those grades up and I can put their names in the paper again. They can't get their grades lying around here watching TV."

"That's the right thing, and I was a' thinkin' it too," Fritz finishes with a nervous grin.

Frank says, "Okay, you kids get your bags and get off to school. Betty, you can take 'em on your way to work."

Fritz looks up and waves the gun past Frank's torso as he points toward the door. "Betty works down at the city clerk's office. She does the water an' sewer bills. Been there fourteen years—ever since we got married."

"I know, Fritz. I see her in there once in a while."

"The mayor treats her good. He gave her a certificate last Christmas and five hundred bucks, too, for doin' such a good job and not missin' a day of work all year...ain't that right, doll?"

"Hush up. Frank don't wanna hear 'bout all—"

A voice thunders through a megaphone. "What's going on in there? Is everything okay, Frank?"

Frank turns back over his shoulder and responds in a loud, measured voice. "It's all right. Everything's all right. Just be calm out there. Betty and the kids are coming out now, so for God's sake take it easy and don't do anything stupid."

Betty gathers her purse and the boys hoist up their book bags. Frank motions them out with a nod of the head toward the door. All the while he watches Fritz reclining with his .45.

Fritz leans forward as the oldest boy begins to open the screen door.

"Jimmy, Johnnie, come here and give your old dad a hug before you go off to school."

The boys scoot back to their dad and he pulls them together, still holding onto the pistol. The boys take much delight in giving hugs to their father with no sign of fright or embarrassment. The younger Johnnie pauses long enough to give his dad a quick kiss on the cheek. Fritz melts to near tears with a blissful grin.

"Now you boys go and get those 'A's and study hard at school. Go make your old man proud. Make sure you kiss your mommy, too, when you get to school."

"We will, Daddy," Jimmy says.

The boys turn toward the door and Betty grabs their hands to prevent them from darting out. She stands and looks back at Fritz with curiosity and sadness.

"Fritz, you're not going to hurt anyone, right? Even if you don't, you know they're gonna haul you off to Mansfield for causin' such a commotion. So don't get all fired up. Go along with them easy and I'll come by after work to bail you out. I'll make you a nice fried chicken dinner when we get home. I'll send the boys over to Sissy's after school, so we can have dinner and talk things through, okay?"

Fritz presses his lips together, nods his head in the affirmative, then responds in a soft voice. "Don't worry, dear Betty. You go onta work. Things will be okay 'round here. I'm just gonna have a nice talk with Mr. Barnett here and then we'll go with the deputies and things will be okay. I wasn't expecting the newspaperman to come by, but I'm glad he did. Maybe he'll put a little story in the paper about my gripes and that will help things get better for all of us."

Frank looks at Betty, masking his confusion about what gripes Fritz may be referring to.

"Fritz and I will talk it out, Betty. You go on with the boys. Maybe I'll put a story in the paper like he wants. Hell, maybe I'll come by for some of that fried chicken tonight too, and we can all have a laugh about it. I'll post any bond needed to get him out."

Fritz chimes in. "Hell, yeah! Having Frank over for dinner tonight would be great! You and the boys go on now."

Betty looks at Frank, forlorn. "Please don't let him get hurt, Mr. Barnett."

Betty pushes the screen open, her fear hidden from the children and the waiting crowd outside. Frank holds the door.

"It's all right now," Frank yells to the officers. "Betty and the boys are coming out and I'm going to stay and talk to Fritz. We'll be out in a little while."

Instead of leaving, the onlookers jostle to get a better look at the distressed family in the doorway. Betty steps out and stares at the ground, ignoring the mob as she leads the boys over to pile into a rusting Ford Taurus that waits under the carport. A low buzz emanates from the crowd as she backs out and maneuvers cautiously around the police cars. She makes her way out of the trailer park as a deputy jumps in a cruiser to follow her out, lights flashing but sirens off.

No one moves to leave, nor have the deputies moved from their ready firing positions.

Phil puts the megaphone up to his mouth, no doubt to reassert his authority. "Tell Fritz he has fifteen minutes to talk. Then we're coming in for him."

Frank says, "For Christ's sake. Just—"

Fritz cuts in. "You don't think I can hear ya, Phil? Why don't ya just come on in now? That would make my day, buddy. But of course, you'd send in someone else to do your dirty work, huh, you big fat chicken."

Frank shuts the screen and stands inside. He turns to Fritz.

"You shouldn't egg him on. Don't give him a reason to come in and make a mess of things."

"Guess you're right. I'll calm down. Is the sheriff out there yet? He's about the only one with 'nuff sense to keep those deputies under control."

"No, he hasn't gotten here yet. You wanna talk to him when he does?"

Fritz looks down at the gun and rubs the barrel on the leg of his boxers to give it a shine on both sides.

"Nah, I don't think I need ta talk to him. You'll do jus' fine."

Frank cautiously moves away from the door and toward Fritz. In the middle of his slow glide, something catches his eye off to the right. He stops midstride and sucks in a startled breath.

Fritz studies Frank's drawn-in mouth and furrowed brows. "What? What's the matter?"

Frank glances to the right, hoping Fritz won't be able to tell.

"What is it? What the hell?" Fritz barks as he slides down in the recliner and points the gun alternately at the door and the window at the end of the trailer. "Is someone comin' up on the trailer? Those bastards better not be comin' up on us!"

"No, that's not it, Fritz. Just take it easy."

"Then what? What are ya afraid of?"

A serene voice from the corner asks, "Yes, why don't you tell him that you're afraid of dying, Frank?"

Frank whirls to see the stranger sitting on the end of the sofa where Betty had been earlier.

"I know you're wondering what I am doing here," the stranger says. "Just know I am here to help you, no matter what happens. You don't have to respond to me. Fritz cannot see or hear me, but I can hear you thinking."

Fritz leans forward slightly.

"Frank, you okay?"

"Yes, I'm fine. I have a little bit of a headache and it's coming at a bad time." He turns back. "Now let's talk about why you're so upset that you made Betty call the sheriff."

Fritz has no chance to respond as they hear a car pull up close to the trailer. The car door opens and then slams shut and a deep voice carries all the way inside. "Okay, what's going on here, Phil?" Phil's response is muffled and drawn out.

Frank says, "The sheriff's here now, so he'll keep the deputies in line out there. You want him to come in and talk with us?"

"No. I just wanna talk to you. You're a smart man and can understand what I have to say. The sheriff's got a job to do and ain't got much time to stand here and listen to a fool like me. I guess they'll say you're my hostage, too. You'll tell them I wasn't holdin' you against your will, won't you? You know you can leave any time you want."

"Yes, I know. We're just talking as neighbors. We'll go out of here together as friends. In fact, I'll tell them you were trying to make me leave, but I wouldn't go."

"That's kind of you. Everyone 'round town knows you're a good man. Let's just talk a while, okay? I'm glad God picked you to come in here today."

Frank eyes Fritz curiously, then glances to the stranger who sits quietly without emotion.

"You think God picked me, huh?"

Fritz pauses. "Well, I don't know if he really did, but I'm glad it's you."

"Frank," the sheriff yells without the megaphone, "are you and Fritz doing all right in there? Fritz, just come out and we'll go over to the station and we can talk about anything you want. I have some nice men out here who want to hear what's bugging you. I could bring some nice hot coffee in and you can talk to them. These fellas with me are real good listeners. Just tell me what you want to do."

"Frank, can you tell the sheriff I just wanna talk to you? I think he needs to hear it comin' from you."

"Listen, Sheriff," Frank yells back. "I'm going to talk to Fritz for a while, then we'll be out. Everything's okay in here."

"Have it your way, then. I'm going to send all the deputies and neighbors away. Anybody that stays around will be arrested for obstruction. When you come out, it'll just be me and these two other guys here leaning against the car. You hear that, Fritz?"

"Yeah, Sheriff, I heard you. You're a good man too. We'll be out soon. Will you have someone check on Betty and the boys and make sure they made it to work and school okay? And tell 'er everything here's okay too."

"Sure thing, Fritz. I'll call my assistant on the radio and tell her to check on them and let them know."

Fritz looks down at the gun and again rubs the flat sides of the barrel on his boxers. Frank takes the opportunity to look deep into the stranger's eyes. The old man gives a slow nod that Frank should listen to Fritz. So, with the intentness of a reporter, Frank focuses on every sorrowful word of Fritz's troubled story. When Fritz finishes his disturbing tale, Frank struggles to find any profound words that would provide absolution for the man's past sins, so he gives an old standard.

"Listen," Frank says, "that was a long time ago. You're a different man now. How about you give me the gun and we'll walk out as friends. I'll ride along with you to the jail and pay your bail. I want some of that fried chicken tonight."

The two men exchange nervous smiles as Fritz rises from his recliner. Suddenly an explosion from the .45 rings throughout the trailer and down the street. The gasps of neighbors and shouts of deputies echo between the homes, igniting a firestorm of confusion.

# Chapter Ten

Frank leans his backside against the front fender of the patrol car next to the sheriff, and the two stare at the trailer encircled in yellow police tape. Several deputies scurry about taking photos of the scene from all angles, inside and out.

Instead of having left, the gawking neighbors have grown in number. Scores of children on bicycles flock from all directions and abandon their rides to vie for the best viewing angles. The weary sheriff slides his cowboy hat off with a sigh and firmly squeezes Frank's shoulder.

"Are you sure that's all you want to tell me, Frank? It's a pretty flimsy story."

"I can't help it. It happened just like I told you."

"You were in there talking for what, twenty minutes? He didn't give you any other hints—no reasons why he was in there with a gun? He only talked about his boys and his wife's fried chicken?"

Frank nods his head, not really caring if the sheriff notices.

A breath of cool fall freshness wafts down the street, pushing the ache and bafflement from Frank's face. He shuts his eyes and raises his nose to the air, then breathes deeply. A slight smile breaks over his face and he takes in another strong, audible nasal breath.

Frank whispers, "Do you smell that, Sheriff? The fall asters? They're in full bloom now."

The sheriff looks at Frank curiously. "A man lies dead inside, supposedly from an accidental, self-inflicted gunshot to the chest, and the only witness to the event is talking about the odor of a dainty sunflower? I don't think asters even have a smell. All I smell is a story that stinks like hog shit."

Frank goes on, undeterred, eyes shut and face up to the sun. "You know, legend has it that the Titan goddess Asteria looked down through the heavens at the earth and saw no stars, and she wept. The asters then grew like twinkling stars where her tears fell. She was said to be the nocturnal oracle of dreams and shooting stars. Other legends say the constellation Virgo looks down from the night sky and weeps stardust onto the earth, and that's where asters grow. Either way, the aster was sacred to the Greeks and they would burn them to keep evil spirits away."

"Well, that's real nice, Frank. Guess we should have burned some asters around here today, huh?"

"Yeah, I guess we should have."

The neighborhood comes to attention as two of the coroner's assistants flanking the ends of a gurney struggle to roll, lift, and maneuver it out of the trailer. The tightly belted body is completely covered in a sheet, on top of which is a blanket that further conceals the bloody torso. The men perform their duty routinely while looking low, from side to side, searching for obstacles. They expertly avoid eye contact with spectators.

Silence falls over the onlookers as Fritz's body is wheeled from the steps to the waiting ambulance. People become still. Kids stop throwing things. Several squatting adults stand for a better view while other townies rubberneck at the lifeless lump on the gurney. A few people cover their mouths while others lean in to whisper to friends. Several of the men place their ball caps over their hearts.

A shooting is an unheard-of event in Le Fleur. This is big news and will be proven so in the *Sentinel* on Wednesday. It will even make the Mansfield cable channel tonight since a small camera crew is now scooping Frank's paper.

"Frank, you go home and gather your thoughts. I'll need you to come over to the station in the morning for complete questioning. This thing just isn't adding up."

"I appreciate the job you have to do, Sheriff," Frank says softly. "But what else is there to tell? My statement won't be any different tomorrow than a few minutes ago. Besides, if you want to talk to me tomorrow, you're going to have to drive to New York because I'm going fishing up at the Niagara River."

"Damn it, Frank. You think I can let the witness to a killing just drive out of state without a formal interview?"

Frank laughs. "Yeah, I think the county sheriff can do just about anything he wants. I'll be back on Monday about three or four o'clock, so I'll come in and talk to you then."

"All right, but you better damn well be at my office no later than four. This is serious. If you don't show up, I'll send out deputies to arrest your ass."

"Yeah, I know it's serious, Bob."

The sheriff looks at Frank sideways. "Why is it that you're the only one who ever uses my first name? Even my wife calls me Sheriff."

"That's because I write it so often for stories in the paper. Maybe I include 'Robert' a lot so readers know you have a real name, like a real person, not just a man who rides around under flashing lights."

Russ approaches hesitantly.

"It's okay, Russ. You can come on over."

Russ parks his backside on the cruiser door and plops his hand on the mirror. "I think I got some good photos. I also talked to quite a few neighbors about Fritz's recent mood to find out if anything seemed to be bothering him. Nobody had anything unusual to say about how he was acting."

"That's a good start, Russ," Frank says. "This is your story now. It's going to be a tough one. You'll have to talk to Mrs. Weggling when we get back from New York, ya know. Giving her a couple days to gather herself will be good, though. You can interview me on the trip. I'll tell you the whole story for the next issue. But you have to write the story like I'm just another person to interview, not the editor or publisher...not your boss."

The sheriff springs away from the fender crossly. "Well isn't that just dandy! The cub reporter gets the story before the damn county sheriff. Ain't that just grand."

"Don't worry, Sheriff. You already know everything I'll tell him. If there's some other detail that comes to mind, you'll know it before it comes out in the paper Wednesday. And by the way, Russ isn't a cub reporter. He's experienced and smart. You need to keep that in mind. He's going to be running the paper someday. He's a damn good man, not a kid."

The sheriff jumps in the patrol car with a scowl and starts up the engine with extended revs, then sticks his head out the window.

"You better damn well be at my office at four p.m. sharp Monday, Frank. Half of me wants you to be late, though, so I can arrest you. I could arrest you right now if I wanted to."

Frank and Russ move out of the way to avoid having their feet run over as the sheriff peels out and throws a few rocks their way.

"He was pretty ticked off, Frank. Are you sure we should go fishing this weekend with all this going on?"

"What's going on? Everything's over now. Fritz isn't going to get any more dead. Besides, you get to interview the witness of a shooting for the whole weekend and you're going to want to pass that up?"

"Well, I—"

"Never mind. You better get back to the office and start writing the opening 'graphs to this story, but tomorrow I don't want to hear about what you wrote. For now, I'm just another resident, just another person to interview."

"Okay. I'll see you in the morning. You're picking me up at nine, right? Anything special I should pack?"

"Is that what I said, nine?" He proceeds to give Russ a short list of stuff to bring with an emphasis on sunglasses.

"Where we staying?"

"The Youngstown Motel, where the Niagara empties into Lake Ontario. It's just down river from Lewiston. It isn't fancy, but the owner keeps it clean and he always has coffee and pastries ready in the morning. Oh yeah—bring a notepad. This is a working trip, after all. So, what time did I say I'm picking you up?"

"Nine o'clock."

Russ nods and walks off down the street to his car. Frank's eyes follow the young reporter. Memories of his father the publisher surface, and he loses himself in them for a moment. James taught Frank the ropes of reporting and photography and carefully prepared him for the Niagara fishing trips. Frank suffers a pang of regret for not being more attentive to Russ and what is happening in the young man's life, just as was the case with his own sons. Just as was the case between Frank and his own father. The throbbing tumor in Frank's head chillingly ups the stakes between the time he has left and the things he needs to say to the young man. Words of advice and caution flash through his mind, and the fear of missing another opportunity to impart wisdom brings a shaking panic.

Frank believes Russ is often too kind and that the young man gives people too much liberty to inflict insult. He has often wondered if Russ is too timid to challenge offenders, or if his thick skin of strength lets the barbs deflect harmlessly away. Frank eases into a comforting belief of the latter and shudders back to the moment.

From a distance Frank sees two women outside the trailer park watching the final preparations of the ambulance. Gloria's brown skin gives her away. The other woman's hands cover her face, but he recognizes the tall, shapely Julie. He ambles toward them, thinking about what he is going to say but is stopped by Tommy the lawn boy.

"Mr. Barnett! This is really wacked, isn't it? I mean, you were in there with the dude when he got shot! How'd it happen?

"You know I can't talk to you about it, Tommy. He gives him a pat on the back. "Guess you'll have to wait for the paper on Wednesday like everyone else."

"That'll probably be one of your best stories ever, Mr. Barnett."

"Well, it won't be my story. Russ is going to write it. I can't write the story if it's about something I am part of."

Frank continues on. Tommy's voice trails after him. "Oh, I guess that makes sense," even though his tone reveals he has no idea why.

As Frank approaches the ladies, he is overcome with grief at the tormented looks on their faces. Their looks of pain bring a biting realization about what could have happened and the devastation they would have felt if he'd died in the trailer.

With a strange, self-startling nervousness, Frank says, "Hello ladies. How long have you been here?"

Gloria eases her way to Frank, puts her arms around his neck and shoulders and begins to cry.

Julie says, "We've been here quite a while. Are you okay? What...what happened in there?"

Gloria steps back from Frank, cups his face in her hands, and in her most fretful, protective voice she says, "Yes, what on earth happened in there? And why did you go in there in the first place?"

"Well," Frank pauses to search for the reason, unknown even to him. "I guess I went in because everyone else seemed frightened to. Besides, I think I was the only one standing around that didn't have a kid or two at home. As for what went on, I don't think I should talk about it until I give my formal statement to the sheriff, but it was all accidental."

Gloria shakes Frank's head in her hands and stumbles for words through her sniffles. "We were so scared. We heard the shot, saw the deputies rush in, and for the longest time didn't see you come out. We thought you were dead. I don't know if I can handle losing you. I didn't understand that until just a little while ago."

Frank holds Gloria's hands and pulls back slightly. He looks into her eyes, then at Julie, and he sees she's been crying too.

"I guess you probably know, huh, Julie?"

"You mean...if you mean, do I know about your condition? Yes, I've known. I've known for a long time. Gloria didn't tell me, though." Sheepish, she continues, "I hear about everything that goes on around here down at the diner."

"Yeah, I guess you do. You know the news before we print it. I'm okay, ladies, really."

He gives Gloria a strong hug and kisses her on the forehead. She instinctively moves away to make room for Julie, who eases up to Frank and puts her hand on his arm.

Julie whispers, "Frank, I'm glad you're safe. I just wanted you to know that." Embarrassed by her blundering words, Julie turns her head to the side, pulls Gloria close, and both women cry tears of relief.

The scene causes a great lump in Frank's throat and he feels his eyes begin to water.

"Ladies, ladies, it's all fine now. Why don't you both go over to the diner and get some lunch. I'll be along shortly, and we can have some Friday fish fry. Julie, when we get there, you eat with us. Marilyn and the college kids can handle things."

"That sounds like a great idea. I'll do that."

The two women walk off arm-in-arm as they maneuver around people still milling on the street, then they ease into Julie's rattletrap car.

"They are the people you love most in this world, aren't they, Frank. You grew up with one, and the other is the real love you never pursued."

Frank recognizes that irksome voice. Grimacing, he turns around to see the stranger sitting on the grassy embankment next to the sidewalk. He gathers his composure and walks over to sit by the old man, but he cannot bear to look at him directly.

"What do you know about those women? How the hell do you know who I love? And why the hell did you leave me alone in there with Fritz? Jesus, man! I thought you were supposed to be here to help me. That poor man is dead, and you didn't do one damn thing."

Calm as usual, the old man replies, "Perhaps many have tried to help him, but he wouldn't accept help. Everyone has to make their own decisions. You were there to help him and you think you failed, but maybe you did help in a way still unknown to you. I was not in the trailer for Fritz. I was there to help you."

"Help me do what? Watch a man die? I could have done that without any help from you. You were there, and when I turned to ask you what to do, you were gone. How is that helping?"

"What is it Fritz wanted?"

"At first I thought he wanted to die or maybe kill someone. But then he told me the same story Phil told me yesterday. When he got that off his chest, he was going to give me the gun."

Frank continues the account the way he wants to remember. "The poor bastard got up to hand it to me and he tripped and accidentally shot himself. How on earth could you leave us there alone and let that happen? Now I have to face his wife after I promised her I'd watch out for him. She's back there in a patrol car crying herself senseless. I couldn't muster the courage to go talk to her. I need to figure out what to say."

The stranger is quiet for a moment. "I only try to help people see things more clearly. That is what I and the others do. However, the actions people choose are completely up to them, just as the course you decide to take will be completely up to you. Do you really believe in your heart that Fritz was getting up to give you the gun? That he tripped and accidentally shot himself?"

Frank looks at the stranger with a fierce expression that he usually reserves for the mayor. "Old Man, you don't know anything about what he said or why he was doing what he did. You left us in there alone. You don't have a clue."

"Are you sure he wanted you to tell Mrs. Weggling that he didn't mean to shoot himself? Or was he talking about the other thing he had done when he was a young man?"

Frank's face grows red with rage and he speaks with deep yet muted exasperation.

"You can't tell me that Fritz *intended* to shoot himself. He was going to walk out with me. He told me the things he needed to get off his chest, and he was ready to pay the price for it. After keeping it in all those years, he felt relief for the first time in decades. He wanted to see his wife and have fried chicken tonight, and I know he wanted to live for his boys. He was going to hand me the gun, damn it, but I hesitated, and he got up, tripped, and accidentally pulled the trigger. That's how it happened!"

"It sounds as though you're blaming yourself, Frank. It was Mrs. Weggling's choice to leave Fritz with you. It was Fritz' choice to threaten to shoot himself or someone else. It was his choice to do what he did so many years ago. Maybe you'll better understand later why he did that.

"Besides, didn't you realize when you went in that things could end badly for you? That would have solved a great deal, wouldn't it. You could then go out as a martyred hero. But when the time came—when you had a chance to take the gun from him—you hesitated. You didn't want him to shoot you after all, did you?"

There is a long silence. Finally, the old man sighs and Frank speaks softly.

"So, are you some kind of angel or some kind of devil? It seems to me you make things worse for people and then invent convenient stories to explain things."

"I don't know that I am either an angel or a devil, Frank. I'm just me. I try to help. It's you that has to decide what I am, and whether I even exist. I can't give you all the answers because even I don't have them all. We have to discover them together. I just try to help you see things more clearly."

"Well, you look kind of strange sitting here on the side of this hill in warm weather with a suit on."

Frank touches the man's tie and feels the fine silk. Then he clutches the tie near the bottom and pulls on it hard, which causes the man to lunge forward. Frank pokes him in the arm and then touches his face. The man has the warmth of a real person.

"Am I the only one here who sees you? If so, how can I feel you, as a real person?"

"Maybe you see and feel what you want, and everyone else around here does the same. Many things are beyond my knowledge, just as they are beyond yours. All I know is that I mean you no harm."

"What is your name, Old Man?"

"I had a name once, but I have no need for one now. I like 'Old Man,' though, if that's what you would like to call me."

"Are you here because my tumor makes me imagine you?"

"I don't know *how* I come to you, Frank. Maybe it is the tumor, but maybe it's some other reason. I was hoping *you* would know why I come to you. Do you have any idea why you might need my help, beyond the fact you are afraid of dying?"

"Afraid? What the hell are you talking about? I am not afraid to die! Maybe I'm afraid of living! Ever think about that?"

"Of course. That's what concerns me the most."

Frank blows a breath. "This talking in circles is getting me nowhere. You provide me no clue about what you're doing. You're just my tumor pressing on my brain, that's all you are. Maybe I hope that's all you are. I don't think I could take it if you're some damn Christmas Carol spirit coming to visit me. I'm going to the diner to see my favorite women, as you call them. Don't bother me unless you have real answers."

Frank bolts from the side of the hill and walks briskly down the street toward the Corvette, all the while feeling the townspeople's penetrating arrows of pity, confusion, curiosity, and admiration as they watch him walk by. He wonders, in horror, if they have all been watching him talk to thin air like a crazy man. Never has he endured so many emotions in such a short time. He refuses to meet anyone's eyes. He hurries to reach the safe envelope of the Lion.

As Frank arrives back at the gleaming Corvette, he sees now that the car appears conspicuously brazen in bright yellow, with its gaudy, oversized, red brake calipers. He clenches the door and stops to gaze up and down the street. People watch him with a blend of novelty and fright. He no longer feels like one of them. He is now apart from their innocent realm, outside their secure bubble.

From behind him in the crowd a deep voice blurts out, "Hey Frank, did your hair blow off while you raced that thing around this morning?"

The raised voice momentarily conceals the person's identity, and Frank cringes as the crowd enjoys a collective chuckle. He turns and sees that the comedian is the opportunistic mayor.

The irritating curmudgeon stands with an escaping shirttail, unruly tie, and pink skin that bakes in the sun. Not a particularly regal look for someone spewing derisive comments about another's appearance, but the mayor lets loose with vigor.

"I think I saw a squirrel playing with your hair over on Ridge Street this morning!"

Frank pauses, then speaks with a belligerent strength stirred by Fritz's bloody death and the disturbing conversation with his mystifying apparition. "Just remember, Mayor, as Steinbeck said, 'The written word punishes both stupidity and dishonesty.' Perhaps I still have a chance to reveal both in you."

For the second time in two days Frank has made a caustic smile melt from the mayor's bloated face. But, unlike in the newspaper office, the mayor cannot deflect Frank's volley. The fickle townspeople watch the mayor shift from foot to foot as he searches his mind for a measured response. The dragging moment and piercing stares of the residents seem to cause a buckling of the mayor's confidence.

Someone from the crowd shouts in to break the silence. "Hell, ev'ry one 'round here knows the mayor is stupid and dishonest. No need to go puttin' that in the paper!"

A great laugh erupts from the mob and continues long past normal expectations. The befuddled mayor is caught off guard as he looks around at the amused, snorting residents. Without a word the mayor straightens his tie, then pushes through the crowd and heads down the street in the opposite direction Frank was walking.

Frank smiles at the residents and they smile back to let him know they are with him. He has unexpectedly won the moment, if not the day. He climbs into the Lion and ignites its roar as a few people clap their approval. A voice yells, "Good job, Frank. You're a brave man, and we're proud of you."

He and the Lion creep out of the trailer park, past the onlookers, and down the few blocks to the diner. Luckily, he finds an angled space in front of the door where he eases the Lion with satisfaction right next to Julie's car. Above the low-slung curtains Frank sees the tops of the women's heads bobbing back and forth in conversation. He watches and wonders how uncomfortable it will become when they pepper him with questions about the shooting. He puts the car in reverse to drive away, but then decides to stay to take his bitter medicine.

# Chapter Eleven

The relentless little bell over the diner door announces Frank's arrival as annoyingly as his departure the day before.

"Hey, Frank," a middle-aged man yells from the end of the counter. "You doing okay?"

Frank recognizes the man but cannot remember his name.

"Yeah, I'm doing fine. Thanks for asking."

As he glances around to examine the details this time, he recalls most of the faces in the diner but remembers very few names except for a small collection of old-timers, fathers of Frank's baseball teammates. Former high school principal Loomis sits at the far end of the counter by himself, huddled over a cup of coffee and a cleaned plate, rocking back and forth in uncharacteristic anxiety. The Adams brothers are wedged in a booth against the long wall with someone who looks like a salesman in a brown corduroy blazer that is too warm for the weather—perhaps a Ford or Case tractor representative.

He realizes all eyes are fixed on him and he nods hello to those he passes, moving on to the table where the women are waiting. He slides into the booth next to Julie and across from Gloria and hesitates in astonishment to see the old man peering at him over a raised menu from the next table.

"Oh, my God!" he says under his breath.

Startled, Gloria asks, "What's the matter, Frank?"

Frank leans over the table and the women bend in so they can hear.

"Julie, do you see an old man sitting at the table behind Gloria?"

"Why of course. That's Larry."

"You know him? How long's he been coming here?"

"Well, a month or so, I'd say. He's a state auditor that's going over the city's books. He's a nice man. A little proper and old fashioned, but very sweet. He's a good eater and a good tipper, too. He's in here for breakfast and lunch just about every day."

Julie lowers her menu and waves at the old man. "Hi, Larry, how are you?"

"Oh, just fine. How are you doing?"

"Well, I'm doin' better now than I was an hour ago. Frank here gave us all a scare when he was with a man who shot himself. It was very frightening."

"Oh my," Larry puffs as he pushes back in his booth.

In a moment the old man is standing next to Frank. "I heard bits and pieces of what happened from folks here in the diner. The whole thing sounds very traumatic." He reaches out and takes Frank's hand from the tabletop and shakes it vigorously.

"You must be Mr. Barnett, the newspaper editor. I'm so glad you're all right. You must be very upset by all of it. It's very sad that poor man lost his life. I'm sure you have a troublesome story to tell."

Old Man Larry continues to clutch Frank's hand and waits for a response, but he gets none. "I've been enjoying reading your newspaper. You do a very nice job with the articles—very thorough and fair. I'm sure you will do a fine job with this unfortunate incident as well."

Frank bites his lip and pulls his hand away. He tries to sound friendly but can't help being annoyed.

"I'm the publisher, not the editor. And yes, the incident was quite trying, Mister... Mister..."

"You can just call me Larry. It's very nice to meet you, sir."

The old man dismisses Frank and offers his hand to Gloria. "And who is this lovely lady, Julie?"

"Oh, I'm sorry. This is Gloria Booker. She works at the newspaper too and keeps Frank in line. Basically runs the place."

"It's very nice to meet you, Miss Booker. Are you from Le Fleur?"

"It's nice to meet you, too. Well, I've lived here most of my life. Originally, I'm from Willard, up the road a bit, just past New Haven. My family moved over here when I was still a teen."

"Oh, I know Willard pretty well," Larry gushes. "I used to live just outside of there when I was a child. My family used to go into Willard, and I played with my cousins quite a bit there when I was a boy."

Gloria's interest is piqued. "You used to live in Willard?"

"Yes, but my family and all my relatives moved away when I was a young boy. That was so long ago, and I'm old now. I am in my seventies now, and mostly retired. But I drive around and do a little auditing for the state a few months every year. It keeps me active and sometimes I see old friends and family around Ohio. I was fortunate enough to get Le Fleur this year. I've always thought Le Fleur a nice little town and it still seems to be. Everyone is as friendly as I remember."

In keeping with friendliness, Gloria reaches out and latches onto Larry's forearm.

"Would you care to join us? There's no point in you eating alone."

"Oh no, I won't interrupt your time together. I suppose you have important things to talk about. I just want to get some of that great fish and finish reading this week's *Sentinel*. You folks have a nice day. And, Mr. Barnett, I'm so glad you're okay. I hope you find some peace during this difficult time."

Frank responds sneeringly, "Thanks. I'm sure I will."

The old man goes back to his table and is soon waited on by a college student who seems to know him. They have a good laugh together.

Gloria reaches across the table and tugs at Frank's cuff. "Well, you weren't very nice to him. In fact, you were downright nasty to that man."

Frank leans in again. "I'm not sure that man's as nice as you and Julie think he is. I don't trust him. Sounds like a bunch of bull about him living around here as a kid. I think you need to be a little wary of him and not take everything he says as gospel."

Julie puts her hand on Frank's to calm him. He looks at their joined fingers, and then into her softened smile and tranquil eyes. His brashness thaws into childlike gratitude as her touch smooths the edges of his anxiety. He has longed to feel her skin and it provides the depth of tenderness he always imagined. Her gracefulness smothers him as her velvety words fall onto his ears like the flow of a poignant violin.

"Oh, Frank, you're just being a skeptical newspaper reporter again. He's a harmless old man. I've spent my whole life reading customers, and I think he's a nice, lonely person who wants someone to talk to. We all want that, don't we?"

Frank resigns with a gentle nod, squeezes her hand tighter, and speaks in a lighter tone. "You always look for the good in people, even in folks like Larry and me. All I'm sayin' is, maybe we all should take what he says with a grain of salt."

Julie and Gloria exchange a few glances and watch Frank as he stares intently at the old man. Larry holds up a glass of water above the *Sentinel*, nods and winks at Frank, then gets back to reading the paper.

"You sure you're okay, Frank?" Julie asks."

"Yep. I'm fine, really. How could I not be when I have two lovely ladies joining me for lunch?"

The young waiter brings three plates of fish to the table with a nervous balancing act and tries hard not to drop anything, but he is too cautious and loses a knife to the floor. He looks at his boss uncomfortably.

"I'm sorry, Julie. I'll get ya another one."

"Don't worry, Sam. We don't really need knives with the perch. We can cut it with our forks. We'll share one of the other knives to butter our bread."

Sam smiles widely at his benevolent boss and hurries away.

"We ordered for you, Frank," says Gloria. "We knew you wanted the fish."

"Yep. I absolutely did."

Frank reluctantly pulls his hand from Julie's and gives her fingers a gentle tap. "This looks amazing, young lady."

He rips into the food, careless about tartar sauce on his face or shirt as he shoves fish and fries into his mouth while giving looks to the old man between bites. The things he wants to say and the gratefulness he planned to express are now subdued, replaced with curiosity for a bewildering old man in a coat and tie—some spirit perhaps, with a smile and a firm handshake.

"Frank, slow down," lectures Gloria. "You're going to choke yourself!"

"Maybe so," he mumbles. "Wouldn't matter much."

"Frank," Julie scolds lightly, "You know Gloria and I would care a great deal."

He takes a drink of water. "I'm sorry. Of course, of course you would."

"How's your fish?" Julie asks. "You're eating so fast, I'm not sure you've been able to taste it."

"It's very good. Actually, it seems lighter and even tastier than usual today."

She smiles playfully. "Maybe it's so good you don't even need to go on your fishing trip."

Responding to Julie, but looking at Gloria across from him, he says, “Hmmm. I wonder who put you up to saying that.”

“Nobody put me up to it. I just don’t feel easy about you going to New York with everything that’s going on. I’m just concerned, that’s all.”

“Julie, I appreciate your concern, but I need to go. There are things I need to do.”

Frank looks past Gloria’s shoulder to see if Old Man Larry is listening, but he appears to be preoccupied with eating his fish and reading the paper.

Julie asks, “There are people you need to see up there?”

“Yes, a few. I want to look up some folks. I haven’t been up there in a few years, ya know.”

Gloria boldly grabs his wrist. “You aren’t going to do something stupid up there while you have my son with you, are you?”

Frank is surprised by her question and takes another drink of water before answering.

“Oh my Lord, Gloria. Of course I’m not.” He takes a napkin to his mouth and coughs before continuing his defense.

“I just want one last chance at landing a big king salmon. I want to be there when Russ gets his first one, too. He’ll be surprised by the fight in those things. Who knows, maybe we can get a nice trophy to put on Russ’s wall.” He follows with a wicked laugh. “That sure would piss off his wife, wouldn’t it? I’d pay for it so he doesn’t get divorced, although that might be the best thing for him.”

There is a long silence. Finally, Gloria sits straight up in the booth. “So, why did you take the gun from your desk? Are you taking that to shoot the salmon?”

His face turns rigid with surprise. He puts down his fork and rests his head on his clasped knuckles in front of his mouth before mumbling a response. “How do you know about the gun? What are you doing rummaging around my desk?”

"It's my job to know everything at the paper. You think I wasn't going to check about the gun after I saw you with it yesterday? I know everything about you and most everything you do. I also know that gun is the one used to shoot my uncle—right in the jail."

Frank snaps to attention. "What the hell are you talking about? What do you mean, it's the gun used to shoot your uncle?"

Frank had spoken too loudly and several nearby patrons, including Old Man Larry, look in his direction. He hunkers down and lowers his voice. "My dad gave me that gun not long before he died. He kept it in his desk for years. He said that every newspaperman needed a gun in his desk in case some nutty reader came in to pick a fight about a story."

"I know your dad gave it to you," Gloria says confidently. "And Chief Wells had given it to him, the very night my Uncle Willis was shot with it."

"Gloria, what the hell are you talking about?"

"Your dad never told you about any of this, did he?"

Julie begins squirming in her seat, trapped between the window and Frank. "I should go," Julie says. "I don't think I should hear this, or that I even want to."

"No, you should stay, Julie," Gloria insists. "You can be a comfort to Frank. He's going to need your hand to hold."

Julie relaxes from her attempt to leave and settles back in the booth. She feels for Frank's hand and wraps her fingers around it. He is again glad for a chance to connect with the woman he's longed to hold.

Gloria says, "That's what Phil told you about in here yesterday, wasn't it? About how his dad, Chief Wells, framed my uncle, then had him killed. Didn't he?"

Frank slips his fingers from Julie's and begins to rub the side of his head. He wriggles his other hand into his pants pocket and wrestles a bottle of pills to the table top. After struggling with the lid, he finally manages to get it off, shakes two capsules onto his hand, and gulps them down with a long drink of water.

All three nurse their water glasses while they hunt for a way to restart the conversation. Finally, Frank swallows hard and begins with a whisper.

"What the hell do you mean, Gloria?"

Gloria picks up her coffee cup to give her shaking hands a distraction.

"Well, Frank, the day Uncle Willis was shot, I was at the *Sentinel* in the darkroom printing some photos. It was near the end of the day and everyone else had left. I don't think James even remembered I was there. I had only been with the paper five or six months, and I don't think he had gotten used to me being in the darkroom. But I heard someone come in and yell your dad's name, then go into his office. It was Chief Wells's voice. Then I heard another voice, quieter, and I couldn't tell right away who it was. Your dad's office door slammed shut and there was a lot of low talking going on. It got louder and louder, with a lot of swearing. From the back room I couldn't hear what was said, but then I clearly heard your dad yell, 'Wells, you're a damned fool! I can't believe you did it. I won't be a part of the cover up. I'm not hiding the gun for you!' It sounded like pushing and shoving was going on, but except for your dad's shout, I couldn't tell what else was being said. Then after a couple more minutes I heard the two men leaving and the other guy said to Wells, 'He'll keep his mouth shut, Chief. He has too much to lose otherwise.' Then I could tell it was the mayor's voice.

"I walked slowly down the long hallway and peered into your dad's office to find him sitting there, rubbing his forehead. When he saw me looking in the doorway, he grabbed a paper and slid it across his desk to cover something up, but I could see the nose of a gun sticking out. He was very upset but pretended not to be. I asked if everything was okay."

Gloria fights back emotion as she looks out the window. "Your dad was so good to me, Frank. He treated me better than anyone else in town. He didn't act like I was a black girl. He just treated me like the eager, young college grad I was. He gave me real work to do. He had so much faith in me."

Her voice trails off as she stares out the window at people passing by, dispersing from the morning's excitement. She forces her attention back to Frank.

"He was fighting back tears, and he seemed shattered. I think he knew I'd heard some things, but he never told me to not say anything. He just said I should go home to be with my family and they would tell me what happened. So, I went home to find my mom and aunts crying and my uncles in a fit of rage. They were talking about storming the police station to kill Wells or burning down his house around him if they had to. They never believed the story about what happened, not from the start. They thought Wells hired someone to shoot my uncle that night. I'm not sure who really did it, and I'm not sure James did either, but he hid the gun and it's been in your desk all these years. He helped cover it up."

Frank talks to his plate. "Jesus, Gloria. Jesus. You never told me about the gun or any of this. Phil said yesterday that he thought his dad let someone into the jail to club the guard and shoot your uncle. Is that what you think, too?"

Gloria covers her eyes and begins to cry, struggling to speak between muffled sobs. "Wells was here in the diner when Willis was shot, pretending to collect evidence about Sarah's death with the county guys. But I think he put someone up to it and he then took the gun to your dad to hide. You know they were good friends. You also know the guard was never the same after he had his skull cracked. He died a few months later as a vegetable in the nursing home. He was the only witness, and he was the only one who could tell the story, except for the shooter. And Wells, of course."

Frank's tone becomes slightly indignant. "You really think my dad would be a part of the cover up? He wouldn't have!"

"Sometimes," Gloria says, her eyes grief-stricken, "people do things they normally wouldn't do. Evil people find ways to make others do things they would never do otherwise."

"Why didn't you ever say anything? You could have told me. You *should* have told me."

A glimmer of humor shows through the cracks of grief on Gloria's face. "Think about your question, Frank. You had just gotten back a few weeks earlier after you dropped out of college. I didn't know you all that well. What was I supposed to do? Start a race riot over things I suspected? Set off my uncles and get them killed too? I had grown close to your dad and I guess I wanted to protect him. I loved this town despite its faults, despite how I was made to feel sometimes. Most people didn't care that I was black, or at least they pretended not to. But I know your dad really didn't care about my skin, and after I got to know you better, I found out you didn't care, either. That was enough for me. I never knew my own dad, and then my closest uncle was gone, and I didn't want to lose anyone else."

"I don't understand how I couldn't have known any of this. Didn't anyone suspect Wells?"

Gloria slowly rubs her eyes and speaks deliberately, trying to not sound condescending. "Oh, my little Frankie. Don't you remember that my uncle's killing was the talk of the town? Some people did suspect Wells was involved and they openly discussed it. They even had some ideas about who the shooter was, but no one ever really put that together. Maybe they clammed up about it around you and your dad."

Puzzled, Frank says, "Jesus, Gloria, you think people thought my dad was involved?"

"I'm not saying they did. Maybe they just didn't want to lump your dad in with Wells and the mayor."

"Miss Julie, this cherry pie is very good!"

The trio is startled by Old Man Larry's exclamation from the table behind Gloria. Sam had delivered the dessert to Larry without any of the three noticing as they spoke of guns, murder, and deceit.

Julie stammers to an awareness of Larry and murmurs a response. "Oh, oh, thanks. It was my mom's recipe, of course."

"Well it's about the best I've ever had. Your mom must've been a great cook—and a great woman too, I bet."

This was Julie's perfect chance to move the discussion in a less serious direction. "Yes. Yes, she was a fine woman all the way around. Her pies were her specialty. I guess they probably kept the place going."

Larry raises his fork and nods with a big smile, pretending not to notice the obvious stress between Frank and Gloria.

Frank speaks softly, "You two know everything about me and what I am up to. Here I sit like an open book and that old man sits over there stuffing pie into his face. You have no idea what kind of man he really is."

Gloria asks, "What kind of man is he?"

Frank finishes a swallow of water. "Well, I'm not sure."

Frank starts to bite a roll, then stops, puts it down, and hunkers in again. He whispers, "You know, I'm not sure he's a man at all."

Gloria blocks Frank's hand before it can pick up the roll again. "Frank, what on earth are you talking about? Of course, he's a man. For heaven's sake, is your head causing you that big of a problem?"

"It has nothing to do with my head. Remember the old man I told you was in my office yesterday? The one you didn't know was there?"

Gloria nods.

"Well, that's him. That's the man who was there."

"My heavens, Julie, he's totally lost it."

"I haven't lost anything. That's him. He was also with me right before and right after Fritz shot himself. He was in my house last night, too. That man, or devil, or whatever he is, just appears out of nowhere, torments the hell out of me with nonsense, then just disappears again."

Gloria covers her mouth in alarm and speaks through her fingers. "My good Lord Jesus, Frank. This is the worst your visions have ever gotten. He's just a nice old man in town to do some auditing of the city's books. You really need to go see Doc Phillips before you go fishing. This is just a crazy vision from your tumor."

Tears trail down Julie's face as she tries to quash a deep sob. Gloria sees the tears, but Frank does not.

"Well, I have an appointment with Doc this afternoon, in fact. I've several other things I want to do before I leave town, but I'll keep my appointment. No need to worry about that."

Gloria presses further. "I think you've seen Larry around town the last few weeks and somehow you've worked him into your visions. Maybe you needed someone to talk to and he looked like a trustworthy soul to insert into your hallucinations. That's what I think. I bet the doc will say the same thing."

Frank turns to Julie for a response and sees that her face is wet and red. "What do you think?"

Julie says, "I don't know what to think. I really don't. So many things are running through my head. I want...I want to..."

Julie takes a napkin to her eyes then gathers herself. "I just want to tell you I love you, Frank. I love you and don't want you to hurt anymore. I've seen you in here lately and you've looked so depressed. Yesterday was the worst of all. No matter what happens, I just want to say I love you and have for a long time."

Stillness covers the table. The three realize that Julie's proclamation is a demarcation between the stifled feelings of before and those profound sensations that will come after. Gloria reaches across the table and holds Julie's hand as Frank appears to be searching the plates and glasses for some appropriate response to magically rise up from the table.

After a long pause, Frank reaches for both of the women's hands. "You know what's funny? Not until today did I realize that I love you both—very, very much. Even the old man told me I did."

The three smile and collectively shake hands for a couple moments until the adoration is shattered by Larry standing next to their table. "Excuse me for interrupting, my friends, but I have to get back to City Hall. I just noticed that you all look a little upset and I just want to say I hope all is well. You're all so kind here. I hope whatever is troubling you passes soon. God bless you all."

"Thank you, Larry," Gloria says. "I...well...I'm sure we all appreciate that. It was a pleasure meeting you and I hope to see you again."

"That is very kind of you, ma'am. Please take care of each other."

Larry nods to the trio and strides out of the diner with the dignity of an English aristocrat.

Frank sniffs, wipes his eye, and slides out of the booth. He pulls out more than ample money from his wallet and lays it on the table.

"Gloria, I don't know what to make of your story about my dad hiding the gun. It doesn't sound like my dad at all. Maybe someday we'll know for sure. But I have a lot to do before I leave in the morning. I love you both. And please, be careful of that old man."

Gloria jumps up to hug him and whispers in his ear. "I know you have to do what you think is right. I won't judge—no matter what you decide to do. Please, just make sure Russ gets back to me."

Frank pulls away and looks curiously at Gloria. He smiles with the realization that she understands, at least a little, his quest to have one last adventure. He leans forward to kiss her cheek and glances over to Julie.

He takes Julie's hand and kisses it lovingly. "Goodbye, sweet Julie. Thank you for always being here to talk. I hope you know how much you mean to me. You always find a way to help me see things better." He reaches to her cheek and pats dry a tear. He holds her warm face in his palm, wanting desperately to lean in the rest of the way and kiss her deeply, so she can feel it. Instead, he pulls away gradually to keep that moment of desire whole and unblemished. The thought becomes greater than the doing.

The door rings him away, but Frank stands briefly outside the window, unnoticed by the women. They slump back into the booth, cry, and hold each other's hands across the table. After a few moments of spying, he looks back to watch the old man walk toward City Hall, but he sees no one. He climbs into the Lion and roars off, again forgetting his jacket, hat, and umbrella.

# Chapter Twelve

The aged lady sitting at the desk to the left of the double-door entrance looks up from her magazine and lifts a corner of her mouth before blurting a welcome as comfortable as a stubbed toe.

"Hello, Mr. Barnett. I hope you're doing okay after that *really* crazy shooting this morning. You look terrible."

Frank stops to answer with all the calmness he can muster.

"Hi there, Mrs. Loomis. So, everyone here at the nursing home already knows about that?"

Mrs. Loomis puts down the magazine like an exclamation mark.

"Well, Fred called me from the diner with the news. All the staff knows, but I'm sure the residents *really* haven't picked up on it. In fact, the staff has been told to keep *really* quiet about it around your mom, so she doesn't get upset. By the way, she is doing *really* well today, just coming and going a bit, but not too bad, *really*.

"Okay, thanks," Frank says feebly. He turns the corner to walk down the long east hall.

Mrs. Loomis barks at him from behind. "We're all so glad you're all right, Mr. Barnett, we *really* are."

Frank looks in the doorways at the people who sit or lie in various levels of awareness and distress. Occasionally, someone will let out a nonsensical shriek or a string of incoherent sentences that go unheeded by other residents and staff. The variety of unique, blended smells of cleaners and uncontrolled bodily functions changes every few steps.

A gangly man named Jim with a gray bush of hair seems more engaged than the other residents. He sits in his wheelchair exchanging banter with the young female orderly dispensing medicine, then looks away from his conversation to give Frank a big smile. He extends his hand.

"Hey, Hemingway, it's been a few days! Good to see you, young man."

Frank stoops down on one knee and puts his hand on Jim's arm.

"Hi, Professor, nice to see you too. You look pretty damn good this afternoon."

"Thanks, youngster. It's good to be on this side of the daisies, don'cha know! Just got back from my bath a little bit ago. Jack does a good job, but I wish I could have one of those cute nurses do it!"

Frank chuckles, stands up, and pushes gently on Jim's shoulder. "Oh, you're such a charmer. I bet you're out cruising the halls for chicks today, aren't you."

"You got that right, Hemingway!"

"So, have you read any good books lately?"

Jim bends forward like he's going to tell Frank a great secret, but with loud delight, howls, "You aren't going to believe this, Hemingway, but I just started *Old Man and the Sea*!"

"You mean to tell me," Frank says with pretend surprise, "you never read that or made your students read it in all the years you taught at the college?"

"That's right! I didn't want them to think I was too traditional. Of course, I read it, but since I can't remember shit, I thought I might as well read it again—for the first time!"

Both men let out strong laughs and Jim starts wheeling down the hallway toward the lobby, chasing the cute orderly.

"Have a good visit with your mom, Hemingway!" Jim hollers back over his shoulder.

Frank always spends a minute or two with Jim when he visits. At nearly ninety he is still intriguing, one of the most astute and funny men Frank knows. He continues toward his mother's room and stops to peek through George Sauer's doorway. The big, well-groomed man sits in a wheelchair on the far side of his bed, his arms and hands hanging useless in his lap. He stares at a television game show that he doesn't see.

"Hey there, George."

George moves his head and his dark, desolate eyes acknowledge Frank. He cannot speak or move any other part of his body.

Frank nods and then moves on past George's door to a shadowbox of mementos on the hallway wall. Each resident has a small wooden cabinet outside their doorway to display photos, small trinkets, or newspaper clippings about them and their family members. The boxes are a good tool to help the cogent ambulatory residents find their rooms. The boxes also remind visitors and staff that the residents were once vibrant, proud people full of dreams, fears, and passions. Most of the boxes contain faded photographs of smiling couples in happy and long-lasting marriages; of friends and coworkers at parties; of children and grandchildren who may or may not be remembered and who may or may not come to visit.

Frank gently pulls up the clear plastic front of George's box as he has several times before to remove two football trading cards. The cards flaunt a golden man with a strong face and bulging uniform from another era of the NFL's New York Jets. Frank turns the 1970-dated card over to read again the small biography next to the statistics.

*George Sauer was a receiver at the University of Texas where he was a member of the undefeated teams of 1963-64 that won the Cotton Bowl and that defeated*

*Alabama in the 1965 Orange Bowl. George is a four-time All-Star in the American Football League and NFL and led the league in receptions in 1967 and 1968. He was the leading receiver in Super Bowl III in 1969, catching eight of Joe Namath's passes in one of the greatest upsets in pro football history when the Jets beat the Baltimore Colts 16-7.*

Frank looks to the bottom of the card where a small caricature of George bangs away at a typewriter, under which reads, "George wants to be a writer when his football days are over."

Also in the shadow box is a typed poem that George wrote about his father, George Sr., a notable football player in his own right and who, like his son, suffered the effects of Alzheimer's disease.

*Wind-driven fight blows in my marrow,*

*light narrows and clouds invite.*

*Bent by long shadows, longer time,*

*an old man dances in my heart—*

*his broken brain rattles mine.*

Frank's own mind drifts back a couple weeks to a hallway conversation with George's sister Dana in which she said that after his playing days, George worked as a textbook editor for a New York publisher. She said that George submitted an unfinished manuscript to his employer in the hopes of furthering his writing, but the idea was rejected.

As far as Dana knew, George never completed that book or any other. She said he spent many subsequent years taking notes and jotting things down on notepads, hoping to form his ideas into stories, but she believed he never finished a single project. She said that George later worked in a grocery store in South Dakota, keeping his football past, Super Bowl heroics, and several failed marriages hidden from his coworkers. She mentioned a 1983 New York Times article written about him in which George was quoted as saying that he didn't like being a public person "where you stick out too much."

Dana said that George loved the athletic beauty of being a receiver but hated the violence of it, so he walked away in his prime. "When all the NFL head injury talk started," she said, "he was against being part of the suit. He knew what football did to his dad and he knew what it could do to him. Even though he hated a lot about the pro game, he knew he wouldn't have had a meaningful life without football. He would've felt like a hypocrite suing the NFL."

Frank carefully places the cards back in the shadowbox and gently lowers the front, then moves to his mother's wooden box near her door. He looks through the plastic as he always does, even though the arrangement of keepsakes has not been changed in months. One of his favorite photos in the box was taken by him in the 1980s of his mom and dad sitting on the sofa near the Christmas tree holding their portly dark-brown dachshund with its belly out toward the camera. His mother Mary and father James had a turbulent life together, and there were moments when divorce seemed imminent and sincerely hoped for by Frank. Mary despised the newspaper, perhaps even more than Frank's ex-wife Brenda, but she stayed with her publisher husband until his sudden, ugly death. Despite the fights, despite the hurt that each gave the other, this one singular photograph displayed a warm but fleeting companionship during one family Christmas celebration.

Frank came home from college that holiday and hoped that either things would improve for good between his parents or that his dad would finally leave.

Maybe there were more happy times like this one for Frank's parents, particularly during their early days when James was home for leave during the height of World War II. James lied about his age to get into the army and his father Paul, publisher of the *Sentinel* at the time, talked to the area's US Congressman, Robert Franklin Jones, to secure his son's war photographer slot. James came home a hero of sorts around Richland County after some of his dramatic photos appeared in the *Sentinel*, other regional newspapers, and even several in national publications. James began working at the *Sentinel* upon his return from the war and was soon named editor and publisher by his father when Paul retired to his farm and shortly died of stomach cancer at the relatively early age of sixty-one. James became as respected in the community as Paul for being a man of principle and compassion. But, by later inheriting the newspaper from James, Frank was left to interpret, varnish, and buff the details of his father's grisly accidental death on the farm at age seventy-nine.

Frank shakes off the shadowbox memories and moves to the edge of his mom's doorjamb to peek into the room. Mary sits on the side of her bed looking out the window at birds flitting from one feeder to another. The feeders were a gift from Frank on Mother's Day to prompt her out of bed to watch the thrushes, wrens, robins, cardinals, and an occasional aggressive blue jay.

Frank eases into the room and sits gently at the end of her bed, unnoticed. For a few moments he is amused by her delight in watching the birds flap about. Her mind has migrated to the outdoor courtyard and it will take some work to bring her back.

"Hello, Mom," Frank says softly. "It's me, Frankie."

Mary continues to watch the birds, still unaware of his presence, so he moves to the side of the bed and takes her hand.

"Mom, it's me, Frankie."

After a moment, a small smile grows into an expansive grin. She speaks weakly, but her hoarse voice carries the tenderness of all loving mothers. "Hello, my sweet Frankie. It's so nice of you to come see me today. I've been watching the birds. They are such sweet creatures."

"I know, Mom, I saw you watching them. I'm glad you like to watch the feeders so much. It looks like the staff is keeping them full of the seed I brought last month."

"Yes, I suppose they are."

Frank reaches into his jacket pocket and pulls out a large Hershey bar. Mary's eyes clarify with excitement as he begins to unwrap the corner.

"I couldn't come to see my girl without bringing her some candy."

"Thank you. I like candy."

"I know you do, Mom. I think you could live on just candy, if they would let you."

Frank often brings Mary her favorite sweets, milkshakes, and McDonald's cheeseburgers to supplement her meager eating habits. He used to bring her boxes of candy and cookies to leave in the dresser so she could have them anytime she wanted, but it was discovered that other residents and even employees were eating more than she was. As he continues to unwrap the candy bar, Mary turns her attention back to the outdoor courtyard. She looks past the bird feeders and waves femininely to someone out in the distance. Frank leans forward and looks out the window, but the courtyard is empty except for a gazebo and lawn furniture scattered about.

"Who you waving to, Mom?"

"James. Your dad's out there."

Frank chuckles, bemused. "Dad's out there, huh? What's he doing?"

"He's just sitting there, reading a book."

Frank watches Mary gaze and wave periodically to her imaginary late husband.

"Has Dad been inside to see you lately?"

"Yes, just yesterday."

"Does he stop by often?"

Mary answers softly without taking her eyes off the courtyard. "He's stopping more all the time lately, but he doesn't talk very much. He's never had too much to say. He usually just sits outside or over there in the corner with his nose stuck in a book, like always."

After a long pause Frank asks, "Does he ever touch you?"

"No. He isn't very cuddly, ya know. He mostly just sits, and we talk about things. Well, I do most of the talking, but he's a good listener."

Her voice trails off and she turns her attention back to the courtyard. She lets out a small, dignified laugh. For a long while Frank sits and watches his mother and how happy she is to imagine James in the courtyard. Frank shudders to attention and looks around the room to see if anyone else is lurking there. Gratefully, he sees no Larry. Mary turns her attention back inside the room and acts startled to see Frank.

"Oh, Frankie, how long have you been sitting there?"

Frank thinks about what the best response might be. "I just got here, Mom. I brought you some chocolate."

Frank breaks off a corner and reaches across the space between them to hand it to her. She begins nibbling on it and savors each little bite as chocolate begins to build up on her lips and the corners of her mouth.

"Mom, the chocolate is melting in your fingers. Just go ahead and put the piece in your mouth."

Mary either doesn't hear Frank or pretends not to. She continues to nibble at the chocolate as it melts. When finished, she licks her lips and each one of her fingers.

Frank hands her another piece and the messy process is repeated until the candy bar is gone.

"That's all there is. Don't touch anything. Let me get a wet paper towel."

Frank goes into Mary's bathroom to get a towel and comes out to find her pulling at her now-stained blouse.

"Mom," Frank says sternly, "you're getting chocolate on your collar."

Frank tries to wipe her shirt but spreads the chocolate around into a wet brown spot. He wipes off her mouth, then her fingers.

"Thank you. Thank you, Frankie. That was good." In a strained but thoughtful pitch she says, "Your dad always brought me chocolate, you know. We'd have a fight and he thought a box of candy would make it okay. You remember that, Frankie?"

Frank is somewhere else. He looks down and rubs a bit of chocolate on his fingers.

More lucid and robust, she says, "What is it, Frankie? What's bothering you so much, my son?"

Her tone of voice surprises Frank back to the present. "What? Huh? Oh, nothing, Mom. Nothing."

"Come now, Frankie. I may not know much anymore, but I do know when my son is hurting. A mom always knows that. What is it?"

"Mom, I'm going away for a little while. I'm going fishing in New York and may go on another trip after that, so I may not be here to see you for a while."

Mary struggles to comprehend her son's announcement but eventually seems to grasp its enormity. These precious moments of clarity are becoming rarer with each passing month.

"Oh, is that right? Fishing up at the lake like you and your dad used to?"

"That's right. But I have some wonderful people lined up to check on you while I'm gone. They'll bring you candy, pie, and milkshakes, and all the things you like—just like I do."

"Frankie, I don't like the thought of you being away. How long do you think you'll be gone?"

"It could be a few weeks, maybe a month, or a bit longer."

"I see. That's a very long time and I'll miss you. But there's something bothering you. You don't look well today, son."

"You don't even have your glasses on. How can you even see that I don't look well?"

Mary gives out a little laugh. "Hmm. I don't need my glasses to tell that something's bothering you. I can still see the lines on your forehead and hear the sadness of your voice."

Frank moves around uneasily and scratches his scalp with both of his hands, then stands up and walks to the window.

"Everything's good. I just need to get away from the paper for a while, that's all."

"Okay, Frankie, if that's your story, but I know there's more to it than that. You just aren't yourself today."

"Neither are you, Mom. I mean, you are doing much better today. I mean, you look so good today."

She builds a strong laugh. "I guess you're trying to be nice, but you mean I'm not as crazy as usual, don't you?"

Frank moves to her and puts his hand on her face.

"You're never crazy. Sometimes you're just a little confused. We all get that way sometimes."

"Yes, I guess we do, don't we? You a little confused right now, Frankie?"

Frank kneels and gives Mary a warm kiss on the cheek as he continues to hold her face. He then leans in to give her a hug and whispers, "Well, like I said, we all get that way sometimes, so maybe a little bit. That's why I need to go fishing and think a bit."

Mary puts her arms around his back and draws him in closer. Her voice is muffled against his neck, but her words are clear enough.

"Frankie, will I ever see you again?"

Frank is startled and pulls back to look at her face.

"Of course you will, Mom. Of course you will!"

Mary holds on to his hand so he cannot move away any further.

"Okay, Frankie. But you know I love you more than anything, and I always will."

Frank kneels down on one knee and kisses her hand.

"You're my special lady, Mom. I'll be back to visit again before you know it. When I come back, I'll bring you the biggest box of chocolates you've ever seen, and we will eat them together in one sitting."

He stands up again, covers his mouth, and chokes back the sadness of his white lie. He exhales and kisses her on the hand once more as she lowers her chin into her chest. She keeps her head down as he eases toward the door. He stops in the doorway and holds on to the jamb.

"Everything's fine, Mom. I'll be back for your birthday in October."

She looks up at him with no apparent emotion.

"Goodbye, Frankie. I love you."

Frank chokes out, "I love you too, Mom," and turns out into the hallway, stopping in front of the shadowbox. He moves up the plastic cover to get a clear look at his happy parents holding their dog. The memory of that cheerful Christmas moment blankets him in comfort. He slides the plastic back into place and makes his way down the hallway. George's door is open, and the man still stares blankly at the television. Frank wants to say something encouraging but cannot think of anything profound. He continues down the wing and comes to Mrs. Loomis at the desk near the front door, then rushes through the exit without a word.

"Goodbye, Mr. Barnett," she shouts at his back. "Hope to see you again soon."

# Chapter Thirteen

The nurse takes the blood pressure cuff off Frank's arm and sets it back on the tray on the wall. Neither of them acknowledge the routine procedure. "Okay, Frank. Dr. Phillips will be in shortly." She shuts the door behind her. Frank sits on the end of the examination table in his underwear and reads the framed poster on the wall opposite him:

***Important Life Lessons***

*Life isn't fair, so find your own good in it*

*Life is too short to waste energy hating*

*A hand-written letter to a friend will bring you closer*

*Make peace with your past to move forward*

*Forgive everyone of all wrongs against you*

*Believe in miracles and you will have more of them*

*Read one of the Great Novels to discover wonderment*

*Help someone who least expects it and you will be helped*

*Find a reason to laugh and it will be contagious*

*All that truly matters in the end is that you loved someone*

"Jesus. What bullshit."

He slides off the table and picks up a *Sports Illustrated* from the adjacent counter and flips through the pages looking at the headlines. He focuses on an article, then looks up at the poster again.

"Bullshit."

Bored with the reading, he tosses the magazine on the counter and lies back on the paper-covered exam table, knees hanging over the end. He stares at the ceiling and imagines patterns in the holes of the tiles. Just as he drifts off, he hears a knock at the door.

"C'mon in," he mumbles.

"Well hello there, Frank. How you doing after all that excitement?"

Frank rolls his head around his neck and scratches his ear. "Oh my God, Doc. You know about that too?"

"Of course. The barber, baker, candlestick maker, and I know just about everything around this town."

"You know I'm going out of town too?"

"Would it bother you if I did?"

Frank looks down at his socked feet. "Guess nothing like that matters anymore, does it, Doc?"

"Have you talked to Dr. Fisher lately? Is he still trying to get you to take chemo again and have the Cyberknife procedure?"

Frank hangs his head. "He keeps checking to see if I've changed my mind, but you and I both know that chemo just makes me sick, weak, and useless. And the Cyberknife isn't going to do anything except maybe reduce the pressure and pain for a little while. We both know nothing is going to make much of a difference."

"So, you're just going to give up, then?"

"Do you think I should go through hell just so I might have a couple more months of sickness? To be helpless and force someone to wipe my ass and clean up my puke? Does avoiding that mean I'm giving up, Doc?"

The stoic Doc approaches with a tongue depressor, and Frank automatically opens his mouth. The poking and prodding continue until Doc positions himself to Frank's side and places his hand above and behind his ear.

"Any pain when I press?"

"No. Not much. About like a kick in the nuts, I guess."

"I can't tell if you're really pissed off, or if you're using that famous sense of humor of yours."

"I'm not pissed off, at least not at you. Guess I'm just resigned to my fate. It's hard to imagine that I'll be dead and in the ground in a couple months."

"Frank, you don't know that."

"Well, I look at the odds and they sure don't look good, do they."

The doctor picks up a chart, scribbling and flipping pages back and forth.

"How are the meds working to control your pain?"

Frank examines his thumb as he picks its nail with his index finger.

"They do okay, but the side effects are annoying. I still have a hard time going to the bathroom even with the stool softeners and I still get very tired and groggy and... and..."

Frank debates his next words and finally mutters, "Those visions I have are getting stronger and more realistic."

The doctor puts his chart down, crosses his arms, and leans back against the counter.

"Is that so? Tell me about them."

"Well, I keep seeing this old, imaginary man. He just pops into my life. He talks to me, and I talk to him. I can't help but think he's real. In fact, I've touched him. He has to be real."

"That's pretty interesting. How many milligrams does Dr. Fisher have you up to?"

"Hell, I don't know, Doc. I pick up the bottles from the drugstore and take a couple pills five times a day, sometimes six or seven if my head gets really bad. I just took a few a little while ago, but I left the bottle out in the car."

Doc leans forward a bit and says, "Dr. Fisher is okay with you taking so many?"

"Yep. He said if I need one or two more during the day or if I wake up at night it's okay for me to take what I need. But it's not the damn pills. They aren't making me see things, if that's what you're getting at."

"Okay, tell me more."

"I thought this old man, Larry, was just a vision, or some kind of damn ghost, and for a while I thought I was the only one who could see him. But then he was in the diner and Gloria and Julie talked to him too. Julie has seen him there for weeks and I know she didn't imagine that!"

Doc rests his elbow on the counter and contorts his face and lips, deliberating.

"Hm. That's very interesting. Maybe he is real—someone you've seen around town—and now he's gotten into your subconscious. Maybe you find him comforting and you bring him into consciousness when you need to."

Frank looks up at the ceiling tiles with disgust.

"Comforting? He's irritating as hell. Oh my God, Doc. Now I know you've been talking to Gloria. She said the same kind of crap."

Doc picks up the charts again and looks for something as he flips through.

"Did you ever go see the counselor I referred you to a couple months ago?"

"What for?" Frank snaps. "So she can tell me to take it easy and not be afraid of dying? What a waste of time. I don't need to see any damned psychiatrists to tell me those things."

"Well," Doc hesitates. "I told you a while back and I am sure Dr. Fisher did too, that your brain could play tricks on you and you might see and feel some crazy things."

"Well, I guess you were right, then."

"It isn't about me being right. You're the one who has to deal with this disease. You know, it's strange, but I'm not really good with these kinds of situations."

Frank looks up, perplexed.

"What kind of situations? You mean people dying?"

"Well, yeah. I'm not good with dealing with patients who have terminal illnesses."

"Guess that makes us even, because I ain't too damn good with it either."

"So, who you going fishing with?"

"C'mon Doc. You know damn well I'm taking Gloria's kid, Russ."

"Yes, I know. You're right. I've talked to Gloria and she told me he was going. He's a good kid, isn't he?"

Without any instruction, Frank begins putting on his clothes.

"He isn't really a kid anymore. He's in his late twenties. He's one hell of a young man. He's going to be running the paper very soon, probably much sooner than he or anyone else even realizes."

"You think by the New Year?"

Frank stops buttoning his shirt and speaks pointedly. "If not sooner!"

Doc crosses his arms and stares blankly as Frank continues to straighten his shirt and tighten his belt.

"Don't worry, Doc. We will have some time on the fishing trip to cover some bigger issues. He'll be ready. Hell, he's ready now. Anyway, the best way to get anything done is to just jump in with both feet. Sink or swim, as my dad always said. Thanks for everything. I'll see you soon."

Frank doesn't wait for a response. He walks out of the exam room and down the hall to the receptionist and signs a form without speaking or looking at her. In an instant he is out the office door to guide the roaring Lion through downtown Le Fleur, not sure where to go to next. Perhaps somewhere comforting, like sitting across the counter from Julie, complimenting her on the apple pie and finally telling her all the things he should have said. He sees himself leaning over and passionately kissing her as they stand alone in the diner. His heart and the Lion's engine flutter with the shifts.

# Chapter Fourteen

Early morning fog hangs over the outfield grass to the height of a man. The air is clear and still over the dirt infield; no other sound of wind in the trees or of anything moving about can be heard. A body lies on the wooden bleachers, one arm outstretched and resting on another plank just below. Clutched in the hand of the lanky arm is a nearly empty pint of Dewar's scotch with half a shot still collected in the corner of the flask-shaped bottle.

The serene break of day is sliced by the distant hum of an airplane. The growling increases as the C-130 Hercules cargo plane continues a slow turn above the treetops several hundred yards away from the small stadium. The baseball field is often the navigation point for the 130s' turn back toward the Air National Guard base in Mansfield. As the grayish-green plane grows larger over the limp body, the rumble of the four propellers cause the decaying press box and bleachers to rattle.

Frank opens his eyes in fright, raising his head to see what is descending upon him. The imposing plane is low enough to allow any sober man to read the identification on the tail. ANG 30488. The word *Mansfield* sits within a red stripe below an American flag, and all are emblazoned over the gray. For Frank, those insignias are just streaks of blurred color.

"Holy crap!" he exclaims out loud to the empty stadium.

Frank notices a bit of scotch left in the bottle. He props up his body and brings his hand in for the final drink. "Damn!" he says when he finishes. His throbbing head and creaking back mix with the welcome sensations of being alive. He is still here and glad of it.

A crow, unfazed by the airplane, sits on the end of a bleacher a few rows below. Frank takes aim and heaves the bottle at the bird, but the crow takes off as soon as Frank's arm begins to move. The bottle sails high and to the left of where the bird ascends. The C-130's loud engines fade and the rattling stops.

"Son-of-a-bitch crows!"

Laughing, he takes pride in the effort and convinces himself that it was a strong attempt. He sits up and looks out over the sleeping field, recalling his days as a catcher and the powerful throws he made to second base. He was one of the best players in the entire county, and the biggest and strongest. Baseball was his all, as it was for most boys in town. He had dreams of The Bigs.

Behind this very home plate is where he felt he could control everything, where he would tell the pitcher what to throw and the fielders where to align for each batter. The coaches knew he could manage on-field strategy better than they could, and he swells with vanity in that memory.

He sits up a bit straighter and recalls his scorching line drives over the infielders and the times he'd punish the ball deep over the fence, sometimes even over the railroad tracks beyond. He stares out and believes he can smell the musty leather of his glove and feel the red laces of the baseball coursing over his fingertips as he rubs them together. The satisfaction of reliving the moments covers him in droplets of bliss. He is full of pride about having given the love of the game to his sons and how good they became before Brenda dragged them off to the east and a rich kid's sport.

The serenity of the memories turns to dispiriting anguish when he remembers hitting home runs, only to look in the stands for his own absent father. Having recreated the hurtful scene in later years for his own sons pierces him with pain, his remorse now a blinding "son-of-a-bitch" moment.

A voice from a few rows above startles Frank.

"Good morning, Frank. Sleeping off the rough night, I see."

Frank turns his whole body toward the voice because of an uncooperative stiff neck.

"Well, if it isn't my guardian angel Clarence, from *It's a Wonderful Life*. What the hell you up to this morning, Clarence?"

"I prefer you call me by my real name, Frank. I don't like being compared to a movie character."

"Well, well, isn't that just perfect. I get a ghost bugging the snot out of me and he doesn't like what *I* call *him*. Perfect. That's just perfect. Okay, *Larry*, what the hell are you up to this morning?"

"Well, if you must know, I came by to see that you didn't sleep too long and miss your appointment to pick up Russ for the fishing trip."

Frank attempts to stand but quivers back down to a sitting position.

"Isn't that sweet? Not only are you my guardian angel, but you're a wake-up service and butler all rolled into one. Boy, didn't I just hit the jackpot with you!"

Larry snickers and takes off his fedora.

"You sure are grouchy when you have a hangover, but you're amusing nonetheless."

Frank manages to straighten his legs this time and stands.

"Just look at yourself, Larry. An old man sitting in a decrepit set of bleachers with dew all about, wearing a damn suit, tie, and hat. Where the hell do you think you are, Mister, the nineteen-fifties?"

Larry places his hat on the bleacher and rubs his neck as though he too may have a liquor-induced headache.

"I guess part of me is still in the fifties, Frank. They were important years to me. I guess all of us cling to what we know and what we remember—or what we think we have lived and think we remember."

Frank rolls his jaws around, licks his lips, and smacks his tongue on his teeth to try and create some saliva. He feels his earlier grand baseball memories falling from his head to roll around the inside his mouth like the stuffed cotton of remorse. His words stumble over his parched tongue.

"What we think we lived and what we think we remember, huh? Interesting, Old Man, 'cause I've been wondering just that. What the hell have I really lived?"

Larry places the hat back on his head and adjusts it to the perfect angle. He speaks with his typical calmness.

"Is that a rhetorical question? I hope so, because I can't answer that one for you, my young man."

"Young man? Really? You haven't noticed that I'm old? I'm getting older by the second and I'm almost dead."

"Well, you are correct to some degree, Frank. You're older than many, but you're also younger than quite a few. This will be the last day on earth for some of those people. Maybe a couple are right here in Le Fleur. To them you're younger and have more time, and they would gladly trade places with you to have a few more days. They'd love a little more time to sit here and think about their days playing baseball."

Frank sits back down on the bleachers, leans against the row behind him, and stretches his legs onto the row below. He responds nonchalantly.

"A few more days, huh, that's all I have? Just a few more days?"

"Well, of course, I have no way of knowing those things for sure. I can only surmise. In your case, I don't know if a few days means three days or a hundred or a thousand. Of course, if you keep drinking and driving your fancy sports car around like you did last night, the end may be closer than it has to be."

Frank's face contorts. "How do you know how I drove last night?"

"I was there in the car with you as soon as you left the doctor's office to go get your whiskey, and when you thought of going back to the diner to see Julie one last time to tell her you love her. I tried to make sure you didn't wreck and kill someone else as you drank. I also made sure you didn't get picked up by a deputy. That could have meant the night in jail and would have ruined your whole weekend with Russ."

The conversation goes silent. Frank shuts his eyes and rubs behind his ear in a circular motion. He leans forward and coughs with ever increasing ferocity, finally bending away from Larry to spit heavily onto the bleacher next to his own resting legs.

With eyes still shut, he leans back and begins to drift into sleep. Just before losing consciousness, he snaps his head forward and grasps at the air in front of him, stabilizing himself with the other hand behind to regain balance. He looks around the bleachers and the field in front of him, trying to solve the puzzle of his location.

"You're scary, Old Man."

"I don't mean to be Frank. I really don't."

"You were with me last night as I drove, huh? I didn't see you in the car."

"I was there. Sitting in the passenger seat."

Frank cocks his head in disbelief and his neck cracks audibly.

"I didn't see you. You weren't there. And even if you were, how could you keep me from wrecking or keep the police from picking me up? I thought it was all about free will and me making my own decisions. You're a little contradictory."

"My presence can add subtle energy. Sometimes a little calm, and sometimes a small nudge. I can't change your decisions once you commit to something, but I can often add a flicker of clarity as you consider options—or as you begin to wander left of center on a dark country road drinking a bottle of scotch. But you still choose. You still decide, and the larger outcome is still of your making."

"Oh, I see. How convenient. Okay, just tell me why you're following me and pestering the hell out of me."

"I'm sorry, Frank. You do not enjoy having me around to converse?"

Frank lowers his head.

"Well, I guess...I guess it's good to have someone to talk to, even if you're just my imagination. But you just pop in and out. You're not always around when I'd like to talk."

Frank bounds to his feet with a wobble and speaks with a resurrected, commanding voice.

"Wait a minute! You can't be in my imagination because Gloria and Julie see and talk to you. You have to be real. I've touched your body and see you breathe, just like a real person. But how can that be? How can you pop in and out of my life and be real too?"

Larry chuckles. "You think you know what is real and unreal, possible and impossible? I don't even know. If you're delusional and I am only in your imagination, maybe Gloria and Julie share in your delusion. Or, maybe you just imagine they see me."

"So, it is my imagination, then?"

"Perhaps. Perhaps not. The universe is a curious place. The reflections of life can bounce around in many ways. The spaces between here and there may be both large and small, flat and round, fast and slow, joyful and sorrowful. As scientists say, maybe it is all a matter of perspective. Keeping a sense of wonder is an important thing—perhaps the most important quality of being human.

"That's the only difference between curious, growing children and jaded, dying adults—the loss of a sense of wonder. If you think you know all and understand everything, wonderment is lost and your existence is hollow and two dimensional. The joy of what you see and experience becomes muted and sometimes altogether lost. Dullness creeps in and you lose your childlike awe. That is very sorrowful."

Larry stands up slowly, just as any old man would.

"You still ask questions, Frank, so your sense of wonder is not lost. This is good thing. However, now you must go."

Carefully, Frank steps down the bleachers to the backstop. He clings to the fence for a moment and watches as a game from the past plays in his head. He then pulls out his cell phone and looks for any messages, but he has none, not even from Gloria.

"I still have to get home and pack for the trip. I'm supposed to pick up Russ in about forty minutes."

Larry reaches out his hand. "Your clothes are packed, Frank. Your suitcase is in the back of your car."

"What do you mean?" He can't keep the fright from his voice.

"You went to my house and packed me a suitcase?"

Larry soothes, "No, no, Frank. Gloria was at your house last night and packed your suitcase. She was hoping you would go home so she could talk to you before the trip. I watched her, but she was unaware. Her worry and love for you were quite evident.

"After she packed up your clothes, shaving items, and everything you'd need, she did your dishes and tidied up your house. She waited for some time, but then realized where you would be. She knows this field is your place of solitude and she came here and saw you passed out. Rather than wake you, she put the suitcase in your car. You left the top down, so your interior will be a little dewy, just as you are."

Frank pats his damp shirt, which brings on a chill.

Frank walks in front of Larry over the stone parking lot toward the Lion.

"Well, I still have to go home and shower and get fresh clothes. How about riding with me?"

He turns back for Larry's response, but the old man is gone.

"Thanks a lot, you bastard," he says into the early morning silence.

# Chapter Fifteen

Frank sits at the kitchen table, relaxed by the shower. His leather satchel lies open in front of him beside a cup of steaming coffee, a half-empty whiskey bottle, and a full bottle of prescription pills. He takes out the gleaming .38 revolver and the box of bullets and places them down on the table. His breath comes fast and deep as he fumbles the box open to allow several shells to fall out.

With shaking hands, he opens the revolver cylinder, slides a shell into a chamber, flips it shut, and spins it. With gun in right hand he pours a shot of whiskey into the coffee and takes a long drink with the left. He raises the gun to the spot behind his ear where he knows the original tumor lays, deeply buried.

With eyes squinted shut, he holds the pose for an imaginary photographer. He imagines photos being snapped from different angles and how they would look in the paper. Then he sees the messy suicide scene and its sensation on the front page. He curses the delay. "Just take the stupid photo. Just pull the damn trigger!" After a few unbearable seconds of writing the news in his head, he places the gun back down on the table and stares at it.

"You coward!" His thunderous voice cracks the silence and reverberates around the kitchen.

He picks up the gun again, opens the cylinder, and fills the remaining five chambers. He then holds it in the palm of his hand while he strokes the bevels of the stainless-steel cylinder. He stands up, points the gun across the room, and fires a round to neatly pick off a lamp in the living room. The tremendous blast and the crash of the lamp cause a demonic squint and a psychotic grin.

He yells a peppered recollection of his wife. “Take that, you bitch! I always hated your stupid, ugly lamp!”

He lowers the gun and begins to look around the kitchen, then the living room. He takes aim again and squeezes. The explosion of the shot and the splitting wood is even louder than the last. Frank laughs with great, twisted delight at the decorative finial of the stairway newel post laying in shards at the bottom of the first step.

“I am one hell of a shot! Not bad for a feeble dying man, huh, Larry?”

Frank looks around again, but there is no Larry to answer.

“What’s the matter, Old Man? Afraid of being shot?”

Frank looks back into the kitchen and points the gun above the stove with a more confident aim. Boom! A small clock above the stove shaped like a teapot falls onto the burners, leaving only the silver handle stuck to the nail on the wall.

He shouts, “Damn! That’s three for three, Larry. You’re missing one hell of a show here.”

Frank rotates his torso from side to side looking for his next target. He takes aim at the coffeemaker just to the right of the stove. The deafening round splits the glass pot; coffee splatters over the counter and the coffeemaker slams up against the tile backsplash.

“Whoohoo! Oh my God. I’m good at this.”

He turns toward the Florida room and aims the gun at an empty scotch bottle on a side table. He peers his aim and blasts another shot but misses, with the round burying into the wall.

“Oh well, I guess no one is perfect, are they Larry?”

Frank looks around from corner to corner of the house, but there is no old man. He moves back to the kitchen table, slides the gun into the satchel knowing one round is left in the cylinder. He picks up the pill bottle, straining his eyes to read the label.

"Those idiot doctors don't know any more than I do."

He tosses the bottle into the satchel, snaps it shut, grabs another sip of coffee, and bolts through the living room and front screen, not even shutting the heavy wooden inner door. He throws the satchel onto the small suitcase in the back of the Lion, hops in like a schoolboy, and starts the mighty engine with a long rev. He guns the yellow bully down the street with reckless speed. As he approaches the edge of town, he can hear the distant wail of sirens behind him headed toward his house to investigate the sound of gunshots.

Frank gets lost in the sinister amusement of shooting at bits of Brenda's tormenting memory. She used to badger and harass him nonstop for weeks leading up to his fishing trips and complain that she never got to go anywhere with friends. He would always respond, "Well, make some friends and go someplace."

He bellows a big laugh over the steering wheel then yells to the sky, "Hey Brenda, I'm going fishing! You make any friends yet?"

# Chapter Sixteen

Frank just drives. Drives and wonders why he couldn't pull the trigger behind his ear. Perhaps he didn't want people to think he was a pathetic quitter. Or, maybe because Gloria, Julie, and Russ would be haunted by the gruesome scene they would be compelled to inspect. A cold shudder rolls over him with the prospect of fading into nothingness when deleted from the masthead of the *Sentinel*. He strained to live a better life than his father and grandfather, realizing now that he may not have done as well as them. Life had not unfolded as he imagined. He never took the trips he wanted or started those flying lessons. The book he often kicks around in his head remains unwritten. Sweet, kind Julie stood right in front of him across the diner counter, never to be pursued. He curses himself for that cowardice. He never went after his boys, or at least stayed in their lives. So little time now. None of it will happen because he's waited too long, let things slide comfortably along, and enjoyed the perpetual ease of his routine days. Self-loathing radiates anger down his arms and into his clenched fingers, choking the steering wheel.

Tires squeal the Lion to a halt as Frank snaps into awareness just in time to avoid running the red light. He pushes the gearshift into reverse, then backs behind the painted stop stripe. He looks around to see if anyone notices his absentmindedness. Pastor Harold stands in front of the church holding a rake, motioning Frank to come. He backs up more to make the left turn into the church parking lot.

Frank eases the Lion to a stop and puts the car in neutral as it continues to idle next to Pastor Harold, who is standing on the walk.

"Hey there, Harold. How you doing today?"

Harold looks the Lion up and down, from bumper to bumper, then does a knee bend to lower his tall, thin frame to the side of the car. He takes off a work glove and puts his hand on the top of the windowless door and leans in.

"I'm doing fine, Frank. Just doing a little yard work around the church."

Pastor Harold extends his neck a bit and looks over the door into the cockpit as though he might be in the market for a Vette.

"Wow. This is some car. Whatever possessed you to buy this thing?"

"I guess I got tired of being so cheap all the time. I've been driving that old truck for so long, I was getting tired of it rattling my bones."

"You got a convertible, too. That's a pretty good idea. If you're going to get a car like this, why not make it really fun to drive, huh?"

Frank gushes with unrepentant zeal, "That's exactly right, Padre! Why not have some fun? Besides, now I know that when I have to cover a story my car is actually going to start, and I can get there a heck of a lot faster!"

The two men have deep feelings for each other and joke around like brothers, only better, since they carry no baggage from growing up together and competing in front of judging parents. Even though they may not speak for weeks, they always retain their closeness and share joys and disappointments, not as minister and newspaper publisher, but with hearts of equals. Unlike other male friends or colleagues, they can see into each other's dark corners of insecurity without calculating the enormity of those faults or how to take advantage of them. They know each must sacrifice to overcome opinions of their respective self-righteous fickle "flocks."

Pastor Harold stands and puts his hand on Frank's shoulder.

"I know you'll be careful in this thing, but maybe you should let Russ drive to New York."

Frank looks up with widened eyes and dropping jaw.

"Oh my stars. You know everything too, don't you? The trip, my cancer, everything?"

"Yes, but don't be mad at Gloria. She really cares about you. In fact, she asks me to pray for you often, including this morning."

Frank runs his left hand over the leather steering wheel while his other hand fiddles the gearshift around the neutral slot.

"I guess the circle is complete. The mayor, the sheriff, Gloria, Julie, Larry—now you all know. Well, I guess it's good to have people who pray for you. You might have to say a mighty powerful one to pull me through this thing."

Frank stops fidgeting and looks up bleakly at Pastor Harold. "I have to tell you, I'm a little scared."

"I know you are. I've been hoping you'd come by, so we could talk about what you're going through."

Frank talks to the steering wheel, "Yeah, I've wanted to come, but I guess I just didn't know what to say about it all. You carry so many burdens already. You don't need another one."

"Don't be sorry, Frank. Everyone has to do things in their own time. You're here now, and we can talk more soon. Besides, burdens are what I live for, ya know."

The silence lingers until Pastor Harold starts up the conversation again.

"Hey, you mentioned someone named Larry a second ago. Who are you talking about?"

"Oh, some old guy that's been hanging around town who says he's a state auditor. Somehow he's cozied up to Gloria and Julie and has been a real thorn in my side lately."

"You don't say? You mean proper old Larry, the guy who's always dressed well and wears a hat?"

"What? You know him too? The old man who's always dressed like he's going to a funeral? He gives me the creeps. How do you know him?"

Harold says, "He's been coming to church pretty regularly the last couple months. He usually sits by Gloria, in fact. You may not believe this, but he's in the church right now. He said he wanted to say some prayers for some of his friends and relatives and mentioned you, too. He seems to consider you a friend."

Frank revs the engine, shifts into first gear, and holds the clutch.

"Well, that sounds about like him. But I'm not sure you should leave him alone in there. You might come up missing some candlesticks or something."

Harold takes off his Detroit Tigers hat, pulls out a hanky, and wipes his brow.

"I don't think you have to worry about that. Hey, you're getting a message." Harold points to the cell phone on the passenger's seat.

Frank looks over to the vibrating phone. "I'm sure it's just Russ trying to find out where I am. I should've been there to pick him up a half hour ago."

Harold crouches again. "I tell you what. How 'bout when you get back from your fishing trip, you take me for a long ride in this beautiful car and we can have a good long talk. I want to feel the wind in my hair while I still have some!"

Frank smiles. "I tell *you* what. You say some good prayers for Russ and me to catch some fish and maybe we'll go for a drive and have a big fish fry to boot."

"That's a deal, Frank!"

Harold clasps Frank's bicep with comforting absolution. Frank can only muster a timid squeeze of Harold's warm hand, pondering why he was reluctant to seek this moment of intimacy. He knows he needs it and that it is always here for the asking. Harold's touch brings a moment of peace, obliterating ten thousand needles of worry and self-doubt for both men. Frank has always thought Harold an earthly example of what Jesus must have been like, supremely patient and totally unselfish. Harold believes Frank to be a model of that reluctant disciple who tussles with faith and wonders if he is good enough for God's light. Harold knows the answer, even if Frank does not yet understand.

They look at each other with an easy serenity, some kind of strange fellowship that neither fully grasps, but each cherishes just the same. Both find it difficult to let this instance of mutual aid slip away, but they let go without speaking, and Frank eases the Lion away and down the street.

Larry exits the church and stands next to Harold as the yellow dot fades down Countyline Road.

Harold's voice quivers, "That was Frank. He's going fishing up at the Niagara River. Do you think he'll come back?"

With unusual worry, Larry says, "I really don't know. All I know is, there's more that he still needs to do in this river called 'Le Fleur.'"

# Chapter Seventeen

Russ sits in his bedroom at a cheap particle-board desk scrolling through fishing images on the computer screen. He clicks the speaker icon at the bottom to make sure the sound is turned off. He types in "Joe Cinelli Niagara River Fishing" and then moves the cursor over small thumbnail photos of people holding large fish. He looks over to make sure Ann is still asleep, curled up in bed no more than ten feet away.

Russ scrolls the small images until he sees one that shows Joe helping a young boy hold up an impressive salmon. He wonders what traits make this Joe character such a dynamic fishing guide. The search is shattered by his wife Ann's grating voice. "Russ! The doorbell! Can't you hear it? Someone's at the door!"

His words crack with anxiety. "Yes dear, I hear it."

Russ clicks off the web page and fumbles shutting down the computer, nearly falling out of his chair to rise and collect himself.

"I'm sure it's Frank here to pick me up."

Ann roars with acidic venom, "Can you tell that jerk he shouldn't be ringing people's doorbells so early on a Saturday morning? Why didn't he text you to let you know he was here? He better not wake up Nick!"

Russ moves to the side of the bed and leans down to give her a kiss, but she pulls the covers up to her ears and exaggerates her fetal position. Russ leans back as he has dozens of times when she wishes to make her displeasure known though cold rejection.

"Okay, dear, I'll tell Frank to be quiet. Bye, honey. I'll see you Monday." Russ waits for a response that does not come, then eases out of the bedroom and down the steps, hoping to avoid any other abuse from his annoyed wife. His packed duffle bag sits against the wall next to the front door, jacket and hat neatly arranged on top. He is startled to see his mother-in-law Janet sitting in the living room watching Nick play on the floor.

"Running off to your fishing trip, Russ?"

Janet's condescending tone sounds remarkably like her daughter's.

"You just can't wait to run off and leave your family and in-laws to fend for themselves for the weekend, can you."

Russ picks up his belongings and responds to her without looking.

"Well, if you must know, my boss is making me go to work on a story."

"Oh really? To catalog his incredible fish stories? Did you even tell him you were having company this weekend?"

Russ looks over to her, then back to his gear. "Of course I did. But he insisted."

"Had to? Humph."

With hat on, jacket over his arm, and bag in tow, Russ moves toward the spiteful woman. She recoils at his approach, which is amusing to him. He bends down and kisses little Nicholas on the head.

"Bye, my sweet son. Don't take any crap from anyone this weekend, my boy. Daddy will be home in a couple days with some big fish and maybe some even bigger fish stories than your grandma can tell."

"Bye, Dada."

Russ smiles at the unpleasant woman and she returns with a tilt of the head and twisted frown. He walks away, relieved he will not have to suffer her barrage of arrows all weekend.

The woman has only grudgingly accepted Russ into the family. Her daughter broke up with a medical student to have an accidental pregnancy and subsequent marriage to him, a poor fledgling newspaperman. She enjoys reminding Russ at every opportunity that he is the consolation husband with skimpy future prospects for wealth, and frequently asks, in front of others, how things are going at "that little paper."

Russ shuts the door behind him with a purposely heavy thud to find Frank sitting on the porch next to his distinguished father-in-law Steve. Between them sits a small table with a breakfast cake and a pot of coffee.

"Good morning, my young man," exclaims the congenial father-in-law. "Mr. Barnett and I have been chatting here a bit and enjoying some java. Care for a cup?"

"No thanks, Pops. I just want to get on the road."

Frank stands and takes a long drink of coffee to wash down a piece of coffee cake.

"Steve told me his wife was already up with Nick, so I thought I'd just ring the doorbell. Hope I didn't wake up Annie. I'm sure she was up to see you off?"

Russ smirks, then his eyes stop at the Lion parked on the street.

"My God! You did buy a Corvette! I thought Mom was just kidding me. So, we're really going to take that thing to Niagara?"

Frank raises his mug to declare, "You bet your sweet ass we are!"

"Well, c'mon then, let's get going."

Frank hands his mug to Steve and sticks out his other hand for a hearty shake.

"Guess I better not keep Russ waiting any longer. We have a long ride ahead of us and I was late showing up as it is. Good talking to you."

Frank tosses the key fob and it hangs on Russ's chest long enough for him to trap it to his shirt. He opens his hand from around the fob and beams like a child as he leaps off the porch and darts to the car for a thorough examination.

Frank nods to Steve and ambles down the walk to watch Russ's uninhibited excitement. Russ opens the small trunk lid, tosses in his duffle bag and jacket, then slides into the cockpit. Frank throws in his small bag, then lowers the trunk lid, then struggles to get into the passenger side. He looks up to wave to Steve, who is standing on the porch in his robe looking as though he could be ready in a minute to go with them, if only the car had another seat.

Steve cups his mouth and yells, "You boys have fun now. I want to hear all the glorious fish stories on my next visit!"

Russ ignites the Lion and gives her some gas. Frank puts his fingers on Russ's hand on top of the gear shift.

"Now you have to be careful with this thing, Russ. It's very powerful. I hope you're good at driving a stick."

Russ responds self-assuredly, "Sure am, Frank. Every once in a while, I get to drive these on Saturday mornings when I help my buddy prep the cars over at the Chevy lot. Mr. Rocket lets me take one out on the highway when I help them out in a pinch. I've driven this very one into the showroom."

"Really? I didn't know that you helped out at the car lot."

"I asked you about a year ago if it would be okay. I said I needed to get out of the house some on Saturdays and could make a few bucks and you agreed, as long as I didn't miss any good stories that popped up."

Frank twinges, realizing another thing has slipped his mind. "I guess you must have told me about it."

Russ takes off with precision, making a cautious left turn at the stop. He looks around, hoping someone notices him driving the pulsating terror. He relishes this chance to be a little greedy, to do guy things without Ann's maddening ridicule or the constant stress of being the dutiful dad and husband. The young man has emulated Frank's steadiness and responsibility, even to the point of marrying a woman he knew did not love him. The unexpected pregnancy was reason enough for him to do the right thing, believing if he treated her well they would find a way to love one another. But, he soon discovered that he could not do enough for Ann as she still pines for the doctor she once dated.

"Which way do you want to go, Frank?"

Frank puts his hands behind his head and sticks his nose up in the air. He shuts his eyes.

"Just head up 61 then head out east on 224 to 71. When you get up north of Medina take 271 to Erie. We'll stop east of Cleveland and grab something to eat."

"Okay, I got 'er from here. You lean back and take a nap if you want and I'll wake you when we get up to 271. I know the exit well since we take that when we visit Ann's parents."

Russ looks over at Frank already starting to lose consciousness. He turns down the radio with the steering wheel control and flips through the stations until he finds a classic rock station.

Out of his shirt pocket he pulls the Wayfarers given to him by his father-in-law the night before. Steve reached across the kitchen table and handed him the case and said, "Young man, I hope these glasses help you see things more clearly on your trip."

The two shared beers while the women in the next room watched a fake reality TV show and fed Nick. Perhaps Russ's father-in-law is always good to him because he remembers what it was like to be a young black man raising a family with a difficult wife when few people wanted to give him an opportunity.

That mix of comfort and unpleasantness fades into the road in front of him as he steers the car out into the countryside, punches the gas, and tilts the needle to seventy miles per hour in no time.

Russ keeps heading east, slowing only for the little burgs in succession. Frank's hands have finally relaxed down to his sides, his head resting in the seam of the seat. Russ guides the Lion past a semi-truck and pushes the sprinting animal to eighty-five with ease. He hears a buzzing and picks up his cell phone from the center console to find out he is not the one getting a call. Frank rolls his head around in apparent anguish, but the phone going off in his pants pocket does not wake him.

Russ says quietly, "I hope you enjoy your sleep, Frank."

# Chapter Eighteen

Dreams are often like that pesky friend who tells you things you do not want to hear, but damn it, someone has to poke you for your own good. You are obligated to listen because you just cannot walk away from decades of companionship. The dream now bubbling to life in his head overwhelms Frank with feelings of guilt for doing too little for his community and those in it who struggle on the periphery. His charity has been a compulsory routine, he is told, devoid of true communion with his neighbors, many who scrape by in the unforgiving machine of life. He did not get to know their conditions or solve their problems, he just wrote about them and wrote checks to causes out of duty. He tries to force himself awake but is doomed to watch and listen once again.

Images flicker in his mind, of sitting on a hard wooden stool in the middle of a gray concrete room wearing only a plain hospital gown. His hands are tied together and rest on top of a *Sentinel* issue on his lap. A stream of light comes through a tiny window in the wall to his right that is no more than several inches square, the only source of illumination in the room. Before him sits an imposing black judge at an enormous wooden desk elevated high on a dais. The judge is supremely authoritative, but his face is an indistinguishable, muted mass of rubbery brown skin. The only dash of color in the entire courtroom is a single red carnation sticking out of a pewter vase in front of the judge. In a calm and meek voice that belies his massive size and imposing, robed persona, the judge asks, "So, what have you done?"

Frank speaks, but he struggles to fathom his own words.

The judge orders, "Speak loudly and clearly. I cannot understand you, Frank."

This time Frank answers brashly, "What do you mean, what have I done? I have done nothing to hurt anyone."

"That may be so, Frank. But what have you done?"

Frank tries to stand but realizes his ankles are tied to the stool.

Frank says frustratingly, "Your honor, I've told the truth and I've obeyed all the laws. I've committed no crimes."

The judge returns only a blank gaze from his squinting eyes. He asks no more questions, but the piercing stare is flustering.

Frank squirms, then becomes free to find himself standing in the middle of the Le Fleur downtown square. He is still in his hospital gown and is uneasy about being so exposed. He reaches behind and pulls the sides of his gown together as cars whiz by him from all directions. The traffic is so heavy and fast he cannot escape the middle of the intersection for fear of being run over. The sidewalks in all directions are full of people moving nearly as quickly as the speeding cars. The Le Fleur residents appear to be shopping for the holidays as they carry brightly wrapped packages and are dressed in heavy coats, scarves, and hats. Snow is falling and blowing around him, but he experiences no cold or wind.

Frank yells to the people on the sidewalk to help him get out of the traffic. The cars halt with squeals and people stand in place, looking curiously at Frank in the middle of the square. He tries to move his legs, but mud is up to his knees and he can't get free. Frank is relieved when two teenage boys and two smaller boys move toward him through the stopped cars. The boys arrive but do not take Frank's hands or release his feet. Instead, they lay their wrapped gifts around Frank, further preventing him from moving in any direction.

"Boys, what are you doing? I know you! Why are you doing this?"

Other residents follow and pile their gifts around Frank until he is buried up to his torso. Still others bring bundles of newspapers and books and begin to throw them on the mound of gifts. The heap grows and grows until finally one of the big, leather-bound books of historical newspapers leans against his face.

Out from the crowd a single man approaches and stands at the base of the widening mountain of boxes, colorful paper, cardboard, flittering pages, and hidden holiday treasures. The man takes off his long shiny metallic coat and throws it on the pile close to Frank's face.

"This is my robe of justification, Frank. It protects me from your barbs and the suspicions they cause for the residents. I won't be needing it anymore. Here, you take it."

Frank realizes it is the young version of the malicious mayor.

The mayor laughs madly and points at Frank, then turns to encourage others to do the same. Their laughter grows deafening. Residents still in their cars start gesturing out their windows and honking their horns into a riotous crescendo.

The mayor turns back to the pile, pulls a lighter out of his pocket, looks up at Frank and smiles, then reaches over to light the end of a newspaper. The flame spreads to the wrapping paper and pages of the books and newspapers. The heat intensifies, and Frank begins to sweat.

There is no pain, yet. Then the coat catches fire and brings the flames close to his face, causing him to scream frantically.

"Frank, Frank! Are you okay?"

Russ manages to speed along the interstate while reaching over to shake Frank by the arm. Frank snaps his head forward, opens his eyes, and looks around in fright.

"It's okay, Frank. I think you were having a bad dream."

Frank wipes his hand across his sweaty forehead several times and then rubs his hand on his jeans.

"Yeah, Russ, I was just having a dream. Everything's okay."

Frank clears his eyes and looks around the blurred countryside.

"Where are we?"

"We just went through Mayfield Heights. By the way, you got a call from Gloria and I got a text from her. I sent her a text back telling her you were sleeping and all was okay, and that we'd call her later on."

Frank shuts his eyes and puts his head back against the seat rest.

"Good, but don't text and drive."

"It was a voice text, Frank. I didn't type it."

"That's good. There's a McDonald's just off 90 up here. We can pull off there and get some breakfast if they're still serving it. If not, we'll get lunch and I can take my medicine again too."

"Sure thing. I'm gettin' pretty hungry."

Frank falls back into a stupor as Russ gets back to passing cars, wind buffeting the top of his head. The eastern sun shines even brighter now, causing the young driver to adjust his Wayfarers and visor to the perfect angles. His exhilaration for this perfect day and his freedom continues to grow.

After a few minutes the Lion eases onto an off-ramp, through an intersection, and comes to an abrupt stop. Frank bobs forward to awareness.

"We're here, Frank. Do you think I should put the top up while we go in?"

"Nah. We'll be able to see the car from the counter and we can sit on this side of the restaurant. It'll be okay."

The two men struggle out of the low-slung Vette, but Russ gains his footing and springs to the restaurant door while Frank stutters his stiff body forward. Russ holds the door for Frank as several other people slip inside before him.

The two men order their food, then Frank moves to a window table in view of the Lion waiting patiently outside. Russ stops at the self-serve soda bar and watches Frank sitting and staring at his food with total disinterest. Russ returns to the table and he begins eating the Egg McMuffin and hash brown in uncomfortable quietness.

Finally, Russ stops between bites and says, "Do you want to talk about the shooting now?"

Frank looks up exhaustedly at the spirited young man. "Not yet. I'm kind of hazy right now. We'll have plenty of time this weekend to go over it. We'll talk when my head isn't throbbin' so much."

After downing a few pills with his Coke, Frank bites his hash brown, drops it, then pushes his untouched muffin toward Russ and looks out the window toward the Lion.

"Guess I'm not too hungry after all. Why don't you eat mine too?"

"No, we'll take it with us. You may want it in a little while."

Russ finishes his food, wraps up Frank's muffin, and walks to the trash bin with his tray of debris where he stands and watches Frank look woefully out the window at the Lion.

Keeping his eyes on Frank, he slides back to the soda bar to top off his drink.

"Move it over, nigger!" says a disgusting voice.

A burly man in a sleeveless orange Cleveland Browns T-shirt and camouflage ball cap begins to push close to Russ.

"I said, move it over, nigger!" the man shouts. "You cut in front of me, you black son of a bitch!"

All the customers are startled at the outburst and stare at the two men in anticipation of a fight, but Russ ignores the insult. He calmly finishes filling his cup, puts the lid on, and moves to the side to get a napkin.

"Pardon me, sir," Russ says.

As Russ turns back to the table, he sees Frank approaching with a red face and clenched fist.

"Hey moron," Frank shouts. "You got a problem over here?"

The burly man sneers, then says loudly, "Not anymore, old man. The nigger got out of my way. Is he your nigger or somethin'?"

The man is surprised when Frank grabs his shirt collar, but he recovers quickly enough to knock his hand away. He puts up his fists and flexes his thick biceps to welcome Frank into a beating.

"You really want to go with me, you old fool?"

Before Frank can decide his next move, a chiseled store manager arrives with a baseball bat lifted above his shoulder ready to swing at the hulking man.

"Okay, that's enough of this bull! You get out of here!"

The big man withers from his fighting posture.

"Okay Mr. McDonald, as soon as I get my Coke."

The manager continues to hold his swinging pose, and Russ puts Frank in a bear hug to prevent him from getting pummeled. The man finishes filling his cup and slowly strolls out the door as if no one else exists and nothing interesting happened. Russ lets go of Frank and the manager lowers his bat.

"I'm very sorry about that, gentlemen. I heard what he said. I was kinda hoping he would press it, so I could knocked his head off. Let me get you some gift certificates for your trouble."

Everyone in the dining room stares at Frank. He skims the faces and a few return small smiles and affirmative nods. His scan stops at Larry, sitting in the corner in his blue suit, drinking a coffee and holding a newspaper.

"Oh no," he mumbles.

Russ grabs Frank's arm. "What's wrong?"

"Nothing's wrong. Not a damn thing. Everything's just great!"

The manager returns and hands each man a stack of gift certificate booklets.

"I am so sorry, gentlemen. We'll keep an eye out for that guy. We've seen him in here before. If he shows up again, we'll call the police."

Russ reaches out and shakes the manager's hand vigorously.

"Thank you, sir. I appreciate you stepping in like that."

Frank says, "Yeah, thanks a hell-of-a-lot," then shoves his certificates into Russ's hands.

Frank bolts through the door as Russ follows behind, frantically clicking the key fob. Frank plops into the Lion, pulls the door to a solid thud, leans his head back, and shuts his eyes to avoid speaking anymore. Russ starts the car without revving the engine and is soon on the highway again with no one to talk to. Russ looks over at Frank, wondering what would have happened had the manager with the bat not shown up to save the day. The various mental images always replay with Frank getting the worst of it, but with him being deeply gratified from the battle. Russ now wishes Frank had the chance to try and hopes there will be another chance for him to release some anger in New York.

# Chapter Nineteen

Russ sings flatly, Frank sleeps with his mouth open, and the Lion hums evenly as it sprints toward Erie. Classic Ray-Bans, taut steering wheel, edgy music from his phone wirelessly connected to the car, soothing sun, and a fragrant breeze shred Russ's troublesome morning into an inconsequential pile of rubbish. Crossing into the corner of Pennsylvania brings a little heavier traffic with a noticeable increase in semi-trucks. A conspicuous rise in cars containing pretty young women gives Russ a straighter posture. In car after car they make evocative faces and wave at Russ and his majestic yellow Lion. A magazine-beautiful, brown-skinned girl with long flowing black hair rolls down the window of a little red sedan in the left lane, leans out with ample cleavage, then blows a kiss to him. Russ's face expresses youthful excitement until the cars slow behind him and exit the ramp marked for Erie College. Russ sticks his hand up in the air to wave goodbye and watches in the mirror as the coed caravan leaves the highway.

The trip is a little under four hours old. Frank has slept most of the travel time, which is both frustrating and relieving for Russ. The young reporter hoped for some great man-to-man banter with his boss, but he is also glad to avoid a reoccurring awkwardness that sometimes springs out of nowhere when he is around Frank. With no conversation to stumble over, meanings of words to analyze, or inflections to interpret, he drives with mental liberation. Driving in solitude provides an opportunity to think about wildly different topics, including why he is often intimidated by Frank, now meekly huddled in his seat with drool glistening on his chin.

Russ has always been respectful to others even when they may not have deserved it. Whether it has been Frank gently pushing him around as bosses sometimes do, or some ogre spewing bitterness in a restaurant, or even a spiteful and unpleasant wife, the young man always maintains his cool to analyze situations for a better understanding of why people act the way they do. Some could interpret this as a wilting weakness, but perhaps it is the strength of enduring intelligence. Russ likes to think it is the latter, without being too smug about it.

Frank revives from his sleep and wipes his mouth and eyes. He looks around in a squint, then rubs behind his right ear.

"How long have I been asleep?"

Russ keeps his eyes on the road. "Almost two hours, I guess. You were really out of it. I don't know how those semis didn't wake you up."

"What is that music you have on? I could hear it in my sleep and I think it caused a nice dream this time. I was coaching third base at my boy's baseball game."

Russ turns the music level down. "I hope it didn't wake you up."

"No, it's fine. I like it. What is it? It's kind of folksy. Something I'd listen to."

"The guy's name is Gregory Alan Isakov. It's called 'The Stable Song.'"

"Hmm, I like his sound. Turn it up a bit. Could you start it from the beginning?"

Frank bobs his head with the melodic and haunting tune.

"This is very nice, Russ. I can actually hear most of the words. They make music like that again, huh?"

"Yeah, they do. I like to listen to the words, myself."

The song is evenly paced, blending guitar, fiddle, and a slowly picked banjo. A periodic, sad violin conjures a strangely comforting gloom. Frank listens and believes the singer is describing reverent songs that bring back memories of people he used to know, who now seem to be familiar ghosts of the Ohio River. The lyrics go on to describe throwing stones at the stars and having the whole sky fall, and Frank interprets this as his rebuking, or at least ignoring, all the good in his life, only to have everything crash down around him. He imagines the singer trying to escape the past, places, and perhaps people he knew, just as Frank himself has tried to leave Le Fleur behind. But the singer is drawn back to the place he roamed, cursing and moaning, until his heart aches—then, finally, it rallies and beats stronger. In these words, Frank imagines himself being drawn back to Le Fleur where eventually his shiny diamonds, or hopes, will be unavoidably turned back into coal.

Frank nods. "That's some song, Russ. It's like a sad and tender lullaby all in one. Can you play me another good one?"

Russ picks up his phone and scrolls down a list of songs. He clicks the phone and touches the steering wheel controls to raise the volume.

"Here is one I think you'll like, too. It's called 'Head Full of Doubt' by the Avett Brothers."

Frank scoots down in the leather seat and listens as he watches the passing scenery to his right. The music fills his head and is as haunting as the first song. It talks of wrong, right, and the fine print of black and white, and being frightened by others who don't see the injustices of the world. The singer describes understanding the dream, but still, with a head full of doubt, he vows to work until the bad thoughts are erased.

Frank rubs his lips at the close of the song and mumbles something unintelligible while still looking away at passing vineyards, long rows of fences, and tidy farms with red-and-white barns.

Russ turns down the volume. "I'm sorry, did you say something?"

Frank turns to Russ with swelling eyes, speaking with a shaky voice.

"I—I'm sorry Russ. I'm very sorry."

"If you mean that little event back at McDonald's, that was nothing. You don't have anything to be sorry about. Don't worry about it."

"Oh yes, I have plenty to be sorry about. McDonald's *was* something—but that's not all."

Frank pauses, then begins again, his voice cracking.

"I've known you all your life, Russ. I was even there at the hospital when you were born, the day after your father ran off and left Gloria. I was around you as much as my own boys when they were growing up. Then, when they were taken, I felt like, in a way, you replaced them and had become my son, or at least a wonderful nephew."

Without looking away from the road, Russ chokes out, "Well, um, that's very kind of you. You gotta know how much respect I have for you."

"I do, Russ. You've always been respectful to me. But I never treated you any better than my own boys, which wasn't very good. I was there for you when I wanted to be and probably not when you needed me to be. Worse than that, I never gave a second thought about what you and your mom must've put up with every day. I think I just ignored how some folks treated you. I heard what some of the farmers said over the years about you and your mom being black and not fitting in, but I ignored it and tried to make what they said unimportant. I guess I pretended that most everyone in Le Fleur felt about you and Gloria like Dad and I did."

Russ alternates looking at the road and Frank to make sure his own message is delivered with at least some eye contact.

"Listen Frank, almost everybody in Le Fleur treats Mom and me great. There's just a few folks in town that give us the cold shoulder. But we don't hold that against 'em, 'cause they might've just been raised poorly. Mom and I treat everyone the same whether they love us or hate us. We're just gonna keep showing people we're bigger than the hate. I think that's helped most everyone see that we're just hard-workin' people like them. But you know what? You can't make everyone love you, no matter what color you are."

Frank reaches out and squeezes Russ's elbow.

"You are a smart young man, Russ. I am very lucky to know you."

"Thanks. You don't even know how incredible of a person you are. I think it's time for me to tell you that."

Frank snorts a laugh and hangs his head.

"Well, I'm glad *you* think so."

Frank points to the interstate service plaza exit just ahead as the Lion approaches the town of Hamburg.

"Let's pull off here. The gas will be cheaper here than up in Buffalo or Lewiston. This is where my dad would always stop on the way up and then for breakfast on the way home. It's a tradition. We can't break that now, can we?"

The two men stretch their legs at the pump. Frank swipes his credit card, then Russ fills up the Lion. Frank pulls out his phone and reads a text message from Gloria. "Hope all is well with my boys. Give me a call and let me know how it's going." He chooses to ignore the request.

"You should probably call your mom and let her know everything's okay. Don't tell her about the idiot back in Ohio, though." Russ gets back in the car and sends a quick text to his mom.

"Russ, pull over there and let's go into McDonald's for a burger. I'm getting pretty hungry. I also need to get a drink to take some medicine, and I wanna show you the walkway over the freeway to the other of the side of the plaza."

Russ pulls the Lion to the parking area as Frank trails him on foot. Frank stops in his tracks, puts his hands on his hips, and yells loudly.

"That son of a bitch!"

Russ hops out of the car.

Frank points to the rear of the Vette. "Come look at this. That moron back in Ohio keyed our car!"

Russ kneels behind the car and rubs his hand along a deep gray gash stretching from taillight to taillight underneath the Vette racing flag emblem.

"Man, that guy was out to do some damage," Russ says.

"Yeah, he probably saw us pull up in the car and he just couldn't stand seeing a black kid driving a shiny new Vette. He was one jealous son of a bitch."

"Don't worry about it. It's just a bump in the road. We can't let something like this ruin our trip."

Frank exhales. "Yeah, you're right. Put the top up and let's go in and see if we can avoid getting into another tussle at this place."

The men use the restroom in the large plaza, then Frank says, "Follow me, Russ."

Frank leads Russ to the walkway that spans the four lanes. The vantage point allows motorists headed west to park on the north and access the restaurants on the south side.

"Stand right here as a semi goes under. It's a very strange feeling."

The two men look out over the roadway with cars zooming below and await the approach of a semi. A large tandem-trailer truck approaches with its nose lined up right at the men, with the leading edge of the first trailer appearing as though it will hit the bottom of the walkway. Russ tenses up and braces for impact. The truck and trailers rocket just a couple feet below the walkway, which reverberates with buffeting from the truck's draft.

"Wow! That was wild. It seemed like that truck was going to plow into us."

"Yep, it sure is! I remember the first time my dad had me stand here. I wanted to stay here and feel that rush over and over. I felt like I was cheating death, even though I knew I wasn't going to get hurt."

The men wait for one more truck and its tantalizing gust, then make their way to the McDonald's counter. Russ pulls out several gift certificates from Ohio to pay for the food.

"That little incident didn't turn out all bad, did it, Frank?"

"No, I guess not, my boy. Let's get this to go and get back on the road."

The Lion's top goes down and Russ finishes his burger while Frank makes it through half. He puts the wrappers in the bag at his feet, pops his pills, and takes a long draw of his Coke. Back on the highway he navigates Russ through a couple tollbooths as they head northeast past the towns of Lackawanna and West Seneca and finally north toward downtown Buffalo. Native American names are emblazoned on highway signs and billboards in the area, including the advertisement for Seneca Falls Casino, which has a "Great Regional Attraction, Thunder Falls Buffet."

"You know what, Russ? I didn't even have to use the GPS to get us up here. I remembered everything!"

"That's great, Frank."

The reinvigorated publisher directs them through various lane changes as they glide into Buffalo past myriads of old homes and warehouses. They finally come to downtown where the northeastern tip of Lake Erie narrows on their left to become the mouth of the north-flowing Niagara River.

"See that round water intake building out there in the lake? We fished out there several springs for small mouth. Boy, the fish love that spot. Everybody would catch forty or fifty, and our arms would be so tired at the end of the day we could barely lift a can of beer. Most of the bass were three to four pounds, but every once in a while, we'd land one five or six pounds. Let me tell you, son, a five-pound smallie can fight just as good as a twenty-pound salmon!"

They glide along Niagara River past the Triple-A Buffalo Bison's baseball stadium and continue past various bridges and overpasses until they drive under the ramp of the Peace Bridge that connects the US to Canada. They proceed north where a toll booth marks the South Grand Island Bridge, a structure that fills the sky before them. Frank has a dollar and a quarter in change ready which Russ tosses into the basket to provide a green light.

The river splits into two mammoth veins as it flows around the roughly thirty-square-mile Grand Island. One branch of the river flows east and one west until they bend back to rejoin at the northwest corner of the island to become one mighty torrent above the falls. The massively girded humps of the Grand Island Bridge are really a pair of spans that serve each direction, rising nearly a hundred feet and stretching nearly two-thirds of a mile across the Niagara River.

Russ drives nervously onto the bridge as the Lion rises and the river falls far below. The locals pass him on the left while he concentrates on conquering the intimidating heights. Easing into the Lion's descent at the bottom of the bridge and onto Grand Island gives Russ relief and a lighter grip on the steering wheel.

"That's some bridge, isn't it, Russ?"

Russ rubs a hand over the top of his head several times before mustering a response.

"Yeah, some bridge. I wish you would've given me a heads-up on that before reaching the toll gate."

"I think that would have just caused you more stress. Sometimes when something is just sprung on a person, they can handle it better than if they had too much time to worry about it. Besides, now that you mastered that one, you'll have no problem with the one up ahead that gets us off the island."

Russ starts to say something but instead swallows heavily as he drives past a serene and wooded environment. In the distance looms the next pair of bridges that rise into the sky over the north river to the city of Niagara Falls.

Frank speaks excitedly. "Now when you get to the top of this bridge, look a couple miles over to your left and you can see the mist rising up from the falls. It's a very cool sight."

Russ glances left and can see where the rivers have rejoined into one as the wide water flows west to the falls several miles past his sight. There it will plummet onto the ancient rocks below where some is sprayed up, perhaps hundreds of feet, depending on weather conditions. The turbulent flow at the bottom of the falls turns north again where it courses a mile or so to squeeze into the tumultuous whirlpool, then rages further downriver into "Devil's Hole," with rocks and rapids, flanked by a state park with the same name where Seneca warriors and British troops did battle in 1763. Past that seething eddy, the water calms as it churns past the three-hundred-foot-high walls of the power plant intakes where some of it falls into the waiting turbines.

Russ turns his attention back to the road for alignment and grips the wheel while managing another peek westward through the neighboring southbound bridge girders. The distant mist rises into the sky above the unseen falls into a rainbow panorama where the water droplets and sun meet over the Niagara. The sight brings Russ a moment of calm fulfillment.

He guides the Lion's descent of the northbound bridge and comes to a confusing array of exits and signs that point in various directions—Niagara Falls, visitor centers, and a host of shops and lanes into Canada. He awaits instruction from Frank, who looks out the side of the car like a bemused tourist.

"Where to now?" Russ begs.

"Just stay straight for a bit more. I'll guide you to the exit before the traffic starts backing up to the bridge to Canada. We'll take one of the last exits before the border crossing. I want to make a quick stop for something, but I'll guide you along. I can't remember the name of the road right off, but I'll remember it when I see it."

The Lion rumbles on as the men study the scenery and Frank finds a new source of giddiness. Just past a giant landfill mound is a forest of electrical poles, transformers, and wires carrying the power from the falls to energy-hungry consumers. The billboards and signs for cheap smokes, tourist information, and outlet malls line the highway. Further past the electric jungle the road spans an enormous channel that is hundreds of feet wide with shear-face walls feeding an enormous lake that extends far to the east.

"What's that?" Russ asks.

"That canal diverts water from the Niagara to the reservoir over here on the right.

"You know, about seventy-five percent of the water in the river never makes it over the falls but is channeled into reservoirs, then into the power-plant turbines. We need to stop by on the way home, so you can see the falls. It's still amazing, even with just a quarter of the flow. It's really powerful. Just imagine if all the water went over the edge."

Russ looks at Frank with surprise. "Damn, that's crazy. I had no idea."

Frank turns Russ's attention back to the road.

"Okay, take it easy, now. I think we're coming up on the exit I want to take before we wind up getting in the border crossing mess."

Russ decelerates, slightly puzzled, and waits for his next command.

"There, right up there. Take the next exit. Slow down and get off here. See that big building up there?"

"What are we doing, Frank?"

"I need to stop a minute at a nursing home just up the road. I'll just pop in and out. Here it is. Turn left here and go past the hospital."

Russ and the Lion obey and stop at the drive for Our Lady of Peace Nursing Residence. The area around the nursing home is surprisingly tranquil, although it sits just a few hundred yards from the congested highway tangle into Canada.

"Wait here. I'll be just a minute."

"You actually know someone here?"

"Yes, I think an old friend of my dad still lives here. The old police chief from Le Fleur, Benson Wells. I just want to run in and get his room number, so I can send him a gift of some kind. I haven't seen him in years. He used to go fishing with my dad. When he got older, he moved up here and bought a house on the river just past Lewiston because he loved the area so much. Then a few years later he had a stroke and came to this nursing home. Later, my dad and I would stop here on the fishing trips to see him. I'm pretty sure the guy's still around. Just wait for me, and I'll be right back."

Russ gets out, looks around in curiosity, and leans against the Lion. The giant building is accented with appealing stone, wood, and muted earth-tone accents. An impressive multi-story porte cocshere adorns the entrance, with a finely landscaped courtyard in front of the building. A large statue of the Virgin Mary sits within a fountain at the center of the yard, with beautiful teak park benches flanking her at the perimeter. This is not the average, economy-minded nursing home that serves tapioca pudding for every dessert.

Russ can see Frank inside talking to a woman at a desk near the entrance. Within moments Frank is walking briskly back and the two men slide into the car. “Okay, young man. That’s that. Let’s go.”

“Is he in there?”

“Yep. I got his room number, so I can send him a nice little gift.”

“But you don’t want to go see him now.”

“No, not right now. Maybe later. He’ll get his gift later.”

# Chapter Twenty

Frank directs Russ away from Canada onto the Niagara Scenic Highway, formerly called the Robert Moses Parkway, that parallels the river heading north. The Lion slithers along the tree-lined road and Frank sits up in excitement to point to the familiar landmarks.

"Look over there. That's Canada on the other side. Isn't that a magnificent view?"

Russ looks back and forth from the road to the vast, western rocky bank on his left that cradles the river in the canyon out of sight below. Homes of prominence appear to teeter on the far cliff as a garrison against a never-to-come American invasion.

Frank exclaims, "We'll be down there by the power plants tomorrow pulling out some hellacious salmon, my young man."

"You mean we're going to fish right down there in that canyon?"

"Yessiree!" The childlike inflection rises in his throat. You're going to be blown away by those salmon. And you're going to love Captain Joe. He knows every inch of this river and these two lakes. He's lived his whole life on Grand Island, and damn, you should see his fancy log cabin. It looks like a lodge with all the deer heads and mounted fish hanging everywhere."

Russ smiles. "Damn!"

The Lion reaches the apex of the parkway hill where the river emerges on the left from its hiding place of declining canyon walls. The river widens northwest at the bottom of the hill around a vast vista of trees and housetops. Several church steeples rise above to exalt the town of Lewiston and the God of its three-thousand people. The scene is reminiscent of those old-fashioned travel posters enticing you to immediately reserve your hotel.

Frank says, "Isn't that gorgeous? I never get tired of it. That's Lewiston down there on the left. It's a great little town, named after Morgan Lewis, a nineteenth-century New York governor. I'm going to have you drive through it to get to Youngstown."

"Okay, Frank. Sounds good to me."

"And, ya know," Frank is compelled to add, "the Niagara is only one of a couple dozen rivers in North America that actually flow north."

Frank frequently provides spontaneous lessons on inconsequential bits of trivia, although he knows it annoys people. He is known around the office as "Frankipedia," but that does not deter his habit. He researches people who have towns or highways named after them, such as the controversial, early-twentieth-century planner and political power broker Robert Moses. Why wouldn't others want to know how much water flows over Niagara Falls, or facts about native tribes that once inhabited the region? "You know, Russ, Ontario is derived from the Huron language that means, 'Lake of Shining Waters.'"

He then goes on to describe how the hard rock at the top of the falls crumbles away several inches a year when the softer layers below are eaten away by the torrent. The falls' rate of erosion was nearly four feet a year in the mid-1800s when the river flowed unimpeded, he instructs. "Theoretically, over the coming millennia, the falls could chew back the twenty miles south to Buffalo and then on further into the eastern end of Lake Erie!" Knowing these facts is as necessary as air to Frank.

He is caught up in the history of Lewiston, the town from where the Americans invaded Canada in the war of 1812, only to be repelled. Later, during the Civil War, townspeople here risked jail to escort fugitive slaves across the river to their new friends in Canada. Then, in the early 1900s, the "alternating current/direct current wars" were fought here between Nikola Tesla, Thomas Edison, George Westinghouse, and J.P. Morgan. The Native Americans, the Red Coats, the militia, the slaves, the risk takers, the industrial giants, and the corporate scapegoats were all here. Even US presidents stayed at the Frontier House stagecoach-stop hotel, still standing in the center of Lewiston. The building's thirty-inch stone walls also had, until recently, housed the town's only McDonald's. It is now used for a more historically honorable office building.

Frank is amazed that others do not marvel about these facts; these people and their endeavors. Were these not daring, worthy souls? How many people even know of Tesla beyond hearing the name of the fancy electric car bearing his name? Each week, Frank tries to help others learn about facts like these and ponders why they are important to him and not to them.

The Lion slides down the hill, exits off the Scenic Highway ramp, and rolls down the active core of Lewiston where historic storefronts flank the travelers. Trendy restaurants and family diners, old-fashioned bakeries, antique stores, sports bars, and Irish pubs line the busy four-lane street. Despite the wide thoroughfare, the town is stuck somewhere in the last century, akin to the little hamlets along the coast of New England. Everyone here will say hello or at least nod when you pass them on the sidewalks. Many wear expensive plaid woolen shirts or field jackets. Humble shop owners live next door to the millionaire Buffalo CEOs, who live next door to factory workers, who live next to the rustic bed and breakfasts. But unlike "downstate," most people here possess a fierce conservatism.

Well-preserved revolutionary war artifacts scattered about prohibit Lewiston from fully entering the present. Despite the historically decorous surroundings, a tinge of grittiness floats about, perhaps left over from the hardscrabble, industrial reputation of Buffalo and the infamous bruising of the 1970s Niagara Love Canal ecological disaster inherited by the Hooker Chemical Company.

"Up there on the right is a good barbecue restaurant, Russ. Maybe we'll eat there tonight or tomorrow. Now just up there a bit I want you to take a left on Niagara Street."

The Lion obeys and coasts down a big hill past collections of neat white houses. The car reaches the street's end at a flat parking area next to the concrete-block building housing the Creek Road Bait & Tackle.

"C'mon, Russ. There's someone here I want you to meet."

Every square inch of the wall space in the shop is tidily covered with tackle, mounted fish of various sizes and species, and photos strategically spaced about reflecting hunting and angling heroes. No store clerk is to be found. The place is quiet except for the soft gurgling of water in the two live bait tanks on either side of the store. Frank yells out, "Is anyone here?" A moment later a tall young woman with striking, angular features exits the open doorjamb from the back storage room. She smooths her strawberry-blond locks and pulls them back over her shoulders as she approaches the counter.

"Hello, gentlemen, can I help you?"

Her smooth voice, womanly persona, crisp white blouse, and designer jeans are oddly juxtaposed against the bait shop's faint smell of minnows and worms.

"Well, yes there, ma'am." Frank falters at the sight of a woman he remembers being not much more than a teen. "My good friend and I would like to get some fishing licenses."

Russ does a double take and considers the reference to a woman less than half of Frank's age as being a "ma'am" and the equally notable suggestion that he was Frank's "good friend" and not just an employee or chauffeur.

"Okay, that's easy enough," she says. "Come on over here to the computer. Have you bought a New York fishing license in the last three years?"

Frank looks at the floor, "No, I'm afraid I haven't been up here for quite a while."

With a perfect smile the young woman replies, "That's okay, just give me your driver's licenses and we'll get you all fixed up. You want the license for a season, a week, or one day?"

"Just the one-day sticker for tomorrow will do," Frank responds.

Frank produces his license while Russ fumbles and drops his to the floor. Embarrassed, he bends over to pick it up and bumps his head into a display of a dozen fishing poles but manages to collect himself and the rods before they slide to the floor. The woman giggles slightly.

"Sorry about that," Russ mumbles.

"Oh, that's no problem. I've been meaning to latch those. A little boy came in with his dad last week and did the very same thing, except he scattered them all over the place."

Being compared to a little boy wilts Russ a bit as he endures handing her his license.

She takes a moment to examine the card and says, "Ohio, huh? Russell W. Booker? That's a long drive to go fishing."

"Yeah, kinda," is all he can gather.

Frank stares at Russ, widens his eyes, clinches his teeth, and nods his head toward the woman as if to prod, "Say something else, you fool, she is trying to start a conversation!"

"Uh, yeah," Russ begins, "we're Buckeyes, but ya know, it's only about a six-hour drive up here and it seems to go fast."

Frank shuts his eyes and shakes his head in mild disgust at the juvenile comment, then turns his attention to the woman punching the keyboard.

"So, young lady, what's your name?"

Russ snaps to attention, incredulous.

"I'm Valerie. Valerie McLaughlin."

Frank's voice raises a couple octaves.

"You don't mean to tell me that you're Maggie's daughter."

"Sure am. You know her?"

Frank is caught off guard.

"Uh huh. She—well, ya know, I had come up here a few times over the years with my dad, and he would bring me in here. Your mom was a young woman then. We got to know each other a bit and I would come back up here in later years to fish with my friends and buy our stickers here."

Valerie looks at the driver's license, then looks up at the man that only faintly resembles the photo. "Oh, is that right, Mr. Barnett?"

"Mmmhuh."

Russ moves closer while fiddling with fishing lures, pretending not to listen. Frank is seemingly lost in adoration as Valerie continues to enter data into the computer.

Frank asks casually, "Where's Maggie now?"

Valerie looks up. "She said she wanted to run to the grocery to pick up a few things. Personally, I think she just wanted to get out and enjoy the sun a little bit. I'm sure she'll be back, though, before we close in a couple hours."

Conversation stalls as the men sign the forms and printer noise fills the shop.

"Here you go, Russ," Valerie says cheerfully. "Keep this in your wallet while you're fishing. And here you go, Mr. Barnett. That'll be twenty dollars and ninety cents, with tax."

Frank has his credit card waiting and surprises Valerie by purposely touching her hand in the exchange.

"That seems less than I paid five or six years ago."

"Yes, the state lowered the price a couple years ago to encourage more fishing and tourism. I didn't think it would matter, but it seems to have actually helped a bit. You say you were in here about five years ago?"

"Yeah, with a couple other old farts. 'Bout this same time of year, now that I think of it. We'd come up here in the spring for the bass up in Buffalo and then down here in the fall for the salmon. But that fizzled out after one of the guys passed away."

"Oh, I'm sorry to hear that."

"Yeah, things weren't the same after Willy died, and our little group just started doing less and less together. Then one guy retired to Texas and the other guy—well, we just don't talk much anymore."

"That's too bad, Mr. Barnett."

"Please, call me Frank."

"Okay, Frank, you going to need anything else for fishing?"

"No. Our guide, Joe, will have everything we need, except for any food or beer we want to take, and we'll get that up in Youngstown. Do you know Captain Joe? Joe Cinelli?"

Valerie responds delightedly. "Everyone 'round here knows Joe. Look over there at that photo above the coolers. He's the best guide for a hundred miles, maybe even all of New York. He wins just about every tournament there is. He catches his limit when other captains come back with only one or two fish—or none."

Both men bend over to look at a photo of Joe holding up a mammoth salmon, standing on his boat with the Niagara canyon walls in the background.

"He sure is something," Frank says reverently. "Joe always made sure we brought in fish. See, Russ, I told you we're in for one hell of a day tomorrow!"

Russ fumbles again with his wallet, trying to look up indirectly at Valerie. She stretches her arms out on the counter. "It sounds like it is going to be a great time and the weather is going to be absolutely beautiful."

She hands the receipt and credit card back to Frank, who takes them with his left hand and extends his right to shake hers.

"It was good seeing you again, Valerie. You must have still been in high school last time. Now you're all grown up. My, how time flies."

"I actually remember you now too, Frank. You and the other guys from Ohio came in here and you all flirted with my mom. But it seemed like you were the only one who knew how to get through her hard shell. I could tell she kinda liked you."

"I remember your mom to be a very special lady, Valerie. I hope to see her again this trip."

"Come back before we close at eight and I'm sure you will."

"Maybe we'll come back in a bit after we check into the Youngstown Motel. Tell her I stopped in."

"Of course, but why are you staying there? Why don't you stay in town here at one of the bed and breakfasts?"

"It's kind of a tradition. The motel over in Youngstown is where the guys used to stay. Besides, I like the drive along the river."

"I sure can understand that. I hope to see you both again."

Frank and Russ share sly looks before making their way out the front door to pile into the Lion.

"I think she kind of liked you, Russ."

"Oh, I don't know about that."

Russ puts the Lion into gear and rolls off, giving a sanguine look over at the bait shop. Valerie stands in the door watching them pull away.

"Who knows, Frank, maybe she thought I was kinda cute when I almost knocked the poles over."

"Maybe so. I think she's pretty, don't you?"

"Uh, yeah, really pretty."

"If you think Valerie's pretty, you should see her mom. Maggie may be the most beautiful woman I've ever known, and she has a real heart of gold. Well, in the top three, anyway. Turn left here on Center. Now, if you were to go straight about two blocks, you'd run into the river."

"Why don't we go down and see it?"

"Not now. I don't want to overwhelm you by introducing you to two mysterious women within five minutes."

A couple more turns and the Lion is moving along 18F parallel to the river and snaking out of Lewiston.

"Keep your eyes peeled, Russ. Except for the California coast, this drive to Youngstown is probably one of the most relaxing drives I've ever made. It's part of the Great Lakes Circle Tour. You're going to love this place."

## Chapter Twenty-One

With a guttural purr, the Lion claws along the river to sneak under the tree canopies as big cats do. Widely-spaced houses to the right brag about old money and big summer parties on stately lawns. The bungalows strung tightly along the river cliff to the left are where the new rich hide on weekends among the massive virgin trees.

The fifteen-minute northerly drive from Lewiston to Youngstown provides magnificent glimpses of the Niagara River that have always reached into Frank's gut and pulled out childlike awe for these old things that were once seen by ancient people and prehistoric beasts.

Subtly mixed fragrances of pine, fall apples, and chrysanthemums flood the Corvette's warm cocoon as its supple leather is fondled by a splendid fall evening breeze. Western sun skirts through fluttering leaves to break apart and bounce over the hood like glistening jewels strewn about. The everyday clutter of billboards, truck noise, and grime are erased by tidiness and the occasional Revolutionary War historical marker.

The old stagecoach road is the adventure—where every dip and rise deliver hauntingly simple testimonials of diverse lives which endured here for eons. A surging calm provides room for contemplation, one uncomplicated epiphany—that singular gasp of austere truth a person craves but rarely attains during the routine of busy days. The casual journey lies branded in the mind, to smolder and take on new hues and facets when later recalled to warm a cold ashen winter day. This slow drive along Niagara provides space to reflect on those with whom this very path was traveled, but who have since departed over that ancient highway into eternity. Their infinite journeys may have been taken over comforting roads like this—tree-lined passages alongside vast rivers of time flowing toward something greater.

Frank hopes Russ will drive here again in the future, possibly with his son Nick, to appreciate the smothering quietness and inescapable compulsion of each personal salmon run. He aches to be remembered, like those souls he conjures today. He can scarcely grapple all the sensations contained within this elongated moment. Still, bits and pieces, certain aromas of this autumn day, will cling fast and provide solace during the hard realities of the days and months to come.

The stands of trees thin on the left as the river widens enough for the travelers to steal longer looks at the shimmering water between the houses that huddle closer together as Youngstown approaches. If Lewiston is a New England charlatan, the small town of Youngstown is a legitimate descendant. It is a place where things great and small are held in reverence and history begs for contribution to its pages.

Frank craves to scribble his lines there but fears his book of life will be buried deeply on a shelf where his concepts will linger out of sight. The prospect of being soon forgotten creates a hollowness in his chest, but the greater fear of appearing feeble in front of old friends here makes him want to turn around and head back to Ohio.

# Chapter Twenty-Two

Frank breaks the long silence. "Watch it right here. It can be a speed trap. Just up there at the middle of the square, turn right, then take a quick left to the motel. You can't miss it. That Irish restaurant, Brennan's, may be where we eat tomorrow night after fishing."

"What kind of food do they have?"

"Oh, just about anything. They have a killer baked pasta, and their wings are huge."

"Do they have any *real* Irish food?"

Frank pauses and looks into the air. "Well, come to think of it, I don't think they have any Irish food at all. Just bar food and some pastas and seafood, mostly. Since when did my black friend become a connoisseur of Irish food?"

"I don't know that I'm a connoisseur of any food, but I like to try new stuff whenever I can. I do like Julie's stuffed cabbage rolls. Those are Irish, aren't they?"

"Hmm. I don't know. Never really thought about it."

Russ approaches Main Street's signal and turns right, past a massive stone structure that dominates the small downtown area with its wrap-around porch and its uncommon three-story height.

"What's that building?"

"That's the Ontario House. That inn's been there for more than two-hundred-and-fifty years. It's basically a bar and has a few rooms they rent out. It's supposed to be haunted. Maybe we can go there tomorrow night to celebrate our huge catch."

Russ sees the ground sign a little further up on his left for the Youngstown Motel. He whips around the corner and immediately left again into the gravel parking lot behind the motel.

He looks up and down the length of the white vinyl two-story motel that has been perpendicularly attached to the house on the corner of Second and Lockport Street.

Russ hesitantly asks, "This is where we're staying?"

"I know it isn't much to look at, but the rooms are big and clean, and the beds are comfortable. Let's go see if Bruce is here."

The men climb out and wade through the freshly laid gravel to a door located where the house and motel meet. Russ lets the screen flap closed behind him and looks around. The men stand in a transition room built during a long-ago remodeling project that added the motel rooms onto the main house. Frank rings the bell, which summons a gruff female voice from somewhere around the corner that asks, "Who is it?"

"It's Frank Barnett from Ohio. Bruce said he would have a room for me for two nights."

The woman responds, "Do you have cash?"

Frank hesitates, then answers loudly, "Yes, I have cash."

"Then leave a hundred and twenty there under the paperweight and take the room key off the desk for 3B. It's all ready for you."

Frank leaves the money and grabs the key attached to a large, flat, 1960-era motel keychain dangle. The men haul their bags up the wooden steps to the second floor. They peek inside 3B and then Frank moves to the far side of the room and places his bags on the bed.

"I'll take this bed. It's closer to the toilet."

"Sure, fine with me."

Russ examines the austere room while Frank dashes to the bathroom. The simple bedroom is scuffed from thousands of fishermen and their tales. A hulking square tube-television sits on a tired wooden dresser. A battered round dining table and two fake-leather chairs droop sadly into the corner. The only hint of adornment in the entire room is a large metal-framed navigational map of the eastern Lake Erie-western Lake Ontario basin with Grand Island and Niagara highlighted in the middle of the two.

Russ flops onto his bed and throws his hands back over his head. He lets out a big sigh that develops into a yawn.

Frank emerges from the bathroom. "Don't get too comfortable, my boy. I have a little chore for you."

Frank pulls two crisp one-hundred-dollar bills out of his wallet and places them on the bed near Russ's feet, then points his thumb toward the bathroom.

"I want you to walk across the street to the liquor store and get me a bottle of eighteen-year-old Glenmorangie. That should be about seventy or eighty bucks." He then points to the wall behind Russ's head. "And then go across the other street to the grocery and get yourself a twelve-pack, a bag of ice, a Styrofoam cooler, and some snacks you'd like to take on the boat with you tomorrow."

"Snacks? What kind of snacks?"

"Anything you want. Chips, nuts, candy bars. If you want, you could get some lunch meat and bread to make sandwiches on the boat. Get a few bottles of water too. While you're doing that, I'm gonna get cleaned up for dinner. You can shower when you're back."

Russ jumps off the bed, picks up the bills, and thinks, *I know who you are really getting cleaned up for*.

As if answering Russ's thought, Frank replies, "I don't want to smell like a dirty hobo when we go back to meet the ladies tonight."

***

Russ trips into the motel room, plastic bags bulging around his arms and hanging off the ends of his straining fingers. He jolts to a stop when he sees the clean and freshly dressed boss lying back on his bed with eyes shut and arms and legs sprawled in all directions. Two prescription bottles are tipped over on the nightstand with a few pills spilled out. A plastic cup lays on the floor next to a small wet spot and an empty pint bottle of whiskey. Russ snaps rigid at the sight of the shiny .38 lying on the floor next to the dangling tassels of the bedspread.

Shopping bags still hanging, Russ moves over to the bed to check for a gunshot wound. No blood or injuries are apparent on the comatose man. Frank takes a startled gasp but remains asleep. Russ releases a forgotten breath of his own and steps back to set several bags quietly onto the table. He makes more noise than he wants when he slumps to a seat and puts the rest of the bags on the floor. Keeping his eyes on the blotchy old man, he reaches down for a beer out of the twelve-pack. Russ drinks and stares while Frank begins to snore raucously. After observing patiently through three beers and a half bag of chips, Russ moves to the end of the bed and puts his hand on Frank's leg.

"Frank, Frank."

This ignites thrashing legs and arms, grunts, and moans, breaking the calm. Bits of words spew vehemently. An internal fight ensues, and Frank is punching the air and pillows within reach. Russ scoots away toward the end of the bed to avoid getting caught in the mêlée. Frank gains consciousness, leans forward, throws his legs over the side of the bed, and lowers his head as though he is going to vomit. He lets out an agonizing wail as Russ's eyes widen with shock.

Frank looks around the room in confusion while pulling on an eyebrow. He closes his eyes, then blurts, "Where the hell am I?"

"We're in New York, Frank. Remember, we came up to go fishing. To catch some salmon."

Frank chuckles in antipathy. "Oh yeah, fishing. Now I remember. The damn salmon run."

Russ pauses to let Frank mutter incoherently some more, but the vitriol finally subsides, and the void needs filled.

"Yeah, we're going out with Joe Cinelli tomorrow. We talked about going back to Lewiston tonight and maybe going out to dinner with Valerie and Maggie, remember?"

Frank rubs his hands over his face and looks for words on the ceiling.

"Maggie. Dinner with Maggie?"

"Yeah, and her daughter Valerie." Russ stands. "We saw Valerie a little while ago at their bait shop in Lewiston and she said we should go back tonight if we wanted to see her mom, Maggie."

Frank's fog lifts a bit.

"Maggie sure is a nice lady. A real nice lady. I wish I could redo the last twenty years. Things may have been different between her and me. Guess it's too late to think about things like that now."

"It's never too late, as they say."

Frank responds sullenly without looking at Russ.

"Never too late? Don't believe that bull, my boy."

Frank slowly eases to his feet to prove he is steady and alert, but instead confirms his imbalance and lingering muddle.

"What's that junk all over the table?"

"You sent me to the store to get some snacks for the boat tomorrow, remember?"

"Oh, hell yeah, snacks for the boat. Where's the whiskey? You got the whiskey, didn't ya?"

"Yeah, I got it, but do you really think you should be drinking? Didn't you take some pills?"

"Don't worry about that, Russ. Those pills only work with scotch. In fact, I know the perfect ratio of pills to scotch. I may even write a research paper on it."

Russ digs through a plastic grocery sack and pulls out a brown bag stapled at the top and rips it open. He pulls the tab around the lid of the Scotch bottle and pulls out the plastic-topped cork with the familiar, wet sound. *Thoomp.* He extends the bottle toward Frank.

"Well, here you go," Russ snaps. "Who am I to stand in the way of medical research? Your cup is on the floor by your feet there."

Frank bends down with calculated measure to pick up the cup. He raises it confidently to Russ.

"Did you get ice? The proper way to drink scotch is with two ice cubes. It releases the true flavor."

Russ takes the cup and reaches into another grocery sack to poke a hole in a bag of ice. He drops two cubes into the cup and pours two fingers.

"Just a bit more, Russ. That's a skinny cup."

Russ obliges and shoves the cup toward Frank and snarls, "Here you go. I guess you don't mind showing up for dinner drunk."

Frank swirls the light caramel-colored liquid around with the ice, then takes a long smell before taking a small sip. He closes his eyes, swallows, and exhales strongly.

"Pour yourself one, Russ. This is good stuff."

"No, that's okay. I had three beers while I waited for you to wake up. Oh yeah—and half a bag of chips and a Slim Jim, too."

Frank can tell that Russ is angry about coming back to find a drunk and confused man lying on the bed. Little does he realize Russ's anger is really a mixture of naiveté and pity.

"You had three beers? Heavens, Russ, it might be you that's going to show up drunk for dinner. You going to be okay to drive?"

Russ sits in quiet incredulity and watches Frank wrestle his stiff bones down onto the side of the bed, so he can savor each drop of his drink. Russ puts the remaining beers in the Styrofoam cooler, pours the bag of ice on top, and rearranges the groceries on the table.

Frank looks over with scorn. "What the hell's the matter with you?"

"There's nothing wrong with me. I'm just wondering why the hell you're sitting over on the bed with that gun on the floor by your foot. Are ya planning on shooting someone?"

"Oh, you saw my gun now, did ya?"

"Yeah, it's hard to miss. Whad'ya bring a gun for?"

"Well, you just never know when it could come in handy. Maybe it could be useful when bumping into a racist asshole at McDonald's."

"Yeah, right, Frank. Ruining your life over someone like that wouldn't make any sense or do anyone any good."

Frank reaches down clumsily to pick up the gun, then flops onto his back. He raises the gun into the air, points it at the ceiling, and twists it from side to side to feel the flawless grip in his palm.

"Well, of course you're right about that. That redneck was evil, but not nearly evil enough to be shot, at least not today. But I'm pretty sure he'll do something in the future that'll make someone mad enough to take him out. And ya know what? He'll damn well deserve it. His years of being a jackass will finally catch up to him. I guess it always does for everybody."

Russ starts stripping his clothes as he moves toward the bathroom, wondering if Frank is going to start picking out targets, or worse.

"The funny thing is," Frank continues while leaning up to put the gun on the nightstand, "the person who takes him down will probably be someone he knows. They'll finally just get tired of his bullying. He's going to piss off a friend or a coworker and that'll be it. A club to the head or a bullet to the gut. It'll be sudden and violent. Years of crap he's dumped on someone will be thrown back on him in a fit of rage. The person who kills him won't even be sorry for it."

Russ searches for some profound response and is mortified that the only thing he can spill out is a tepid, "Maybe so," as he shuts the bathroom door behind him.

He takes a deep breath in front of the sink, then turns on the shower. He climbs in to let the warm water melt away the strange day. While shampooing, he listens for a noise, a gunshot, a suicide. The trickling stream should relax, but it only creates more anxiety.

"What the hell is he going to do?" he murmurs.

# Chapter Twenty-Three

Night shrouds the Great Lakes Circle Tour road back to Lewiston, which now seems longer, less familiar, and much less spectacular. The hushed, nearly black surroundings provide an exaggerated sense of wilderness that belies the proximity to the fanciful falls and abrasive Buffalo. Russ coaxes the Lion between the lines and around each subtle curve.

He glances over at Frank, who seems to be rehearsing unspoken words over his lips. Even the dim cabin cannot hide the boss's fragile and pale appearance. Frank's nervousness about not being recognized by an old flame is evident through his twitching fingers, tapping foot, and bouncing knee.

"Be careful, Russ. There's a lot of deer around here."

The unexpected comment slightly startles Russ, and he straightens behind the wheel and burbles back a weak, "Okay, Frank." Instantly a doe jumps from the trees along the bank out in front of the Lion and bounds off to the other side.

"Shit!" Russ slams on the brakes and comes to a stop. "Son of a bitch, Frank! Did you just conjure that deer our way?"

"No, I don't think so," he laughs. "They're just all over the place up here."

Frank reaches over and grabs Russ's arm. "Now wait a minute. Don't go yet. Where there's one, there's more. This happened to me once about ten years ago when we were on the way to the boat real early in the morning. Just missed a big buck then."

Two more deer bolt out to chase their leader across the road.

"Okay, that should do it. Go on."

"Are you sure, Frank?"

"Not really, but we can't sit here forever. Just be careful."

"How can you be careful when they just come outta nowhere and run in front a' ya?"

Russ eases the Lion forward, then picks up the pace, clenching the wheel and bouncing his eyes back and forth to the road's edges. His own nervous twitches replace Frank's, who now appears oddly composed.

Lewiston grows closer and the comfort of approaching street lights and neat salt-box frame houses along square blocks replace the fear of backwoods wildlife. The low grumble of the Lion faintly disturbs the peaceful neighborhoods as Russ navigates the lefts and rights into downtown. Main Street is full of cheerful couples, and pub windows shine with jovial patrons who live for these autumn weekends before bitter winds and biting snow engulf the valley.

The final turn down the hill to the bait shop reveals a raging fire pit illuminating two women sitting at a picnic table. The Lion's headlights cause the women to shield their eyes, and the men look at each other with a mix of fear and delight. Russ turns off the car and the women bathe in the flicker of flames.

"Relax, Russ. Just be yourself."

Russ scrunches up his brow. "Me relax? What about you? You're a nervous wreck."

"Maybe so. I haven't seen Maggie in a long time.

"Well, she sure looks happy to see you."

Frank smiles. "I think her daughter looks pretty happy to see you, too."

"Her name is Valerie, remember?"

"Oh yes, Valerie, that's it."

Frank sits motionless as Russ opens his door.

Russ speaks, trying not to move his lips. "Frank, we need to get out of the car."

"I know. Just give me a second."

Frank swings his door open, climbs out, and walks toward Maggie. Russ reaches Valerie and extends his hand. She clasps both of hers around his, beaming.

"Sure glad you guys made it back tonight. We were wondering if you'd show up," Valerie says.

Russ inhales, nearly gasping with delight in a moment that he knows holds some special meaning, but which will take time to resolve. He lets his hand linger in her supple touch for an extended moment. Her gentle assurance of instant friendship smothers any remaining anxiety. He gently pulls away to speak, with a smile and newfound confidence.

"Well, there wasn't any reason not to come back."

He looks at Frank to see if what he just said was as awkward as he thinks it sounded, but apparently his boss's mind is elsewhere.

Maggie doesn't try to hide her excitement. She moves toward Frank and gives him a generous hug and a tender kiss on the cheek. Frank is caught by surprise, but he manages to lift an unnerved hand onto her back and apply a timid squeeze. Maggie recognizes the unease she is causing and moves back from the embrace.

"It's so good to see you, Frank. I couldn't believe it when Valerie told me you stopped by the store. It's been a long time. And you must be Russ. Very nice to meet you, young man."

Russ gives a hearty shake. "Nice to meet you too, ma'am."

"Oh, please call me Maggie."

Russ dips his head in acknowledgment as she leads the group toward the Adirondack chairs that encircle the fire pit beyond the picnic table. She picks up the poker and gives the logs a half-hearted stoke.

Maggie says, “You sure have a nice car there, Russ.”

“That’s not mine. That’s Frank’s. He just got it a couple days ago to drive up here.”

“Is that right, Frank?”

Frank looks at Russ in semi-disgust. “Yep. That’s about the size of it, I guess. I didn’t think my old truck would make it up here. We call the Corvette ‘the Lion.’” He cringes at the absurdity.

“That’s a good name,” Valerie says. “Very fitting.”

Maggie realizes the car subject is making Frank uncomfortable and changes the tone.

“You boys want to sit for a while and have a drink before we go get dinner? I have some beers there in the cooler, a few bottles of wine, and I just opened an old bottle of scotch. Or if you want, instead of going out to eat we can just do some hot dogs on the fire and have some cheese and chips. Sometimes it’s really hard to talk in a loud restaurant. This might be a more relaxing way to catch up.”

“Oh man.” Frank livens right up at this. “You always were a good hostess, Maggie. Did you get that whiskey just for me, or have you taken up an appreciation for the good stuff too?”

“Well, you always said it was the nectar of the gods. Who am I to argue with that?”

Maggie’s recall of his well-worn quote causes Frank to relax enough to laugh deeply. He carries the buoyant mood toward Russ with the clever influence of a used-car salesman.

“So, waddaya say, my boy? You wanna just stay here and do some dogs on the fire and drink some beers and whiskey? Sounds like a pretty good deal to me. Whatcha think?”

“Are you kidding me?” Russ says. “I’d love to sit around the fire. Beer and dogs sound perfect!”

Valerie reaches into the cooler and tosses Russ a can of beer as Maggie leans down to a basket and pulls out a plastic tumbler, three cubes of ice, and the full but opened bottle of single-malt scotch. She hands Frank the glass and her fingers caress his with artful casualness. She puts in the cubes and pours a substantial drink.

"Thanks, Maggie. You gonna have a drink?"

"Well, of course. Friends don't let friends drink alone."

Maggie reaches into the basket again to pull out a half-full bottle of red wine and pours glasses for her and Valerie. The group strategically chooses their locations so each can sit close to their paramour.

Maggie raises her glass. "Let's toast our guests. May God smile upon you and may you have your best-ever fishing day tomorrow."

Frank raises his glass. "Thank you for that. Now I have one. May God keep you and your daughter healthy and wealthy for many years to come."

The conversation moves to updates about the newspaper, the bait shop, and expectations for excellent weather and fishing. Frank announces the promotion of Russ almost as an afterthought, and the ladies heap congratulations on the young man. Frank cuts short the praise by rushing to give Russ an enthused history lesson of the area and an account of the "Niagara escarpment's geological uniqueness." He leaves enough room for Maggie and Valerie to fill in some details that only locals could verify.

Hostess Maggie passes out long metal campfire sticks with red wooden handles, and the group cooks their hot dogs over the open flame before loading them onto buns with ketchup, mustard, and relish. The chips and cubes of cheese are passed 'round and the simple meal brings gushing thanks from the two men. Frank finishes the last bite of his dog and puts his hand over his mouth for a quiet but obvious burp.

"Man. That was a good dog. Could I have another one?"

Maggie opens the cooler for another dog and threads it onto the end of her stick. "Here, let me do the honors for you."

Russ wipes his fingers across his mouth. "Wow, Frank. I haven't seen you eat this much in months!"

Maggie rotates the wiener over the flame as more drinks are poured and Frank begins a rundown of his Niagara experiences. He bubbles with yarns of fishing the river and the neighboring lakes during the early years with his father's troupe. Then he moves to the later years with his own buddies. His emphatic laughs punctuate the stories he perceives as funny. Then solemn moments of looking into the fire litter his accounts of those whom he now misses, some because of death or others who have left over ill feelings. Both reasons provide a harsh finality in the storyteller's textured recounting of brotherhood's ebb and flow through the highs of unwavering support to the lows of competitive agitation. But, the brighter memories of camaraderie carry the moment and provide a balm of comfort. He says he is better for having known them and all the pettiness is forgiven. After all, he says, guys who feel like true bothers always have a few scuffles of honesty that friendly acquaintances would avoid.

Frank's stories stall as Maggie hands him the prepared dog and no one picks up to fill the quiet. They all stare toward and beyond the bonfire as Maggie puts on another log and Frank munches.

Finally, Valerie interjects, "Wow, what a gorgeous night. Russ, you want to go down to the river and look at the stars?"

Russ piques with obvious excitement but cannot seem to find words to respond.

Valerie had saved the moment. She snaps up an open bottle of wine off the picnic table and coaxes, "Come on, it's a short walk."

She grabs Russ's arm and the two disappear down a trail toward the river to leave the elders staring into the fire.

"Well," Maggie says, "those two sure seem to have hit it off, haven't they?"

"Yes, it sure looks like it," Frank mutters. "I just hope they know what they're doing. Russ is married and has a kid."

Maggie looks at Frank curiously. "I know that, Frank, and so does Valerie. Just because they're going down to the river to look at the stars doesn't mean they are as stupid as we were."

Frank, embarrassed at insinuating that Valerie might be leading Russ astray, looks up from the fire curiously.

"How does she know Russ has a kid?"

"You don't remember that he mentioned his son a little while ago? I guess you were digging in the ice for another drink."

"Damn, I'm sorry. I guess I am a better talker than a listener. Guess I rambled on like no one else had any thoughts to share."

"It's okay, Frank. I think everyone appreciated your stories. It was nice to hear you talk about your fishing trips, your dad, and your friends. I've seen you quite a few times over the years, but I never got too many of the fish stories. I really liked the one about how you dropped your dad's prized coconut cream pie at the boat launch and the seagulls swarmed in to eat it. I can just imagine the look on your dad's face."

Frank chuckles, then picks up the poker to enrage the flame. "Yeah, he was looking forward to eating that pie while out on the boat. Before heading home, we had to make another trip back to the pie lady's house way over by Olcott to get another one. That cost us an hour, but he wasn't leaving without getting some of that pie."

He tosses on a couple more pieces of firewood and then pushes them in place to build the perfect Boy Scout campfire. Frank is mesmerized by the flame as his mind wanders to some other place.

"What is it, Frank? I get the feeling you want to tell me something."

"Just thinking about Dad, I guess. He was a pretty good man, despite all his faults."

"He seemed like a good person. He was very kind to my mom."

"Yeah. He treated everyone like they were the most important person in the world when he spoke to them. I saw how nice he was to your mom when we were in the bait shop. Ya know, she seemed like a really sweet lady, too."

Maggie takes a gulp of wine and blurts, "You do know that they had an affair, don't you?"

Frank stops poking the fire and stands to face Maggie. "They what? What are you talking about?"

"Surely you knew that, didn't you?"

Frank turns to stab the fire again so he can avoid looking at her. "Your mom and my dad? You serious?"

She sloshes some more wine into her glass, slumps back, and takes a couple trembling sips and stares off in the direction of the path where the youngsters fled.

"I guess I shouldn't have said anything about it. Not sure why I did. It really doesn't matter."

"My dad and your mom, huh? No, I really wasn't aware of that. Are you sure? Really?"

"Well, yeah, I'm positive. Every time he came up to go fishing, they would sneak off back to our house and spend some time together and I would watch the bait shop. Hell, I think I was only sixteen or seventeen and she would let me watch the store all by myself. Mom said that in order to get away from his friends your dad would say he wanted to go for a drive and have some 'alone time' to think and look at the stars. Of course, he was having anything but alone time. As I got older, mom told me about it. I think she really loved him. She leans forward to pick up a stick and poke at the fire, releasing a plume of sparks.

"You know, I think he loved her, too. He would come up once in a while by himself to see her, just like you came up every once in a while to see me. He'd drive up to Buffalo and she'd go down to be with him, just like we used to do."

Frank rubs behind his ear and neck and moves around the other side of the fire ring for a different perspective of Maggie, awash in waves of orange and gold. He picks up another piece of wood and tosses it haphazardly onto the fire, only to have it roll off to the edge of the metal ring. He reaches in carelessly to grab the end of the log while flares dance around his jacket sleeve.

"Careful, Frank. You're going to get burned."

Frank ignores the plea for caution and places the log at the apex of the fire before pulling his hand out.

"Guess I'm more like my old man than I realized. Like father, like son."

Maggie laughs. "And like mother, like daughter, huh?"

"So, does Valerie know about us? Did she suspect anything?"

"Well, I think she was beginning to, but then you stopped coming up and you just faded from her mind, or so I thought. Then a couple years ago she asked about you, which surprised me. She said, "Mom, how come that guy from Ohio doesn't come up anymore?" I just told her that your group of friends kind of scattered to the wind. I think she was hoping that you'd save me from being alone. She probably knew more than I realized."

Frank asks, "Why didn't you say anything about our parents before? You had plenty of chances over the years."

Maggie bites her nail. "Well...I was a little embarrassed about it. My dad was missing in action somewhere out in California and your dad was married. I guess I just felt that was their business and didn't want you to think about them when we were together. I didn't want you to regret making the same decisions your dad did, then maybe it could have turned out different for us."

Frank looks at the fire a long moment, then his attention is drawn to a house behind Maggie's shoulder where someone is sitting in the darkened side yard.

"Who's that over there watching us?"

Maggie turns around to look.

"Oh, that's just Louis. I call him Saint Louis. He's a good old soul. He likes to stargaze, too. Funny though, I thought he was going over to St. Catherine's to visit his cousin for a week. He asked me to keep an eye on his place. Guess he didn't go after all."

"You sure that's Louis? It looks like an old man I know, and he seems to be watching us."

Maggie is surprised by Frank's comment. "Well, of course. Who else would be sitting on his patio? Besides, he watches everybody."

Frank responds uneasily, "Yeah, of course, who else could it be?" He then picks up the energy, "So, Valerie thought you needed to be saved from being alone, huh? You never got serious with anyone?"

Maggie scrunches up her plump lips, rubs her model's chin and clears her throat. "Well, you know me, Frank. I'm kind of particular."

"Yeah, I remember you telling me that a few times. That's why I never thought I really had a chance with you."

"Never had a chance? Didn't you know I was madly in love with you?"

The flickering flame shows the color gathering in both of their faces. "Loved me?" Frank says. "You never said anything of the sort."

"No. I never did. *You* didn't, either."

"How could I say that," Frank says brashly, "when I saw you no more than a few times a year?"

"Well, Frank, you must be the densest guy in Ohio. You know we had to see each other, and we always picked up right where we left off. I never really saw anyone between your visits. What's more, I've only been on two or three dates since you stopped coming up here five years ago—and I never even asked them in!"

Frank pours out the watered remnant of his drink, then throws a crinkled napkin into the flame to watch it burst brightly like a magician's trick. He looks over to the neighbor who is now standing, pretending to look at stars.

"You sure that's Louis over there?"

"Jesus, Frank, don't change the subject. Did you love me or not?"

"Hell, I don't know. I don't know what I thought or what I knew. I'm here now, though, aren't I?"

She counters, "Yeah, so why are you here now? Why now, after five years of staying away? Did you come all the way up here just to torment me? To tease me?"

"Come on, Maggie. You know I'd never do anything to hurt you."

She moves to the edge of her chair and leans forward. "You wouldn't? You didn't think disappearing without so much as an explanation wouldn't hurt? Well, you're pretty damn wrong on that one, bud."

Frank takes a deep breath like a surfacing oyster diver and rubs behind his ear where the malignancy eats at his brain. He stops rubbing to put his forefingers in the corners of his eyes for deep digs.

"You going to tell me why you're here, or not?"

Frank begins to scour his eyes almost violently.

"Let me save you the pain, Frank. Let *me* tell *you* why you're here. You came up to say your goodbyes. You came up to tell me you're dying."

Somehow Frank settles even further back into his chair. He is suddenly a frightened child who has yet to learn to speak—as if he knows words mean something but has no understanding of them. His fright turns to hurt and confusion as he bites the forefinger of a clenched fist while resting his elbow on his horizontal wrist. His eyes well but he fights off the emotion.

The slouching child grows defiant and jumps up to toss his glass to the ground with a thud and demands, "How the hell do you know that? How do you know I'm dying?"

"Frank, my darling, you have no idea that I know Gloria? Yes, I know you're dying, and she wanted me to come visit you, but I couldn't do it."

Perplexed, Frank asks, "What do you mean, you know Gloria?"

Maggie stands, hands on her hips, and ignores his question. "I thought you were done with me, and I couldn't just show up there. I came close, though. I came so damn close. I couldn't bear the thought of not seeing you one more time. You're the man who stole my heart, then crumbled it like a cracker. But even more than wanting to see you, I couldn't stand to see you dying. I wanted to keep the thoughts of how you were—how we were. And now here you are, and I can't love you and now I can't even remember you the way you were. Damn you for taking that from me, Frank!"

She reaches down for more wine then drinks it straight from the bottle.

"And one more thing! I know you're in love with Julie, too!"

Frank steps toward her but stops as she holds her ground. He says, "I can't believe this. Gloria told you all this stuff? How'd you get to know her? She told you I was in love with Julie? I've never even dated Julie! What else do you *think* you know about me?"

"You mean what *don't* I know? I've been talking to Gloria for years, even before you stopped coming up here."

His pasty face stiffens. "Oh my God. How did all that start?"

"You're so silly. She called up here to talk to my mom and help arrange your dad's fishing trips. Then, you had her call up here to help arrange your early trips. I took some of the calls and hit it off with her. I guess after a while—women's intuition—she knew I was in love with you. I guess I was too inquisitive about you and what you were up to in your life. She'd call back sometimes just to talk and see how Mom and I were doing. I think she wanted to make sure I was never going to hurt you. Then, when she and I became phone friends, she wanted to warn me about how fickle you were and make sure that you weren't going to hurt *me*. She even sent flowers from the paper when Mom died. I've never even met her in person and she sent flowers. I never asked her, and she never told me, but I think she knew about your dad and my mom, too. She's a pretty smart lady."

"God, this can't be happening. Did she call to tell you I was coming up here this time?"

Maggie laughs with sarcasm. "Of course she did. She was looking out for you. That's how I knew to have all this ready and to have one of your favorite whiskeys. This night's no accident, Frank. Valerie was even in on it at the shop to tell you to come back while I was out getting all this stuff."

Frank fakes a chuckle and bends to pick up the glass. "Whoo-boy," he says as he drops a cube, splashes in some scotch, and expertly twirls the drink.

"I remember Gloria planting the seed a month ago that I should come up to relax and get my mind off things and to catch a few salmon. She even suggested that Russ would enjoy something like that. Boy, you women sure do know how to manipulate us men, don't you?"

Frank gulps his drink, then tosses the glass into a pile of mulch.

Maggie's posture relaxes. "I guess some women are better at it than others, but I didn't ask her to plant the seed. I told her that I didn't want to see you again and hoped you wouldn't come up. I guess she didn't believe me. I was a little mad when she called to tell me you were on your way up here."

A strong gust of wind flows across the fire pit to kick up embers and drag them through the open space between Frank and Maggie. Most fly off toward the darkness of a small open field adjacent to the bait shop. A single glowing ember lands on the top of the cooler which Maggie deftly knocks off with the back of her hand as if she were smacking the lid for being so careless.

Frank sits down and rocks his body back and forth trying to think of something to say. Maggie sits motionless.

"You really didn't know I loved you, Frank?"

Frank pulls on the back of his collar and tries to say something. It comes out an inaudible, slightly drunken mess. He stops speaking and crosses a leg over his knee, clumsily grabbing his ankle.

He coughs and tries again.

"Maybe I did know. I guess I wasn't sure. I just didn't know you gave up your life hoping I would love you back. I think there were so many things that I just ignored. I just pretended they weren't real."

Maggie says quietly, "Apparently I wasn't good at manipulating you to love me. I couldn't even get you to lie to me and say it."

"Let me ask you this. Are you glad that I'm here now?"

Maggie eases to Frank and holds his hand as they stand closely together. "Yes. I'm so very glad, Frank."

***

After leaving their elders, Russ and Valerie head down the well-worn path that snakes lazily through the brush. The trail is marked by dim blue lights on low posts, similar to airport runway beacons. After fifty yards the walkway opens to the platform of a descending wooden stairway illuminated by four yellow lights on higher posts. The water below is difficult to see, but the sound of a muffled surge clearly suggests that the fast-moving power of the Niagara is somewhere at the bottom of the wooden steps. Stretching in both directions along the American bank are small docks, also with yellow bug lights marking the river's boundary. A hundred yards across the river along the Canadian side is a marina where several dozen boats sleep for the night.

"It doesn't look like much right now with no moon," Valerie apologizes, "but when you can see the water it is pretty impressive."

Russ stares out over the void to the Canadian lights. "I think it's pretty impressive now, without even seeing the water. How far down is it?"

"Oh, I don't know. Forty, fifty feet, I guess. Maybe a bit more."

She pulls Russ's arm to lead him to the first step.

"C'mon, let's go down to the water."

Russ resists. "Are you serious? I can't even see ten feet. You want to go all the way down there?"

Valerie chuckles. "Oh, c'mon, Ohio. I won't let anything happen to you. Besides, the river is pretty calm by the docks and the moon will be up later. It'll be almost full tonight, and we'll be able to see up and down the river forever."

Russ gives in and Valerie deftly slides her hand down to curl her fingers around his sweaty palm before taking each cautious step toward the water. He gains more confidence with the descent, until at last they are standing on the floating rectangle.

She turns to him at the bottom with an enthusiastic smile glowing in the soft yellow light. "See? That wasn't so bad now, was it?"

"Not so bad. I'm just glad you were in front of me and knew where you were going."

She lets go of Russ's hand, takes her shoes off, and tosses them toward the middle of the landing, then eases onto the side of the dock, rolls up her jeans, and plunges her feet and calves into the darkness of the water.

She turns back slightly to see Russ standing safely in the center of the dock with mouth agape.

"Well, aren't you going to come over and put your feet in?"

He frowns as if the question were purely bombastic and not in need of a response.

"C'mon, it's okay."

"Uh, isn't it cold?"

"Just for the first few seconds, then it seems warm."

Russ takes off his tennis shoes and low-cut socks and tosses them over to where her shoes lay. He moves up next to her, but slightly behind, then sits cross-legged, too far from the edge to even get his toes wet.

She leans back, grabs his sleeve, and pulls him forward while he makes calculated and deliberate moves to scoot even with her.

She says devilishly, "It's okay. I'm not gonna to push you in."

He grudgingly rolls up his jeans to his knees, then slowly slips in a toe, then a foot, then down further until the water surrounds his shin. The insertion of his other leg is quicker, finding Valerie's tender skin where he lingers to massage their calves. The current creates eddies between their rubbing legs and the platform.

She asks in a soft voice, "There, that's not so bad, is it?"

Russ takes the opportunity to place his arm over hers and grasp her hand in mock fear.

"Well, if I fall in, you're coming in with me. So don't get any ideas."

"Oh, you're such a baby. Nobody's fallin' in."

She pauses. "But if you do, just let the river take you along and swim at a slight angle to a dock downriver. Just don't panic and try to get straight back to the bank. The river will win that fight."

Russ's bewildered look presses Valerie to add a guarantee. "But I've got you, so you aren't going anywhere, Ohio."

Russ forces a laugh. "Well, like I said, if I go in, you're coming with me, N-Y!"

Valerie turns Russ's pretend-fear-handholding into a tight squeeze of security and affection. He slides his hip closer to blend with hers. The water laps and roils around the platform and other nearby docks. Beyond the rhythm of those small waves the surging, unseen part of the river creates a steady resonance, like a summer wind over a swaying Kansas wheat field.

"So, waddaya think?"

"Well, the water isn't so bad after you get used to it."

"See, I told you. Now you just have to watch out that some giant sturgeon doesn't come along and bite off a toe."

Russ looks mortified.

"Just kidding! But there really are sturgeons in the river. They're leftover relics from the dinosaur days. Bet you didn't know that."

"No, I didn't. Not sure I'm glad to know now, either."

Valerie twists off the lid to the wine bottle, takes a couple big gulps, and hands it to Russ. He takes an even longer drink, then hands the bottle back. Valerie screws on the lid and sets it aside and lays back on the decking. She puts a hand under her head and pulls Russ back to join her. A tall tree at the top of the bank behind them forms a small canopy, but it is back far enough from the river to allow a good view of the India-ink sky and piercing stars.

Valerie says warmly, “If we lay here long enough, we’ll see a satellite or two go over.”

“Well, if we lay here long enough, I’m going to fall asleep from all the alcohol.”

“Stay with me, Ohio. This magnificent night can’t be wasted. We have to be awake for the view when the moon comes up.”

“I’m with you. I’m okay.”

Valerie points at the sky. “Look, right there above us. There goes a satellite.”

“Where?”

“Right there about eleven o’clock, headed to one o’clock.” Russ adjust his angle and squints his eyes but says he cannot see the moving dot.

She tries again. “Okay, see that little clump of three stars right there? It’s going right under them now.”

“Yes, there it is. Man, they move fast, don’t they?”

“Yep. It’ll get all the way around the world and back this way in about ninety minutes. The ones in geosynchronous orbit are visible up there too, but the human eye can’t tell them apart from the stars because they stay in the same spot over the earth.”

Russ turns to her, a bit amazed. “My goodness, you know a lot about the night sky. It’s rare to find such a beautiful science geek like you.”

“I’ll take that as a compliment, Russ, but I don’t know about the beautiful part. I’ll take the geek part, ’cause I think it’s important to be curious about stuff. If that makes me a geek, that’s okay by me.”

They lay still, scanning the heavens for more satellites. The cool, still air provides a crystal panorama that flaunts a dazzling Milky Way of distant worlds.

Russ asks, "Do you think there's life out there?"

"I think so," she says confidently. "If you think about the hundred billion or so galaxies in the universe, each with hundreds of billions of suns, I think there has to be some kind of life. Maybe not exactly like us, but given the sheer odds that earth just didn't happen as a one-off, unrepeatable event, there has to be some kind of smart beings out there. Don't you think?

"You've thought about this a lot, haven't you?"

"Well, nature just keeps repeating itself everywhere. I believe the chemistry is the same and the physics of space has to be the same everywhere. The same math, the same odds, so why the hell not?"

Russ moves even closer.

"Good point." Russ sighs. "Maybe some aliens are laying on their backs looking at our little sun wondering if we exist."

She sighs along, "I think they could be. Reminds me of Carl Sagan's book *Contact*. Did you ever read it?"

"No, but I saw the movie. One of my favorites. Jodie Foster was Ellie, right?"

"Yeah, the movie was pretty good too. Remember early in the story when Ellie told the evangelist that she didn't believe in God because science couldn't prove it—that she just couldn't take things on faith? Then after she traveled in time and met the alien, she told the congressional committee that they should believe her story even without proof. The only person who believed Ellie's story just happened to be the evangelist. He reminded Ellie that science couldn't prove everything, and some things just had to be taken on faith alone. The committee wouldn't believe her, but the preacher did, just because of his faith in her."

"Do you think he really believed her? Or did he just want to believe her because he was in love with her? They had a pretty interesting relationship, after all."

"Hmmm, that's pretty insightful," she says. "You think his love for her caused his faith in her?"

Russ shrugs. "Maybe."

The two lay in silence looking at stars while stirring the river with their feet. Several times they let their skin touch and linger.

Russ breaks the quiet and points to the sky. "Look, Ellie—that's what I'm going to call you now—there's a satellite right there. See it?"

"I was just getting ready to point it out to you."

He takes his hand out of hers, leans up to look out over the emptiness between the riverbanks, and kicks some water into the air.

"Hey, wasn't Carl Sagan an atheist?"

"I think he was agnostic," she says. "I don't think he believed either way. I guess he had trouble accepting things without proof, just like Ellie. Funny thing, though, the way the book ended, it seemed like he left the door open to accept that some things are possible even without evidence."

"Well, I can't see much beyond this dock," he declares, "but I *know* there is a lot of water between us and Canada over there, 'cause I can feel it and I can hear it. And you know what else? I have faith that this Captain Joe character is gonna lead us to some salmon tomorrow!"

"I sure hope so, Russ." She leans up and opens the bottle for a drink, then hands it to him. "Can I ask you another question?"

"Sure."

"Do you think Frank really just came up here because he wanted to fish, or was it an excuse to see my mom? Do you think he loves her?"

Russ finishes off the bottle and sets it behind them, then rubs his mouth across his sleeve.

"Uh, not sure. But you know, that's really several different questions. Maybe he wanted to come see her. Don't know about the love part. I didn't know your mom or you existed until we got up here, so it's hard for me to get a read on that. Maybe Frank loves your mom and doesn't really know it."

Russ stammers a bit as he continues. "I mean, think of it. How does somebody really know they love someone else—and how do they prove that love—even to themselves? They can say it and they can do all the things you would expect to show compassion, but how do you really know what they think or feel?

"I *can* tell you one thing, though. When we drove back to your bait shop tonight, it's like I could hear Frank's heart starting to race. He got all sweaty and it was like he was scared to get out of the car. Maybe his being scared to see your mom is some kind of proof he loves her."

Valerie has steel in her voice. "Or maybe he was just scared that mom was going to slug him or say something to embarrass him in front of you because he just flat out stopped coming up here. You know, he never got back in contact with her."

"Well," he concedes, "Guess that could have been it."

With sadness she says, "Or, maybe he was concerned that she wouldn't recognize him because of his cancer."

Baffled, Russ says, "How do you know that Frank has cancer? How would you know that?"

She continues, "Well, I'm—well, my mom, uh, she talks to Gloria in your office now and then. Gloria's told Mom all about what's going on with Frank. They've talked for years ever since she called up to arrange his fishing trips. Gloria knew that my mom has always had a thing for Frank. Well, she used to anyway, before he stopped coming up and he never called her to say why."

Valerie places her warm hand on Russ's cold fingers, squeezes tightly, and continues uneasily.

"I've, uh, I've known about you for a while, too."

He answers with no surprise in his voice. "Oh, have you now? And just exactly what do you know?"

"Well, for starters, your mom thinks you are a magnificent son. She told my mom several times that you saved her life."

"Saved her life?"

"She said you gave her purpose when your dad left."

"You know about that? If you know things like my dad leaving, I suppose there isn't much else you don't know."

"I just know bits and pieces, really," Valerie says apologetically.

The talking stalls and Russ pulls his feet out of the water to put his heels on the edge of the dock and wrap his arms around his knees.

"My feet are getting cold."

He begins to say something else, then interjects with a booming, "Wow! Look!" He points above the houses on the Canadian side. Did you see the trail on that one?"

She nods. "Oh yeah. That was really something, wasn't it? It may be left over from last month's Perseids. On clear nights like this before the moon comes up you can see several pretty good ones per hour. That was one of the brighter ones I've seen in a while. You should be here for the Leonids in November or the Geminids in mid-December—now those will be some great shows if we don't get cloud cover. This is supposed to be one of the best Geminids in years. I've been planning for that one on December 13.

"You know what's funny?" she continues. "Some people are fearful of meteors. They think if you see one, it means someone is going to die. My dad used to say crap like that. Of course someone's going to die. People die every day under meteors, whether you see them or not."

Russ turns his head to Valerie and places his cheek on his knees, still hunched over and hugging his legs. He looks at her, marveling, seeing an exquisite puzzle to be solved. She is still scanning the sky.

"You know, Russ..." She stops as she realizes Russ's gaze has been fixed on her. "What is it? What are you staring at?"

"Oh, sorry. I didn't realize I was staring. I just find you amazing. You seem so strong and so smart."

"Oh, I don't know about all that," she dismisses. "I guess maybe when you grow up without a dad, it can make you stronger and you have to figure out certain things. You did it too, so you're probably stronger than you even realize."

"Yeah, you may be right. You know my dad left my mom. So, what happened with your dad? Where's he?"

She stretches to the sky, arches her back, and lets out a moan of fatigue and petulance.

"I was waiting for that one. Well, I might as well tell you. A good newspaper guy would find out anyway. My...my dad jumped into the upper Niagara when I was just a little kid. He was really sick, dying actually, with some rare cancer that we think he got at the chemical company. He just couldn't take it anymore and he jumped and went over the falls."

She turns to him with radiating anger.

"I've never forgiven him for it. He chose to die instead of spending even a few more days with me and Mom. I've always thought it was selfish. I was just a kid and Mom didn't even get to say goodbye. And Jesus, you know what else? Captain Joe found his body floating just a little way up from here. The poor man snagged the body and kept it close to his boat until the river patrol came to pull it out. Can you imagine that shit?"

Russ lets go of his knees and leans over. He puts his arm around her shoulders. "I'm so sorry. That had to be rough."

"I think it was harder on my mom. Grandma had just died a few months earlier, too. My grandpa ran off to California with some woman about ten years earlier and Mom was left with lots of bills, a crappy little bait shop that my dad actually hated, and a kid to raise.

"But you know what? Joe got the town to rally around her. They raised money to pay bills and saw to it that the bait shop got fixed up real nice. The people here basically adopted us. They did all kinds of repairs to the shop. New roof, new furnace, new floors, and paint. Everyone helped, never wanting a penny in payment. Then Mom made it a successful business, paid those people back anyway, and raised me at the same time."

Russ smiles sympathetically. "That's pretty awesome. She did one hell of a job, too. That's sort of like back in Le Fleur when my dad left. Me and my mom and a few aunts and uncles were the only blacks in town. But a lot of folks saw to it that we would be okay, especially Frank and his dad. They put a lot of faith in my mom and me at the paper. But my mom really worked hard. She accepted no excuses and paid what she could for my college, and she got student loans. Mom never said it, but I think Frank really paid for a lot of my college. He never let on, of course."

Valerie picks at the edge of the wooden dock while Russ puts his feet back in the water and leans forward to try and see the vortices around his legs.

"Russ, how long do you think Frank has? I've seen photos, and he doesn't look very good compared to those."

He tries to hide his surprise at the question by yawning and rubbing his forehead. He breathes deeply and thinks about his answer. He starts to speak, then thinks some more.

He bites his thumbnail and mumbles, "I'm not really sure. A couple months, maybe."

He straightens and speaks more clearly. "Part of me thinks he came up here to end it, to kill himself."

"Oh my God, Russ. Why do you say that?"

"I'm not sure, really. Just the way he's acting. Some things he's said. It's like he's trying to do some things really quick, for the last time."

"Well, he does know he is dying, so why wouldn't he want to do some things first?"

He pulls a small shard from the decking and rubs it between his fingers before tossing it into the river.

"No, it's different than that. It's like he's in a hurry, like he's on a mission. He came up here for something, something serious. And he brought a gun with him. He's got it in the car right now."

With a manic pitch she asks, "A gun? He's got a gun? Holy crap! You don't think he would hurt Mom, do you?"

"Oh, God no. He'd never hurt your mom. I'm not sure he could hurt anyone, except maybe himself. I do think he wants to die up here, though. He loves it here, and I'm not sure he ever wants to go back to Ohio. There's too much hurt back there. Just yesterday, he was with a guy that shot himself. The guy died right in his arms. I think that's gotten him close to the edge."

Valerie moves around onto her knees facing Russ. She brushes her hair back and leans in for more details. But Russ just closes his eyes, then breathes deeply again to collect the smells of wood, trees, flowers, fish, seagulls and the lower Niagara.

"You mean, a guy shot himself and Frank was there?"

With a resigned exhale he recounts Fritz's standoff, then says, "Frank told the sheriff that the guy was finally giving up—going to give him the gun. But as the guy was getting up, he tripped and shot himself in the chest. That was that."

Valerie leans in closer to dissect Russ's face.

"Oh my God. That's terrible."

"Yeah, it wasn't a pleasant sight when they wheeled the guy out. Frank was pretty stunned. But in a way, it seemed like he wasn't really surprised, like he'd already foreseen it. I'm supposed to interview him this weekend and write the story for the paper. I think the tragedy got him thinking about taking his own life and having someone witness it and tell the story about it. Maybe me."

She jumps up and the platform rocks, forcing Russ to grab the edge under his knees to avoid falling in the river. In a whirlwind she gathers the socks, shoes, and wine bottle, and pulls on Russ's hand.

"Jesus! Come on, let's get back." She bounds up the stairway and into the darkness.

"What about the moon?" he begs. "Aren't we even going to wait for the moon to come up?"

"Sorry, but that's just not going to happen for us tonight," she squawks.

Valerie takes off in a near run along the path then stops at the clearing, causing Russ to bump into her. They collect themselves, seeing Frank and Maggie embracing by the fire pit. The neighbor watches from his patio as the former lovers hug and weep together.

"Well," Russ says, "Looks like they made up. Hope it sticks."

# Chapter Twenty-Four

Joe expertly backs the trailered boat down the ramp into the water of Lewiston Landing. At the precise depth he jumps out of his pickup, scampers around to climb onto the trailer hitch, flips a lever, and cranks the winch loose to float the boat back. The silver hull is emblazoned with blue letters, "Cinelli's Niagara River Guides." He then scrambles onto the dock to tie off the boat before hopping in to fiddle with the GPS and depth finder near the steering wheel. He accomplishes in sixty seconds what would take most seasoned captains several minutes to achieve.

Frank and Russ finish their descent of the thirty-foot wooden stairs to the concrete pier. They lower the cooler and bags of snacks to the ground and alternately flex their arms and exercise their hands. Russ looks out over the river. He flares his nostrils to gulp in the damp, misty air while straining to make out the veiled Canadian shoreline to the west.

A cheerful Joe yells, "Hey, sleepyheads. Glad to see you guys decided to join me."

Frank tries to be enthusiastic. "Hey Joe, how you doing, young man?

"I'm doing pretty good, but I'd be a hell of a lot better if you slackers got over here and helped with the boat. We're wasting daylight!"

The novice fishermen pick up their loads and move to the side of the boat and lower them again. Joe leaps out to give Frank a hearty bear hug.

"Wow, it's good to see you, Frank. It's been too long, my friend."

Frank holds on for an extended moment, then the men clumsily separate. "Yes, it has. Way too long."

Before Frank can make an introduction, Joe extends his arm and grabs Russ's hand.

"You must be the brains of this outfit."

"I don't know about that. I'm Russ. I'm a reporter at Frank's paper."

Frank interrupts. "Bull crap. This is my new managing editor. He's one smart, hardworking little shit. A better writer than I ever was."

"Well, that's good to know," Joe laughs, "because I've seen some of your work. Hopefully he's a better fisherman than you, too. I haven't managed to teach you a thing in twenty-five years. It's good to meet ya, Russ. I hope you'll have some good fish stories to tell when ya get home."

"Well, I've heard a lot about you and how great a fisherman you are, so I'm pretty hopeful to get a salmon or two."

"I don't know that I'm such a great fisherman, but I have a feelin' we just might get lucky. It's going to be a gorgeous day."

"Is the limit still three per man?" Frank asks.

"Yep. Since there are three of us, our boat can bring back nine and I won't be catching any. So, which one of you will get the most?"

"I'm just a beginner, so Frank is bound to get the most," Russ says.

Joe climbs back into the boat and reaches up to grab the cooler and bags and places them neatly along the inside hull where fishing poles are clasped to the wall.

"Well, we sure aren't going to get any fish tied up here. Hop in, boys."

Only a couple years younger than Frank, Joe has the energy of a much younger man. He helps Frank into the boat and tries to hide his surprise at his old friend's unsteadiness. Frank missteps onto the deck and Joe's eyes meet Russ's with unease.

"Okay, make yourselves comfortable, guys," Joe says as he jumps back up onto the dock. "I'm going to take the trailer up. I'll be right back. We'll be catching fish before you know it."

Frank and Russ study Joe as he darts to his truck and drives up the steep road to the top of the cliff. Joe does everything fast. No wasted motion. Abundant confidence. He has spent a lifetime around the river, around boats and inexperienced weekend fishermen. He has honed his skills of teaching and entertaining and has become widely known as the best guide from Erie to Rochester. He wins nearly every fishing tournament in the area and often bags the biggest buck while hunting on Grand Island. However, his reputation as the best outdoorsman in the Niagara region hasn't changed his humble approach to life. Doing things with passion and precision is all he knows. He just *does* and lets everyone else talk about it.

His guide business used to be his only job and he made a fine living. As the most sought-out fishing guide on the Niagara, he has hosted trips with politicos, professional athletes, outdoor writers, and numerous hosts of television fishing shows. But the trips he cherishes most are the ones with novice fishing parents and their kids. These are the people that come back time and time again to forge lasting friendships.

Joe now fishes less as life and career have migrated beyond the river. For the past decade he has been working full time as an engineer in nuclear power plants, traveling around the country overseeing equipment repairs. His brother Chris has filled the void as a full-time fishing guide and is building his own stellar reputation. Now, Joe only has time to host a few fishing trips a year with very special clients, his true friends. He picks and chooses when he wants to work and fish, so he can spend ample time with his beautiful wife and two daughters.

The good and simple parts of life are not a mystery to him. Humor, friendship, honesty, and a few well-placed, mildly salty jokes keep the fishing experiences relaxed. He gives everything he can to his friends, family, and Grand Island's Whitehaven Road Baptist Church. Having always admired Joe, Frank would choose to be him if it were an option.

Russ continues to stare at Joe parking the truck high above them while Frank sits down on the edge of the hull with a labored groan.

Russ turns at the sound. "Are you okay?"

"No, not really. Kind of queasy."

"Well," Russ continues mockingly, "Maybe you shouldn't have finished last night and started this morning with pills and whiskey."

He pauses, then adds, "And, you should have eaten that cinnamon roll I brought you from the coffee room."

Frank rubs the back of his neck and then pulls his stocking cap back down over his ears.

"Maybe so, but I just have trouble eating in the morning."

Frank stands again to prove he is well enough and they look at each other's faces in wonderment, imagining what this day will bring. Perhaps there will be hearty laughs about bumbling misses of fish to provide a reprieve from the routine of life and the thought of what comes at the end of it. Or, perhaps the day will be a sobering reminder of the intermittent strengthening and weakening of this relationship. As most people do, the men have spent years assuming there would be ample time to corroborate their shared admiration. Trying now to convey those sentiments would seem insincere, with words falling like rain of regret to rust the nostalgic affection.

"Did you call your mom this morning, Russ?"

"Yeah, I talked to her while you were in the bathroom."

"Everything okay back there?"

"Yeah, of course. You know she can handle anything."

"Yeah, I know. She always has."

Russ's smile fades. "She is awfully worried about you, though. She said you haven't returned any of her texts. How come?"

"I'm on vacation. Besides, I've got you to take care of me."

Russ's smile returns. "Yeah, that's what I told her."

Joe bounds down the tall wooden stairs, unties the boat, and jumps behind the wheel at mid-starboard side. He turns the key to snarl life into the one-hundred-fifty horsepower outboard Honda motor. He pushes buttons on the GPS mounted on the dash, puts his jacket on over his sweatshirt, and looks around to see that everything is securely in its place.

Frank asks, "Joe, you want us to sit on the floor while you go fast upriver?"

Without looking up Joe says, "Not right now. We're going downriver and out on the lake to troll the ledge out by the red buoy. We're in a period of transition. The salmon have been out there staging before they come into the river to spawn. You guys can just sit up in the seats for now."

Frank responds with faint disappointment. "Oh, okay." He had hoped to fish in the gorge by the power plants where the river is fast, the cliffs are breathtaking, and the challenge of holding the reel and setting the hook pits man's skill against the cunning of the fish. Trolling the lake puts most of the contest on the speed of the boat and action of the downriggers to hook the fish, with little chance of failure. The upper river is the experience he wanted Russ to conquer. The two guests maneuver to the elevated swivel seats, with Frank at the bow and Russ taking the stern. Joe pulls the throttle back slightly to reverse the boat from the dock then pushes the lever forward and turns the wheel briskly to move out into the river.

Joe has spent his adult life watching and interpreting his clients' dispositions and can tell Frank is not enthusiastic about fishing the lake. He says, "You know, if we don't find the fish out on the ledge they've moved up toward Devil's Hole and we'll go up there and knock the snot out of them."

Frank snaps back to attention. "Okay, that sounds great."

Joe slowly guides the boat out, not far from the docks, and drifts downriver with the current. As he navigates, he studies the water on the side of the boat closest to the shore. He puts the throttle into idle, grabs a long pole with a fine mesh net on the end, dips the net into the water, then pulls out an animated load of flopping minnows. He opens the live well below Frank's feet and deposits the net into the water with a swirling motion.

Joe says, "Those might come in handy if we want to switch for walleye or smallies."

He guides the boat to the middle of the river and studies the surface as he leans forward to scan both sides of the bow. Frank asks Joe what he is looking for.

"Just checkin' to see how the water looks today."

Joe finishes his scrutiny and guides the boat to the middle of the river where the current pulls the boat along.

"Hold on, guys. We're going to go a bit faster."

Joe pushes the throttle forward with ever-increasing force and the twenty-one-foot aluminum Lund Pro-V effortlessly pushes the water aside. The men are pressed back in their seats as the boat cuts a moderate pace up the border between the neighboring countries. Now and then Joe looks forward from side to side of the bow to absorb more clues from the river.

Russ scans the ridges of the tall cliff edges on either side of them where the brims have begun descending toward Lake Ontario. Houses that were once perched sixty feet above the banks back at Lewiston are now only twenty or thirty feet above their heads. The houses on the Canadian side appear to be grander with their white-columned porches, and they sit back further from the cliff. The Canadian shoreline is punctuated with a few large marinas, while the US bank projects more numerous, private docks. The Lund approaches Youngstown on the right where the historic retail buildings rise above the treetops. The crown of the silver water tower next to the motel peeks just over the rooflines. Masts of congregated sailboats create a forest on the water where a concrete ramp comes down to the ever-widening river. Just ahead is the opening to Lake Ontario. Frank nods over to the sailboats.

"Hey Joe. Tell Russ what those things are."

"Those things floating in the water over there? Those are speed bumps!"

Frank and Joe laugh, but Russ has to think for a moment.

"Oh, speed bumps!" he finally says. "I get it. Good one, Joe."

Frank closes his eyes in mock embarrassment.

"Okay boys, you're going to want to climb down now. You need to sit on the floor and lean back against the platforms. And Russ, turn your hat around. We're going for a quick ride out to the ledge."

Joe secures his hat and puts on his sunglasses. He pushes the throttle forward to build thunder in the motor and push large wakes to the sides. The hull periodically smacks the water and tosses spray into the air, which sometimes splatters on Russ. Frank feels the bouncing intensely on his back and in his throbbing head. He is uncomfortable but enjoys watching the pleasure on Russ's face.

Frank yells, "You ever been this fast on a boat before, Russ?"

The noise deafens.

"What?"

Joe turns back to repeat Frank's question. "He wants to know if you've ever been this fast in a boat before."

Knowing he won't be heard, Russ shakes his head no, takes off his hat, and whips it around the air like a cowboy busting a bronco.

With a devilish smile, Joe pushes on the silver lever to unleash more of the big motor's fury onto the lake. Russ strains his neck to see past Joe and Frank and over the raised bow where the expanse of open water spreads out before them. He squints from the cold wind slicing at his eyes and cheeks and reaches up to hold onto his hat. He roots around inside his coat with his other hand to find his sunglasses, puts them on, and gives Frank an exhilarating smile and a thumbs up. Frank purses his lips and returns a wink and a nod.

Past Youngstown sits an enormous stone-walled fortress where the shore juts to a point before sliding to the east. American and British flags are joined by a white flag, all flying above the tourists milling about the manicured lawns. Russ points to the massive garrison and says something inaudible. Frank smiles, points at his ear, and shakes his head in deafness.

The shorelines spread away to the east and west to untie the men from civilization. Before them is a watery horizon with small ripples created by a light, unfettered breeze. Joe keeps pushing the Lund in a straight line while Russ looks back to see where the houses blend into a dissolving tree line. After a few more minutes of moderate speed, Joe smoothly pulls back on the throttle, allowing the boat's bow to settle down on the smooth water.

"Okay Russ, you can jump back on your seat. Frank, I'll bring your seat back here on the floor close to Russ in a minute."

He pushes on the GPS buttons, then hops about the hull to prepare fishing poles with bait and nestles them into downrigger sleeves to trail behind the boat.

"Watch the two poles left of the motor, Frank, and Russ, you watch the two on the right. If a fish strikes, the line will release from the cable and the rod tip will snap up. When that happens, grab that pole out of the holder, steady the crank, and pull up smoothly. Don't jerk too hard or you might pull the hook right out of the fish's mouth. Then reel in, nice and steady."

Joe moves back to his dashboard seat and eases the throttle forward to push the troll slowly eastward. Frank turns to watch the poles facing the distant shores while Russ turns his seat to watch the poles toward open water.

"Look, Frank," Russ says. "There's a big ship out there."

Frank swivels around for a glance, then back to watching his rods.

"Sure is. Hey Joe. Remember that time we went out of St. Catherine's and that big freighter went by about a hundred yards from us? I thought we were going to get smashed."

The two men carry on the conversation without looking at each other.

"Yeah, I remember," Joe says with fondness. "We were out about ten miles trolling in the big boat that day. I think you all crapped your pants. Your dad kept asking, 'Joe, you see that ship coming at us, right?' I kept saying, 'What ship?' He thought I'd lost it."

Frank laughs. "Yeah, I think he'd already had half a jug of wine by then and was a little tipsy. It was the funniest thing to see him so scared and slurring his words. I think that ship had a hammer and sickle on the smoke stack, didn't it?"

Joe responds while staring at the depth finder.

"Yeah. It was a big old Russian freighter, I think. Man, that was a long time ago. What, fifteen years?"

"More like twenty. We were just in our thirties then. Well, at least I was. Maybe you weren't thirty yet."

"Holy cow, we're both old farts now, aren't we? My God, Frank, you started coming up here before my girls were even born. Now they're almost out of college."

"Oh, my, that doesn't seem possible. How are the girls?"

"Amanda and Alyssa are fantastic." Joe beams. "They're magnificent women, gifts from God. Ingrid has been a wonderful role model for them. They had no choice but to turn out good."

"You know you had a big part in it, Joe."

"Maybe, but moms are the real force in kids' lives."

"I think you may be right," Frank admits.

The conversation stalls. Joe keeps pushing the boat toward the red buoy a couple hundred yards ahead. He watches the water and finder intently for depth and marks for fish. Frank and Russ keep watching the rod tips as the sun breaks through the mist. Scattered boats troll in both directions at different distances from the ledge. Frank breaks the silence after a few minutes.

"So, Joe, you been fishing much lately?"

"Naw. Not really. It's been pretty busy at work all summer and I've been traveling a lot. Sure glad you're here, though. I needed this as much as you guys."

"Well, it's been a long time," Frank says. "I just needed to get out of the office. I thought Russ could stand a little time away from a crying baby and nagging wife, too."

"You have a new baby, Russ?" Joe asks.

"He's not much of a baby anymore. Really a toddler. His name's Nicholas. He's a great little kid. I love being a dad."

"Yeah, there's nothing like it. Greatest thing in the world."

Russ looks behind him to see the delight on Joe's face.

"I think you're right. I can't imagine anything better."

Frank says, "You remember when we stayed out at Four Mile Creek State Park and you and the girls came out for the bonfire and hot dogs?"

"Oh yeah," Joe smiles. "They couldn't have been more than five or six."

"Dad thought they were the best things ever. I think he regretted never having any daughters. He talked about your girls all the time."

Joe doesn't answer right away but keeps looking at the finder.

"Okay guys, we're marking some fish. Keep an eye on those rod tips."

"I think I'm going to be the first to get a fish, Joe!" Russ says.

Frank chuckles. "You may be the first, but I'll betcha I get the biggest."

"Oh yeah? You wanna bet?"

"Well, maybe I do," Frank says.

Russ asks, "You wanna get in on this bet, Joe?"

Joe crosses his arms. "Well, who's paying for the trip today?"

"Why does that matter?" Russ asks.

"Whoever writes that check always goes down in my record book as catching the biggest fish. How do you think I've stayed in the charter business so long?"

Frank enjoys a deep belly laugh, then the duped young man grows his own smile and shakes his head with amusement.

"I should have known you two would conspire against the rookie."

Joe responds unsympathetically, "Just wait until you have to pass the rookie initiation."

Frank laughs again. Russ rubs his chin and wonders about that ritual.

The men shift in their seats in anticipation of a strike. The moments pass with no rod bouncing to life while the Lund keeps moving in a straight line. Watching of poles and instruments continues. The big red buoy slides past the boat about twenty yards on the left.

"Joe," Russ asks, "You mind if I have a beer?"

"Of course not. I'll get it for you, sport. You keep watching your lines."

Joe slides to the cooler and pulls out a beer, then pauses. "You want one too, Frank?"

"Not right now. I might have some whiskey in a bit."

Joe opens the beer and hands it to Russ.

"Here ya go. A beer before seven-thirty in the morning always helps the fish bite. Every time someone gets distracted, the fish decide to show up."

"Man, I hope so."

The troll continues without strikes and the minutes lag into boredom. Frank stands up to stretch his legs and remove his outer windbreaker. Joe alternates watching instruments and looking back to the men and the bent poles. Nearly simultaneously Russ and Frank yawn, stretch, take off their hats, and scratch their heads. Russ finishes off this beer and sets the can next to the hull wall.

Frank fractures the quiet. "Hey Joe, can you reach in that bag and toss me that bottle of scotch?"

Joe looks at his watch. "Eight o'clock. I think that's a perfect strategy."

Frank pulls the cork with a *thwump* and takes a swig right from the bottle. He smiles in delight, reaches into his pocket, throws a couple pills into his mouth, and washes them down with another swill. He closes his eyes, breathes deep, and gives a small cough.

"You want a nip, Joe?"

"No thanks. I need to be stone sober if either the Coast Guard or game warden comes up to check us out."

Frank takes another hit, recorks the bottle, and reaches it out to Joe.

"Okay, but that stuff sure clears a man's head."

Joe takes the bottle, scans the label, and puts it back in the bag.

"That's good stuff. I'll have a drink when we get back to shore and start cleaning the fish."

"Hey Joe," Frank says, "Is the state of New York still putting thousands of fingerlings in Lake Ontario every year?"

"Oh yeah. But it's more like several million with all the species combined."

"You know, Russ," Frank says, "the salmon go upstream to spawn, but most of the fish aren't fertile. They're just going through the motions, but somehow their instinct keeps driving them up that river, even though they weren't hatched there. Somehow they know that's where they're supposed to die."

Russ stops staring at his lines. "Is that really true, Joe?"

"Well, kind of. The fish are still mostly fertile and there is some spawning in some of the lake's tributaries, but the water temperature and silt level in the Niagara keep most of the eggs from making it to hatchlings. So, Frank's right. Without the fingerlings being released every year there wouldn't be much salmon and trout fishing around here."

"How long do the fish live?" Russ asks.

"About two to four years for the king salmon. A few will make it to five or six, but they all die after spawning. The females live a few days after the run and the males a few weeks."

"Why do they die?"

"Well, salmon don't feed much while spawning. They have one mission, and that's to get upriver and reproduce. They die of starvation and exhaustion. But the trout make it back to the lake after spawning and they can live longer, but they don't get as big."

Russ asks for another beer and a Little Debbie oatmeal sandwich cookie and Joe tosses them to him.

Russ sighs. "Well, at least the salmon get to go out with a bang."

"You got that right," Joe says. "I'm like the salmon. When I can't do it anymore, I might as well die and be ground up into fish food."

Joe realizes his comment may have made Frank uneasy. But he also realizes he cannot appear to be overly empathetic about a situation of which he is not supposed to be aware. The comment passes flippantly, just as it would have in years past when discussion of death would have been just another topic to pass the time.

Without a single strike Joe reaches the point of impatience. "Okay, boys. We're outta here. There's been a big change from Friday's report. They must be getting upriver. Frank, you jump back up front for a minute while I get the rods."

Joe replaces Frank's seat onto the bow and the men settle down onto the floor as Joe pushes the throttle well forward. The rush of wind and smacking of bow on the water seem even more intense on the trip back toward the river. The bow slams down hard and water is sprayed into Russ's face, cold and invigorating. He takes off his sunglasses, wipes his face with his arm, and smiles.

Frank is glad to be going up to the gorge where he wanted to start the day's experience but feels an unease about the possibility of not catching any fish. That would make for an expensive boat ride and dampen Russ's desire for ever returning. A haunting thought of the tradition ending once and for all brings a hollow shudder of melancholia.

***

The boat continues cutting south and zips into the river past Youngstown, Lewiston Landing, and then the dock where

Valerie and Russ deliberated existential uncertainties. The river is soon squeezed hard by the rocky walls, and the water's turbulence grows. Tall trees cluster thicker at the top of the cliffs to paint an early autumn burlesque show. Niagara turns a bit to the left, and once around the bend the boat passes under the massive Queenston-Lewiston Bridge. The steel arch stretches across the water more than three hundred feet overhead to connect the two countries.

On the right just past the QL Bridge are the imposing walls of Ontario's Sir Adam Beck Hydroelectric Generating Station. The tan walls have vertical columns embedded in the concrete that appear to grow out of the turbine building along the water. The colossal structure stretches several hundred yards along the gorge to form a buttress that reaches to the bluffs high above.

Further upriver to the left on the American side are similar walls of New York's Robert Moses Power Station. This wall is not as long as the Canadian plant but seems even taller. Balanced at the top is the Power Authority's large square indoor viewing area that resembles a glass-and-steel fort. Here tourists can see miles downriver to the lake and upriver to the mist of the falls. Or, they can look straight down several hundred feet and see men battling on the shoreline for their own salmon trophies.

The river between the two power plants appears as a roiling pot of water just before it breaks into a full boil. The bottom of the gorge is still in the shadow of the American bluff, but the deep green glass-bottle color of the water changes hues slightly with the reflected sunlight bouncing off the Canadian cliff. At the ends of the giant power plant walls are rocky outcroppings punctuated by car-sized boulders. Here a few fishermen scale down and risk falling and drowning for the chance to haul in a week's worth of meals.

Just ahead, at the entrance to Devil's Hole, other boulders peek up in the river to prevent the Lund from navigating any further. A dozen millennia ago a taller Niagara Falls sat in this spot. The face of the prehistoric falls receded several feet each year until it finally arrived at its current location, around the bend and several miles upstream. The fall's erosion has now been reduced to a couple inches a year, thanks to the diversion of most of the river's flow into channels and reservoirs above the cliffs on each side. From there, tunnels feed the hungry power plant turbines far below at the river's banks. Given enough time, perhaps millions of years, the falls will recede all the way back to Buffalo and Lake Erie. When that happens, Lake Erie will spill out to flood the basin to connect with Lake Ontario. The city of Buffalo, if it were to still exist, would be wiped away in the midst of a conjoined super lake. Frank read this and told others, who either did not believe or seemed not to care. That puzzled him.

Joe pulls back on the throttle where rocks have made the water broken and choppy. The hull lowers and the boat moves ahead slowly, just a few feet from the rocks.

"You guys can jump back up now," Joe says, pushing the throttle to idle. "We'll start here."

He scurries to the bow, bends down around Frank, and plunges the trolling motor into the water. Then he rises to toe-tap the trolling control pad on the bow platform. He steps away from the pad, and the electric motor stops while the boat continues to drift downriver at the perfect angle. Joe takes a rod from the portside wall brackets, opens a small cooler, and removes a one-inch round skein of roe. He nimbly baits the hook and joins Russ to the rear.

"Here you go, Russ," Joe says. He hands Russ the rod and reel. "You ready?"

Apprehensive, Russ says, "I—I guess so."

Joe goes through a dizzying array of instructions for dropping the line, managing slack and bouncing sinker, avoiding snags, and setting the hook.

"Okay, Joe. I think I got it."

Frank watches in amusement as his young protégé holds onto the pole like a baffling lightning rod ready to be jolted from the heavens. Russ pushes the button and line drops straight down. The sinker hits bottom, and he turns the handle to engage the reel and bring the tackle just up off the riverbed. The rod bends slightly from the weight of the sinker and the tip bobs up and down a few inches each time the lead weight hits and bounces. The line lingers behind the boat. After a few moments the rod straightens, which indicates the sinker is dragging on a rise in the riverbed. The line slackens from loss of tension.

"There's the slack, Russ. Reel it in a bit," Joe says.

Russ complies, and the slack disappears. The rod tip bends and bobs again from sinker weight. Russ inhales deeply, trying to stay calm.

"That's it, Russ," Joe says. "Just keep lifting a bit when you need to get that line taut. If there's a lot of slack, reel up some more, but if you can't feel the bottom any more, let more line out. Gotta keep that bounce on the bottom."

In seconds Joe has another pole baited and hands it off to Frank at the bow. Frank releases his line toward the middle of the river. Frank hasn't forgotten the strategy and smiles are exchanged between captain and learned student.

Joe glances back at Russ, who is concentrating intently on his mechanics of bounce, lift, drop, and crank. Joe baits a third line, then reaches the pole out over the side and tosses the line a few feet out toward the shore. He sets the depth and clicks up the reel, continually scanning back and forth from Frank, who appears confident, to Russ, who seems unsure. The boat leaves lines and sinkers behind as it drifts downriver toward the power plants.

Frank's energy builds as his proficiency grows in keeping the sinker at the correct depth and out of a snag. He is relaxed. He is alive. He can breathe and concentrate on something he controls and forget about what is controlling and killing him.

Joe watches the currents. He steers the boat slightly, working his rod. He watches Frank and Russ. He watches the shore and the approaching power plants. He watches Frank and Russ again. He watches everything.

"OK guys, just another couple minutes on this drift, then we'll head back up and start all over."

The river moves the boat fast relative to the men fishing from the bank. The constant din of Niagara's mighty flow fades into background noise. Without direction, Frank reels in his line to check his bait and removes a piece of weed. He feels that the skein is still firmly hooked, then lets the line fall again with a plunk. The men work their poles as the boat drifts toward the wall of the Moses Power Plant turbine house.

The sound of a strange, muffled turbulence grows as the boat bobs closer to the garage door-sized openings that feed the turbines. "Okay guys, reel 'em up," Joe says. "We're going back up."

The men obey and begin to reel in their lines. Joe increases the throttle and begins to turn the wheel, then stops, alarmed. He takes up his binoculars and peers at the far end of the turbine wall.

"Oh my God. Gentlemen, you won't believe this!"

Frank stands up in front of his seat and turns in fear back toward Joe.

"What's wrong?" Frank says.

"Turbine fourteen is turned off at the end of the plant."

"Is that dangerous?"

Joe laughs. "No, it isn't, unless you call catching all the fish you want dangerous. They're going to be stacked up in there like cord wood!"

Russ asks, "What do you mean, Joe?"

"They're probably working on the turbine or something and when one is off, the fish will go there and rest in the calmer water before finishing their runs. We'll go over there and give them their last meals."

Joe keeps his eyes fixed where the power plant wall meets the rocky cliff as he steers the boat out to the middle of the river to drift past the idle turbine.

Russ asks, "So, you think we'll get some big fish in there?"

"Russ, I guarantee you're going to catch the biggest fish you've ever caught, probably bigger than you've ever seen. If you don't, your boss here doesn't have to pay for the trip!"

"I'll take that guarantee," Frank says. "And you know what, if I catch *my* biggest fish ever, I'll pay you double!"

"No need for that," Joe says. "But I'll also guarantee that your biggest fish beats Russ's biggest fish."

"That's okay by me, Joe," Russ says. "But I'm kind of worried about what I have to do for my initiation."

"Ha! You should be," Frank adds.

Joe works feverishly to rebait the poles as the boat glides under the QL Bridge and downriver. He hands off the baited poles to the fishermen and begins rigging the third as he shares his strategy for getting the limit.

"Here's the plan, guys. We're going back up to that turned-off turbine and I'm going to hold the boat smack dab over that calm water." The excitement builds in Joe's voice. "You guys will drop your lines straight down for a few seconds. When they hit bottom, you'll start reeling up slowly, and you'll get a strike before you know it. You don't have to worry about drift, bouncing your sinker, getting snagged, or anything. When you feel a tug, it's gotta be a fish. You just set that hook, lift up, and reel it in. The fish aren't really in a mood to eat, but that bait floating in front of their faces just ticks them off. They'll strike at it just to keep it from annoying them."

Joe turns the boat and heads back toward the turbine wall. Just past the QL Bridge they see a boat that appears close to swamping as it rotates in a huge eddy. One man in the imperiled boat is fighting the steering wheel and engine controls, while the other struggles at the stern to reel in a fish.

"What's going on over there, Joe?" Russ asks.

"Sheer stupidity. That guide has no idea what he's doing. It's his first year on the river and he doesn't know you don't take your boat close to a whirlpool. He's gonna get 'em both killed."

"What should he have done?"

Joe doesn't hear Russ's question as he maneuvers to hover about thirty yards away from the struggling men.

"Grab the big net, Frank. Put your life jackets on and Russ, you grab a couple more life jackets from that door on the side wall. We may need to fish these guys out in a minute."

The men put their poles on the deck and do as they are told. They watch in horror as the other boat spins, with its stern dipped into the vortex and bow angled up into the air a good twenty degrees.

"Saving these jerks is going to kill our chances for getting our salmon. What assholes," Frank says.

Joe shakes his head and sneers. "The captain should have cut the damn line. His client has a lunker on there and he can't stand to let it go."

The man fighting the fish at the descending stern throws his rod and reel angrily into the whirlpool, scampers to the bow, and grabs the front transom. The man at the wheel lays on the throttle and the boat finally escapes the current. Violent hand gestures and swearing erupt as the fortunate men head downriver toward Lewiston.

"Wow," Frank says, "I'd love to hear their conversation when they get back to the dock." He lets out a sigh of relief. "Glad we didn't have to go in there after them. Now we can get back to the fish!"

Russ picks up his pole. "I wonder if the captain is going to make the guy pay for the rod he tossed overboard!"

The men laugh, and Joe resumes the push against the current to the power plant. He slows the boat as it approaches the convergence of the turbine house and the rocky cliff wall. He then jumps to the bow and dips the trolling motor in the river and hurries back to the steering wheel. He taps the throttle slightly to find the perfect idle to float the boat over the calm water.

"Okay guys, this is it. Come down off the platforms and stand on the lower deck to fish. Frank, you drop your line on the side toward the bank. Russ, you drop yours on the other side. I'm going to drop my line off your side too. If one of you gets a fish hooked, the other guy needs to reel in fast, so we don't get tangled up."

Joe watches the two men drop their lines with successive plunks and makes sure they set the cranks and begin to reel up slowly before he drops his own line.

"That's it, guys. Good job."

Within a few seconds Frank snaps up his rod violently and begins to crank. The weight on the end of the line is gone, and the sinker and bait are near his rod tip.

"Damn it, I screwed that up!" Frank yells.

"Don't worry about it. Your bait looks good. You just jerked a little too hard. Drop your line again, you'll get it."

"Joe! I got one," Russ bellows.

Joe turns to see that Russ's rod is seriously bent as he strains to turn the crank. Joe snaps up on his own rod and walks it to the front of the boat and hands it off to Frank.

"Here, put your rod down and you get this one up while I help Russ."

Frank lays his rod against the side wall and begins to struggle with Joe's pole.

Joe moves back, picks up the big net and leans out over the side of the boat in anticipation of Russ's fish breaching the surface.

"You have a nice steelhead, Russ."

Russ keeps his eye on the line that now extends farther out into the river. "How do you know that, Joe?"

"I can tell by the fight. I've been doing this a while."

Russ's line goes slack and he reels with no resistance. He slumps the handle to his belt and moans dejectedly. "Oh crap. I lost it."

"No sweat, Russ. You let him swim back toward you and weren't reeling in fast enough to take up the slack. Gotta keep that line taut. Finish reeling up while we get Frank's fish."

Joe moves forward with the net and leans out again. Frank cranks the handle evenly but with strain.

"You got a small king on there, Frank. Okay, stop reeling. Keep that rod tip up and walk back to the middle of the boat."

Frank nearly trips as he steps back, and Joe catches him by the waist.

"Easy, big fella. We got this."

Joe leans out a bit further, extends the big net into the water, makes a swipe, and captures the angry salmon. He lays the net on the deck with the fish still struggling to escape. He turns the boat toward the middle of the river to start drifting downstream while Frank and Russ huddle around the flopping salmon.

"Man," Russ says. "That's a good-looking fish. Could be the biggest one I've ever seen."

Frank takes a deep breath. "God. That was fun."

Joe moves between them with a pair of pliers and a club. He raps the flopping fish on the head to stun it, removes the hook, and untangles it from the net.

"Well, this one's only a couple years old, about twelve, twelve and a half pounds. We're going to get some a lot bigger than this one. Russ, you got a camera?"

Joe grabs Frank around the shoulders and hands him the fish by the gills while Russ pulls out his phone to snap a photo.

"Take another one, Russ. Frank, hold that fish out in front of you a bit more. Yeah, that's it. Make it look a little bigger."

Joe takes the fish and opens a large live well in the deck floor. He gently places the fish in the hold and moves it back and forth in the water to revive it. He drops the door shut and gets into the cooler for bait, then rigs the poles again. In a couple minutes he has the boat back upriver to the turbine wall to start all over again.

Frank and Russ are poised to drop their lines. They know they are in a race to get a fish hooked since the other has to reel in and watch the action.

"Okay men, drop 'em."

The men release their lines, wait a few seconds, and reel up slowly.

"Joe," Russ says, "That fish Frank caught really doesn't count for him, does it? I mean, it was you who set the hook."

Joe smiles. "What do you think, Frank? Should that count for your total or mine?"

"Well, anyone can set a hook, right? The real work is getting it to the boat. So, yeah, I'm counting that as my catch."

"There you have it, Russ. Frank one, you nothing. But remember, I might be handing my pole off to you next, so it may all even out."

"Well, I'll be ready then."

Frank yells, "Got one, Joe!"

Russ reels in his line dejectedly, and Joe gets busy attending the angle of the boat to allow drift away from the turbine house and into the flow of the river.

Frank's pole is bent to near maximum arch.

"Easy, Frank. You have a giant king on there. Could be close to thirty pounds. He's gonna run out into the river. Just let 'im take the line when he wants. Whatever you do, keep that rod tip up. If you feel any slack, that means he's coming back at us—then you keep that rod tip up and reel in like the devil. You remember that?"

"Yep. I got this."

"This may take a while. You up for it?"

Frank nestles the rod handle on top of his belt buckle for support and holds the arching pole high above his head.

"We'll see. I'll go as long as I can. If I get too tired, I'll hand it off to Russ. You okay with that, Russ?"

"Sure, but I bet you can take this guy."

The boat begins to float swiftly backward, downriver. The line stretches out over the bow toward the eddy where catastrophe nearly struck earlier. The unraveling reel whines as the monster fish swims away. The reel stops unwinding as the fish pauses and Frank manages to lower, crank, and lift. After a few turns the reel hums again as the salmon heads further upstream away from the boat.

"Damn it!" Frank gasps.

Joe keeps the boat pointed toward the fish and the swirling vortex. "Okay, Frank. I'm going to take the boat up to it. Try to reel in fast as we go toward it. Remember, no slack."

Perspiration forms on Frank's brow even though the fight has lasted just a few minutes. Russ has moved next to Joe at the steering wheel to video the struggle with his phone. Frank winds in the sagging line feverishly as the boat eases toward the fish and the whirlpool.

Russ looks away from Frank's fight.

"Joe, I'm sure you know that you are headed toward that whirlpool, right?"

"Yep. No worries. I know how to deal with it."

The boat is slightly faster than the fish and Frank continues to crank in line feverishly. The distance to the fish closes as the line moves into the outer edge of the whirlpool where Joe guides the boat close to the swirling water.

Frank glances back a bit to pant. "Uh, Joe. Is this gonna be okay in here?"

Joe responds with complete calm.

"You just keep reeling fast. We're good. I'm going to speed up and we'll get up to the fish and then past it. When we catch up, you step back here to the left side of the boat and keep reeling. As we pass it, walk to the back of the boat, stop reeling, and just let the fish take the line back out. Got it?"

"Got it."

The boat cruises to the fish just as Joe described, and Frank keeps cranking hard. He eases back and staggers to the side of the boat to get even with the fish that now hangs off the outer edge of the eddy. The boat slingshots past the fish and beyond the whirlpool's influence. Frank stops reeling and line hums off as he walks to the rear deck. The fish stays near the whirlpool, and Joe steadies the boat in place only twenty yards from the edge of the vortex. Joe's maneuvers have closed the gap to the fish by forty yards. He moves back to Frank and reaches in to adjust the drag button on the reel.

"Okay Frank, the fish won't be able to take line out so easily now. We're going to see if we can't pull him along and turn back downriver. If he takes line, you let him take it and don't reel against his run. If he stalls, keep reeling down and lifting. But don't lower too much to give slack. We're going to see who gets tired first."

Frank spits sweat off his lips. "I think he's already won that battle."

Russ stops recording and slips his phone into his pants. "You want me to take the pole?

"Nah, I think I'm good for a few more minutes. I'll yell when I'm ready, though."

Joe moves the boat upriver another thirty yards, then begins the sweeping left turn toward the American shore. Frank holds the pole steady without cranking and the fish rotates around the whirlpool then out into the fast flow to be pulled downstream behind the boat.

The fish resists steadily but takes no line. The pause gives Frank a chance to adjust his hands on the rod and reposition his elbows against his rib cage. He reels down and lifts up several times, then stops to gather his breath as the line stays taut. He holds the pole up high, the boat drifts downstream, and the fish comes along grudgingly. Frank's left arm and hand supporting the rod begin to shake. He adjusts his arm angle and grip on the cork handle again to relieve the stress.

Joe asks, "You doing all right?"

"Okay for now."

Russ takes his phone out to resume recording. Minutes pass and the fish periodically takes several feet of line and Frank reels down and lifts up to bring back the same amount. The process is completed over and over with no line gained or lost. The QL Bridge passes overhead and provides a fleeting shadow from the intensifying sun. Frank shifts his shins against the rear platform and displays new resolve in the fight.

He struggles to ask, "How long have we been going, Joe?"

"It's been almost twenty minutes. How you doing? You need Russ to take over?"

"No. I'm good for a few more minutes."

"Okay then. If you can, keep reeling down and lifting. Those few feet at a time will tire out the salmon."

With a burst of energy Frank reels down and lifts ten times. The arduous task brings the fish within twenty yards.

"Great job, Frank," Russ encourages.

Frank breathes heavily, then shouts gleefully, "I think I'm winning, Joe. I think I'm going to get this done!"

"I think you will too. Now be ready because when he sees the boat, he may take off."

On Joe's cue the salmon runs and the line hums out. Much of the line that was gained is now lost.

"God! Oh, my God," Frank howls.

Russ lowers the phone from his intermittent recording. Joe nods to him that he should move to the back of the boat to help Frank.

Russ moves alongside Frank and says softly, "You sure you don't want me to give you a hand?"

"If you could just hold the rod for me a minute so I can move my arms around and get some blood flowing, that would be great."

Russ gets behind Frank in a bear hug, then reaches around and lifts up the rod handle from Frank's belt buckle. Frank raises his arms to the sky and shakes them around several times.

"Thanks, Russ. Just hold it for a minute if you could."

"I got it. Take all the time you need. It looks like the fish is resting too."

Frank flexes his hands and fingers, takes off his stocking cap to wipe his brow, then throws it down. He breathes deeply several times and adjusts his sunglasses, rotating and flexing his neck.

"Okay, Russ. I'm ready. Thanks."

"Are you sure? I'd be happy to hold it a little longer."

"No. I'm okay for now. Just stay close and be ready, though."

Russ eases the pole back into Frank's hands as he settles his shins forward against the stern platform and repositions the butt of the handle into his belt buckle.

"Okay, you bastard, let's go!"

Frank reels down and lifts up twice, then rests. He repeats the process several times, with each interval of rest lasting longer than the one before.

"You're doing great, Frank," Joe says encouragingly. "You just take your time and reel when you're ready. I don't think he's going to run again."

Frank grunts something and continues his rhythm of dragging the fish closer.

"How long's he been going, Joe?"

Joe looks at his watch. "Over thirty minutes now. A little longer and we'll be back at Lewiston Landing."

"You have many go this far downstream?" Russ asks.

"A few. Not a lot. You don't get into one this big every day. How you doin', Frank? You got this? Only about another fifteen yards to the boat, if you can do it."

"I can't quit now."

Frank's hands have become various shades of red and purple while his left arm has petrified into an "L" of steel. His right hand still cranks with each lowering of the pole, but the rotations have become uneven grinds.

"Wipe my face, will you, Russ?"

Russ picks up a clean shop rag and swabs Frank's forehead and cheeks.

Joe asks, "Frank, you want Russ to put some ice water on that rag and put it around your neck?"

"Yes!"

Russ dips the rag into the cooler and wrings it out before tucking it into Frank's shirt collar.

"How's that?"

"Oh man, that feels good. That could be what I need to finish this guy off."

The silhouette of the salmon is now close to the surface, just ten yards from the boat. It slowly swims back and forth to nowhere while Frank points the pole to follow its course. Its tail lazily breaks the surface with each turn. It resists, but it is too tired to run out. Frank reels down and lifts four times to bring the salmon within five yards. He pants exhaustedly and strains to keep the rod pointing up. His arms and shoulders shudder, veins bulge in his neck, and he blows sweat from his lips with each exhale.

"Holy crap," Russ yells from behind his videography. "Look at the size of that thing! It's ginormous!"

Joe stands at the starboard side with the large net.

"All right, Frank, keep that rod up and walk backward to me, nice and easy. When you get him close, I'll net him. That's it, that's it. Okay, just keep walking back to the bow. Keep going!"

Russ videos Frank stumbling back to plant his butt on the forward platform. Joe reaches over to dip the net under the salmon and captures it with a grunt. Russ points his phone back to Joe as he pulls the shaft in, hand over hand. He grabs the rim of the net like he's picking up a bushel basket of potatoes and scuffles the massive fish on board to drop it with a thud on the deck.

Unlike the first fish of the day that flopped around, this giant salmon lays nearly motionless, with just his tail and gills flexing periodically. Joe deftly removes the hook from the fish's mouth and uses two hands to lift it up for Russ to capture on camera.

"God bless, Joe, that thing is almost as long as your body!"

Frank staggers to his feet and holds his shoulder, rotating his arm. Joe raises the salmon higher for the benefit of the gawkers on Lewiston Landing.

"Awesome job, Frank. C'mon, let's get a photo. I can't hold this thing forever."

Joe continues to hold onto the gills with both hands while Frank reaches in with a mix of misery and elation. Russ videos the men holding the fish and then snaps off a couple photos. Frank collapses behind the steering wheel while Joe gets the big scale to weigh the fish.

"Holy cow. This bad boy is thirty-six-and-a-half pounds! I've only caught five or six salmon bigger than this in my life. Good job, my friend! You should get this mounted for your office."

"Release it, Joe."

Frank covers his face with both palms and rubs his eyes, pretending to wipe the exhaustion away, but the smeared moisture and the snort of a breath divulge some mixture of relief and suffering.

Joe stands dumbfounded and Russ cuts in, "Release it? Why would you do that?"

Frank continues to rub his face to fend off any full-blown weeping. "I just want to," he manages.

"Frank," Joe says, "if we release it, it'll never make it back up to spawn. It's just going to die down here within the hour."

Frank finally reveals his face without regard to tears or judgment. "Well, maybe it deserves to die here in the river where it lived and not in the hull of a fishing boat. I won the battle, let it win the war. Let it swim away with some pride left."

"Are you sure about this?"

"Yeah, Joe. I'm sure."

"Okay. Come on over here and see if it can swim away."

Frank stumbles forward and Joe leans over the side to place the fish in the water. He holds onto its tail and gently moves the fish back and forth to get water running through its gills.

"Reach down here. You should be the last person to touch this guy."

Joe pulls the fish closer to the boat and Frank reaches down to grab onto the tail. He feels the salmon struggling to find strength, with a desire to live on and go somewhere deep in the river that is familiar and comfortable. He imagines the fish feeling his hand and knowing that the grip is by a creature with empathy and benevolence. There is a moment of gratifying mercy that he realizes has been an uncommon trait for him. He believes the fish and he have simultaneously absorbed the bluntness of mortality, but it brings comfort and not anguish. He holds on for a few seconds, then pushes the fish forward to help it on its way. The big salmon floats just a couple feet from Frank's lingering hand to labor in place before moving its tail. It slowly slides forward to disappear.

Frank struggles to stand and Joe turns from the boat's side to surprise him with a hug.

"You did great, Frank. Just great. And it was a nice thing to release the trophy. When it dies, other fish will get strength from it. You ready to head back up and get into some more?"

"Let's go back up, but I think Russ will be the only fisherman from now on. I'm going to sit and watch. Maybe I'll video Russ and eat a sandwich. That's the best fish I could ever catch. I'll finish on that one."

Frank opens a beer, gulps down a couple pills, and lays back on the rear platform to watch the gulls circling overhead. Sweat trickles down the side of his cheek, his arms are stiff from overuse, and his head and back pulse with pain from the struggle. He feels, and it is a welcome ache. He shuts his eyes to simmer in the eternal page he has just written in the river's book of significant events. He knows the day will be talked about long after him. He quietly mouths to himself, "That was a good thing, wasn't it Larry?"

Joe turns the boat and heads back upriver toward the power plant wall. Perhaps there is another trophy lurking there to help Russ write his own pages into the river's history. Frank breathes fully in agonized triumph. Russ looks at the video on his phone, replaying the release over and over.

# Chapter Twenty-Five

The banter and the drinks flow smoothly at the crowded restaurant. Russ and Joe provide enthusiastic highlights of the day while they prod Frank to interject a few grunts to confirm that his struggle was great, the weather was fantastic, and the shut-down turbine was boundless good fortune. He sits in a hazed awareness of his companions while thoughts of his coming deed flush him with a sobering anxiety. He realizes his actions within the hour may cloud their every memory of him. Regardless, he promises himself to muster the courage and follow through.

Maggie and Valerie are captivated by the fish stories, laughing and sharing in Russ's delight while viewing the videos and photos. They particularly enjoy the picture of Russ's required initiation of kissing the first fish he caught. Joe's wife Ingrid works on her wine and pasta, smiling pleasantly and nodding to the accounts she has similarly endured dozens of times over the years with some of her husband's closest clients.

Maggie lifts her glass of beer. "Here's to Captain Joe, Frank, and Russ. Congratulations for a great day on the river, rookie Russ bringing in the limit, and Frank catching one of the biggest salmon we've ever seen! That picture is going to look great in the bait shop!"

All but Frank raise their beers to clink their glasses with cheerful exclamations. Maggie, Valerie, and Joe tap the bottom of their glasses on the table in the Irish way before drinking. Everyone sips while Frank's mind is elsewhere, rehearsing his scheme. Maggie calls his name several times to snap him back into the moment. He jolts back and unceremoniously tosses back all of his remaining scotch.

Russ says, "I still can't believe Frank let that huge bastard go."

"Yeah, tell me about it," Joe says. "Unless it's a sturgeon, I'm just not used to releasing trophies."

"Frank," Maggie asks, "Why did ya let the fish go? It sure would've looked good hanging in the shop."

Frank rubs his hand, still aching from the fight, searching for an answer. He then focuses on Maggie.

"Well, I guess I just realized what it is like to be near the end. That old fish deserved a better fate than dying in the hull of a boat. I wanted it to just settle nice and easy on the bottom of the river where it belongs. And besides, I guess I needed to start releasing trophies. It felt good to let something go that meant so much. You know, I'll have to start doing that a lot from now on."

Eating and drinking stops. Smiles run off into small trickling streams of melancholy.

"C'mon everybody," Frank begs, "It's all right. Everybody knows this is my last trip up here. We all know I'm on bonus time. It's okay."

Maggie's swelling eyes catch everyone's attention before she weakly objects.

"Frank, you don't know that. You don't know what the future holds."

"Oh dear, there's no need for us to dance around it anymore. We all know my days are numbered. Now I've finally said it, and everyone can stop pretending. I just want you all to know that I'm glad to be with you right now. That's all that matters."

A net of awkwardness is cast over the table until Joe pulls it away.

"Frank, all I can say is, I'm glad to know you. Always have been and always will be. No matter what happens, you know we're all here for you."

Frank rubs the napkin across his mouth and stands.

"I know that, and I appreciate it a lot. You all mean a great deal to me. This is the best trip up here I've ever had. Now, I'm going to take the Lion out in the country a bit and look at the stars. Maggie, I'll stop by the bait shop in a little while and pick up Russ. Maybe we could end the night with a bonfire?"

Maggie says defiantly, "Frank, don't be silly. You're in no condition to drive out in the country by yourself."

"I'm fine. I've only had a couple drinks. Don't worry. I'll be back in an hour or so."

Frank drops a wad of cash on the table and begins to walk away. Russ halts him with a grab of the shirt.

"Let me go with you. I like to look at stars too, you know."

"Nah. I just need some fresh air and a few minutes by myself to think. I just want to absorb the day in a little quiet. Why don't you stop by a liquor store to pick up a bottle of scotch then go to the bait shop with the ladies to get the fire started?"

Frank shoves some bills in Russ's hand. "Here." He pulls away.

"Frank," Joe says as he stands. "How about you all come by in the morning for breakfast and see the girls on your way out of town? Maggie, you and Valerie come too."

"I'd love that, Joe," Frank says. "Ingrid, you okay with that?"

She stands next to Joe. "Absolutely. The girls would love to see you."

"Okay, it's settled then," Frank says. "Maggie, I'll see you and Valerie in a bit back at the bait shop with Russ. Joe, I'll see you guys at your place in the morning for breakfast. What time should we be there?"

"How about nine-thirty? Is that too early?"

"I think that's perfect. You all good with that?"

Heads bob.

"That sounds great," Frank says with forced enthusiasm.

He gazes around the restaurant and bar area as if searching for someone, then settles his looks back to his friends. He starts to say something but gives up on that idea to weave his way through the crowded dining room and leave everyone pondering.

The puddles in Maggie's eyes overflow, but she does not wipe them. Instead, she sits and clasps her hands on the table, stoically watching Frank leave. The roar of the Vette can be heard over the din of the patrons and everyone settles back down to sip on their drinks.

"Mom, you don't think..." Valerie says.

Maggie says strongly, "No. He'll come back."

Joe looks puzzled. Russ says, "Frank brought a gun with him. We think he may want to end things up here—shoot himself or even jump in the river. He's been acting weird."

"No," Joe says confidently. "He's not a coward. He wouldn't do that to all of you. He cares about you too much. We'll be having breakfast with him in the morning."

Doubtful, Russ says, "I hope you're right, Joe. I hope you're right."

# Chapter Twenty-Six

The Lion creeps down Lewiston's Center Street and onto the ramp for Robert Moses Parkway. Looking up, Frank can see bright stars fighting for attention within the Niagara light pollution. All of his senses sizzle with fullness as he breathes deeply. He is resolute with purpose. He feels frightened, young, like that blissful night decades ago when he drove nervously to pick up the prettiest girl in high school to take her to the prom. His mind momentarily wanders from his looming task to recall the face of that girl, that dance, and what could have been.

He snaps back to the present as regret melts that memory. The Lion bears left onto Lewiston Road where it climbs to the top of a long hill. A left turn to cut through Niagara Falls Country Club brings eerie calm in its desolation. The hearts of both the Lion and Frank are pumping in steely rhythm. A right onto Mt. St. Mary's drive causes his sweaty hands to nearly slip off the steering wheel, but he manages to cautiously pull the Vette into a stubbed road to nowhere that is just a hundred yards from the retirement home. Reaching back into his satchel, he pulls out the fully loaded .38, rolls it over in his hands several times, then gets out of the car and tucks the weapon neatly between his back and belt where the cold metal causes a slight spasm. There is no turning back. It is overdue. Purposeful strides pull him down the dark, deserted road where there are no buildings or anyone along the way, but he still looks around to make sure he is unseen.

Turning the corner of St. Mary's nursing home parking lot, he moves out of the blackness and into the glare of the huge courtyard. The circular wall of the fountain with a sculpture of The Madonna and Child needs to be caressed. He rubs his hand on the concrete, then reaches in to cup some water. He pats the coolness onto his face and breathes deeply several times while surveying the lobby where the receptionist desk sits empty. He gulps air again, wipes his hands on his hips, and walks calmly through the sliding doors, past the desk and down the right hallway. The corridor is empty except for the waist-high handrail along the wall and a single chair that appears to be haphazardly placed outside of a resident's room.

Frank enters a restroom just before his destination, splashes some more water on his face at the sink, and rubs it to the back of his neck. He slowly opens the door, looks both ways down the hall and then slides into the adjoining Residence 1317.

Sitting there in a wheelchair under a hanging lamp is a small plump bald man. The unconscious lump sleeps with head drooping forward, causing shallow, strained breaths. Frank shuts the door, reaches behind to pull out the gun, and aims it at the old man.

"Wells," Frank says in a strong but quiet voice. "Wake up."

The man tries to breathe as he continues to sleep. Frank punches the old man's shoulder.

"Wells, wake up."

Wells raises his head and tries to focus on Frank before him. Slowly swiveling his head, he clumsily raises his hand to shade his squinting eyes.

"Who's there?"

Frank keeps pointing the gun but doesn't say anything.

Wells asks, "James, is that you again?"

Frank lowers the gun.

"What did you say?"

"James, you're back. I knew you'd be back."

"Wells, who're you talking about?"

"I'm talkin' 'bout you, of course. You–James Barnett."

Frank's hands begin to tremble.

"This is Frank, James's son. I've come to kill you for all the things you did back in Le Fleur. You don't deserve to live anymore, you son of a bitch."

Wells opens and closes his eyes several times and chomps his dry, toothless mouth. He finally musters strength to bow forward for an assessment.

"Frankie? That's you? Little Frankie Barnett? How can that be? You look just like your old man."

"Yeah, it's me, you damn prick. I've come to shoot your brains out."

"You've come to shoot me? Did your dad send you?"

"Of course not, you old fool. He's been dead for more than fifteen years. I came to shoot you because I found out what you did thirty years ago. Your son told me that you framed Willis Booker. Then you got Fritz Weggling drunk and paid him to shoot Booker in his cell. Now Weggling's killed himself out of guilt and left his sons without a dad because of you. When you went into that diner that morning, Sarah was still cooking away, wasn't she? She had a heart attack when you were there. You let her die on the floor, took the money, and framed Booker. Now it's your turn. You don't deserve to live."

Wells gains strength and sits up straighter.

"Listen, you little shit, Sarah had a heart attack when I went in to get coffee, but I tried to do CPR. It just didn't work. She was a great lady and I wouldn't just let her die, but she did. I wasn't going to waste that opportunity, though."

Wells refocuses. "Your dad sent you. I know he did. He was here a little while ago giving me hell. He had to send you."

"Shut up, Wells. No one sent me. Dad's been dead a long time. I'm here because I wanted to come. You ruined so many lives. Someone should have killed you long ago."

"That's probably true, Frankie. I thought your dad might someday. I've even thought about killing myself, but I got too feeble to even do that. But James, oh, he knew he was nearly as guilty as me. He knew what happened and he kept the secrets. He had to keep the secrets, ya know."

"What do you mean, he had to keep the secrets?"

"Frankie, my boy. You really don't know?"

"Know what, you bastard?"

"That your dad was in the Klan too."

"Klan? What the hell are you talking about?"

"Oh, little Frankie, you don't know anything. James came to a few meetings. We even snapped some photos. But somewhere along the line he got all uppity and thought he was better than us. When we took Booker out, James knew he couldn't blow the lid, 'cause we'd take him down with the rest of us, thanks to those photos of him at some meetings. He didn't even know they were being taken 'till I showed him. Of course, your dad wasn't in on the killin', but he couldn't let the town find out he used to be a Klan sympathizer."

"That's all a lie. My dad would've never supported the Klan."

"You go ahead and think what you want, boy. You keep that perfect image of your dad as long as you want. But we had our little club, and he was there a couple times. There were about ten or twelve of us. I think a couple of them still live back in Le Fleur. Of course, most of them were just as gutless as your dad and stopped coming to the meetings. But I didn't. Me and a few others kept the faith."

"Yeah, like you, the mayor, and Weggling, right?"

"Weggling? Oh, heavens no, that idiot wasn't in the club. He was just a pawn in the game that needed money. But, there's no need to talk about that, Frankie. You came here to do a job, so you might as well get it over with. I want to see if you have any more guts than your dad did."

Frank raises the gun and aims it at Wells's head. The longer he points, the more his hand begins to tremble.

"C'mon, Frankie. Do it. Do it, you damn coward. You're as big a coward as your dad! C'mon Frankie, be a bigger man than him."

Frank lowers the gun.

"You want me to kill you, don't you, Wells? You want me to put you out of your misery.

"Maybe so. Who'd want to live like this? I can't walk and can barely lift one arm. Sometimes it's just the right time to check out. Your old man knew when it was his time."

"What?"

Wells's laugh turns into a cough. He recovers to give Frank an evil stare.

"You think James *accidentally* fell into the corn silo and suffocated? Oh, Frankie, you little boy. You don't really know anything, do you?"

Frank points the gun again.

"Shut up. Just shut up."

Wells's wicked grin is a revolting meld of gums and drool.

"He was weak, Frankie. He couldn't live with the fact that he knew what really happened to Booker. But more than that, he was scared to death that people would find out about him. He told me he was going to jump into the corn, and he did. I didn't think he had the balls for it. But it was called a farm accident, you know, and his life insurance would pay for an accident. I never told anyone about that. Not even my son Phil."

Frank charges and clutches Wells's robe. He shakes the old man, then raises the gun above his head to bludgeon him.

Wells develops a perverse smile and his eyes brighten in fanatical anticipation.

Frank pushes Wells away and the wheelchair skids back.

"No. You want me to kill you. No, damn it. You aren't getting out that easy. You just sit there and rot. I'm not doing your work for you."

Frank reaches around to put the gun under his shirttail and walks backward to the door.

"You just sit there and rot, Wells. I hope you live another ten years and rot, bit by bit. I hope you live in a kind of agony that you haven't even imagined."

Frank pushes the door open and collects himself in the hallway. Wells moans pitifully like a child throwing a tantrum over a wanted toy.

"No! Frank, come back. You've got to come back. Please, you've got to get me out of this hell. C'mon, you coward. Don't be a damn coward!"

Wells's pleas turn into uncontrolled weeping and Frank cultivates his own vile grin in realizing that Wells's living is the perfect punishment. He straightens his clothes and looks up to see if anyone is coming to check on the commotion. Staff is not alarmed as the clamor blends among the various wails of other residents.

Frank is startled to see Old Man Larry sitting a few doors down on the hallway chair with his hands perched on top of his umbrella handle. Larry has no discernable emotion while the two stare at each other. Frank opens his mouth, but he can't talk. He takes a step forward and Larry just stares. Frank opens his palms and gestures to ask *what*. Larry's eyes pierce as moments drag. Frank grimaces fiercely and finally turns back into Wells's room to interrupt the old man's yowls.

Between sobs Wells says, "You came back. You came back to do it after all."

"Yeah, I came back, but I'm not going to do it. You're going to have to do it. Let's see if you have the guts that you claim you have."

Frank places the revolver on the corner of the bed and pushes the wheelchair up so Wells can reach it with his good arm.

"There. I'm not sure why I'm doing this, but you can shoot yourself and start your trip to hell with your own gun after I walk out. The police are going to have fun with this one. They're going to wonder how a feeble old cop in a nursing home got his hands on his old service revolver and killed himself. Funny, don't you think?"

Wells nods yes with some kind of pitiful, astonished gratitude.

Frank turns away and slips back into the hallway to find that Larry has left. He passes doorways to see residents watching TV, some telling agonizing stories to themselves, and orderlies handing out medicine. He makes it to the entrance where a lady is reading a newspaper at the receptionist desk. The gunshot behind him sounds like the pop of a single firecracker. The alarmed receptionist looks down the hall without seeing Frank leave through the front doors.

***

Frank is soon feeling alive and alert behind the wheel but drives calmly and carefully to obey the lines and speed limits down the hill to Lewiston. The wind has grown refreshingly cool as it dries the beads of perspiration from his temples and around his neck. He looks up through the open roof to see that stars are brighter against the darkened eastern backdrop away from the lights of Niagara. The sweat is now gone. There are no trembling hands, no fear of police, no fear of anything, at this one serene moment. He looks at the empty passenger seat.

"Well, Larry," he mumbles, "it's done. Is that what you were supposed to help me do? Help me kill another man? Seems like something the devil would do. Are you the devil, Larry? Have I become a devil too?"

Frank aggressively exits the ramp for Lewiston and has to press the brakes firmly to stop at Center Street.

"I should've just floored it and plowed into that tree over there, huh, Larry? I could 'a ended it all so quickly. Just like Wells did."

He waits for a response that doesn't come.

"So, what's up, Larry? You abandon me again? I don't have the gun anymore, so I guess I'm going to have to get creative. I wonder if anyone has ever driven a Corvette over the falls. That'd sure make some headlines now, wouldn't it, Larry?"

Frank moves along Center Street, watching and listening for police or ambulances, but they never come. Turning left down the hill to the bait shop reveals his friends and lost love milling about the bonfire. As he gets closer, he sees Joe's truck parked off to the side. The group watches uneasily as Frank thrashes awkwardly out of the Lion.

Frank gathers himself. "Joe, you stopped, too?"

"Yeah, the thought of a bonfire just sounded kind of nice. Haven't had one for a while. I got you a real nice bottle of whiskey, too."

"You didn't have to do that, Joe. I gave Russ money for it."

Joe grabs a bottle of Johnny Walker Blue off the picnic table and holds it up as Frank approaches.

"I had to, Frank. Anyone who catches a salmon over thirty-five pounds deserves a bottle of Blue."

"Jesus, Joe, that's a couple hundred bucks. That's damn nice of you. Go ahead and open 'er up."

Joe had already removed the wrapper before Frank's arrival. He pulls the cork and Maggie fills each glass with several cubes and hands them around. Joe slides along the semicircle to pour drinks for everyone.

"Here's to Frank," Joe smiles. "The second-best fisherman on the Niagara River."

Everyone cheers and sips with only Ingrid and Valerie coughing with fiery discomfort.

Joe laughs. "Well, we know who doesn't drink whiskey now, don't we."

Chuckles and grins bring an extra glow to the flame. Frank downs his drink and holds out his glass for Joe to pour another.

"Well," Frank begins seriously, "thank you all for gathering here with this fine whiskey to honor my heroic accomplishment."

"It really was somethin', Frank. I don't think I could've landed that salmon," Russ says.

Frank tastes and swishes the whiskey over his teeth before taking a hot, deep breath to continue his speech.

"I'm not talking about the fish, Russ." Frank pauses and they all look around curiously. "I'm talking about the fact that I came back tonight. When I left the restaurant, you all thought I was going to kill myself."

The group twitches and shuffles with unease.

"It's all right," Frank says. "I have to admit that when I left, that thought crossed my mind a time or two."

To fill the speechless void, he goes to the woodpile and lifts up the largest log and staggers it to the top of the pyre.

Finally, Maggie musters, "Frank, we—well, we were concerned about you. You looked pretty upset when you left."

Frank avoids looking at her or anyone else. "Yeah, I guess I was. Things are closing in on me fast, darlin'. My brain may be getting eaten up with cancer, but there's still a lot bouncin' around in there. But, ya know, I'm glad you all got together, whether it was in fear of my suicide or to celebrate my unexpected return. And you know what else? I'm glad I came back. Just think, I could have missed this chance for a bottle of Blue!"

Maggie surprises Frank from his blind side with a massive hug while sniffling and rubbing her nose. Valerie collects her mother close and also begins crying while Ingrid moves into stoic Joe's arms. As the odd man out, Russ stares down into the fire to take a long sip.

"Okay, folks. I'm not dead yet," Frank says. "Let's all have a seat, watch this magnificent fire, and polish off this nice gift bottle."

The group lets go of their hugs to dry their eyes.

Frank tries to brighten the mood. "Well, Russ sure made a haul today after I quit fishing, didn't he? Maggie, you and Valerie are going to have salmon all winter."

Maggie answers shakily, "You and Russ should take some of that fish home. I'm sure Russ would like to take some to his wife. It's right there in the bait shop freezer."

Russ flings a wood chip into the fire. "No, that's okay, Maggie. Annie doesn't much care for fish. I'm afraid it would just go to waste."

"Well, take some home to your mom, then," Maggie insists. "Surely she would enjoy it."

Russ gets up to pour himself another drink and looks at Frank.

"Probably so, ma'am, but I don't think Frank is going to want salmon stinking up his new car on the drive home."

"See, Joe," Frank snickers, "I told you he's one smart little shit. You're going to love having him up here in coming years to bust your balls."

Joe picks up the bottle and reaches over to give Frank another splash. “I’m looking forward to that. But I bet you’ll be with him to give him a run for his money.”

Frank lifts the glass to his lips, then pauses. “That would be nice.”

Everyone gazes into the bright, crackling pile of wood to contemplate their fears, hopes, and the uncertain future. Bonfires have a way of drawing out unsettled thoughts like little moths flittering about the flame until they get too close and finally disintegrate. The shared bottle of whiskey is a comforting ointment that convinces everyone that this night, this moment, living right now, is all that matters.

# Chapter Twenty-Seven

A fall chill greets Monday morning. Gently swaying, upturned leaves foretell of a building squall, but for now the climbing sun still rules most of the sky. The Lion waits patiently for the red light at Youngstown's Main Street intersection with no other beasts on 18F coming from the north or south. A few of the leisure crowd wander in and out of The Village Diner that blocks the view of the river straight ahead. Several locals sip their lattes in Ashker's Coffee Shop on the corner to the left while the Ontario House on the right sleeps, recovering from its rowdy weekend.

"Turn right, Russ."

"But Joe's house is the other way."

"Yeah, I know. We're going to make a stop before we go to Joe's."

Russ takes a right to head north out of town and soon passes the massive Fort Niagara where tourists are collecting in the parking lot. A little further, 18F sweeps a curve to the east to become Lake Road that follows Ontario's shoreline. The elevation continues to fall as they pass grand houses roosting on the bank above the lake. Sparsely placed trees provide an unobstructed view of the water's vanishing horizon.

Frank says, "About a half mile up the road we'll come to a 'T' intersection. Take a left there. We'll go past Four Mile Creek State Park where we used to camp out."

Russ comes to the stop and again follows orders.

"Where we going, Frank?"

"Up here on the right is the pie lady's house. We're going to get a couple and take one to Joe and Ingrid."

"Wow. They must be something for you to come all the way out here to get 'em."

The right side of the road is perfumed by vineyards and apple orchards heavy for harvest. Fence rows and farm houses in varying states of repair are sprinkled between the trees and vines.

"Here, turn right here. It's that light blue house. Pull in."

Russ slides the Lion into the driveway and turns off the engine.

"Frank, I don't think anyone lives here anymore. The place is run down and looks like the grass hasn't been cut all summer."

Frank gets out of the car and snoops around the property. A dilapidated swing set is crumbling to the rear of the side yard and debris peeks through the tall weeds.

He takes a few steps toward the front door where he reads a sign posted to the outside of the screen: 'FORECLOSED–Niagara County Sherriff's Office Order to Vacate.' The rest of the lettering is too small to read from a distance.

Frank turns back to the Lion and barks, "Well, I guess the pie business wasn't so good after all."

"Or maybe business was really good, and she had to find a bigger place with a bigger kitchen. Maybe she just rented this place," Russ says, trying to ease the sting.

"Maybe you're right. Maybe this place just didn't work for her. Hell, she could have left years ago for a better spot."

The wishful thinking cannot hide Frank's disappointment. "Man, I was looking forward to a piece of that coconut cream later today. And damn, you would've loved her blackberry crumble. Best pies ever."

Russ tries to provide company to the misery as he directs the Lion back toward Youngstown.

"Yeah, I bet they were something. Nothing like a homemade scratch pie. You know, though, Julie makes killer pies too. How 'bout we get a nice piece of her Dutch apple with ice cream when we get back tonight?"

"That's a great idea. After I meet with the sheriff, we'll have your mom join us and you can show them the videos on your laptop of you catching all those tiny little fish."

"Very funny. I know you caught the biggest, but I caught the most."

"Only because I was wore out and let you catch a bunch to make up for my trophy!" Frank looks out to the lake to see a few boats trolling along the ledge where he and Russ were the day before.

"Those guys out there must be rookies. They don't even know the fish are up in the river now. I wonder how long it will take them to figure it out since Joe isn't out there to follow around."

Russ acknowledges with a forced laugh.

"Hey Russ, turn into Four Mile Creek State Park when you get up there. I want to take a last drive around."

"You sure we have time? We're supposed to be at Joe's in about half an hour."

"It'll be okay. We'll be just a few minutes."

Russ turns into the park entrance and drives up the long road, admiring the tall tree canopies. He comes to a stop at the security hut where a young woman leans out the window with a wide smile. She ogles Russ and the flashy car.

"Good morning. Could I help you?"

Frank bends over onto the console to take charge of the conversation.

"Good morning, Miss, I was hoping that my friend and I could take a quick drive through the campsites. I used to come up here years ago on fishing trips and I wanted to show him around a bit before we get back on the road."

"Uh, sure. I guess that would be all right. Just take it slow and beep on your way out so I know when you leave."

"Thanks, young lady." Frank smiles and directs Russ into the campground and around the twisting roads. Several large motor homes, smaller pop-up campers, and a few tents are strewn about. Most of the two hundred fifty-nine sites have been vacated while remaining campers squeeze out a few more days of relaxation before the park closes for the winter.

"Up there on your right should be a clearing with a large Boy Scout cabin on it. Pull in there."

Russ turns into a small parking lot next to the big log building that stands in the middle of a hundred-yard-wide meadow that is another hundred yards from the lake. Frank gets out with surprising energy, and motions for Russ to follow him to the water. Five feet from the edge of the cliff he climbs up to sit on top of a lone picnic table. Russ finally catches up and looks out over the lake thirty feet below.

"Pretty nice view, huh? Look over to your left a bit. You can see the Toronto skyline."

Russ squints through the morning vapor.

"Oh yeah, now I see it. That's pretty cool. How far is it over there?"

"I think it's about thirty, thirty-five miles, if I remember correctly. You can really get a great view of it at night. My dad and I used to sit here after dark and look out over the lake and solve all the mysteries of the world. Most of the other guys would stay back at the fire, but this was our place to connect. Most nights we would bring our sleeping bags over here to lay on the ground and look up at the stars. We'd have a little competition about who could spot the most satellites. He didn't even know you could see them with the naked eye until I pointed one out to him. Ya know, he was a smart man, but he just didn't bother to learn some things. Then, after he saw his first satellite, he wanted to search for them every time we came up."

Russ slides up on the tabletop next to Frank. "You really loved your dad, didn't you?"

"Yeah, I guess I did. I thought he was bigger than life. He ran the paper, ran his farm, and everyone in town loved him. He told me all the time that he loved me and was proud of me. Funny, but he never really said what he was proud about, and I never asked."

Russ says, "That's still great that he said it. I remember him pretty well, even though I was just a kid when he died. I know my mom thought a lot of him. I remember her crying like a baby about him even weeks after the funeral. That's one of my strongest childhood memories."

Frank bows his head and rubs the back of his neck. Russ notices a single tear running down Frank's face and quickly looks away. Frank scratches the top of his head and tries to casually rub his face to conceal his physical and mental pain.

"I didn't even know my dad," Russ bursts out as he gazes off to the glimmering water. "Mom says that after he took off, no one ever heard from him again. There were rumors from relatives when I was a teenager that dad was a drug addict and tried to rob a convenience store down in Florida with a toy gun. They said the clerk shot and killed him. Mom said she never knew anything about it, and I couldn't find any newspaper stories about it, but I'm convinced she knew. Our fathers sure took different paths, didn't they? Your dad was a saint that wrote about jerks like my dad."

Frank reaches to the sky and lets out a bear-sized groan. He rubs his knees then picks a nut out of his tooth left over from the morning's motel breakfast of Danish, pills, and scotch coffee.

"Well, Russ," Frank says softly. "I don't think I believe in saints. I'm sure both our fathers had their demons, just like we all do. No one really knows what's in a man's heart, and sometimes not even the man himself knows. Most people just try to do the best they can in whatever circumstances they are thrown into."

Russ contorts his face in understanding and picks at the wooden table, trying to think of a profound response. He is disappointed there is none.

Frank continues, "Maybe your dad left because he was afraid he'd ruin your life if he stayed. Ya know, maybe he went into the store with a toy gun because he wanted to get shot. Maybe his pain was too great to go on. Maybe he was a spent salmon that knew it was his time to die. Who knows?"

The men watch boats headed in each direction on the lake. Some speed out to the ledge and some scurry back toward the river, all in search of prize fish and a few crystalline moments of splendor.

"Frank, can I ask you something personal?"

"Sure."

"Are you afraid of dying?"

Frank takes a deep breath then licks his lips.

"I don't know, Russ. I'm not sure what I feel. I think I'm a little less afraid of dying now than I was a couple days ago. What I'm more afraid of is disappointing people. I just don't want to let anyone down."

"Waddaya mean? How could you let anyone down?"

"Well, I think people in Le Fleur have looked at me and my dad as being insightful people. I'm not sure we really were. I don't think we did our best for folks. I don't know. It's hard to explain."

"That's kinda silly. You do a great job at the paper and have done a lot for the town. You support every cause there is. You're being too hard on yourself."

"Maybe so. But I feel I could have done better. I don't think I really did my best. It got to the point that I wanted to crank out a paper every week, get the ads mostly right, and get the damn thing printed and on doorsteps every Wednesday afternoon."

Russ poses an objectionable look. "What about all the awards? They don't give awards to bad newspapers."

"Yeah, well, maybe we were just a little less crappy than all the terrible little newspapers out there."

Russ's protest turns to mutiny.

"Listen, Frank, you're a great writer. I've learned a lot from you. I hope I can do half as well as you did. What you do is important, too. The town looks forward to the paper every week. Just look at how many get it online. You know there are only a handful of houses that don't get it one way or the other."

"You're an incredible young man," Frank says apologetically. "You work hard and really do a magnificent job. You do all the little things right that I used to do years ago, before I got tired and lazy. You're a fine writer. The paper is in better hands now."

Frank can sense that Russ is searching for a response, so he jumps back in to take away his unease.

"Anyway, we need to get going. We're gonna be late getting to Joe's. I know you're wondering—we'll talk about Fritz when we get back on the road after breakfast."

Frank slides off to scramble back to the Vette, Russ following. The Lion growls awake and heads for the camp exit as fast as the narrow, circuitous road with kids on bikes will permit. Russ slows for the speed bump, tosses a wave to the smiling girl in the window, and gives a couple short beeps.

"Hey Russ, turn right onto the ramp for the parkway. It'll be a lot faster. We don't need to go back through Youngstown or Lewiston. Just follow the signs to Buffalo."

The Lion hums along and is soon up the hill toward the power plants. The rocky gorge to their right where they fished yesterday begs for parting respect. Frank stares, long and unbroken; Russ steals looks while staying mindful of the increasing congestion. The mist from the falls rises miles ahead and to the left past the power plants and the bridges as a signature calling card for tourists.

Frank says, "Sorry we don't have time to stop at the falls. I didn't even think about that when I agreed to have breakfast at Joe's."

"Oh, that's no problem. I'm sure I'll be back up again in the future."

A tinge of remorse smothers Russ's last few self-centered words, but Frank moves quickly to straighten the yaw of guilt.

"I hope you do, Russ. You round up some friends and get back up here to start your own traditions. Maybe you can go out to the campground and look at stars and satellites someday with Nick. Maybe you can tell him about me." He pauses. "Just be careful, though. A woman like Valerie up here could really complicate things for you."

Russ puffs acknowledgment. "Yeah, I hear ya...and you know I'll tell Nick about you since you mean more to me than just about anybody but Mom."

The following silence heightens the profoundness of the compliment and the bleak realization that Frank will never return to the Niagara River he has grown to love. He will fight to hold onto the memories, smells, and emotions of this personal nirvana as the cancer continues to ravage his mind and temperament. Recall of this place may be the only drug to bring any kind of relief, until it too loses its potency near the end.

Russ navigates the spaghetti ramps onto I-190 to stay in the US and presses on past the reservoirs, giant electrical substations, mammoth landfill, and outlet malls. The Monday morning rush hour into Buffalo is the antithesis of the calm left behind on the parkway. Russ handles the toll booth and Grand

Island Bridge with ease this time. He reaches down to press "go" on his phone for the directions to Joe's house he had entered last night. The proper British voice directs them toward the Whitehaven Road exit and through several turns of country roads. Finally, she instructs Russ to turn right into a long drive and announces, "You have reached your destination."

Frank remarks, "Damn, that thing really works, doesn't it?"

The car barely rolls to a stop as Frank works his way out. He climbs up onto the log home's porch before Russ can even take off his sunglasses. Russ surveys the well-trimmed surroundings and the log cabin home's simple stateliness and three-car garage with all the doors up. He is struck by the uniqueness of the garage bays also having doors to the rear that allow vehicles to pull through. In the garage bay closest to the house is a new red Mercedes Benz sedan, Joe's pickup truck in the center bay, and the fishing boat at the far right. He recognizes Valerie's car parked to the side of the driveway, causing an inhale of anticipation. Russ turns his attention back to Frank on the porch who is waving him onward as Joe opens the door.

"Good morning, Frank." Joe wraps his arms around Frank for a manly hug. "So glad you made it. The food is just about ready."

Joe leads Frank past the living room's massive stone fireplace that separates the finely appointed kitchen where Ingrid is pushing bacon around an iron skillet. Maggie and Valerie are sitting at the counter drinking coffee but leap off their stools to greet Frank.

Russ stumbles through the doorway just in time to hear Maggie say, "Frank, you actually came! I'm so glad you decided to stop. We weren't sure you would really want to come."

Frank is showered with more love as Russ stands alone in the living room to study the hearty leather furniture and other stylish furnishings that belie the exterior's country cabin guise. An elk-head trophy adorns the fireplace wall, but no other mounted beasts are visible to suggest this is the domain of an accomplished outdoorsman. He finally glances to Valerie who returns a flicker of the eyes and slight smile. He joins the group in the kitchen while she hands out hot coffee and small plates of warm cinnamon rolls. Russ grins with gratitude and squeezes her arm in thanks before taking a plate and cup.

Frank glosses over Russ's stupefaction. "Thank you, my dear. You are so kind."

Russ awkwardly blows the steam and sips as he tries to think of something to say. Ingrid rescues him. "Why don't you all just have a seat out there in the living room while I get the food ready?"

The accidental hostess toils in the kitchen to execute perfect timing of the food, while the others gather in the living room to coddle their coffee, nibble on rolls, and do their best to generate any small talk that would quash the awkwardness of this peculiar communion.

Frank says, "Joe, after breakfast, you need to take Russ down the basement and show him your man cave."

"Absolutely will."

Frank's attention is drawn to the huge flat-screen TV on the far wall where a reporter on the Buffalo morning news delivers a segment about a shooting at a nearby nursing home. The sound is barely audible as the image shows medics wheeling a body out of the facility's front doors. The tagline at the bottom of the screen reads, "Former Ohio Police Chief Dead in Apparent Suicide."

Russ and Joe join Frank in watching the report, while Maggie and Valerie disregard the news to discuss the flakiness of the cinnamon rolls. Russ's brown face turns a shade of inhuman chalkiness. He looks at Frank, tilts his head to the TV, and raises his eyebrows as if to declare silently, *you did this?*

As men often do, the three speak among themselves with just their eyes and facial expressions. Frank finally puckers his lips and shrugs his shoulders. The hollow denial is all the proof Russ and Joe need as they try to act normal by biting rolls and washing them down with coffee. Russ is making connections in his head while Joe clicks off the TV and simmers in confusion.

With fortuitous timing, Ingrid invites all to the kitchen with a homey, "Okay, come and get it."

The men scatter around the kitchen table while the women dish out food and distribute plates. Maggie and Valerie heap praise on Ingrid for the wonderful breakfast while the men shove food in their faces to avoid saying anything about what they just saw on the news.

Uncharacteristically abrupt, Joe snaps, "All right, if you guys are done, let's go down to the basement."

"Joe," Ingrid reasons, "They haven't even finished eating yet. Maybe they'd like some more eggs or bacon."

"No, that's okay," Frank says. "I think we're getting pretty full. Those first servings were huge. Isn't that right, Russ?"

Russ looks up with chipmunk cheeks full of food and glumly bobs his head. He swallows and washes it down with orange juice, then catches up with Joe and Frank who are already at the basement door.

On the descent Russ can tell that this basement isn't going to be the typical manly sanctuary. Instead of the usual big-screen television, one wall is adorned with mounted fish of a dozen species, a turkey with wings spread wide, and three deer heads with enormous antlers.

Another wall displays hundreds of brackets that hold thousands of lures, hooks, leaders, rolls of fishing line, and devices with purposes unknown to Russ. There are racks supporting every type of expensive waterproof fishing jacket as well as all the vests, camouflaged hunting clothing, hats, and gloves available to outdoorsmen. Behind the stairs are three large gun safes that are chock-full of every kind of rifle, shotgun, handgun, and corresponding ammunition needed for hunting and target shooting.

At the far end wall are glass cases that extend nearly the width of the basement in which dozens of lures and fishing reels are laid out in museum fashion. Above the cases hang dozens of photographs from perhaps thirty years of various outdoor adventures. Like everything else in the basement, the photos are hung with exhibition-hall exactness.

“Well, Russ,” Frank probes, “Whaddaya think? Pretty damn impressive, huh?”

“This is incredible,” Russ says. “I feel like I’m in a sporting goods store. Is there anything you don’t have for hunting and fishing?”

Joe scratches his forehead. “Hmmm. I guess about the only thing I’d really like to get are a couple antique lures I’ve been looking for. I could get them online, but they’re asking too much for them. I’ll find them someday in a bait shop somewhere.”

“What about all the stuff in the display cases? Are all those lures and reels antiques?”

“No. Just a few of them are worth anything. The others are just ones that have special meaning for me.”

Joe leads Russ to the case and points to a collection of ten lures laid out next to their original boxes, which are slightly faded or deteriorated. Most of the lures are in excellent condition, only a few having rusty hooks or scrape marks. Each lure has a small tag identifying the maker, type, and year.

“I’m kind of fond of these few,” Joe says casually. “They’re pretty old, and handmade.”

Curious, Russ sees names like Friend-Pardee Kent Frog, 1907; Lane Automatic Weedless, 1912; Moonlight Dreadnought, 1918; Pflueger Rubber Decoy, 1892.

Joe slides to the other end of the display case where he bends down. "Those other lures are fun to collect, but these are the things that mean the most to me."

Russ leans over to examine an assortment of bright lures and three reels with more modern names—Zebco, Garcia, and Shakespeare.

"They aren't valuable at all, except to me," Joe says. "These are the first lures and reels my dad gave me when I was a kid. They're my most prized possessions. When I die, those will be with me in my casket."

Russ asks softly, "Is your dad still living?"

"No, he's been gone for about fifteen years now. He had cancer from the chemical plant. It was rough watching him fade away like he did."

"Sorry about that," Russ says. "You don't want to pass these reels on to your daughters?"

Joe straightens, looks Russ in the eyes, and speaks solemnly. "The girls have their own things that he gave them when they were little that have special meaning for them. And I have some other things of his they'll get, like watches, pins, and photos. But these are sacred things he gave me—his hands were on mine when he taught me to use them. I'll never be separated from them."

Joe points to the wall of photos behind the case. "These are pretty important to me too. Take a look at that one with the blue matting."

Russ leans over the display case to study the picture of Joe posing with several men with their catch at the Lewiston Landing sign. He leans in closer to see Frank and his dad with several other unrecognized men. Frank reaches in to glide his finger across the glass.

"Yep. There's Dad and that's me. There's my former brother-in-law Mike, my golfing buddy Dave, and there's

Police Chief Benson Wells, the old man on the news who killed himself last night."

Frank turns to Russ and Joe. "Yeah, I visited him last night. I went there to kill him. But I couldn't do it. He begged me to, but I couldn't. So, I just left his gun with him."

Joe is expressionless while Russ's mouth is wide enough to swallow a huge sturgeon lure.

Russ gulps air, then asks, "Why would you go there to do that?"

"That's one of the things we might talk about on the drive home. Joe, I guess you'll just have to have Russ tell you about it someday."

Softly but emphatically Joe says, "You don't owe me any explanations, my friend."

Frank struggles up the stairs to leave the others in the basement, mumbling softly.

"Frank," Maggie shouts, "You want something else to eat? More coffee?"

"No, we have to be heading out. I have an appointment back in Ohio that I need to keep. Thank you, my dear, for everything."

Russ and Joe make it upstairs and everyone gathers on the front porch to hug Frank and Russ, exchange forced farewells, clumsy words of tenderness, and poignant looks. Joe gives Frank another bear hug and surprises Russ with his own manly embrace.

"It was my honor to take you guys out yesterday. Have a safe trip home. Send me a copy of that video."

Maggie leans in and puts her hand on the back of Frank's neck to pull his head lower. She raises on her toes and softly puts her lips to his. She backs away with no words and Frank says nothing. He reads her eyes for several moments, then skims the other faces before leaning in to give Valerie a light kiss on the cheek. He turns and steps gingerly down from the porch and twists into the Vette without looking up at his friends.

Russ says to no one in particular, “Goodbye. I hope to see you again,” before hurriedly bounding down the steps to the car. He starts the engine and looks up. He gives a timid wave while Frank continues looking down at his trembling hands. Russ turns the car around and heads down the driveway, noticing that Frank is looking in the side mirror at the frozen mannequins on the porch whom he loves but will never see again. The morning continues to fight the dark veil pouring in from the west and golden trees lining the driveway vigorously wave goodbyes.

“Stop at the end of the drive and put the top up, Russ. It’s going to rain.”

# Chapter Twenty-Eight

The Lion fluently scales and descends the south Grand Island Bridge amid thinning traffic. Russ sets the cabin to a soothing seventy-four degrees as light mist beads on the vibrant, blond fiberglass. Moisture-sensing wipers pick up their rhythm as the drops fall heavier with a calming patter on the convertible top. The semi-trucks slow down and Russ keeps a measured speed through the spray. Buffalo is dispatched as Hamburg draws near on I-90 west.

Half an hour of silence is enough for Russ. "Frank, do you want to stop at the traditional place?" A mute Frank just looks out the side window. Russ asks again a bit louder to pressure a response.

"Oh, no. Sorry, Russ. I was just thinking about stuff. We don't need to stop unless you need to use the bathroom or get a drink or something."

"No, we'll just keep going."

The wet side window serves as Frank's canvas for imagining the faces of the people left behind on the porch. He tries to remember each little nuanced wrinkle, contented laugh, or twinkle of the eye. He hears their voices and inflections of kindness. The reminiscing is a chorus of comfort and torment.

The Lion speeds under the covered walkway where people stand to defy illusory death as cars and trucks zoom under their feet. Russ looks up to see children wave, but Frank just keeps looking at the window to imagine the droplets of rain as being the tears of those he loves standing at his funeral. He sighs that image away to collect scrambled thoughts for the stories he is about to tell Russ, then to fantasize about one more night in the arms of Maggie. The alternating, burning flashes of regret and yearning are equally crushing for a man with limited spirit and even fewer options.

Russ says just above the din of the rain, “Frank, can we talk now?”

“Okay, Russ. You’re the reporter, so ask away.”

Russ pauses to form his own thoughts and then, while minding the road, asks, “Well, you went to the nursing home to kill that sheriff. What the hell was that all about?”

With empathy Frank says, “That has to be very troubling for you. Well, I’ve been thinking that might be a story for another time. Maybe after you get the paper out this week. Right now, you need to concentrate on the story you have to write about Weggling.”

“All right, then. Tell me what you and Weggling talked about before he shot himself.”

Frank smiles at his protégé. “Now, that’s a pretty good question, Mr. Editor. Except one thing. How do you know he shot himself? Maybe I shot him.”

Russ looks at Frank, shocked.

“Oh, don’t be silly, Russ. You know I didn’t shoot him.”

Frank looks back out the side window for more staring but is interrupted again.

“Well? You going to tell me, then?”

Frank turns back to focus on Russ’s hands on the steering wheel.

“Okay, I’m going to tell you two versions of what happened. First, you’ll hear a version that could be true. Then, a version that may be closer to real. But ultimately, you’re the one who’s going to have to decide why our little paper exists and what people need to know.”

"Two versions? Just tell me the truth. Why don't we go with that?"

"Like I said, I'll let you decide what the truth should be."

Russ bounces several puzzled looks between Frank and the wet windshield.

Frank continues. "You saw all the commotion at Weggling's before I went in. That is what it is. You'll do a great job describing that. And, of course, you'll describe all the shouts exchanged through the screen door. And you'll do a good job talking to Mrs. Weggling and she'll tell you about how Fritz loved his family and about his exemplary military record. Then all his neighbors and the guys at the VFW will say what a great guy he was. The big question is, why did Fritz shoot himself, isn't it?"

"Sure. Of course."

"Well, Mrs. Weggling was telling the truth about Fritz not laying a hand on her or the kids. Betty was sitting on the couch as calm as can be and the kids were on the floor watching cartoons with empty cereal bowls by their sides. After Betty and the boys left, Fritz told me that he only had the gun out because he was having nightmares for years about the Gulf War. It was a reoccurring dream about his camp being raided and that everyone in his platoon near the perimeter of the base was killed. In the dream he just happened to be at the supply depot on the other side of the base, so he lived."

Frank pauses for a modest cough, then continues. "Well, apparently that dream carried over into his waking hours when he was afraid the deputies would storm the house, like it was his base. He was paranoid about the deputies, for some reason. The only time he felt safe was when he had his gun in his hand to protect his family. He didn't know who to tell about his dream or his unfounded fear of the deputies, and he needed someone to talk to that could get him some help. That ended up being me.

"I told him that I would get him some counseling through the VA and the county. I thought I had convinced him it was going to be okay. He said he was going to hand me the gun and we would walk out together and get him the help he needed. He turned the gun handle toward me, but as he was getting out of the recliner to hand me the gun, he tripped, and the gun, still pointed at his chest, accidentally went off. As he was lying on the floor, he told me to tell his wife and boys that he didn't mean to shoot himself and that he loved them very much."

"Is that how it happened, Frank?"

"Kind of. I may have changed a few things."

"What do you mean, you changed a few things?"

"Well, he had nightmares, but not about the Gulf War. His nightmares were different. He described them as a cancer of the mind that was eating him alive. He wanted to end it all before he became crazy and a burden to his family or even hurt them. He'd spent decades agonizing over something he had done as a young man before the war and said he had to tell someone about it so then he could kill himself. He said he deserved to be shot for what he had done, and he didn't want his boys or wife to find out about it. He felt the only way to pay for his sin was to confess out loud to someone, so God could then forgive him. But I told him that he only needed to quietly ask God to forgive him and he didn't need to tell anyone else. I also told him that he wouldn't want his boys to remember him giving up and killing himself in their home.

"I also told him that if he killed himself, Betty's work insurance wouldn't pay because of suicide. That really alarmed him. He thought for a couple minutes before he told me that he was going to hand me the gun. He said he wouldn't kill himself after all—that it wouldn't be right. Then he told me about what he did when he was a young man. He cried and apologized for it. I convinced him that it was a long time ago, and that it didn't matter anymore. I told him he led a good life and raised good kids. He prayed out loud for God to forgive him. Then he turned the handle around like he was going to give me the gun, but when he got up to give it to me it went off. The more I've thought about it, I think he meant for it to go off. I think he still wanted to kill himself, but he wanted it to look like an accident, so Betty and the boys could get the insurance.

"When he was on the floor, he said, 'Frank, make sure you tell everyone it was an accident.' I thought at first he had a look of fear and shock about being shot. But now I think it was a look of pleading; he was begging for me to say that it was an accident and that he had tried to give me the gun. Then he said something else that caught me off guard. He said, 'Tell them I wasn't keeping you hostage. Tell them that you were my friend and that I asked you to leave, but you wanted to stay with me. Thank you for being with me, Frank.'"

"Jesus, Frank! What was it that Fritz did that he was so sorry about?"

Frank clenches Russ arm. "That's something we don't need to discuss right now. We can talk about that later too."

"I think I need to know, Frank. It's pretty damn important to the story."

"Editor, it's only important to one of the stories. If you decide to tell the second story, then I guess I'll have to tell you. But, if you write that version, the insurance company will surely claim that Fritz intended to kill himself all along—that it wasn't an accident at all. Perhaps even worse, if you write that, his kids are going to think their father committed suicide. And you know what? If I tell you what Fritz did as a young man, his wife and kids may think it was worse than suicide. So, Mr. small-town newspaper editor, how you gonna write the story? What do people really need to know?"

"Damn, Frank. You want me to write a story and make up stuff?"

"I don't want you to make up anything. I've told you two versions, and I'm fuzzy about some of the details in both. You didn't make up either story—you would just be quoting me. It's up to you how ya want to do it. But I need to know which story you're going with before we get back to Le Fleur and I go over to Mansfield to meet with the sheriff. Our stories need to match."

"Jesus." Russ's face reddens as he stares at the rear of a semi-trailer. Painted on the door in big bold letters he reads a Bible verse: *Therefore, having put away falsehood, let each one of you speak the truth with his neighbor, for we are members one of another.*

An avalanche of edgy quiet returns. Mean clouds shroud the lake beyond Erie as Pennsylvania eases into Ohio. Summer has officially declared its retreat and blustery autumn is now in command of the landscape. For the warring months to come, the sun will only periodically fight its way through the ruling curtain of gray before timidly withdrawing. As a transition state, Ohio suffers from an identity crisis of allegiance, not being fully in the camps of either the Northeast or the Midwest. The state's schizophrenia bounces between jumbled temperaments that both regions readily repudiate. Ohio's hope for a benevolent winter's reign is its only strong commonality with neighboring brethren. Frank thinks about this being his last winter and also yearns for an easy one.

# Chapter Twenty-Nine

After dozens of miles of Russ's silent stewing, Frank finally reaches to the dash to tune the radio to 1100 WTAM. Cleveland Indians announcer Tom Hamilton bemoans in salty caramel voice that the weather may prevent today's game against the rival Detroit Tigers. The 1:05 p.m. Monday contest would have been an "off-day" makeup from a rain-out earlier in the summer. But, as Hamilton describes, depending on the Indians' success over the last days of the season, "The Tribe may be far enough ahead of the Tigers by week's end that the game may not need to be made up at all."

"Damn, I would've loved to stop and catch that game. I haven't been to a game in years, and the Tribe may finally pull this thing off. Francona is making these guys really believe they can do it. You still an Indians fan, Russ?"

"Yep."

Frank listens for more but knows Russ is too angry for anything beyond curtness. He pushes for an answer anyway.

"So, when was the last time you went to a game?"

Russ doesn't bother to look at Frank. "Well, I guess that was when I was about eight or nine when you and your dad took Mom and me." He adds an extra sting. "As I recall, that was just a couple weeks before your dad died."

The wipers scrape louder, and a greater chill fills the car. The trip's promise of excitement and possibilities for profound bonding has eroded back to the foulness of life's chaffing truths. The once cozy padding of the carefree weekend is now an oncoming, bare concrete wall of obligations and mortality.

Frank begins to say something but breathes it back in. Miles roll. Russ's stern concentration on passing through the bouquets of mist churned up by truck after truck is broken by Frank's request for Russ to play some Van Morrison. Frank gets lost in the music while Russ cringes an obliging tolerance. The Lion swims on. Frank fiddles with his hands.

He finally cracks the clamor of nothingness. "Well, Russ, whadya write about for the editorial this week?"

Russ turns down the music and keeps his eyes on the road. "I wrote about the great anticipation of a road trip and thrill of what it must be like to fish the Niagara."

"I see. So was the trip what you imagined?"

Russ pauses to think. "The fishing was all I hoped it would be."

The unsaid "but" prickles Frank back to silence for a long while.

Finally, he says, "Let's stop at the next exit and go to that McDonald's."

"Okay," Russ says. "You getting hungry, too?"

"No. I just need to get a drink so I can take my pills."

"Oh."

At this stop there is no racist. No turmoil. No benevolent manager. No old man in the corner. Just a quick restroom break with a couple well-timed medications. The gift certificates are used for a to-go order of two quarter-pounders and Cokes—no fries. The Lion bolts back onto the freeway, gets up to speed, and Russ devours his burger. Frank nibbles at his sandwich, then shoves most of it into the bag at his feet along with Russ's burger box. The Lion pushes harder on I-90 through lighter rain and thinning traffic.

"Have you talked to your mom today, Russ?"

"No. I've texted her a couple times. I just did while you were finishing up in the bathroom. She said she's sent you several more texts, but you still haven't been answering her."

"Yeah, I turned my phone off yesterday. What'd you tell her?"

"I told her all was good, and we'd be home in a couple hours."

A nearby bolt of lightning startles the men.

"Wow, that was close," Frank says. "I bet that wasn't more than a hundred yards."

"Yeah," Russ continues with controlled worry, "I hope our convertible top doesn't get struck."

"No, that probably wouldn't be good," Frank says. "So, how you going to write the Weggling story?"

Russ is caught off guard by Frank's clunky segue, but rebounds smoothly. "Well, what have you decided to tell the sheriff?"

Frank rubs behind his ear and leans his head back.

"So, it's going to be a Mexican standoff, huh?"

"I don't think it's a standoff at all," Russ says coolly. "You'll have to go first with the sheriff tonight. My story doesn't need to be written till tomorrow night."

"So, you're going to write it based on what I say, huh?"

"Yeah, that's the idea. But I know which story you're going to tell the sheriff because I know you want to protect Fritz and his family."

Frank nods and smashes his lips together.

The Lion eavesdrops while obediently stretching on toward Le Fleur. Rain stops, and clouds break to blue with sunlight peeking around the edges. The traffic on I-71 south is unusually light for a late Monday afternoon. The roadway is drying, but the infrequent semi-truck still churns up just enough annoying moisture to activate the wipers.

Frank turns the radio back to the Indians network. It is still raining heavily along Lake Erie behind them and the ballgame has been officially called off. A makeup will only happen if the

Indians unexpectedly lose their seven-game lead in the standings by the end of the season.

"Okay," Frank says as he turns off the radio. "I'll talk to the sheriff tonight, then you come by my house in the morning to interview me, so we make sure we have all our facts straight."

"All right," Russ puffs. "You're still the boss. Whatever you say."

The Lion eases off the highway at Lodi and heads west on the two-lane road. Frank lays his head back to try for sleep. Russ puts on his sunglasses and pushes the pedal to eighty. It is too fast for this unpredictable road of semis, pickup trucks, old ladies on their way to the market, and the occasional piece of farm equipment hogging the road. Frank subdues his alarm and fades in and out.

The farms and tiny towns finally spill into a truck stop at the intersection of little New Haven. Russ turns south as Frank sits up to gather himself and wipe the drowsiness from his eyes.

"Russ, could you pull into the cemetery up on the right? I'd like to stop and see my dad's grave."

"Sure. No problem."

Russ eases into the sprawling Maple Grove Cemetery and the Lion slowly climbs the modest rise through the grave markers and scattered, majestic oak, maple, and walnut trees. The immaculate grounds thrust up the different colored marble and granite tombstones that glint in the western sinking sun now nestled between horizon and clouds. The splashes of sky blues, grays, oranges, and yellows merge with the colored trees that drip the earlier autumn rain.

Frank points to guide Russ to the area where many of the Barnetts are buried. "Right here. This is good."

Russ pulls off to park in the grass and asks, childlike, "Do you want me to stay in the car?"

"You don't have to, but I'd like a few minutes alone, if you don't mind."

Frank timidly approaches his father's tombstone, then kneels on the damp ground at the granite face. He gently runs his fingers over the name of James S. Barnett and the dates 1922–1999. Beside his father's name and date is "Mary Barnett 1924–" which is yet to be completed. A bronze American Legion World War II service marker star about the size of a hand is pushed into the ground near the concrete base. The star is cloaked by an eagle with wings and legs spread and opposing talons clutching arrows and olive branches. A small American parade flag rises from behind the eagle's head. Frank pushes the post of the marker deeper into the ground and firmly straightens the flag.

"Well, Dad, I made the trip one last time. We got some nice fish and I caught one monster and killed another evil one. He talked about you. Maybe you already know that, huh? Ya know, I guess I'll be laying a few feet from you pretty soon—maybe just a few weeks now, I guess—probably by the New Year, anyway."

Frank reaches down and pulls a few blades of tall grass from the corner of the tombstone.

"Guess you know I saw Maggie in New York. Her little daughter Valerie is all grown up. You'd like her. I think Russ could have been crazy about her in another life."

His eyes moisten and words are hard to form, but he needs to say them out loud to make them real.

"Dad, I thought I hated you for cheating on Mom and what you did with the mayor. Wells told me you killed yourself. That made me hate you even more. But on the ride back from New York, the hate stopped. I just realized that you probably did the best you could, given the position you were in. You probably had the same kinda issues with Grandpa, too. I figure I'm a lot like both of you. I just did the best I could, but I'll see if I can make the little time I have really worth something. Dad, I'm going to tell the truth so everyone knows. I hope you're okay with that."

Frank sees a figure approach from his peripheral left and jolts to his feet. The panic melts at the sight of the old man in his suit, top coat, and fedora, carrying his umbrella.

"Christ, Old Man! What the hell are you sneaking up on me here for? You scared the crap out of me."

Larry stands with a quirky little smile that somehow provides some comfort. Frank looks back to see Russ sitting in the Vette playing with his phone, then refocuses on the old man. "So, what? What is it? Why are you here?"

Larry flicks his umbrella toward a small headstone to the left of James's. The inscription reads, "Our Beloved Son, Larry Barnett, 1943-1952."

Frank inspects the headstone and begins to tremble. His breathing becomes erratic as his head oscillates between the stone and the old man's sympathetic face.

"No. No," Frank pleads. "Don't say it. Don't say you're my brother Larry."

The old man's smile grows strangely wide while Frank's quivering intensifies.

"Is it that difficult to believe, Frank? Didn't you even think of me when you heard my name was Larry?"

Frank holds the back of his head, then scratches deeply.

"I've met a lot of people over the years named Larry."

The old man laughs. "But none of them appeared to you like I have. Of course, I died long before you were born, so I was never part of your life. In that respect it isn't surprising that I'm not at the forefront of your thoughts."

Frank wipes his face on his sleeve and catches his breath. "How do I know you're my brother?" How do I know that all this time you haven't just been the tumor pressing on my brain? Maybe I'm just imagining you right now."

"Frank, I can't make you believe in me. Either you have faith that it is possible, or you have no faith at all, in anything. But, again, if I am your imagination, how is it that your friends have seen me and talked to me?"

Frank calms. "Larry, you died when you were nine. If you're my brother, why do you look like an old man?"

"I've come to you at the age I would have been now. You wouldn't have let me through to you if I spoke as a child. I have the wisdom of an old man when I come to you as I would have been now."

"Why, Larry? Why are you here?"

"Frank, I had told you that I was here to help you figure some things out. But mostly, I have been here because your heart has been alone. Being alone is far worse than your tumor or the prospects of dying—you saw that with Wells in New York and Weggling in his home. But you have friends. You have Gloria. You love Maggie and you love Julie. In fact, you love that young man sitting over there in the fancy car. But you can't bring yourself to tell any of them you love them.

"You had a girlfriend in high school that you loved, but you didn't tell her. You had a wife, but she didn't believe you loved her. You had sons that you loved, but you haven't seen them since they were children and they do not know you.

"The things you are doing for your friends are nice. You are wiping out their debts, giving property, all of your money. It will make their lives easier. They will appreciate it. But even with all of that, they will not know that you love them and appreciate them. That is what they really want, just your love."

Frank murmurs, "I guess it's too late for that now."

"Why is it too late? It's just a matter of courage. Tell them and say it with conviction. It cannot be said without feeling. They will know if you mean it or if you are just saying words. But, most importantly, you must let them love you.

"Remember when I said I do not know how I am able to be here? That is the truth. I really don't have all the answers, Frank. To me, 1952 was an instant ago. Your life has seemed long to you, but it has been less than an instant. I'm not in a place. I'm in warmth. I'm consumed in love. I was fortunate that when I died as a child, I didn't fear the accepting or the giving of love. There is fear in taking the risk to love someone. This fear grows stronger with age until it becomes very difficult to give freely."

Larry leans on his umbrella. "The fear of living and of death comes from the prospect of being alone. You must love in order to overcome the fear and be in the warmth. You must let others love you, then fear will go away."

"Larry, you had to be in such pain from the fire. Do you remember all of that?"

"Yes, I remember the fire, but I do not remember the pain. Mom was at the hospital for ten days and covered me with her love. Mostly I remember how she loved me, and I returned that love with my eyes and I let her know that I was going to be fine. Our love for each other made the fears go away. She knew that I would be covered in love forever."

"Was Dad always at the hospital too?"

"Yes, almost all the time, but he wasn't in my room much. I know now that he loved me deeply, but he didn't know how to show it. He never said it to me in the hospital. He was crushed by knowing I was going to die. He was fearful and had a hard time accepting love. But you knew that about Dad all of his life, didn't you?"

"Yes, I did. Larry, did Mom and Dad ever love each other?

"Yes, especially during the war when I was a baby. But later they began fighting when Dad was drinking a lot. They stayed married, but my death caused an even bigger rift. They got a little closer again when you were born, but that faded as you grew. Dad started drinking again and was at the paper all the time. Mom never had forgiven Dad for something when I died, and it caused a wound that never fully healed. My death could have brought them closer forever, but it didn't. Dad was afraid to ask for forgiveness, so Mom never forgave. There was no asking so there was no giving. Each waited for the other to show love."

"Did Mom blame Dad for the fire and not getting you out of the house before being burned?"

"No, she didn't blame him for the fire. I'm sure you heard about it, though, on New Year's Eve?"

"Yes, I heard about it," Frank whispers. "Mom talked about it a few times. She said all you kids were upstairs playing while the adults were downstairs playing cards. The space heater in the upstairs bathroom was leaking gas. The kids wanted a light plugged in but couldn't move the dresser, so Mom's sister Anna went upstairs to move it for them. Mom said Anna clicked her lighter to see the electrical outlet and that's when the gas blew up. Mom said Uncle Stan and Aunt Connie got burned badly too when they ran up to grab Anna and the kids. Stan and Connie lived through it with scars on their arms, but you and Anna weren't so lucky."

Larry says, "That's pretty much how it happened. Anna only lived two days, but I lived ten. Because Mom stayed with me, she never really got to mourn the loss of her sister. Fortunately, none of the other kids got burned at all."

"So, if it wasn't the fire, what was it that Mom never forgave Dad for?" Not spending time with you in the hospital?"

Larry pushes his umbrella further into the grass and places his hands on top of the handle. "No, that wasn't it either," he says. "It was really a little thing that became larger than it should have. I had gotten a new bicycle for Christmas, but Dad wouldn't let me take it outside because it was so snowy and cold. I begged and begged, and Mom tried to convince him it wasn't that bad outside, and they got into a huge fight. But he said the weather needed to clear up before I could ride it. Then the weather between Christmas and New Year's got even worse. I never did get to ride the bike and Mom never forgave him for that. It started as a small seed of pain that grew into a giant oak as the years passed. I don't think he ever forgave himself for it, either. He carried that pain forever. He is forgiven now, though."

"Larry, I'm sorry. I'm sorry for so many things. Mostly, I'm sorry for not knowing you when you came to me and not trusting you."

"Oh, my brother, it wouldn't have been natural for you to know me or trust me right away. You had to take this time for your mind to search possibilities, to create some room for faith. Thinking about things on that salmon run was a good thing for you."

"So, now what?"

"Well, Frank, I can't tell you what to do. Let it come to you. Think about truth. But you must choose what to do. After all, it's still about free will. But I hope you let people love you."

"Will you be with me, Larry? Will I see you again?"

"I'll be in your heart and mind, like a big brother should. Beyond that, I don't know what is to happen."

"Will I die soon?"

"I don't know what the word 'soon' means anymore."

Frank looks over to Russ, who is still playing with his phone in the car and unaware of the conversation at the grave markers.

"Okay then, will—"

Larry is gone. Frank kneels between the headstones.

"Brother, don't leave me now. I'm going to need you with me. I can't die alone."

Frank runs his hand over an inscription carved in Larry's stone just below the dates:

*I am waiting for you*

*For an interval*

*Somewhere very near*

*Just around the corner*

# Chapter Thirty

The rooms in the house are dim except for the kitchen, where Gloria reads the *Sentinel* that was delivered this afternoon. The quiet amplifies the refrigerator hum and the rhythmic downspout drips at the back door. Tranquility like an empty theater fills the space, while a curtained stage invites the actors and patrons to come experience something unusual. Perhaps tonight it will be a comedy. Perhaps a tragedy. The dying lead actor will provide the improvisational cues.

From the table Gloria can keep an eye on Frank as he sleeps in the shaded sunroom on the hospital bed delivered to make him more comfortable. He no longer has the strength to climb the stairs to his bedroom and often struggles to the downstairs hall bathroom.

She has been here around the clock for the past six weeks to take care of Frank as he continues to decline. She only gets short breaks when the same home health nurse comes for a few hours each morning, except for Sundays. The kind aged soft-spoken nurse gives Frank a sponge bath every day and dresses him in clean pajamas. She massages his muscles, tells him jokes, and softly plays the guitar for him, occasionally singing a hymn. It is a ritual that helps them both challenge the veracity of the hopelessness. Frank often tells the nurse she must be an angel, and she usually responds that he helps her be one for a few hours every day.

Gloria reads Russ's front page story about the VFW's plans to host a holiday party to launch a college fund for the

Weggling boys. Only she knows that Frank has already had Fenton change the will to provide funds for their educations.

Frank has given away nearly everything. Gloria controls a trust that includes the paper, the farmland, most of the downtown properties, bank accounts, and the new Chevy Malibu. The house, stocks, gas station, and of course the Lion, are in another trust controlled by Russ. To avoid excessive taxes, Julie has been "sold" the shiny new Camaro and her restaurant building with upstairs apartments by making miniscule payments to Gloria's trust. The New York bait shop's mortgages have been assumed along with all of Maggie's and Valerie's debts. Sizable sums have also been put into the Community Fund for youth causes, the local food pantry, adult work training programs, and several high school scholarship programs. The church's mortgage has been paid off and additional funds put in its foundation. Harold is not to speak of the donation's origins, but most in the congregation know it had to be from Frank.

Most dramatically, it was revealed in last week's *Sentinel* that Frank provided the final funding needed for the new art gallery set to open in February. Russ printed the article, although Frank asked him not to. For his donation, the board of directors named the gallery the James & Mary Barnett Visual and Performing Arts Center and added Gloria, Russ, and Julie to the board as Frank requested.

All that Frank retains are his meager personal belongings and a small salaried title as Publisher Emeritus that provides health coverage for medical bills and enough life insurance for funeral expenses.

Since Gloria spends most of her time caring for Frank, she asked the paper's accountant to temporarily manage the business side of things. Russ also hired a couple of part-time reporters to help pick up the slack while he comes over every afternoon to sit beside Frank's bed to talk—to listen, really, about the events that need to be told and maybe even be written.

After the fishing trip, Russ got the details about Fritz Weggling being a young, directionless young man when Chief Wells got him drunk then sent him to knock out the guard and shoot Booker in his cell before he could be transported to Richland County. Russ sits dumbfounded and listens as Frank angrily condemns men who burned crosses and explains how a police chief took the diner money and had an innocent man framed and later killed. Frank says the mayor swept it all under the rug out of fear for his own safety from the Klan and that James chose not to expose it all to protect the innocent townspeople, especially Gloria, from the world's vulgarity. All those details were omitted from Frank's story to the sheriff and from Russ's sanitized *Sentinel* article of Weggling's death. The Weggling family as well as the community's perception of reality were protected. But the innocence of Russ's Uncle Booker remains buried as well.

However, Frank did tell the sheriff, the mayor, and Deputy Phil how he helped Chief Wells end his wretched life with his own gun. The sheriff was surprised but did not seem to care much; the mayor pretended to find it morbidly humorous; and Wells's son Phil appeared relieved, almost thankful.

Chief Wells's suicide up by the Niagara got a brief, four-inch, matter-of-fact story on page two in the *Sentinel* and fifteen seconds on the Niagara television news channels. The Niagara stations were unaware that Frank provided the gun, and Russ chose not to share the fact in the paper. It was his second act of withholding information. For their own diverse reasons, the sheriff and the recently reelected mayor have told no one about the gun's source.

Attending Wells's funeral in New York were only his son Phil, two people from Our Lady of Peace Nursing Residence, a priest, a funeral director, and a couple grave diggers.

When the pain in Frank's head subsides enough, he remembers and confesses to Russ about having had the intoxicating urge to shoot Wells. He also admits his glaring failings as a dad and husband and absolves his father James of many human frailties. Frank surmises that James hoped the town's bigotry would die a natural death and approvingly concludes, "It appears almost dead now. Maybe it will finally go out with me and guys like Old Man Loomis."

He also told Russ, "Booker's framing and murder is in your hands now. But you have to decide if it should be told." He said the details could make for a good series—maybe one that could even win a few Ohio Newspaper Association awards and finally undo the mayor once and for all. "But you have to decide if taking him down and clearing Booker is worth what it would do to Mrs. Weggling and her boys. The truth about Fritz would devastate them and many others in the town."

Frank also tells Russ that all the details are in a notarized document in a bank deposit box somewhere—to be released by Fenton if anything ever happens to Russ—and the mayor knows it.

Frank also shares warmer stories with Russ. Just a few days ago Frank recounted, for the third time, his last visit with his mother shortly after the fishing trip. Frank delighted in sharing a giant box of chocolates with Mary and singing "I'll Fly Away" with her that evening. It was a visit filled with love, calm, and appreciation. The next morning, he found that she had peacefully flown away, asleep in her bed. He said Mom would have been pleased with her beautiful service with an overcrowded sanctuary, but also slightly embarrassed by Harold's touching sermon about her being the strongest woman in town.

Frank affectionately recounted Mary's story about conversing with a nine-year-old Larry just a few days before she died and how excited she was to know she would soon be with him. He also wondered aloud about his mother's joyous reunion with Larry and if he would get to see them both again when he died. It was also the first time Russ had heard the story of the tragic fire and the sorrow of the Christmas bicycle. But Frank said nothing about Larry visiting as an adult during the time around the fishing trip. He feared it would have sounded like the tumor had already won the battle.

After telling the tragic house-fire story to Russ, Frank pointed to the shadowbox in the hallway that displays Larry's 1950s-era ball glove and Roy Rogers' knife, ring, and spur.

"Russ, when I die, I want you to take that shadowbox and Larry's photo off my wall and display them in your house. They are my greatest possessions. When people ask you about them, you can tell them that the things belonged to my brother. I want them to know that Larry lived and was a real boy and had real hopes and dreams."

Frank also apologized on several occasions for not being able to attend the funeral of football player George Sauer. He said he should have spent more time with George, talked to him, and held his hand just to let him know someone remembered him as a Super Bowl hero.

"Ya know," Frank had said to Russ, "George never wrote that book he wanted to write, and I never did either. I think he could have written a pretty good book about the Jets team and what it was like to hang around Joe Namath that crazy Super Bowl year. I think George knew about both the violence and the beauty of football but didn't know how to describe it before it was too late. It would have been a good book.

"Maybe I could've written one about the sins and the goodness around this town. You know, it's all right to show the ugliness to prove there is beauty, right? Maybe now you and Gloria can write about that for me—for us. I'm afraid Le Fleur hasn't seen enough of its foulness to really appreciate its simple majesty."

Frank has more difficulty talking about Professor Jim, who now cannot even remember his own name or the colossal Hemingway persona. The literature he loved lies dormant somewhere, never to be retold with his colorful theatrics. Frank said he hopes Jim's tales live on in the students he taught.

Last week Frank told Russ, "I'm not afraid anymore to die, but I get sad to think that all my thoughts and feelings will die with me, like Jim's will. Between the pains, my mind still races with strange ideas and possibilities. I can't explain them all to you, and they will be buried with me. I wonder if Jim still thinks about his stories but just can't tell them. Maybe he is tormented by that. He and I are sorta like George Sauer. When we go, people won't know what mattered to us, the things we really cared about, or that we even existed at all."

Frank talks less these days. But when he feels well enough, he reads brief passages of the great books that he had promised himself his entire life he would devour. Sometimes a page or two from the great creators is all he can muster before the headaches, coughing, and vomiting throw him down hard. Other times he is well enough to manage a couple of chapters, several magazine articles, and a few written notes to friends and acquaintances. He writes to people he has not seen for months, years, or even decades, about how they helped shape his life or brought him joy. In some notes he asks for forgiveness for his real or imagined petty crimes against them. His spirits soar when notes of pardon and well wishes are mailed back. Frank rarely uses the Internet, but a couple of weeks ago, in a sense of urgency, he sent long-time friend Dave an email of reconciliation. They grew apart when Frank soured after his divorce. He now anxiously awaits a response.

Frank says blinking electrons are impersonal; hand-written notes exude sincerity. He says, "Writing lasts. They can keep my notes and know that I really lived and that they really meant something to me."

Le Fleur residents, especially members of the town's service clubs, often call to ask if they can stop by to visit with Frank, but Gloria has been instructed to politely tell them no. His pride will not allow anyone except his closest few favorite people to see him in his advanced, deteriorating condition.

One of those allowed to come sit at the bedside is Pastor Harold, who every few days brings cheeseburgers and milkshakes for lunch. Frank manages only a little of the burgers but does drink most of the shakes. Gloria goes for walks or to the store while the two men explore redemption and dive into the profoundness and contrast of the Greek definitions of the four loves. Their bond brings them a great appreciation for the Biblical expression of agape and philia. Both men bask in this most primal form of Church, with each believing that the hour is more meaningful and comforting to them than the other. Frank always has Harold recite Bible verses before leaving. He often asks for Revelation 22:1-3 which begins, "Then the angel showed me the river of water of life, as clear as crystal, flowing from the throne of God and of the Lamb." Naps are always more restful after that.

Then there are the times he cherishes most—Gloria sitting with him pretending all is well, recollecting funny stories of the newspaper office and events that happened in the community over the years. Those sessions often end with Frank talking about how he now understands James and appreciates him like never before. Once he told Gloria, "Dad had his cracks and I have mine. We're all broken in some way, aren't we? I guess it's not the cracks that matter. Sort of like a sidewalk—all that's important is to try and patch 'em up so other folks don't trip over 'em. You know, Jim told me that Hemingway said the world breaks everyone, but some get stronger at the broken places. I'd like you to remember that Jim told me that, Gloria."

"I will. But you remember how it ended for Hemingway, right? And someone also said that we're all a little broken. We don't need more varnish—we need a carpenter."

He grimaced that day and said, "You always need to throw a little religion in, don't you?"

# Chapter Thirty-One

The front door creaks and Russ stumbles into the living room, shaking his coat sleeves and dabbing the moisture from his face.

"The rain's lettin' up," Russ says. "Should be clearin' soon."

Frank rolls over in a state of half-sleep induced by pills. Gloria raises her finger to her lips in Russ's direction as he sheds his coat and shoes. He goes to the coffee pot to pour himself a cup, then joins her at the table.

Russ whispers, "How's he doing today?"

"About the same as yesterday. Good, then bad, then a little better again. He's been sleeping for about three hours. I imagine he'll wake up soon. He'll need more pills."

Russ rubs the rim of his cup. "Mom, how long do you think he can hang on?"

Gloria takes a deep breath and blows out hard and long. "I think every day may be the last one. Then, sometimes, I think it could be weeks or months. I know he would like to see the dedication of the art gallery, but I don't see that happening."

"What'd the doc say yesterday?"

Gloria pours herself more coffee. "He really doesn't know. He said at this stage it was a guessing game, and it comes down to when Frank is tired of fighting and ready to go. He said people have the ability to will themselves to live a few more days or to throw in the towel when they are fed up. He said when Frank stops eating altogether, that'll mean he's done. I guess that's the state of modern medicine—it still comes down to the will to live versus the desire to die."

Frank starts flailing around the bed as he begins to awaken. His eyes finally open with fright until his awareness of place and companions catch up to his fears.

Gloria chirps lightheartedly, "Well, well, if the man of leisure hasn't finally decided to join us."

Frank tries to respond, but hacking coughs overtake his attempt. Russ starts to rise to go to Frank, but Gloria grabs his arm to hold him back.

"Give him a minute."

Frank gathers himself and manages to swing his legs over the side of the bed. The effort causes heavy breaths as he searches for more energy.

Gloria says, "Do you need the bedpan?"

"No, I want to use the bathroom—like any man would. I'm feeling pretty good. Really, I am."

Gloria and Russ join him at the bed and gently lift him to his feet. They flip on light switches as they shuffle down the hallway to the bathroom. Russ helps Frank while Gloria waits in the hall. Frank clings to this shred of modesty and Gloria obliges. Frank wants to wash away the sleep and brush his teeth before Julie arrives. Every couple of days Russ shaves Frank and even applies some cologne. Today is that day. Frank will not allow the nurse to shave him since he believes only another man can understand how to navigate a face with a sharp razor.

Julie comes by most evenings and brings dinner for everyone and helps Frank choke down a few bites. Mashed potatoes and gravy work best. Once in a while she even manages to get Frank to take a few bites of pie as she holds his idle hand during the ordeal of feeding himself. Other times when his strength is low, she has to feed him but will always wipe his lips and kiss his cheek when he is finished. Gloria and Russ will sit and watch Julie in wonderment, hiding their tears while she patiently dotes over Frank.

Russ finishes the shave, and Frank smiles widely with an appreciative nod. The trio make it back to the kitchen table where Frank is helped to sit. Gloria pours him a half cup of coffee and a glass of water.

"Frank, there's a piece of mail for you on the table. You want me to open it for you?"

"Yeah. Who's it from?"

"It's from your old buddy Dave."

Frank's eyes widen as Gloria opens the envelope and hands him the card. Frank trembles to put on his glasses and reads the note with softening, contented eyes.

Dave had been the closest person to Frank for many years, as close as a brother—uniquely cleaved, similar to Pastor Harold. Dave and Frank were like family that would discuss almost anything—things that men who are wholly confided in each other would share. However, over the last few years they had a parting of temperaments. When Dave moved to Texas, each waited for the other to take the first step to mend the brotherhood. But men can be silently stubborn in their self-perceived virtue. That was until Dave knew he had to seek reconciliation when the news arrived about Frank's condition. This note delivers the long-desired news that Frank craves—Dave is flying up next week to visit.

"Well? What's it say?" Gloria asks. "You want to talk about it?"

Frank cannot speak at first, then manages, "Not right now. Maybe later."

She knows the card has good news, but he simply folds the note and slips it into his pajama shirt pocket. He shuts his eyes, rubs his cheeks, and lets a weight slide from his shoulders. Gloria smiles, knowing that this is the card he wanted most of all to receive.

"All right, folks," she says buoyantly, "I think we should do something tonight."

Frank winces. "Gloria, I told you, I don't want to put up any Christmas decorations."

"No, it's not that, Frank, even though I think we should do that too. Right now, I'm talking about something different."

"Oh yeah? What's that?"

"After you go to bed later and sleep a few hours, I think we should get up, drive out to the country, and watch the meteor shower. It's at its peak tonight. And it's clearing up. It's going to be almost fifty, and the moon will be down. Should be perfect for watching."

Frank and Russ look at each other, then at Gloria, in astonishment.

"I'm not kidding," she insists. "I really think we should do it. It'll be fun. We'll wrap you up in blankets and we'll take those recliners from the patio and a thermos of coffee."

Frank asks, "Where on earth would we go?"

"We could go to your big field out at the end of North Street. It should be nice and dark out there."

"Yeah," Frank perks up. "There's a lot of stone at the entry to the field so it wouldn't be muddy at all. No tall trees or streetlights or anything around there, either. But you know what? It isn't my field anymore, it's yours."

Russ gets up to get more coffee. "Are you guys serious?"

Frank straightens up. "Why the hell not," he bellows. "We could head out there about two o'clock and lay back and watch the stars. Even if we don't see any meteors, it'll be great to get out and get some fresh air for a change. Gloria, do you think Julie would go too?"

"I know she would."

"You've already asked her?"

"Well," she pauses, "It was really her idea. She brought it up a few nights ago after you fell asleep."

Frank settles back with satisfaction.

"Damn. This is a great idea. I don't think I've looked up at the stars since the fishing trip."

The front door opens with a racket and Russ moves quickly to help Julie carry several bags of food to the kitchen table.

She says, "Well, look who's up, sitting there all clean and polished."

Frank's glee pours out. "Julie, you sweet little thing. I'm so glad you're here. You know what Gloria told me?"

"Well, I think I might have an idea."

"Yep, we're going to go out to watch the meteors tonight. That's a brilliant idea, sweetheart!"

Julie puts one hand on his shoulder and holds his elbow with the other. She leans in to kiss his cheek with a softness borne from years of stealing looks at him from across the diner counter while hoping for something much more. He reaches up to smooth back her hair with equal tenderness.

"You sure you're up to it?" she asks. "It's kind of a crazy idea. I didn't know if you'd really want to do it."

"Don't be silly," he says. "Of course I do. Gloria has it all worked out. We'll go down to the field at the end of North Street and take the recliners. Hell, we can even take some wood and have a little bonfire. No, wait. That wouldn't be good. We need darkness. A fire would wash out the view. But we could take coffee, and all lay there and watch the show. Gloria said it's going to be clear and fifty. Perfect. Just perfect."

"Okay, okay," Gloria interjects, "we'll see if you are up to it tonight."

"Oh, we're gonna do it. I'm going no matter what. You have to set the alarm and get me up. I'm cutting back on the meds tonight so I won't be so damn out of it. We're gonna do this. Now Julie, whadya bring to eat? I'm starving."

The food is unpacked and Frank attacks it. The others wonder if he is overdoing it.

"Frank," Gloria mothers, "slow down. You're going to make yourself sick."

"Now, that's funny, Gloria. Sick. I'm going to make myself sick. You funny woman. Julie, this is fantastic meatloaf. The candied carrots are great too. I can taste everything. What kind of pie did you bring?"

"Pecan."

"Holy cow. Gloria, heat it up and get the ice cream out!"

Gloria obliges. Frank devours his pie and ice cream and lets out a mammoth belch.

"Damn good, Julie. Incredible."

"I'm glad you enjoyed it. That's the most you've eaten in weeks."

Russ picks up the to-go boxes while Julie cleans and kisses Frank's face and helps him take a half dose of pills with Coke. The team then steadies him for a trip to the restroom.

"I got this, ladies," he quips, giving Russ a wry grin. "No help needed. I can make it down the hall."

He succeeds in the trip and hobbles back to the bed and sits on the edge. Julie climbs up next to Frank while the others pull up closely.

"Thank you for dinner, Julie. Thank you all for taking care of me the last few months. You all know you're my family, right? The three of you are all I have. I didn't want to be a burden to you like this, but I'm so lucky to have you in my life. I love all of you. I know you'll take care of things after I'm gone, too. That gives me peace. Now, I want to talk about the funeral."

"Frank," Gloria whispers, "we don't need to talk about that now."

"No, we do. It's the perfect time. My head is clear and I have strength."

Julie puts his hand in hers. She wipes her eyes but holds back the sobs. He strains upward to kiss her on the head, then arches his back with purpose.

"I've written everything down about how I want the funeral to be, and I gave it to Harold when he came to visit a couple weeks ago. He's a wonderful man, probably more like Jesus than any person I've ever met. He probably knows me as well as anyone but the three of you."

Julie looks at the floor to avoid breaking down as he continues to talk out the window.

"Gloria, no matter when I die, I want the funeral to be on a Friday evening. I'd like it to start about seven. Harold has all the stuff I'd like for folks to read and the music I want played."

He turns his attention back to the trio. "Russ, you're going to need to download a couple songs and give them to Harold. At the start I want the song 'Ancient Highway' by Van Morrison played. It's almost nine minutes, so that should give everyone enough time to get settled. A lot of folks are going to think it's a weird funeral song, but it's my favorite, so they'll just have to suffer through it.

"After the funeral I want 'Amazing Grace' played outside on bagpipes and then the wake to be down at the VFW Hall. Fenton's got all the details on that and everything's paid for already. I want everyone to have a lot to eat and drink. I want a big party—well, that is, if anyone else besides you guys show up. The burial can be Saturday morning, with just Harold and the few of you there. I always liked Saturday mornings, so I guess that's a good time for a sendoff at the cemetery, but I don't want to ruin Saturday for other folks.

"I also gave a list to Fenton about who should get some of the things around here. Ya know, most everything's junk that needs thrown away, but there are a few little things I'll want each of you to have. Fenton's got the list, but Russ, I want you to be in charge of making sure everybody gets what they should."

"Me?"

"Yep. You're the man now, as they say."

"Okay, Frank. I'll do whatever you want."

"And one more thing. My sons. At some point, they'll find out I died and show up to claim whatever I left them. Fenton has a box of stuff for them. Everything they get is in that box. Russ, I want you to be there when Fenton gives it to them. There's a note taped to it and I want you to read it to them and be my voice. I want them to know you've been like my son in their place, but I also want them to know that they have never been out of my mind through all the years. I've never blamed them or their mother for what happened. Maybe the things in there will help change their opinion of me—at least I hope they do."

Russ's voice cracks. "Okay, I'll handle it."

"And I want to be buried next to my brother Larry. He's next to my parents, because he's their firstborn. I'll be on the other side of him. The plot and headstone are already paid for. Shelby Monuments already has the inscription on the stone."

"Frank, please don't," Gloria begs. "We don't need to talk about this sadness now."

"Gloria," Frank assures, "the saddest part isn't that I'm dying. The real tragedy is that I didn't start to think about living and loving until I found out there was so little time left. I want you to know that I love you three more than anything, and I have found peace in your love for me."

Gloria and Julie reach for the tissue boxes and cover their faces as they cry. Julie buries her head into Frank's shoulder while Russ envelopes his mother.

"I'm sorry," Frank concedes, "but I needed to talk about this stuff. I needed my family to know these things. Now, there's something else I need to tell you and I know you're going to think I'm nuts."

Curious, they draw closer.

"You know that old man Larry that was hanging around town back in the fall and who we saw in the diner? Well, he was really my brother. He came back here to help me through all of this. He would appear out of nowhere and talk to me. Remember that day in the office, Gloria, when I said some crazy man was there? That was Larry. He was also there when Fritz got shot. And I saw him a couple times in New York too."

"Oh Frank," Gloria gasps. "We've talked about him. Larry was just a nice old man that had a way of making everybody feel good. He went back home to Cincinnati. Your brother Larry died in the fifties, long before you were born, when you were just a child. It must have been the medicine or something that caused you to get the two confused."

"No. I'm sure of it, Gloria. The last time I saw Larry was when Russ and I stopped at the cemetery on the way home from fishing. He spoke to me by his grave. It was my brother, all grown up, as an old man, as he would be had he lived."

Gloria goes into the kitchen to get more coffee, while Julie goes to the hall bathroom to regain her composure. Russ is left not knowing what to say.

"You believe me, don't you, Russ?"

"Well, I guess so. But I didn't see an old man at the cemetery."

"No, you wouldn't have seen him because you were busy playing on your phone. You didn't notice anything that was going on around you. That's a dangerous habit for a good reporter."

Gloria returns to sit next to Frank and wraps his hands around a cup of coffee.

"Here, Frank, take this. I put a little scotch in it. It should help you relax a bit."

"Well, thanks. I'm already pretty relaxed, but I've sure missed the taste."

Frank relishes his elixir as silence grates the time. Finally, Russ gets up to pour his own scotch coffee.

He stammers, "I think I could use one of those too."

Julie emerges from the bathroom with reddened face and puffy eyes, having done the best she could to subdue her weeping and fix her makeup. She sits across the room in Frank's preferred worn chair with sturdy arms and sunken padding where he has collapsed so many times.

"Okay, Frank," Gloria says. "Let's say that Old Man Larry is your brother. How's that possible? We've all seen him around town. We've all shaken his hand. He feels like a real person to me. So, what, he just appeared to you like a ghost?"

"I don't know how he appeared to me. He just did. At first, I thought it was my tumor playing tricks on me, but now I know it was really him. I touched him, too. He was real, but he wasn't. I don't know, I guess it's one of those weird mysteries you always hear about. But I have complete faith he was my brother."

Frank shuts his eyes and lowers his head to let a wave of agony course through his head and neck. During these attacks he loses cognitive and verbal abilities but has learned that crossing his arms close to his chest before the worst of it will help him gather enough strength to battle the insurgency. Gloria opens a blind and raises the window to allow the reinforcements of bursting sunlight and clean air to aid Frank in his cerebral skirmish.

In recent, lucid days he has tried to shore up his mental fortress by reading heady scientific journals. One article that fascinated him examined the "duality paradox" of light; how it may exist as either particles or waves, depending upon different physical settings or one's perspective. He surmised that he and Larry communicated through a unique, shared viewpoint of light, thanks to some quirky, molecular quantum physics even the worthy scientists cannot fully understand.

The explosions in his head subside and he finally wins this little battle. But the assaults always return to chip away at the castle wall of the brain. All fortifications in his head and throughout his body will soon be breached and the victory flag of cancer resolutely planted.

Frank finally drifts back from the fray with a couple of deep breaths. He scratches his face and refocuses on Gloria as though he never paused.

"You're a fairly religious person, so you have faith in things you can't see and don't understand, right? Why not this? Why can't you have faith in Larry coming to me as my brother?"

Gloria quietly moves to the window to bathe in the rain shower's lingering moistness. She runs her fingers from her forehead through the silky black hair to her shoulders. She begins to speak. She stops. She rubs again. Defending religious faith is perilous when convictions have been severely tested by doubt. She fears her well-rehearsed, balanced sermon of poignancy will melt into insolence now that uncertainty has grabbed onto her lectern.

She mutters, "Well, I guess with God, all things are possible, aren't they?"

"You guess?" Frank quips. "You don't know? I thought you talked to God every day."

"Well." She delays, stretches, and inhales hard. "I'm finding it harder to talk to him. I think we're mad at each other."

"Mad? You think God is mad at you?"

"I don't know. Maybe. Perhaps he has a right to be."

"Why is that?"

"Oh, I don't know. Maybe because I haven't been so faithful."

"I see. Is that because you've prayed for me to be healed and you know it isn't going to happen? You feel deserted, maybe?"

"Maybe a little bit," Gloria admits. "I just believed God would heal you."

Frank scrunches his face. "Well, that really would be a miracle at this point, wouldn't it? Maybe you're just praying for the wrong thing. I've prayed for lots of things the last couple months but being healed wasn't one of them."

Gloria is surprised. "*You've* been praying?"

"Sure. Imminent demise can do that to a man. You want another shocker? I've lain here the last month and read the Bible from cover to cover. Bet you didn't even know I was doing that, since it was mixed in with my other books and magazines. I'd wake up in the middle of the night and read for a while. Harold brought it to me and we prayed together. I think you were at the grocery at the time."

Gloria looks over her glasses, astonished.

Frank nods to Julie. "What about you, darling? Do you think God gets mad at people?"

Julie tries to sit up.

"I don't think God gets mad." She pauses. "I think maybe he gets disappointed. Maybe more like hurt, like when a parent gets let down when a child does something thoughtless. The parent feels the pain, but mostly for the kid. He just wants to grab and shake the kid and tell her she's wasting chances and can do better. Then he hugs her, forgives, and believes she will be kinder, or at least hopes she will."

Frank clears his throat roughly. "How would you understand that? You don't have any kids."

She talks through her bit lip. "No, but I have a dad. And I've hurt him plenty of times, but he always forgave me."

Frank flickers her an approving smile. "Yes. Yes. Forgiveness. So important, isn't it?" He picks up strength again. "But, ya know, I think it's a lot easier to forgive than to ask forgiveness, don't ya think?"

"What do you mean?"

Frank repositions himself on the bed.

"Well Julie, when you said or did something to hurt your dad, all he wanted was to know that you didn't want him to hurt anymore. He was eager to hear that you were sorry and forgive you. Everyone, except for the most scornful, maybe, are eager to forgive. But, taking the first step for you to admit you were wrong and recognize that you hurt him—that's the tough, prideful part. It requires a lot of humility. That kind of humility is a hard thing for people."

Gloria goes into the kitchen to pretend to tidy up, wipe things down, and do anything to be elsewhere than part of that conversation. Russ stays and listens closely.

Julie says, "You're right, Frank. I felt his pain go away when I asked for his forgiveness. When I asked, he knew I cared about his hurt, that I loved him."

Frank waves Julie over and she slides onto the bed, drapes her arms around his neck, sniffles, and kisses his cheek.

"I'm sorry, Frank," Julie pleads. "Will you forgive me?"

"For heaven's sake, what are you talking about?"

She pulls back to look Frank in the eyes. "I need to take that pain away you talked about, the pain I've caused you. I've loved you for a long time, but I played hard to get. I should've been more receptive. I should've let you get closer. We should've been together."

Russ now feels like a voyeur. He slips to the kitchen and joins his mom with faux cleaning and pretending not to listen to the lovers who never were, yet always were.

Frank wipes a tear from Julie's cheek.

"Listen Julie, of course I would forgive you, but there's nothing to forgive you for. You've been here every day. Brought me food, fed me, loved me like a wife. You, Gloria, and Russ—my God, you've all shown me so much love. Love that I didn't earn. But that didn't matter to you. You loved me anyway. I've felt it in my soul these last few months. I'm the one who should be asking you for forgiveness. I'm the one who should have shown you love from the start. Years ago."

The two hug and kiss like young lovers would, the closest they have ever been. New tears of absolution smudge across their lips, eyelashes, noses, and earlobes. They fall back onto the bed and hug through alternating sobs. They stay embraced for a long minute until they remember the others.

Frank raises up. "Dammit, I have to pee."

He slides off the bed and scoots to the hall bathroom. Julie wipes her face in her shirtsleeve and slinks to the kitchen and pours a drink.

"Since when did you start drinking whiskey?" Gloria asks.

"Just this second. Funny, huh?"

"Well then, I guess I should give it a try too."

Gloria uses a bowl to scoop ice out of the freezer and the three caretakers sit around the kitchen table and pass the Glenlivet.

Julie and Gloria sip, gasp, and cough. Russ smiles and enjoys the fact he can drink the liquor without all the theatrics. "C'mon, don't you know this is the nectar of the gods? That's what Frank says, anyway."

Frank comes back down the hall and stops at the kitchen in surprise.

"What's this? You're all drinking my scotch? Man, I'm glad I have a couple extra bottles stashed above the fridge!"

He awkwardly fills in at the table and takes the glass from Julie for a sip, then hands it back.

"Boy, that's good isn't it?"

Julie snorts, "Well, I don't know about good, but it sure gets your attention."

Laughs circulate among the improbable group of new drinking buddies. Frank laughs at them, then asks, "Russ, could you go and reach up over the fridge to get those two other bottles down?"

"Frank!" Gloria snaps. "You aren't planning on drinking those now, are you?"

"No sis, I just thought we might take those with us tonight to the meteor show."

She sighs. "Why on earth do you need to take two?"

Russ says, "Damn, that's a great idea." He jumps up and stretches to reach into the high cabinet. He pulls two rectangular boxes down and stares at them.

"Jesus, Frank, these are twenty-one-year-old bottles. What are these, like two hundred a bottle?"

"Almost three hundred," Frank mumbles.

Gloria's jaw drops. "Three hundred bucks for a bottle of whiskey? That's crazy."

Frank proudly extends his neck and talks with his hands. "Well, I was saving them for a special occasion, and I think tonight would qualify as that."

Julie puts her glass of ice down and stands behind Frank with her hands on his shoulders.

"It's a special night indeed, Frank. Very special."

Gloria drops a few more cubes into her glass, pours a short drink, and takes a sip. She speaks timidly.

"Well. It's a special night for sure," she begins. "We've heard about Frank's ghost brother visiting us all, so I guess there's something I might as well tell everyone too. Guess this time is as good as any."

Her resolve grows. "Julie and Russ, you should sit down. Julie, I'm glad you're here, 'cause you're really part of the family, and I want you to hear this too."

Puzzled, Russ lays the boxed bottles down on the table and takes a seat.

Julie sits next to Frank. She takes his hand serenely, as though expecting to hear about the weather.

"Well Gloria, what do you have to tell us?"

Gloria drains the glass, then looks Russ in the eyes.

"Russ, you know James and I were very close. I loved him very much. He was a proud and complicated man. But he was always there for me. He never let me down."

A long pause floods the room with pregnancy of a grand statement.

"He never let me down. Remember that. But I have to tell you this, and you may not like it."

She bites her thumbnail and sighs softly.

Russ begs, "Okay, Mom, what, already?"

Gloria blurts, "Russ, James was your father."

Silence.

Russ finally asks cynically, "What? Are you kidding me?"

"No. I wouldn't joke about something like this. You and Frank are half-brothers."

Russ stands and backs up to the sink as if the table were on fire.

"Jesus, Mom. What the hell are you saying? You and James? You were messing around?"

Frank leans in. "Sit down, Russ. Don't be disrespectful to your mother."

"Frank," Russ continues, "Did you hear what she said? Your dad and my mom. You gettin' this?"

"Yes, I'm getting it. Are you? Let your mom talk."

Russ sits down again with resignation.

"Okay, Mom, what else you got?"

"Well, we weren't messing around, as you say. We each had one night of loneliness. It was one night, and we were both afraid of some things. He was in his office crying, and I went in to see what was going on with him. I told him things were going to be okay and I just hugged him. Then things just happened."

"Oh my God. You did it right there in the office. Right there?"

"It was just the one time, Russ."

Russ rubs his hands and stares at his fingers.

"I know you're shocked," Gloria says, "but I thank God every day for you. You saved me, and I love you more than life itself. I also believe God has forgiven me for my indiscretion."

"Well, I guess I'm kind of shocked," Russ says, "but I have to tell you that I often wondered if I might've been Frank's kid. I guess I wasn't too far off, but I never suspected James, since he was older."

Russ's tone softens. "So, you two just went about your business after you got pregnant? Did Dad know? Well, the guy who thought he was my dad—did he know?"

"No, Dwayne thought he was your father, but he just couldn't handle the responsibility, so he took off back to his drugs and women. James made everything possible for you. Anything you needed, he paid for."

Russ leans back and stares at Frank, trying to comprehend that they are half-brothers. He examines Frank's face as if discerning the meaning of some strange, contemporary painting in a museum.

He finally asks, "So, did you know about this, that we were brothers?"

Frank licks his lips and makes a chewing sound to get moisture into his mouth before answering. "Yeah, I've known for a while. Gloria told me after we got back from the fishing trip. She thought I should know. We were wondering when to break it to you. We thought maybe we shouldn't even tell you."

"Well, I'm glad you did. I just don't know what to say."

Gloria moves to Russ's side and touches his face. "I know, son. I didn't like keeping it from you. Not sure why I picked now to tell you. It just seemed like the right time."

"Well, Julie," Russ asks, "Whaddaya think about all this?"

"All I know is that you have two people here that love you tremendously. Well, three, actually, because I do too. And, you have a brother. That's all pretty good, isn't it?"

Russ leans in toward Frank.

"Okay, brother, what do you think about all this?"

Frank bends in closer and holds Russ's hand. "Well, I've always felt close to you and Gloria, like we were a family. I'm honored to have you as my brother. I've always felt like you were a son to me, but you were my little snot-nosed brother all along. I always wanted a brother, ya know. And you know what else? I'm an uncle to Nick. How cool is that? Actually, I'm pretty happy about all of it. I just can't wait for Ann to find out, though—she may blow a gasket."

"Yeah, Ann," Russ laments. "I have a feeling she isn't going to be all that crazy to find out I'm a Barnett. Of course, she wasn't even happy when I came home with the Corvette. She said it was a stupid and pointless car—that it would help ruin the environment for Nick and his kids. She finds the worst in everything. Her glass is always half empty."

"So, then," Gloria says, "don't be like her. Your glass is not just half full, it's completely full. Rejoice in this, son, and be proud of who you are. Be proud you are my son and Frank's brother."

Frank gets up and wobbles stiffly, like an old man, to the refrigerator.

"Hey brother, how about a piece of pecan pie? I'm gonna have one."

Russ cackles. "We're talking about all this big stuff and you're gonna have pie?"

"Hey, when you are in my condition, any time is pie time."

"All right, Frank. I'll have a piece too."

Frank returns with half a pie and small plates and forks and cuts slices for him and Russ.

"Anyone else?"

The ladies shake their heads no.

Julie says, "Frank, this is the best you've been in a long time."

"Yes it is, darlin'. I feel great. I have your love, a new brother, and some sort of stepmom, I guess."

Everyone laughs, then Gloria says, "Oh my goodness, that's not true, but it is all weird, isn't it?"

Frank lifts a bite of pie with his fork and holds it in the air.

"Here's to my brother, his wonderful mom who acts like my boss, and sweet, precious Julie who loves me like a wife. I give thanks for all of you. And this pie. I mostly give thanks that I can eat this pie."

"Oh, Frank," Julie says, "you're silly."

"I'm glad you think silly and not crazy, with me telling ghost stories and all. Now, how about you and Gloria go to the store? Surely there is something you two need to go shopping for. I want to spend a little time with Russ, if you don't mind. Just two brothers chewing the fat, or the pie in this case. You ladies good with that?"

"Sure," Gloria says, "You men can have a nice talk. We'll be back in about an hour."

Gloria and Julie gather their purses and jackets and stop at the door to look back at the men hunched over the kitchen table. They wonder if the brothers will summon the courage to squeeze out candid answers to all the big, bewildering questions.

## Chapter Thirty-Two

"Well," Frank treads softly, "Why don't you tell me how you feel?"

Russ picks up the bowl Gloria used for ice and gets up to dig out his own supply from the freezer. He arranges two of the used glasses, opens one of the old Glenlivets, and pours carefully.

"Whaddaya wanna know?"

Frank asks, "First of all, what do you think about being my brother?"

"How about giving me a minute to think about it while I savor your expensive whiskey?"

Both men take healthy sips and wait for conversation. Russ finishes off his drink then pours himself a double.

"So?" Frank asks.

"You want to know how I feel about finding out that you're my half-brother?"

"Yeah, but mostly, I want to know what you're going to do with the information."

"Whaddaya mean?"

"Well, you gonna let people know? You gonna be resentful toward your mom? You gonna hold it against my dad—our dad?"

"I don't know. I can't be mad at my mom. I guess I can't be mad at James, either. Without him I wouldn't be here. I guess it's all just surprising. I don't know what I think about letting people know, though. What's it to them?"

"Yeah, it's not their damn business, is it? Who gives a crap what they think? But, ya know, if someday you wanted, you could shout it out in a seventy-two-point headline that you're my brother. That'd send a buzz around town, wouldn't it?"

"Yeah, it would. But I don't think I'd want to embarrass Mom. And what about your family? Everyone would know your dad messed around."

Franks swirls the ice in his glass. "Not sure they'd find it all that surprising. I think he had a reputation. Anyway, you don't think half the people in this town didn't do the same thing?"

Russ takes a drink while he muses.

"You damn well better believe they did," Frank declares. "Anyway, I guess it's just strange when you find out something that's been hidden from you your whole life, huh?"

"Yeah, you can say that again. I guess it's sort of like when you found out about Wells and the whole Klan thing."

Frank nods slowly, shuts his eyes, then rubs the back of his neck and head.

"You all right, Frank?"

"Yeah. I guess I kinda overdid it this evening. Lots of food and lots of whiskey. Kinda shocked the system, I guess."

Frank summons a small well of stamina to continue. "Russ, I wanna tell you some things that I hope you remember."

"Okay." Russ looks concerned, as if he is about to get a scolding.

"First, you're one of the finest people I've ever known. You're honest, hardworking, smart, and very kind to people. You're so much like your mom."

Russ is relieved. "Thanks, Frank. You saying that means a lot." He reaches into the pie pan with his fork and digs out another hunk and lets Frank continue.

"Also, if you ever want to share the story about being a Barnett, I would be proud if you did. I would kinda like the world to know that I had a brother as smart and kind as you."

Russ smiles widely. "Thanks. Maybe I inherited some of that from Mom and some from James. You got your mom and dad's good parts too, ya know."

"Maybe so. Maybe our parents gave us the good stuff—the instincts for survival, I guess."

Frank takes a sip, then continues. "Another thing, Russ, I'm happy that you're connected to Larry. With you carrying on, it's like a bit of him and me will still be around. Just wish I could have known him growing up, to share more stories about him with you. Maybe if he had lived, things would have been different between my parents. Who knows?"

Russ licks the fork as a thought incubates. "Yeah, but if that were true, maybe I wouldn't even be here."

They look at each other to assess the weight of that strangely probable consequence. Russ changes the subject.

"Frank, you really believe the old man was your brother Larry? Have you seen him lately?"

"Yes. He's my brother, and he was here. I mean he is *our* brother. I just know it's true. But no, I haven't seen him lately. When I said the cemetery was the last time, that was really it. Wish I could see him, though. There's so much more I'd like to ask him. But having seen him gives me the courage to die."

Russ shifts around nervously, wondering if he should ask the next question. "What did you and Larry talk about in the cemetery?"

Frank rubs a growing exhaustion all around his face and takes a deep sigh.

"Well, he said life was all a matter of perspective. Things we think we know can really be different depending on how we look at them, or maybe how others experience them. And the important thing is to never lose a sense of wonder—to never stop asking questions, and to never believe you have all the answers. He said when you think you understand everything, you'll become less childlike, and you'll lose a sense of joy and become dull, and your existence hollow."

"Um, that makes sense, I guess. So, he was saying that you shouldn't be so full of yourself, huh?"

Frank nods and stares somewhere across the room. Russ sees that he is drifting away in his thoughts and clumsily tries to bring him back.

"So, besides not having Larry around growing up, do you have any other regrets? Never mind, you don't have to answer that. That's stupid. I shouldn't have asked that."

Frank's attention returns. "It's a good question, Russ, a good reporter question. Who wouldn't wanna ask a dying man that?"

"Frank, you don't have to..."

"No, it's okay. I want to answer this."

Frank focuses on his hands, breathes deeply, and relaxes his posture.

"You know, I only have a few big regrets, I guess, which is pretty good at this stage.

"First, I wish I would've been better to Brenda. She deserved better. I could've tried harder but didn't, and I lost her and my boys because of it."

"Are you kidding me, Frank? From what I hear, she treated you terribly. My God, she stole a bunch of your money, ran off with the kids, and wouldn't let you see them! *She* deserved better?"

"Yes, Russ, she did. I wasn't a very good husband. I really didn't pay attention to her. By the way, she didn't steal anything. She just took money from an account we shared. I had several others she couldn't get to. She needed that money for the boys, and I was kind of glad she had it."

He rubs his hands as if trying to warm them, then scratches his head as though thinking about a great mystery. Russ sits patiently for the next thought to gel.

Frank begins again with a soft but strong voice. "Listen, you have to do your absolute best to make things work with Ann. I don't know what her issues are, but you need to be the best husband you can and help her through them. Listen to her closely. Find out what's important to her. Find out if there is a sweet woman under all that salt."

"I hope there is," Russ says. "I've tried hard to find it."

"But don't throw in the towel until you've dug to the core and found out what she's always stewing about. The trick is trying to discover that without losing yourself in the effort. You really have to give her your best, but don't go overboard and kill yourself if you find out that she's all salt after all. If you start to lose yourself and become someone else, then it's time to quit."

"How will I know that?"

"Not sure, but I think you'll know somehow. Maybe Gloria will let you know when you aren't you anymore. Moms know more about you than you can even imagine. They see your heart. No. Really, they are your heart."

"Okay. I promise to try and make it work with Ann. I really do love her."

"Then do everything you can to show her. Maybe then, if she never shows you love back, I guess you'll know it won't ever work. But don't forget to let her love you and let her know you feel her love—if she has any to share."

Frank pauses to wipe sweat from his forehead and cough softly. He looks at the floor for some more words, then looks deeply into Russ's eyes.

"Whatever happens, though, you have to be there for Nick. He's going to need you more than you can imagine. But of course, you have to realize he'll never fully understand you. Parents watch their kids grow from virtually nothing into adults—if they're lucky, anyway. We get to see them change into different people throughout their lives. But they only see us one way, as adults who try to boss them around and tell them what's good for them."

He coughs more vigorously and breathes hard to regain his strength.

"Kids don't understand that we used to be different people—that we were once little kids and teenagers just like them. We may understand being like them, but they have no idea what it's like to be adults like us. They'll only get that part when they have their own kids. Then their perspectives about us will change. Sometimes we may look better, but sometimes we may look worse. Then they'll fear becoming the older versions of us, just like we feared becoming our parents."

Frank struggles to his feet and slowly makes it to the bed as Russ follows, ready to catch him. Frank scales the bed, sits on the edge, reaches over to punch up a pillow and draw it close to his chest as he gets lost somewhere in memories of himself as a kid, playing baseball and bringing home a piece of crude art or funny essay he wrote at school. He recalls his dad sitting at his desk working on a story and barely acknowledging him or the essay that won the classroom contest and chocolate Easter bunny. He begins to tell Russ about that stinging pain, but stops as he remembers committing the same crime against his sons. He lets that memory melt away into the pillow he hugs.

Russ tries to bring him back. "Yeah, that's an interesting point of kids not really knowing us except as adults. Never thought of it like that, but since Nick was born, I've been thinking more about my dad and what it might have been like for him. I wish I knew why he had so much pain and why he was so frightened of staying, of being here to watch me grow. I wonder what really happened to him."

Frank shrugs. "I don't know."

The newfound brothers share sorrowful smiles and compassionate looks of connection that were forged long ago, but which were never fully discussed, not even on the fishing trip. A flood of tears could overtake them now if only they allowed the moment to grow. But they are men, and men have a way of circumventing emotion. They just keep swimming up that swift, cold river of murkiness, mostly alone.

Russ regains composure. "Anything else you want to share?"

"Yes, there is," Frank says. "I regret never making it to Ireland and England. I always wanted to go and thought there would be time. Now that dream dies with me. Maybe you could take Ann there, to both places. Make it a second honeymoon without Nick—go first class. Maybe you could be my eyes and I could see it all through you. Crazy, huh? Who knows, maybe that could be the start of something really good for you two."

Surprised, Russ says, "Okay. I promise to go for you. I think that would be great for Ann and me, too."

"Good. I'm glad you would do that. Take a couple things of mine and leave them in each country—bury them next to a wall or courtyard or someplace peaceful, maybe even a cemetery. I know that sounds weird, but then I would always be connected to the places. You should see if you can find any of my mom's relatives, the Adamses and Kirkpatricks, up in the north of Ireland. And go to the Ring of Kerry and look at the stars. I read about this little town called Waterville on the west coast. It's supposed to be one of the best spots in the world to stargaze. Go there and look at the stars for me.

"And go to a little town in Norfolk in northeast England called 'Scarning.' Go to the church there and look for my dad's last name in their records. I still think there are some Barnetts living there. See if you can find them and tell them hello for me. That would make me happy."

"I'll do that, Frank. What should I leave over there for you?"

"Don't know. Use your imagination. Something you think is fitting."

"Okay, I'll think about that."

More resolute now, Frank says, "You know, you're so much bigger than that little paper. You should sell that thing. Do something else. Papers are dying out, but you and your mom now have the means to do whatever you want and for whoever you want. Get out there and do something you really love for the people you love. Think about living somewhere else to get a different perspective of the world."

Surprised, Russ says, "Well, I really love the paper, and I love the town. I love the people here. Not sure I want to do anything else or live anywhere else."

"I know," Frank replies. "I just don't want you to wait until you're an old man to challenge yourself. First of all, you may never get to be an old man. But if you're lucky enough to grow old, you'll wake up one morning, look in the mirror, and wonder what happened to the younger you.

"And ya know, as you grow older, the fear of change just becomes deep mud around your feet. Moving forward to do anything different will seem scary. Then the routine of standing still in the mud becomes cool and comforting, a convenient excuse to stay where you are.

"But that routine can be overcome by doing for others first, 'cause then you have purpose and you're not worried about yourself anymore. Doing for others is really the only thing that can get you out of the mud. Besides, when you do for others, it's the only thing that can last for generations to come."

Russ nods. "Yeah, I guess you're right."

"And Russ, you really do need to scare yourself. Jump into something tough. Learn another language, pick up an instrument, paint a picture, join a choir, or write a damn book—anything—just pick something to express yourself.

"I've only recently learned that you have to dive into to that chilly fright. You have to pick at your doubt and pull back at the mystery of things. You may not be very good at the start, so it's okay to fail. The real wonder is in the trying, ya know—creating something new or different, even if it's just writing down some crazy idea you've never had before and coming back sometime later to try it. Even if you fail, share it with someone you love, maybe with Ann. Let her celebrate the trying with you. You can't be afraid of failing in front of her. If she won't celebrate the trying and accept you failing, maybe she isn't really there for you after all."

Russ stares at his teacher in amazement. He wonders where all this sage advice was hiding. He can manage only a curious mumble. "You think so?"

"Yes. If she doesn't love you when you fail, she doesn't deserve you when you excel. But I really think it can be good to fail. Just remember, you can fail a hundred times and have more joy in the trying than the person who tries once and instantly wins. Don't be seduced by the easy wins. The bliss is in the ninety-nine times where you learned something and made it better in the end."

Frank coughs some more and searches for another thought.

"I never knew the beauty of failing and having to climb back up over and over. I never experienced the satisfaction of really testing myself. I never started anything from scratch, except for this dying thing. I think I got this one down."

Frank laughs weakly at his macabre joke and Russ nervously tries to join in, then sits very still, somewhat perplexed about what to say.

Frank whispers, "Do you remember those kaleidoscopes when you were a kid? Be like one of those and let the light roll over those rocks in your head to make something different. And you have to let Nick see the best of you. He needs to see what it's like for his dad to try to do scary things. Then he will try, too.

"I hope you take him up to fish in the Niagara and go back year after year so you both can learn about what it meant to my dad and me and to make your own special memories. Then someday, he might want to take his kid, and they can talk about how awesome you were.

"And one last thing. When you try some scary new thing, don't be afraid to ask for help. We all think we have to walk through our private darkness alone, but we don't. You just have to ask, listen closely for the answers, have faith, and be open to unexpected and crazy possibilities. And ya know, those who love you will want to help. That's how I know you, Gloria, and Julie love me."

"Frank," Russ begins in a soft, frightened weep, "I'm not ready for you to go. There's so much more for you to teach me."

Soothingly, Frank says, "No my brother, it's past time for me. The species only gets stronger when the old salmon passes on. That's the only way families can improve, you know. It's your time now, then someday when you've done all you can, it'll be Nick's time. You'll find out how important it is to release those shiny trophies you tried to protect, things you thought were yours, but you really just borrowed. You'll need to hand them down to others and let them try to make them better."

Frank looks around the rooms in search of something, or someone. "You know, Russ, before I became ill, I wondered what it would be like to grow old. What it would be like to be in my seventies or eighties. Would I be an old curmudgeon living alone and afraid? Well, I'll never get that old. Right here, right now, this is my old. This is how it ends. But I'm not alone and I'm not afraid. That's not so bad, is it?"

Before Russ can answer, Frank continues, "That's all I got, Russ. I think I've overdone it tonight. I need to sleep now."

Frank coughs violently for a moment, then crawls onto his side and curls into a ball. He speaks to the smart speaker device on his side table and commands it to play the sounds of a thunderstorm. Instantly, the storm rolls into the room from a more expensive speaker to which the device is connected. The audio is amazingly realistic. It appears to be raining hard just outside the window. Faint thunder in the distance grows and rolls in the speaker, then subsides as it would on a late-summer evening. Water seems to trickle through a downspout as falling drops patter on the imagined roof of an outdoor covered patio. Russ wonders if this is randomly generated noise or an actual recording. He wants to ask but cannot dare to break the lulling mood of gathering comfort.

Frank falls into a dream of driving the Lion along the Niagara in a light rain that reflects pleasant hues in his mind to smother the pain. He is finally there again in the campground next to Lake Ontario listening to the raindrops drumming onto his tent. He is warm. He is calm. It is real to him. He looks ahead to later years and sees Russ and Nick within their similar salmon run moments that provide them comfort when the suffocating haze of doubt tries to push away their hope and faith.

Russ stands, a bit unsatisfied, as Frank slips deeper into sleep and dream. The young man wants more days like this, to dig down deep into this simple but intellectual man he has mostly taken for granted. Only now can he fully grasp the compassionate wisdom of his boss, friend, and brother. He hopes Frank can see similar complexity in him. He smiles because he believes it may be true.

Russ is surprised to find himself wanting to be close to his brother. He gently crawls into bed to snuggle close and drape his arm around Frank's chest. He listens to the sounds of amplified rain and distant thunder and believes they are real and that he is in some different place, maybe as a child in a home growing up, hugging the brother he always wanted on some scary and stormy night. He suddenly realizes, that with Frank and Larry, he has had two brothers all along. His once lonely life blends into some kind of strange, deepening sense of family tenderness that is so new, so peculiar, so reassuring. He pulls the thin blanket up to their shoulders.

"Good night, brother."

The sounds of water and rumbling thunder continue as both men sleep and dream of Niagara. They both see the other there with them. There is no talking, only being together and looking out over the lake to see the sun setting as a sparkling jewel of absolution.

Gloria and Julie return and enter the front room, surprised to see the two men sleeping on the bed. The women pull close and hold hands, not knowing what to say, so they say nothing. They stand for a long moment before walking quietly into the room. They sit. They watch. They listen to the synthetic storm. They are flooded with baffling sentiments that cannot be described, so they do not try.

# Chapter Thirty-Three

Gloria gently shakes Frank's shoulder and whispers in his ear that it is time to go. He grunts and turns over. She waggles again and speaks a bit louder. He groans, sits up to scratch, looks around to see a lit Christmas tree in the corner, and snorts his amusement. She explains that she was tired of the house not having any seasonal decorations at mid-December, and he grumbles some sort of resignation to her decision.

He asks where Julie and Russ are, and she says that they have already taken the recliners, blankets, coffee, snacks, and of course, old scotch to the field for viewing the meteor shower. Frank's excitement grows as he efficiently completes his trip to the bathroom by himself and begins dressing in the warm clothes Gloria has laid out. He again reads the card from Dave, then puts it in the pocket of his favorite flannel shirt before slipping on a thick Eddie Bauer three-button cable-knit sweater. His pleasant grin assures Gloria of the great news of Dave's note. Several sips of coffee and a half-eaten cereal bar provide Frank with a little more momentum.

The serene drive through the stillness of downtown Le Fleur reveals the Christmas wreaths and white lights wrapped on the street poles that are juxtaposed against the unseasonal, spring-like night. Frank scans each passing building, many of which he used to own. He gives extra attention to the window of the diner that is decorated with a beautiful holiday scene hand-painted by Julie. He remembers several years ago when he declined Julie's invitation to help paint that year's Christmas landscape because he had to eat quickly and run to cover a story. As he mulls that prickly regret, Frank believes he sees the figure of an old man sitting at the counter drinking a cup of coffee, but as they move down the street, he reasons that it had to be the outline of the cash register and the cuss bucket.

Gloria turns down North Street and before long makes the sweeping curve to cross the short bridge over the Black Fork Creek where Old Man Loomis had run off the road into the bloated river so many Christmases ago when Frank had to rush out to cover the event. Rumors circulated in town that Loomis and his famous bald tires skidded into the water while chasing and shooting at Booker's pickup truck. Booker never reported the incident, although several townspeople said they had seen bullet holes in his tailgate before it was clumsily patched and painted. Loomis's alleged handgun was rumored to have disappeared into the swift floodwaters as he flailed his way to the bank and to the rescuing EMTs. Loomis told no one but his Klan buddies about the incident, who then later finished the job.

Gloria slows but nearly overshoots the dark entrance to the big field. She turns in as the headlight beams bounce over the large gravel, then settle onto the figures with flashlights standing next to a pickup truck. Several recliners and camping chairs are arranged around the truck.

Frank asks, "Who's with Julie and Russ? Oh heavens! It's Joe, Maggie, and Valerie. And who's that over there? Oh my God, it's Pastor Harold. What the heck's going on?"

Frank slides out of the car and rushes awkwardly to hug everyone in group fashion. Laughs swathe the embrace.

Frank sputters, "What—what are—what are you all doing here?"

Joe says, "Julie called us all a few days ago and told us about this plan to watch the meteor shower tonight. The weather looked like it was going to clear up, so we drove down this afternoon, got settled in the hotel, slept a bit, and got up to come out."

"I can't believe you crazy fools drove all the way from New York and then came out here in the middle of the night."

Maggie steps back from the pack and puts her arm around Julie.

"Frank, Julie knows how much we all care about you. She wanted us here for this, to celebrate with you. She's a hell of a woman. I can see why you love her so much."

Frank is not sure how to answer. He clenches the top of his sweater collar sticking out of his coat, bunches it close to his chin, and changes the subject.

"Harold, why on earth did you come out here at this hour?"

Harold puts his hand on Frank's shoulder. "Remember a couple weeks ago when you were going on about the coming meteor shower? I just had to be here to see if it was as good as you said it would be."

Frank gives Harold a manly hug. "You guys are incredible. I love you all very much. God's blessed me with all of you."

Joe says, "Okay everyone, grab a seat and lean back for the show. Frank, we've already seen some really good ones. I think this is going to be one of the best meteor showers ever."

Everyone settles in and turns off their flashlights to let the darkness fall all over them. Frank picks a recliner as Julie and Maggie slide into theirs on either side of him; he reaches out shakily to hold their hands while Gloria wraps his chest in a blanket and gives him a kiss on the forehead. She then moves back to lean on the hood of her car to listen to everyone ooh and aah at the streaking meteors and eavesdrop on their light-hearted stories. Joe says Frank is now a minor celebrity in fishing circles thanks to his salmon struggle video posted on Cinelli's newly-created Niagara Fishing website. Harold tells Frank that although the Indians were eliminated early in this year's playoffs, next year they will be in the World Series because two of their injured pitchers will finally be back, healthy. Russ and Valerie are in charge of the ice and whiskey distribution, and everyone takes at least a little.

Russ lifts his glass and says, "To the Barnetts—the only folks in town who really believed in Mom and me."

Everyone reaches into the dimness in front of Frank to clink their glasses, then Gloria returns to the hood of her car to watch and quietly listen some more to the scattered topics. There is talk of Niagara's majesty, the importance of the new art gallery, the warm early-winter weather and the wonderment of how mysterious cosmic wormholes may implausibly and fancifully blend space and time beyond credence. Frank listens to the words, tasting each syllable as a delicate diner pie crust.

A gentle wind rustles through the low shrub line to the left and the stars shimmer like far-away lighthouses begging for visitors. A magnificent spark of light streaks across the sky and disappears to leave an afterglow of green and silver. Everyone gasps and points and agrees that it is the most magnificent shooting star they have ever seen.

Tears tumble, hands clasp tighter. The calm breeze and heavenly pageant provide a profound serenity. Tender glances through the dark supplant the coarseness of unspoken, graceless words, which would, by their mere utterance, shatter wistful thoughts and the feasting on this moment of grandeur.

# Chapter Thirty-Four

Frank awakens and looks around the sunroom. The Christmas tree glows in the corner as muted rays filter through the slits of the blinds. Near the tree, a gleaming new bicycle with a big tag stating "To Nick from Frank" reflects a glint of gold. Russ sleeps in the big cushy chair next to the bed with his hand resting on Frank's arm. Harold is sprawled out asleep on the other overstuffed chair, and Joe is on the floor sticking out of a sleeping bag. The four women chat with buoyant, hushed tones in the kitchen while making breakfast. The delicate blue asters Julie picked up at the grocery this morning stand cheerfully tall in the glass vase on the table. Warmth seeps into every shadow, into every gleeful resonance of women's soft voices, and into every breath laced with succulent Christmas pine.

Frank stirs through the strong pain meds to focus on the end of the bed where a youthful, beaming Larry stands, hand extended, appearing just like his last black-and-white childhood photo that hangs in the hallway next to the shadowboxed ball glove. The beautiful child places his hand on Frank's foot; the swaddling comfort is transcendent. Frank whispers, "Forgive me." Young Larry smiles and nods absolution. Frank breathes deeply and comfortably with understanding of the trip they are about to take together and shuts his eyes. The pain and all those trophies he once guarded melt away as their journey begins along that soothing river into the mystic.

The coffee and bacon smell glorious.

# Author Bio

SHANNON DAVID HAMONS was born in Shelby, Ohio, and grew up in the nearby small town of Plymouth. He graduated from Bowling Green State University in northwest Ohio with a degree in Education. He also attended The Ohio State University in Columbus, living in nearby Westerville for twenty-five years where he raised his two children. Soon after college he was a reporter, editor, and general manager for a chain of weekly newspapers. He later worked in municipal government economic development and then became vice president of a private development company. After a short period in the Dallas, Texas, area, he returned to Ohio to become Development Director for the small city of Harrison, Ohio, near Cincinnati, where he lives with his wife Joy. *Releasing Trophies* is his first book; his second book is underway. Entitled *Working,* it is a collection of humorous short stories about the many odd jobs he had as a child.

CPSIA information can be obtained
at www.ICGtesting.com
Printed in the USA
FSHW010624081220
76555FS